SOCIAL BITES

from fan girl to fang girl

By: Amanda Maehill

Table of Contents

Author's Note

Dear Reader,

This is a work of fiction, as we all know that vampires aren't real, even ones cosplaying on social media. I, the author, am Autistic and ADHD (Attention-Deficit/Hyperactivity Disorder). There's a very common expression that if you've met one Autistic person, you've met one Autistic person, because we are all very unique. The same goes for ADHD. Many of the traits of Autism that our main character, Katrina, displays in this book do mimic a lot of my own traits, but I also relied on shared experiences of Autism and ADHD from my wider community. We are learning that both Autism and ADHD have been severely underdiagnosed, and in the coming years, you'll probably be learning of one or more people in your life who is Autistic and/or ADHD.

There is also a character with DID (Dissociative Identity Disorder), which you may know as Multiple Personality Disorder. MPD was renamed to DID in 1994. I attempted to be as accurate to someone with DID as I could. But just like above (and you'll find with any human with a disability), each person with DID is going to be unique. For the sake of the story, I've taken some liberties with how easily my character switches between alters. People experiencing DID may have as few as two alters, however there are recorded cases of over one hundred alters, and many in between. Alters are created as a survival mechanism by the brain, resulting in an unintegrated personality created by dissociative barriers. Each alter, for the most part, is an individual with their own preferences, voice, memories, and style. Think of it as many people sharing one body. There is a lot of misinformation around DID, and it is usually portrayed in the media as "psychological thriller" or "horror." But people with DID can live fairly normal, if not challenging, lives. It is a childhood trauma disorder and most people with DID are not dangerous—they are all survivors themselves.

In this book, I make every attempt to normalize Autism, ADHD, DID, and a few other disabilities. Autism and DID both have a lot of unnecessary stigma around them. Many people with these disorders mask and hide their disorder as much as possible, which only causes further trauma. There is nothing wrong with being Autistic, having DID or ADHD, or any disability. Disability is not a dirty word. It is morally neutral, not good or bad. It is a variation of the human condition. And the disabled community asks that you use the word "disabled" to refer to one of its members instead of euphemisms that just imply their disability is shameful.

With that, dear reader, I hope you enjoy this book. I enjoyed writing it for you.
Sincerely,
Amanda Maehill

Content Warnings

On a serious note—delivered with a light-hearted wink—this book dips into some real-life topics beneath all the vampire flirtation and romance fun. It's meant to be a mostly feel-good story full of connection and charm. But what's totally fine for one reader might be a no-go for another. I believe in transparency without judgment, so here's a friendly heads-up on what you'll find inside—spoiler-free, promise.

- Consensual vampire biting (because, of course). One past-tense memory involves a non-consensual turning. Violence in this scene is minimal and emotional safety is prioritized. (ch. 13)
- Mentions of blood—human, murine, bovine, and porcine—but nothing graphic or gory.
- Open-door sex scenes featuring enthusiastic consent, emotional intimacy, and occasional teeth.
- A central character with Dissociative Identity Disorder (DID), portrayed with respect, input from community voices, and without sensationalism. DID is caused by extreme childhood trauma. This isn't a trauma story, but there are brief, non-detailed references to that past. I don't believe mental health conditions require a content warning, but childhood trauma references do. If DID is new to you, I invite you to read with curiosity and compassion.

What's *not* in this book?

Graphic violence. Sexual assault. Gore. Trauma as shock-value. I don't write that way. This story was built with kindness and care.

This list isn't exhaustive—if you have specific sensitivities, feel free to reach out. Your safety in your reading space always matters to me.

Now... back to the vampires, cute librarians, and social media meet-cutes.

—Amanda Maehill

Chapter 1
An Idea Forms

Montgomery

"You've got to leave, Nikolai! I go Live on VidVibe in less than fifteen minutes. Having you playing Zelda in the background would completely undermine my vampire image." Frantically, I rush around trying to finish putting on just the right amount of eyeliner to make my blue eyes appear even more icy, while also attempting to get my best friend, Nikolai, to go home.

"Oh, come on, Montgomery, I can play quietly in here while you do your weird vampire routine in the den. I won't be loud. I'm right in the middle of this dungeon and I can't figure out the last piece of the puzzle." Nikolai doesn't even glance up from the enormous TV hanging on my wall in the game room, controller still in his hands. He lounges on one of my two black leather sofas in what I think is a pretty sweet game room setup. I had been slowly adding LED lights that you can change to different colors to suit your mood, and they are currently set to a brilliant blue. On the walls I had hung artwork depicting scenes from some of my favorite video games. I have a soft spot for Mario, so among my decor there's a heavy influence of Mario, Luigi, and the rest of the Nintendo gang, but I also have Sonic the Hedgehog, Metroid, and of course, Zelda. Honestly, I might be a vampire, but I'm a big gamer at heart, and I was meant to be in this era. Thinking back on my earlier life, it's hard to even imagine how I survived without Wi-Fi, Bluetooth, LED lights, and my Nintendo Switch. Not to mention my smartphone! How did anyone survive before smartphones?

"Now! Leave!" I smooth my fingers through my long black hair, glancing in the mirror to make sure my costume looks put-together. Yes, vampires can actually show up in mirrors. Most of the things humans learned about us have been wildly blown out of proportion. We're *mostly* normal. I lean into an absurd vampire costume to give humans what they expect to see when they hear I'm a vampire. My silk shirt, a deep wine color, is layered under a black leather jacket with a lot of pewter buckles, studs, and hardware that look "vampire gothic," at least I think. Since the symbol for eternal life holds a lot of meaning for me, the black choker I put on as a last touch, features a silver ankh.

After adding one last ring to my already overloaded fingers, I think my look is complete. I just have on black jeans tonight because I feel like being comfortable and will mostly be waist up on the camera.

These types of clothes are not usually what you'd find me in! I'm a jeans and T-shirt kind of guy. Heck, I've even been known to dress like the locals and put socks on with my Birkenstock sandals. But not too often, I promise, mostly just if I'm darting out to check the mail. I do have a very impressive T-shirt collection with Marvel superhero logos on them, along with other funny gamer-type shirts. Nikolai is more preppy. He likes wearing polos with his jeans, but both of us are really just average gamers.

"Alright, I saved. I'm out of here," Nikolai says as he tosses the controller on the couch where he'd been sitting all day.

"Finally!"

"Have fun tonight. Hope all the girls swoon over you," Nik teased.

"Oh, they most assuredly will," I smirked back at him.

"I still think this whole VidVibe thing is hilarious—you know you don't need to do it right?"

"I do," I said as I ushered him towards the door.

"We both have so much money neither of us need to work," he responded as he slowly shoved his feet in his laced up shoes adding, "but it does pass the time."

"Mhmm, and that's why you keep your job as a bartender? To pass the time?" We both knew there were plenty of other things he could be doing, and we both knew why he didn't quit.

"The hours are right, and let's be honest, it's a great way to meet girls . . . or cute boys . . . " He trailed off already thinking about the conquest he'd be meeting during his next shift.

"Have your fun tonight, Nikolai, I'll have mine. I've got to get in front of the camera, and I still need to pour myself a glass of red wine." For some reason, holding on to a glass of deep red wine just really makes the look complete—the fans are obsessed. While I can drink wine, I really don't love it. It's all a part of my act.

The whole VidVibe thing started as a joke. One night a couple years ago, Nikolai and I were hanging out (no, not upside down, that's another weird vampire myth). We were hanging out like two normal undead guys, playing video games together. He was playing a Mario game and I was scrolling on SnapFoto. My account, Montgomery1690 (a tiny nod to the fact I was older than people would suspect.) However, I rarely post on it. For one thing, when you are over three hundred years old, your human friends sort of come and go in cycles. Nikolai and I have been friends since childhood, but we hadn't been in Portland for that long. It's crucial to move around and change things up every few years to avoid humans noticing we never appear to get older. But anyway, as I was saying, I was scrolling on SnapFoto and I kept seeing these videos pop up with a logo that said "VidVibe." I'd heard about VidVibe for a while at that point, but had mostly ignored it. The more I kept seeing these VidVibes in my SnapFoto feed, the more an idea started to form in my head. From what I could tell, VidVibe was just these short videos of people talking about all sorts of random things—and dancing, there was lots of odd dancing.

That day sitting in the game room, I looked over at Nikolai playing yet another video game and I got this crazy idea. "Nik, what if I made a VidVibe account?"

"Sure, buddy, whatever you want to do," Nik said, not even looking over at me as he quickly dodged a fireball heading towards his character's head.

"No, Nik, listen man. Do you even know what VidVibe is?"

"Yeah, videos of people doing silly dances and lip synching, right? I think some people pull pranks and film it? That's what you want to do? You better not be planning on pranking me—you know I don't like that!"

"Yes and no. Apparently that is what some of VidVibe is, but there are also all kinds of videos of people doing random things. There seems to be a whole niche of cosplayers that dress up. What if I got on VidVibe and pretended I was a vampire?"

"Uh, Montgomery . . . I hate to break it to you, but you ARE a vampire?" Nikolai finally looked up from his game, brows pinched. At this point we'd only been in the new city for a couple of months and the game room wasn't decked out

14

yet. Sometimes we lived together because of convenience, but after spending over three hundred years as someone's best friend, there comes a time when you need your own space. Our last move was to Vancouver, Washington, just across the river from Portland, Oregon. We usually just say Portland because most people think of Vancouver, BC in Canada when you say Vancouver. For this most recent move, we decided to get houses close to each other. Somehow he still ends up at my house most of the time. Some things just never change. At least I can send him home when I need some alone time.

"Hahaha! Nikolai, the look on your face! I know I'm a vampire, but if I wore a costume depicting how people think vampires are supposed to dress in these videos, people would *think* I was just acting. It could be a fun diversion. I'm just so bored lately. We haven't lived here long, we haven't made any new friends, and I am dying for something new to do."

"It could be fun. I wonder if it will work . . . Do you think people would be interested in watching someone "pretending" to be a vampire? You can't do any magic. That'd take things too far."

"I don't think I'll be teleporting or using telekinesis on VidVibe. Well, I could use telekinesis on video, but everyone would simply assume it is a camera trick. Still, you're probably right. I won't take it that far." All vampires can glamor in a variety of ways and it's a skill that strengthens with age. Something to do with bio-camouflaging. Glamor at a basic level will hide our fangs from human eyes when they are descended, but we can also change a lot of other aspects of our appearance or surroundings.

All vampires can teleport, heal fast, and glamor. We also all have super speed, senses and strength. Then most of us have our own unique abilities. It's fairly common for us to have powers like telekinesis or telepathy, but some vampires have more rare abilities such as invisibility, weather manipulation, elemental control, and I'm sure some others. Nikolai can use telepathy with humans, but thank the gods it doesn't work on other vampires! I don't want him in my head. We spend enough time together as it is. Our powers, for lack of better terminology, are supposed to help us hunt humans, but more on that later.

Back to my VidVibe idea. The more I played around with the idea of creating a VidVibe account to discuss life as a vampire, letting people believe it was all cosplay while being as truthful as possible, the more fun it sounded. So that's how a couple years and 1.6 million followers later, I'm rushing around trying to get ready for a Live event. I do Lives about once a month and my fans just go crazy for them.

Settling into what I affectionately call my throne, which is actually a black leather and ebony wood carved wingback chair, I put my now full wineglass on the small stone table in front of me. Thick dark red velvet drapes cover the window on one side, and a crackling fire in an ornately carved fireplace sits on my other side. When I first started making videos, the setup was much simpler, but over time, I've added quite a bit of Vampire Chic Ambiance to this corner of the room. Wood sconces wrapped with hammered cast iron metal are on the wall to the side of the fireplace, with a large oil painting of a voluptuous woman in a dark yellow dress lying on a green chaise lounge painted in the Renaissance style of Raphael. I found it at a Goodwill and it was just over the top enough that it fit nicely into what I call "my set." I turn on some classical music, look up at the camera nestled in the tripod, then further got into character by dramatically lowering my eyebrows to match my slight scowl, and hit record.

"Good evening, kindred spirits. I hope you are as cozy as I am tonight. I have about an hour to spend with you before it'll be time for me to go hunting—a vampire's got to live, right? I can't sustain myself on wine forever. Who's got questions for me? I'll answer as many as I can tonight."

Chapter 2
Four Friends in One

Katrina

There's an old saying that birds of a feather flock together. Well that's also true for people and their neurotypes. Neurotypical people are the majority brain type out there. Almost everyone you run into has a neurotypical brain. Then there are those of us who fall under the neurodivergent umbrella. It's very common for neurodivergent people to seek each other out as friends. The NTs, as we like to call them, stick together too. A lot of people think neurodivergent refers only to ADHD or Autistic people, but there are actually quite a few disorders or conditions that are neurodivergent. I happen to be both Autistic and ADHD, but my best friend has a disorder called DID; it stands for Dissociative Identity Disorder. You may know it as Multiple Personality Disorder, but the name got changed a while back. And let me tell you, having a best friend with DID makes for a very interesting life! Unfortunately, it's not all fun. DID is a childhood trauma disorder and it shows how truly amazing the brain is at survival. The brain splits into different people when DID forms in childhood.

My friend doesn't go by her birth name (Sarah) with her close friends; she either goes by her system name or by whichever alter is fronting at that moment. Alter is the scientific way of saying "personality." She calls her system: The Rainbow System. This means when it's unclear which alter is fronting (who's hosting gets blurry sometimes) or if the situation requires referring to the group of them, I say Rainbow System (or just Rainbow.) They have four main alters: Jessie, Max, Sky, and Arleigh (pronounced "ar-lee" Arleigh is an elf, an it's common for systems to have nonhuman alters. It's always a guess to who will be fronting at any given moment of the day! It keeps me on my toes. Fortunately, all the alters can mask (that means "pretend at a very deep level") as Sarah and they accept being called Sarah at work, which is where I'm at now. I met Rainbow where she works at the PacNorthwest Vet Clinic. They are a vet tech and I'm here to pick up my cat, Data, who has been acting very much like he might have another ear infection. You may have caught that *Star Trek* reference. I admit it, I'm a Trekkie!

When your bestie has DID, you can usually tell who's fronting right away. At work I stick to calling her Sarah unless I know for sure she's alone. Society has a thing about norms and people who look or act differently get treated poorly. Unfortunately, the world isn't ready for Jessie to start the work day and come back from lunch as Arleigh the elf. Most likely, Rainbow would lose their job if they disclosed the fact they have DID. The stigmatization towards DID is worse than towards Autism, which I encounter daily.

I'm in a small room waiting for either the vet or a tech to tell me what's going on with Data, but I'm hoping Rainbow will be the one to bring him back to me and let me know if it's another ear infection or if he's just being extra. The door opens and in pops Sky, one of Rainbow's alters. Rainbow's body is thirty years old, but the alters each have their own internal experience of themselves that doesn't necessarily relate to the body. For instance, Rainbow's body is fairly androgynous, with a round face, button nose, and short shaggy hair that is that cute styled kind of shaggy. But each alter has a specific way of carrying the body that makes them uniquely themselves. So when I say Sky came in the room, I immediately knew it was her from the way she swayed her hips as she more sauntered in than walked. Internally, in their headspace, Sky is twenty-two with very long straight blonde hair. As a girly-girl, she exudes fun. If she didn't have to be in scrubs for work, she'd be wearing a tight mini skirt and tank top, if I had to guess. Since we are alone, I feel comfortable saying, "Hey Sky, so give me the scoop. What's going on with poor Data? Is he really sick or is he only looking for more attention today?"

"Katrina, you were right to bring him in! Yep, his ear is infected and it must have been bothering him pretty badly. The poor boo! These things can get nasty fast. We cleaned it out and gave him some antibiotic drops. He'll be totes fine soon. Doc wants you to give him some oral pills for the next week—think you can manage? Or one of us can come over after work and help you if you need it." Sky would talk much more professionally if she was masking as Sarah, but in front of me, she's all young adult.

"Oh no, poor Data!" I take him from Sky and gently put him back in his cat backpack. I got it off Amazon and it's the coolest carrier I've ever seen. You can wear it like a backpack and it's got a clear plastic bubble with holes so the cat can see out. I wasn't sure if Data would like it, but surprisingly, he took to it right away and sometimes, if I leave the closet door open at home, I'll find him napping in it. "I should be able to manage giving him the pills, but I'll let you know if he gives me trouble. Do you have a few minutes or do you have to jet back to work?"

"Today's been kinda chill. I can take a breather while I pretend to show you how to do the meds. What's up?" she asks, petting Data.

"Oh, I don't know. I've just been feeling a bit antsy lately. You know I love spring so much and I'm ready to spend time outside, but it's so hard planning anything because you never know if it's going to be raining or not! I love Vancouver so much, but the rain really does get to you by the time spring finally comes around! Anyway, I was just wondering, if it's nice this weekend, do you want to go on a hike? If it's rainy maybe we can stay in and watch a movie or something? Do you have plans?" One of the absolute best things about living in the Pacific Northwest is the gorgeous hiking trails. My favorite is a fairly short one around Lacamas Lake. There's an old dam at one end of the trail and I always stop to take a bunch of photos of the rushing water. Everything around the lake and trail is a serene green, with soaring pine trees reaching toward the sky, mossy wet boulders, and busy darting squirrels. A variety of birds are always flitting about— tiny finches, blue Steller's jays, and, on lucky days, you may see a bald eagle. It's one of my favorite places to be.

"Yeah, you know me, all my friends have soooo many plans this weekend. What do you think? You know if we're not hanging out with you, then we're usually on our computer playing *Stardew Valley*. You know I don't really do outdoorsy stuff, but Max would probably love to front and go on a hike with you. We'll play it by ear, but one of us will totally hang this weekend."

"Sounds like a plan! Alright, well I have to get Mr. Data home and then get myself back to the library. I'm on a long lunch break but work until closing today. Thanks for taking care of Data."

I gather my sweet Russian Blue cat in his comfy backpack and head out towards my car. I really do need to book it back home and then to the library as fast as possible. I always have to be on time for things. My ADHD side can get easily distracted and lose track of time, but my Autistic side needs things to be precise and orderly. It's a constant battle. I should be able to get Data home and back to the library in plenty of time.

"Hello Mrs. Humphrey," I call out quietly as I step into the bright sunny library. Mrs. Humphrey is the head librarian and she's the epitome of motherly. I couldn't ask for a better boss. There is a break in the misty rain—something we call a sunbreak—and the light streams through the library's floor-to-ceiling windows. Every time I walk through the library doors, a feeling of peace washes over me. For a lot of Autistic people, libraries become second homes—all the information in the world at our fingertips to go into deep research dives on any topic imaginable. I mostly work in the back; ordering books for the library, program management (helping come up with events for patrons and the community), checking our inventory, and I've even gotten really good at repairing books that have seen better days. There are a lot of behind-the-scenes things that go on in libraries that most people don't even know about. One day a week, I run the children's desk. It works out for me, because too many people can cause sensory overload for me and trigger a shutdown of my nervous system. But I do love children. They aren't afraid to ask any question that comes to their mind. I just absolutely enjoy that they are still learning about the world and haven't had the wonder stamped out of them yet. If they want to know why I'm not looking directly at them when I'm talking to them, they just ask. The other day, a little boy asked, "Hey, Ms. Katrina, why do you look at my ear when I ask you to find a book on whales?"

I gave him a smile and told him the truth. "I'm Autistic. That means my brain processes the world differently than most people. Looking at people when I'm talking to them makes it difficult for me to focus. I think better when I don't look at you. That makes it easier for me to remember where we keep those books on whales. Hmm, I am pretty sure 'whales' will be shelved at 599.5. Have you ever heard of the Dewey Decimal System?" I had asked the freckled little kid as we walked over to the science books in the children's section. He had gotten his book on whales and taken it over to a table to study it.

Today, I'm working in the back, reviewing a long list of book purchase requests submitted through our library's online system. I am really looking forward to working through that list and then going home for the day. The library closes early at 4 p.m. and I have plans to finish working on my latest crochet project. I want to wrap up the last few steps on the stuffed animal I'm making and film a VidVibe about it to upload this evening.

I don't have many followers on VidVibe, just around 3,000. But that's okay, I'm not on VidVibe for fame or fortune. I just enjoy showing off my crochet projects and I'm shocked that anyone follows me at all, honestly! Also, if I finish in time, one of my favorite VidVibers is planning on going Live tonight and I am secretly hoping to catch it. I can't believe I'm admitting this, but yes, I'm fangirling over a VidViber. His account name is MontyTheVampire and there's just something very intriguing about him. Yes, there is the obvious: that he is capital H-O-T. Like, off the cover of a men's fashion magazine sizzling hot. He has a tapered jaw, with just a light amount of scruff and piercing blue eyes that make me wonder if he wears contacts. His long black hair has a small amount of wave to it, and his whole look is just mesmerizing. I could watch him for hours and never get bored.

Autistic people do something called stimming. It's really normal for us as a way to regulate our systems. People who aren't very kind often call it "hand flapping." But it's way more than just flapping our hands. Yes, some of us do wave our hands around to stim, but there are a lot of healthy stims. I like to play with fidgets and have a big supply of fidget toys both at home and work. I also sometimes will rock back and forth, or—one of my favorites—when I really am feeling pent-up I do what I call "chicken wings," where I tuck my hands near my armpits and move my elbows up and down. You should try it. Even Allistic (non-Autistic) people can benefit from stimming. But stimming behavior can also occur with any of your senses. Watching the dam at the lake I mentioned earlier is a form of visual stimming, as is lava lamps, fairy lights, or anything of visual interest. Watching Monty on VidVibe is definitely a visual stim. He is so compelling, especially his eyes. In person, I don't like looking someone directly in the eyes, but behind the screen I can get lost in his icy blue ones.

Smelling favorite scents or touching favorite textures are also ways to stim. Many Autistic people like to chew on things too, but that isn't something I find helpful.

But back to MontyTheVampire. His real name, or so he says, is Montgomery, and he's just so interesting. He's cosplaying as a vampire but he never breaks character. I can't put my finger on it, but there's just something that my

Autistic and ADHD brain can't quite figure out and I love a good puzzle. Autistic people are so good at pattern recognition and figuring things out! I want to watch his Live and hopefully have a chance to ask him a question. He's got so many followers though, that getting a question answered is a long shot. I haven't told anyone about this whole vampire fascination I have, not even Rainbow. I'm not sure why, but it's just my own private little hyperfocus!

Chapter 3
Asking an Important Question

Katrina

"Data! Data!" I call as I walk through my townhome door. "I'm home, sweetie. How are you feeling after the vet today?" Data comes trotting up to the door to greet me and I know he must be feeling a bit better. He follows me into the kitchen so I can open a can of food for him. He doesn't actually really like canned food very often, but I figure he might want a treat after a visit to the vet.

I finish making my little Junimo crochet project. It's a character from *Stardew Valley*, shaped like an apple. It is a beginner project, but still super cute. I made it for Sky because she loves *Stardew Valley*. The funny thing is, I like to crochet, but I rarely keep my own projects. It's more the act of crocheting that brings me joy, not the finished piece. A way to stim with my hands while watching TV or listening to an audiobook. All I have left to do for the Junimo is to stitch its little stick-like black arms and legs onto the granny smith-green body and stitch in some cheek lines. Those are actually trickier than they look. You've got to get the perfect angle or the face doesn't look right. But I am able to do that while filming it and get the video uploaded to my VidVibe in time for me to sit back with a mug of my favorite tea and watch MontyTheVampire go Live. I think for a second how different our channels are. He's got 1.6 million followers. I can't even comprehend that. I have just under three thousand followers and that itself blows me away. I'm excited if *anyone* likes to watch my little crochet videos. I do it for fun.

The rich aroma of my tea hits my nose as I wrap my hands around the mug and take a deep inhale. The first sip is always my favorite and I take a moment to linger over the smooth vanilla and the sweet caramel flavors of my favorite black tea. I know I shouldn't have caffeine this late at night but my herbal teas just weren't sounding good. This vanilla caramel black tea is my absolute favorite right now and my other teas are probably feeling left out, but I can't help it. It's delicious!

I curl up on my favorite chair in my living room, another ADHD purchase. Note to anyone who's listening: when you buy furniture, remember that you'll probably be keeping it for eight to ten years—most people don't replace big pieces that often. I don't know what was going through my head the day I bought this incredibly oversized red—yes, red—chair. I've been emotionally over the color for several years now, but we are a unit: my cozy red chair and I. For better or for worse. It is comfortable, which is good, because if it wasn't for that, I probably would have found a justification to rehome it by now. The best thing is I can sit in so many comfortable ways in this chair. Right now I'm sitting with one leg tucked under me and one knee up. I've pulled my auburn hair up into a curly messy bun on top of my head and I'm in comfy cotton pajamas with thick fuzzy socks. It doesn't matter the time of year, I have to have socks on my feet! I can't stand the feeling of dirt or cat hair from the floor on my bare feet. I've got my tea next to me on the tree stump side table and I go to pull up VidVibe on my tablet so I can watch Monty on a bigger screen than my phone. Plus, that leaves me able to text Rainbow if I get the whim to do so.

I've spent half the day trying to think of a question I can ask in the comment box for when Monty goes Live. This all feels absolutely out of character for me! I've never before felt so drawn to a social media content creator. I can't explain it. One day I was flipping through the FYP (For You Page) on VidVibe, and one of his videos came up. Instead of just flipping to the next video, I sat there enthralled. I couldn't look away. The guy was so handsome, I assumed he was using a filter. But there was no filter tag. That didn't necessarily mean anything, but I did notice. After a couple of months of, er, lightly stalking Monty, I really don't think he uses filters. I think his eyes really are that blue. His voice is a deep baritone that just hits my brain and soothes away any anxiety. And his content is the coolest. He talks all about being a vampire, which at first was just slightly uncomfortable. As an Autistic person, I don't usually catch satire or sarcasm. I can't tell if people are joking or being serious. But he's so serious—he's one hundred percent committed to his character, which is pretty neat. Also, he talks about history and I'm a sucker for the educational content on VidVibe. His approach to telling history with the twist of being told as if it's first person from a vampire? I'm in.

Tonight though he said he was going to do an AMA (Ask Me Anything) and that's why while driving Data to the vet and doing some of my mindless tasks at the library today, I was trying to think of a question that would grab his notice. I watched his last Live but I didn't try to ask a question. This time, I want to at least try. And if he doesn't pick my question, at least I'll learn some more things about his "character." I'm so curious if he'll be able to maintain the façade or if he'll break at some point. Monty is a really great actor.

I have a few more minutes, so I pull out my phone to message Rainbow on ChatBox. I'm still not ready to tell them exactly what I'm up to, but I need some help with my question. We actually have our own ChatBox server we use for messages. There's a general chat for when I don't know who's fronting, and then each alter has their own chat channel. I pull up Sky's channel since she was around at the vet   today.

Me: Hey Sky, are you still around?

....

....

Jessie: No, it's me now. Sky went innerworld.

This is even better because Jessie loves social media as much as I do. Innerworld is also known as the headspace. The alters can actually interact and talk to each other inside the mind. Innerworld, Jessie is the same age as the body at thirty, but she has thick black curly hair. Sometimes I feel bad because I have long, curly red hair, and I know Jessie wishes her hair matched the way she sees herself innerworld.

She loves my curls but she explained her curls are tighter ringlets in her mind (while her body has short shaggy hair), my red curls are much looser, probably due to the length because my hair goes about halfway down my back. It's my absolute favorite physical thing about myself. Jessie sees herself as having a squarish jawline and green eyes. When she's fronting she often pulls out big round green glasses that match her innerworld eye color. Eventually, I got used to looking at Rainbow, but in my mind, visualizing the presenting alter as they describe themselves. For instance, Rainbow's body has short shaggy hair, but when I'm talking to Jessie I do my best to picture the black curly hair she has innerworld.

Me: What are some really intriguing, thought-provoking questions?
Jessie: Uh, what do you mean? That's a bit broad. What are you doing?
Me: Well, uh, there's someone I've been following on VidVibe and they are going Live here in a few minutes. They are doing an AMA and I thought I'd try to get a question in for fun. It's kinda how Data and I are spending our Friday night.
Jessie: Ah! Hum. Give me a second.

Whew, I don't want to get too detailed just yet. I don't know why I haven't told Rainbow about my Monty obsession. Is it really an obsession? I'm sure it's at a healthy level. I follow a lot of VidVibers. He's just so fascinating!

Jessie: What about asking where they grew up? Or you could get philosophical. Who is it? Maybe I'll pop on and watch a few minutes too.
Jessie: Oh drat. Never mind, Max is wanting to bake. I'm going innerworld, so I'll catch you later and hope you come up with a good question!

Rainbow has been in therapy for a long time and their System has gotten pretty good at controlled switches. Max loves cooking and baking. He must be wanting some cookies, and I hope he makes enough for when I go over tomorrow to hike—or whatever we end up doing.

Just then, MontyTheVampire logs on. I'm still thinking about my question. I may post a couple just to see if I catch his attention. I know the best time is in the first few minutes, before the chat fills up with his fans. And OMG he looks amazing tonight. His hair is down around his shoulders, and while normally a man wearing eyeliner would seem strange to me, it just works for him. His eyes are all but piercing me through the screen. I think his lips are naturally that red against his pale skin. It doesn't look like he's got makeup on other than his eyeliner. He must buy an expensive foundation to achieve that porcelain complexion, or maybe he simply avoids going outside to maintain his VidVibe persona. He's wearing what looks like a silk shirt and a lot of silver jewelry.

@Katrina_Crochet - Hi Monty!

I start to type, then delete it. That is so pedestrian! Why does this have to be hard? I'm just going to ask the question.

@Katrina_Crochet - Have you ever wondered if reality is just a collective illusion we've all agreed upon?

I decided to go with Jessie's idea of a philosophical type of question. It seems to fit, what with him pretending to be a vampire and me pretending he's not pretending. That is what is happening, right? Now let's see if he catches it. I may type it in one more time if he doesn't. Otherwise I'll just sit back, sip my tea, and enjoy his performance for the next hour or so.

Chapter 4
MontyTheVampire Live on VidVibe

Montgomery

Just a few seconds after hitting the record button, the number icon showing people have joined the Live starts going up really quickly. I honestly don't know if this will ever get old. Actually, I do. When you've lived as long as I have, everything gets boring after a time. But for now, doing these VidVibe videos and Live events has kept the boredom at bay. It amuses me so much that I can just sit here and (mostly) tell the truth about being a vampire, and everyone assumes I'm cosplaying.

Some might say by doing this, I'm breaking vampire laws. We have our own entire laws and court system. We live among humans and follow many, but not all of their laws. One vampire law is that we cannot widely tell people vampires exist. I know I'm skirting it very close with my VidVibe videos, but it's the perfect situation. I get to talk openly about being a vampire in a format designed where humans literally won't believe it's true. Sure, there is the odd human who might suspect, but no one takes them seriously—because it's all too ridiculous to even consider. The law is about protecting the secret, and the only way to keep it is to make sure humans think it's fiction. VidVibe, with its entire cosplay niche, does exactly that.

It's interesting the types of fans I get. I have the ones who follow me only for my looks and don't care about anything I have to say. Becoming a vampire actually makes us more attractive. I don't spend a lot of time thinking about my looks, to be honest, but it's an intrinsic feature of our glamor that we don't control. We appear more beautiful in the eye of our beholder. It developed evolutionarily as a way for us to draw humans in for the hunt.

History Buffs are another type of fan that I have. Assuming I'm just an academic, they actually like my perspective on history. Honestly, these are my favorite fans to engage with in the comments. Then there are other cosplay vampires. They get right in on the act and talk about their ideas of vampire culture. I have seen one of my actual real vampire acquaintances in the chat on occasion. I'll get a message from them later that they can't believe I'm pulling this off, but that they're also impressed. Occasionally an angry person shows up too, usually a male, telling me I'm full of it and I should "act my age" and stop playing dress-up. I just ignore them, but sometimes I like to toy with them.

The questions quickly start populating the screen. I figured out how to slow the questions down so they don't scroll by too fast. I of course can't answer all of them, and some get asked so many times, I'm over repeating myself. Hopefully tonight will bring in some amusement.

@MontyFanGirl123 - Monty!!! OMG!!! You are SOOOO amazing! Will you have my baby!?
@CattyGurlz - Monty, how old are you? Do you really drink blood?
@GingerSnapper27 - How were the pyramids formed?

@user4938751098 - You need to get a life!! Get a real job. Your such a loser!

Yep, a bunch of the normal types of questions and comments. "At least learn to spell 'you're' correctly, user4938751098," I think to myself. But I'm going to ignore him for now. If I have to block him, I will, but for now he's a harmless fly.

"Thank you MontyFanGirl123. Nice username you got there. Unfortunately, as an undead, I cannot have your baby or anyone else's."

I start off the Live using what I've learned is my sexiest voice possible. Seriously, if these people knew that I mostly sat around playing online games for hours, would they even give me the time of day?

"Ginger, I'm old but not quite that old! I was born in England in 1690 on a rural farm. I was the youngest of my siblings. My Mother had given birth to nine kids before me, but only five of us lived past the age of one. My brothers and sisters all married but I preferred just working the farm with Mother and Father. I had planned to eventually settle down, but somehow I never got around to it. Then when I was twenty-seven, I was turned. I know many of you've heard this story, and I have videos up on the page that go in more detail, so I won't explain it all tonight. What other questions do we have?"

@Katrina_Crochet Have you ever wondered if reality is just a collective illusion we've all agreed upon?

As my eyes skim the question, I subtly straighten up, almost imperceptibly. Now this is interesting. Not the usual Baby-Daddy-type question I'm used to getting. The thing is, in a Live, you've got to think pretty quickly. Questions and comments are flying at you and it's hard to read, think, and talk all at once. I really should get a social media manager, but that just sounds complicated, and I don't really want complicated.

"Katrina, my sweet dear mortal, what an interesting question you pose. Have I ever wondered if reality is just a collective illusion we've all agreed upon? I've witnessed the ebb and flow of beliefs across the centuries. Reality, to me, is the ever-changing perspectives of leaders controlling the masses to their realities for a time. Whether it's the truth or just an illusion, our perceptions shape our existence. What is very real may seem like an illusion, and with media we can now create illusions that appear to be so very real." I decided to stop talking because I was feeling very self conscious about my answer. Did that even make sense? I was just trying to show off. I probably should have skipped that question! But it definitely grabbed my attention. Something above the mundane.

Questions keep flying at me for the next hour, and while I do love deep philosophical queries, having to think of answers in character on the spot makes me almost sweat there for a moment. I mean, if I *could* sweat. Semantics, you know. When the hour wraps up and I say my goodnights, I feel satisfied with how the Live went. My subscriber count grew by a couple hundred, which is always fun. I wonder if I'll make it to two million by the end of the year. Although, honestly if my account gets too big, I'll probably have to quit and move again, and I'm really liking Vancouver. I can't get too famous though because then it'll be difficult to stay under the radar long-term.

Katrina: Jessie, I know Max is fronting right now baking cookies, but I just had to tell you! That VidViber I was telling you about? He answered my question. I went with a philosophical one like you suggested. I can't believe it. I'll have to tell you about it tomorrow. Hope Max saves me some cookies.

I can't believe Monty answered my question. I'm shocked he even saw it. Even though I entered the Live just as it started, within the first five minutes there were already over a hundred people in the room, and the questions were going by so fast, I figured there'd be no way that he'd even see mine. And he called me a Sweet Dear Mortal. I wish I had been screen recording! I jump out of my chair and start stimming, bouncing from one foot to the other, with excitement. I have more energy than my body can contain and I just have to let it out. It is growing late and I really should start getting ready for bed, but letting myself fangirl for just a while longer will be okay.

Suddenly, I get an ADHD urge to send him a direct message (DM). He probably has DMs turned off. Usually anyone with more than several thousand followers understandably turns off DMs. Some even turn off the ability to stitch videos or mention their usernames. But if he doesn't, I probably only have one chance to send a message that he'll even notice. He may not notice it. Maybe I should think about this. But now is when he might remember me. Maybe? He probably already forgot my question. It was at the beginning of the hour and he talked on so many other topics—a strange mix of surprisingly accurate history (not that I'm an expert or anything, but I've always had an interest in history) and his vampire cosplay fantasy lore.

According to Monty, vampires can drink wine but they can't eat food. They do need to drink blood, but not as often as most myths would have us believe. Listen to me, I already sound as if I believe him. He's such a good storyteller that it all seems believable! No wonder he has so many fans. Apparently, according to Monty, vampires can live off animal blood too. He says he often uses pigs' blood. He said that as if he was letting us in on a big secret, because he normally plays it off as if he's out hunting women all the time. His way of saying things like he's letting us in on secrets while also playing up stereotypes makes everything he says sound even more true. The guy is a genius. I have to remind myself he's actually just an actor.

After thinking about it for a few minutes, I decide it'll be more fun if I tell all of this to Jessie or Sky. Maybe they can help me craft a message tomorrow to DM Monty. Max would roll his eyes at me. He's just as supportive as the rest of Rainbow, but he's much more reserved and serious. Okay, that's the plan then. A good night's sleep and then tomorrow, at Rainbow's house, I'll finally tell them about my silly internet crush on Monty.

Chapter 5
Sliding Into His DMs

Katrina

"Hello! I'm letting myself in!" I call out as I walk into Rainbow's apartment late Saturday afternoon, stepping over a couple Amazon boxes in the front entryway, which reminds me that I think I have a package in my mailbox I need to pick up on the way home. "Jessie? Sky? Rainbow? Who's here?" Their calico cat, Pixie, runs between my legs to greet me and I lean down to give her a good scratch behind the ears.

"Back here! How is Data doing? Did he take the elixir that Sky gave you without any troubles?" Arleigh's musical voice calls out to me. Did I mention Arleigh is an elf? It's common for people with DID to have alters that are nonhuman. DID, like I said, is a childhood trauma disorder and the brain often forms alters it needs to survive traumatic experiences that are happening. This leads to alters who are dragons, aliens, and storybook characters. Arleigh is very much aware that they are in a human body and not actually an elf, but in their innerworld, they look and feel like an elf. Arleigh has told me she's got long straight golden brown hair and a general human hippie vibe, along with the pointy ears, of course. She loves wearing long flowy skirts in earth tones and is often mixing various herbs and edible flowers, making intricately involved tea mixtures and other tinctures. Arleigh is also very much into psychology and would probably have a thing or two to say about my crush on Monty, telling me that it's a parasocial relationship and that I should focus more on my crochet and not on a minor internet celebrity.

"The meds?" I confirmed. Arleigh always has to use the fanciest words, such as elixir. "Like a champ! I just put it in a bit of cheese and he gobbled it up. He seems to be feeling a lot better this morning and was even playing with his catnip toy. What's in your Amazon boxes?"

"Oh yes, I think it's something Jessie acquired from an online establishment," Arleigh says with a deep sigh. One of the struggles of being a System is that each person in the System has their own hobbies and interests. There is sometimes some overlap, but it can be very expensive trying to buy things for each alter, not to mention figuring out storage. Rainbow's apartment has a lot of shelves, and every single surface has stuff stowed away. Arleigh's sigh indicated that she probably didn't approve of whatever Jessie bought. That gets me curious, but I'll probably learn what it is later. "Let's make our way towards the kitchen so you can have one of the delightful cookies Max concocted last night," Arleigh continues. "I found them this morning when I woke up, accompanied by a corresponding annotation on them announcing they were for you." Another thing about being a System is all the Post-it notes. Sometimes the alters can communicate innerworld or be aware of what is going on outside when they are inside, but not always because of amnesia barriers, and Post-it notes save the day.

"Oh, chocolate chocolate chip! My favorite!" I say as I pull up a worn but still serviceable barstool at the kitchen counter. "I'm kinda sad it's raining so hard and a hike wouldn't be fun, but also I'm kinda glad to just spend some girl time hanging out." In the Pacific Northwest there's a saying that there's no such thing as bad weather, just bad clothing. For me, an Autistic girl who cannot stand the sensory experience of being wet or cold—and definitely not both at the same time—there absolutely is such a thing as bad weather. Thankfully Rainbow totally gets that about me and we save hikes and outdoor activities for Katrina-approved weather days.

As I talk, I notice Arleigh sort of get really still for a moment, and her eyes grow soft around the edges. I stop talking because I know a switch is happening. Sometimes switches, especially controlled switches, happen quickly. Other times, it takes a while for an alter to ground themselves to the front. I just let Rainbow have a moment while I check out the cookies. Max really is an amazing baker. It shows how individual the alters are, because Sky can't even boil water. In that regard, it's a good thing she shares a body because she'd have to live off frozen dinners!

With a few rapid blinks, Rainbow's entire posture changes from the relaxed flowy manner Arleigh carries the body to Jessie's typical posture. She tends to hunch her shoulders forward and, well, it's hard to really say, but it's just different. "I popped in because I really wanted one of these cookies! Plus, Arleigh always gets a reaction when she eats chocolate. Can you imagine not being able to eat chocolate??? Ugh. OMG these look so good. I haven't seen them yet. So, how are you? Did we go through all that yet? Did Arleigh ask about Data? I wasn't really paying attention until I smelled these cookies."

"Hi Jessie, it's so good to see you. I was happy to see Arleigh this morning, but I have something I really wanted to tell you! And yes, she asked about Data. He's doing great this morning. Took his meds and is now back to his playful self."

Jessie nods as she takes a giant bite out of a cookie. "Ahummmm, nomm nom. Max should sell these. Oh wait, like when would he have the time? Oh well, more for us! So, what's up?"

"Remember last night when I told you I was watching that VidVibe Live and I needed an interesting question to get the creator's attention?"

"Yeah, who is it anyway? You never said."

"I know." I try to keep the guilty look off my face. I don't know why I'm so nervous about telling my best friend that I've suddenly become obsessed (infatuated?) with a vampire. She, of all people, should understand, sharing a body with an elf! "Well, I've sort of been avoiding telling you about him."

"Ooooh! Now I'm really listening. Why would you avoid telling me?"

"I guess because he's an enigma that I can't figure out. He came up on my FYP a couple months ago."

"Months!" Jessie interrupts me. "Months? You've kept this for months? Now I need to know what's going on, Katrina. You don't usually keep anything bottled up. You're the exact opposite of bottled up."

It's true. I've been accused of being an oversharer by more than one person in my life. Part of that is because I just process stuff out loud—when I talk to my friends about stuff, it helps me figure out what I'm feeling about something too. Which is probably why I'm suddenly needing to tell Jessie about all of this, because I need help sorting it in my own head. "Like I said, he came up on my FYP a couple of months ago. His video was interesting and I watched it but didn't think much of it. It's not like I started following him right away. But the algorithm would show me more of his videos, and I got more and more hooked. I finally did hit 'follow' and now have been watching pretty much everything he puts out.

But there's more . . ." I sort of fade off, still working up the courage to say he thinks he's a vampire. Because I know he's just cosplaying but it seems so real! And, well, along with "oversharer," "gullible" and "naive" are also two descriptions which follow me around.

Looking anywhere except at Jessie's face, I say, "He's a vampire. I mean, his whole account is him cosplaying a vampire. He never breaks character! Also, he's um, absolutely yummy-looking. Like, I'd take him over this chocolate chocolate chip cookie any day and, well, you know I don't usually pay attention to looks that much." I spit it all out and then screw my eyes tightly shut, waiting to hear Jessie's response but unable to look her in the face.

"Ha hahaha ha! That's what you've been keeping from me? That you have a crush on a vampire?!"

"Someone COSPLAYING a vampire," I interject, trying to keep some semblance of normalcy in this conversation. But, honestly, what is "normal" anyway? It is really amazing to me how I hold space for Arleigh absolutely being an elf innerworld as normal but the idea of someone cosplaying a vampire is a struggle. I think it's because Arleigh understands that she's an elf because of her DID. If Monty said, "I'm cosplaying a vampire" upfront, it'd be more comfortable. But pretending that someone isn't pretending they are pretending makes me very confused.

"Tell me more. So you said you asked your question. Did he answer it? What did you end up asking?"

"I went with a philosophical question." Leaning back in my chair, I'm now able to glance up at Jessie. She's smiling, taking all of this in stride. I knew she would, but still, it wasn't easy to share it with her. I think partly because it's been a long time since I even had a crush on anyone. I'm usually content doing my library thing, crocheting, playing with Data, and occasionally going out to dinner with Rainbow or another one of my friends. I lead a pretty mundane life, but I like my mundane life. Routines are comfortable.

"I asked him, 'Have you ever wondered if reality is just a collective illusion we've all agreed upon?' Honestly I'm not even sure where I got that question. It might have been inspired by a poster in the library. But I asked it, and, yes, he did answer! Jessie! I wish I had been screen recording. I've got to show you some of Monty's videos. His name is Monty, short for Montgomery. His account is MontyTheVampire. His voice is so dreamy. And in that incredibly sexy deep voice, he said, 'Katrina, my sweet dear mortal,' and I screamed at my tablet in a total fangirl way. You should have seen me. I started dancing around my living room, and I almost missed the rest of his answer." Jessie can't get a word in edgewise. Once I start to open up, the floodgate bursts wide and I can't stop talking.

As I tell her all of this, I pull up VidVibe on my phone and go to Monty's profile. I hand the phone over to Jessie with his page pulled up on the screen.

"Yep, I can totally see it. Yummy. I can't believe you've been keeping this eye candy from me for months!" She teases. "His hair is gorgeous. I normally don't like long hair on guys, but I can see why you are into him. So what exactly does he do on there?"

"That's the best part—he's actually quite educational. He talks a lot about history. Part of his story is that he's like three hundred years old, so he talks about things that have happened in the past three hundred years— in England and the US, but some world history stuff too. Click on the video titled 'My Siblings.'"

Jessie, still holding my phone, scrolls through his recent videos until she finds the one I'm talking about, and clicks on it.

I hear Monty's voice. *"In the late 1600s it was common for women to have a lot of children. We lived on a farm, and as soon as we were old enough, we were given farm chores. My mother had nine children, but only five of us lived past the age of one—myself, two boys, and a set of identical twin girls. Then she had a series of stillbirths and babies that didn't make it past infancy. Three more boys and one more girl. I never met them, as I was the last baby to be born. There was a significant age gap between me and the older siblings, and I was always treated like the baby of the family. Even back in the 1690s, I got spoiled more than most kids did. I think somehow my mother knew she wouldn't have any more after I was born."*

"What do you think?" I ask.

"I can totally see why you're interested in this guy. The way he tells his story really is captivating. I might be fangirling a bit myself!"

"I call dibs," I say half-jokingly.

"Do you know where he lives? Has he ever said it in any   videos?"

"I don't think so. Almost all of his videos are done in that leather chair. I think he's recorded a couple outside, but not enough to know where he's filming from. Anyway, after that question last night, I wanted to send him a DM. I know it's such a long shot that he'll answer me, but I just have to try or I won't be able to think of anything else. I know Arleigh wouldn't approve, but you understand, right?"

"You'd be surprised. I think Arleigh would be fine as long as after you send him a DM, you don't get upset if he doesn't answer."

44

"I was thinking about it. He has a SnapFoto account too, and I may send the DM there instead of on VidVibe."

"Why? Does it matter?" Jessie arches her eyebrow.

"Just being a little devious. His VidVibe has 1.6 million followers, and he probably gets hundreds of DMs a day. But on SnapFoto, for whatever reason, he 'only' has 10K followers. He might get less messages on that platform. I just want to stand out." I realize I sound a bit like a stalker the moment the follower counts spew out of my mouth, but I convince myself everyone knows how many followers their favorite content creators have.

"I guess we aren't watching a movie today after all," Jessie jokes as she stands up and walks to the living room. She sits down on the purple couch Sky bought from a garage sale one day, and crosses her legs under her. I plop down on her bean bag chair, taking my phone back from her and pulling up SnapFoto.

"Nope! This is my current hyperfixation and I've got to do this so I can focus on something else! Oh, that does remind me though . . . I have a surprise!" I lean over and grab my purse where I had thrown it earlier as we had gone to the kitchen. I dig out the Junimo and present it to Jessie. "Uh, well, it's really for Sky, but I don't want to forget to give it to her. Can you set it where she'll see it? I put a note on it already."

"Sure thing—she'll love it. It's so cute! What an adorable expression!"

"Oh, and Arleigh said you had an Amazon package by the door," I remind Jessie while looking down at my phone. Montgomery1690 is his SnapFoto account. It may have taken a little bit of hunting to find it. Most big creators keep the same name across platforms, but it seems Monty keeps his content separate. His SnapFoto account contains a few beauty shots of himself, but isn't that active.

"Okay, here goes nothing. Maybe I should type it in the Notes app first. I don't want to accidentally send it before I'm ready." I switch to the app and stare at the blank screen.

"You'll probably want to reference your question from last night. What else did he say about it?"

"I'm not even one hundred percent sure. I was in so much shock he picked my question. Something about his perception changing with time or something like that."

"Start it off with something like 'Oh my dearest sexy Monty, will you have my baby?'" Jessie giggled. "Sorry, I couldn't resist. I bet he gets those types of messages all the time. How about 'Monty, I watched your Live on VidVibe last night and it was such a pleasure to hear you talk about blah blah blah'—fill in something he said that was interesting. Then go on to say, 'I was excited you answered my question about the perception of reality. I was surprised you saw it.' How does that sound?"

"I like it."

@Katrina_Crochet: Monty, I watched your VidVibe Live last night, and I enjoyed everything you shared about the history of England. You tell stories in such a compelling way, it's hard not to believe you weren't actually there. You have such a gift. I was excited you picked my question about the perception of reality. I like that you are willing to have deep conversations, especially in a Live. Your answer was so interesting! I have another question for you from the perspective as a "vampire," although I think it's likely one you've considered before. What do you think defines a morally good action?

"Should I put an exclamation mark after saying his answer was interesting? I can't believe how much we have to debate punctuation online. Did you know adding a period or not to a text means such different things to different generations? People are so hard!!! But I digress . . .What do you think?" I hand Jessie the phone as I bombard her with my tangents.

"It looks good. Send it off, and we'll see if he responds!"

Chapter 6
The Reply

Montgomery

As I log off the VidVibe Live, that one question from Katherine, Karina, no . . . Katrina—yes, Katrina—sticks in my head. You meet a wide variety of humans online, and most of the usernames and questions just become a blur. But every once in a while someone will stand out and catch my interest for a moment. I wonder if she's ever commented on any of my other videos? I don't remember the rest of her username, though, so I guess there's no way to find out. I think there's a way to save your live streams, but I've never found a need to do so before. Now I wish I had made that a habit.

I head to my bedroom, trying to put Katrina and her question out of my mind, and start to get out of my costume. I mean it is and isn't a costume. I genuinely think the outfits I pick are badass in a totally cosplay kind of way. If I was headed to some cosplay event and wanted to dress up as a vampire, this is definitely a vibe. But it's a far cry from my everyday wear. I pull my hair back into a low ponytail at the nape of my neck, and put on some comfortable relaxed fit jeans and my Captain America T-shirt. It's starting to fade, which is sad because it's one of my favorite shirts. It's getting late and I do need to find something to "eat."

I usually only feed once a week, but there's no hard and fast rule. There are a couple ways to go about it. In the past, blood had to come straight from the source—human or animal. But now I usually put in an order for porcine or bovine blood through an online order and it comes right to my door. DoorDash for vampires if you will. Yeah, you can actually have blood delivered. Apparently people use it to add to homemade dog foods and there's a recipe called blood pudding which uses bovine blood. I rotate my order from a couple different places because, again, I don't want to draw attention to myself. Human blood is the best, and I'll admit, I'm not proud of it, but there has been an occasion or two where Nikolai and I have procured blood from a blood bank. We can use our glamor to entice humans to believe any far-fetched story we tell them. So, we'll walk into a blood bank and tell them we are inspectors, or some other wild story, and our glamor confuses them enough that they believe us and don't think twice about how wild our story sounds. We can also just teleport into the blood bank after hours, take a few packs of blood, and teleport home.

The blood has been donated for people to live, right? Is that a weak excuse? I mean, yes, Nikolai and I are undead, but without sustenance, we'd cease to exist eventually. In extreme situations, we can go for a while feeding off squirrels or birds, but that isn't very filling and it's not something either one of us would prefer to do. Being able to acquire donated blood keeps us going.

Fresh blood from the tap is the most refreshing. Yep, straight from a human. Back in the old days, we'd seduce women, or in Nik's case, men too, using our glamor, and they'd offer their necks up without any complaint. It doesn't hurt; they actually feel pleasure, and we never drain them. At most, they might feel a bit tired afterwards and have no memory of us. These days, we're all about consent. And so when we "hunt" people for blood we ask before taking. They won't remember us when we leave, but we don't use any magic or suggestive push to do anything they don't fully agree to. Nikolai likes to act the part of a player, but he really respects the men and women he seduces, just as I always value the women I enjoy.

Rain patters against the window and that bums me because I was going to join Nikolai at his bar tonight, but I'm just not feeling like going out in the rain. And while I could teleport there, I think I just want to stay in. I think I'll grab a glass of blood from the fridge and go binge watch some *Doctor Who*.

I blink my eyes open. Apparently I fell asleep on the couch. I don't do that very often but after watching more episodes of *Doctor Who* than I really want to admit to, I must have just drifted off. Thank goodness the curtains were drawn, as it looks like I slept through the entire day. Yes, that's another myth. We technically can go out in the sun as we get older. A new vampire will incinerate. And we do burn very easily. We typically avoid high noon at great lengths. I spend most of my days asleep and most of my nights awake, but again, I can be awake during the day if I need to, with limited exposure to the sun, by staying indoors as much as possible. I look down at my smartwatch. It's almost Saturday evening. Stretching, I look around and realize I never put my cup away from last night. I go to clean that up and pull out my phone. You'd think with millions of followers I'd be getting hundreds and hundreds of DMs, comments, etc. I do get a lot of comments actually, which is why I have notifications turned off on those. But I only get around twenty to fifty direct messages a day. Most of them are spam, some are companies or other creators wanting to do collaborations, and a few are from actual fans or sometimes people who feel they have to take time to tell me how awful I am. Those are an easy block—I don't have patience for them at all.

Scrolling through my VidVibe comments reminds me I forgot to film a video last night after my Live, so I need to get in costume today and film a couple to throw in my drafts folder. Most of the comments are from a recent video I did about how I eat. This is an endless fascination for people. And it's so funny all the responses I get. I actually don't tell people that I can feed from live humans (unless it's in a joking way). For one, I think that'd get me banned from VidVibe. I stick with the porcine and bovine stories. I sure don't tell anyone about how I "liberate" blood from blood banks. Even still, straight up telling the truth, even if it isn't the whole truth, makes people just think I'm cosplaying. It's a never-ending amusement for me. Despite people not believing me, there's a part of me that loves being able to be my true nature in public. After centuries of disguising myself, it's thrilling to just be me.

Next I open SnapFoto. I don't even check it every day. Before I started my VidVibe account, I actually posted silly photos of Nikolai and I goofing off and doing "human" things. But I went in and deleted all of those photos so I could keep up my vampire persona across platforms. Sometimes I do miss being able to show off the other half of who I am. Because, yes, I am a vampire, but who would believe a vampire that likes to play *World of Warcraft* and beat my best friend at *Mario Kart*? The icon shows I have twenty-six new DMs since I last checked the app. Clicking on the direct message icon, Katrina_Crochet jumps off the screen at me. That girl from last night was named Katrina. I immediately wonder if it's the same one. Tentatively I open the message and quickly scan it, verifying it is her. It most definitely is!

I feel my fangs wanting to descend as my anticipation grows at the thought of texting with Katrina. Part of me can't believe I'm getting this worked up. I have no idea what this girl looks like or how old she is—her profile photo is a crocheted frog. But something about her questions just really intrigued me. Before I answer, I feel like doing a bit of snooping. That is, *if* I answer her. I can't get ahead of myself. I click on her profile picture. Thank goodness SnapFoto doesn't show when someone's checked your profile like VidVibe does! But all I see are crocheted items. No selfies. Who doesn't post selfies! Her little stuffed animals are cute, I will give her that. OMG. A Junimo? A Mario Mushroom? A BOO! She's even got a Dalek. This girl has definitely grabbed my attention now.

She has one current Story. I click on it and yes! Finally! A photo of two individuals that I assume are her and a friend. I don't know who is who, but at least I can get an estimate of her age. Not that I guess it really matters. I'm over 330 years old. I was turned at twenty-seven, so I'll forever look that age. The women in the photo look to be somewhere between twenty-seven and thirty-two, but estimating age is so hard. So what's three hundred years, give or take a few? It's then it dawns on me that I'm thinking enough about this woman's age, it could suggest I want to talk to her. I'm getting several steps ahead of myself. I shake my head and refocus on the photo. It's of two women, one with very long fiery red curly hair. Wow, that hair is what fantasies are made of— absolutely stunning. I can't make out her eye color, but she seems fairly short, at least shorter than the girl next to her.

52

The other girl is cute too, with a much shorter shaggy hairstyle and round sweet face. But I can't take my eyes off the redhead. Katrina sounds like a redhead name, right? I'm totally making that up! I could check out her VidVibe, but she'll get a notification that I clicked on her profile, and I'm not ready for that.

I tap my phone absentmindedly, staring off into space, trying to decide if I should respond right away (because who am I kidding, I am absolutely going to respond to her) or if I should wait a day. As much as I like playing computer games, games of the heart are not my usual speed. Nikolai wouldn't understand the intrigue I'm feeling from Katrina's message. He thrives with constant change in who he dates. He's bisexual and goes back and forth between dating men and women fairly equally. I haven't dated in a while because I've gotten tired of people coming in and out of my life so quickly, I don't even have a chance to connect to them. But something in Katrina's message has unfurled the hope that I thought had shriveled up. Maybe there's something to explore and maybe not, but at the least, it's a diversion.

@Montgomery1690: Katrina, I do remember your question. It stood out from the usual types of questions I get. What defines a morally good action, from the perspective of a "vampire"? Well first, let me remind you, I am a vampire so the perspective I share will always be from that view.

Just like reality, what is moral has shifted so much over the decades I've been alive. In more recent years, human society has become much less prudish and judgmental in their morality. Although there are still groups that have taken to book banning again in the name of purity. In the past, what was moral benefited the community. Now there's a mix of groupthink and individual thinking. The internet especially allows group-based morality to be amplified with collective outrage. But these days there is an emphasis on personal ethics and critical thinking, and I'm on board with that.

As a vampire, I find consent something that I hold above all else. I need humans to survive, but I won't feed from someone unless I'm invited to do so. But there are still things I do to survive in a human-dominated world that would be considered morally gray. I'm curious what made you such a deep thinker?

I take a minute to look at what I wrote, wondering if it's too much. I think it's important to be truthful about the fact I am a vampire, even though at this point I know she will think I'm still just in character. I never enjoy lying, even when I have to do it for survival. I edit a few words and check my spelling and just decide to hit send. Tucking my phone in my pocket, I head back into my closet to change into one of my vampire costumes so I can film a few videos before Nikolai shows up at my door wanting to hang out again.

Chapter 7
Blow Up My Phone

Katrina

I am sitting on the floor in front of Jessie. After showing me her new sunglasses, we spent some time talking about Rainbow's VidVibes. They make VidVibes talking about veterinary stuff, and just like at their job, the System works together to mask as one person. Their VidVibe account is about the same size as mine, and it's something we love doing together even though we are in very different niches. Today she used Pixie (who stars in many of her videos) as a model to show how to properly clip a cat's claws. I acted as her camerawoman.

Now, we are settled in to watch the latest *Doctor Who* episode, eating a pizza we ordered for dinner, when all of a sudden my phone pings with a new notification.

"Katrina, I thought you turned off notifications!" Jessie lightly scolds me.

"I did, I did, I promise! But um, I turned them back on in case Monty writes back." I say bashfully, grabbing my phone off the table and almost dropping it in my haste to see who the notification is from.

"Come on, you know that's a long shot! Don't set yourself up for failure like that, Kat." I only let very dear friends call me Kat. Normally I can't stand nicknames. My first sentence growing up was "My name Katrina Prescott, I am myself!" (Not grammatically correct, but I was just over a year old.) As an Autistic kid, undiagnosed until twenty-two, I didn't understand the concept of nicknames. Why call someone something that wasn't their name? It didn't make any sense to me. But as I got older and learned many people use nicknames as a form of endearment, I grew to like them, but only from people I trust and feel are close to me. Monty calling me his sweet dear mortal doesn't really count because he was in character and I am practically in love with him anyway. (Did I think that out loud? What is WRONG with me? I'm letting this crush get out of hand.) But honestly I can't help it. Hyperfixations are part and parcel for Autistic people and Monty has obviously become my new hyperfixation.

"I know, Jessie. But you're wrong. Look, HE DID WRITE BACK!" I jump up off the floor and twirl around three times. "I can't read it. I can't! Let's go back to watching the show. I'm going to ignore it. I can't handle knowing what he said."

"Who are you kidding? I'm not going to sit here and try to watch The Doctor save the world while you're vibrating with excitement over a DM. Just open the damn thing."

"Here, you do it!" I shove the phone at Jessie. "No wait, never mind. I'll read it," I say, just as quickly pulling my phone back towards my chest. I fall down in the bean bag and squeeze my eyes shut just after hitting the open icon in SnapFoto DMs.

I read through the message, taking each word in and holding my breath the entire time. "He remembered me! He liked my question!" I yell.

"I'm right here. You don't have to shout. What did he say?"

"He talks about how morality has changed over the years he's been alive. He also reiterated that he's a vampire. I

56

told you, he never breaks character. He does mention he does morally gray things though . . ." My voice drifts off because that makes me a bit uncomfortable to think about. I'm a rule follower. Or I think of myself that way, but if you really held me to it, I'm only a rule follower when I feel the rules are just. Maybe he's the same. I'll need to keep that in mind going forward though. Also, how much of this is him and how much is his character? This is all very difficult for my brain to tease apart. I stare down at my phone, the rest of the world fading away as I think about what to write. "He asked me a question back," I mutter under my breath, all but forgetting Jessie is still in the room with me.

"Hey! Earth to Katrina!"

I look up with a sheepish expression on my face. "I'm sorry, Jessie, I'll put it down. I came over to hang out with you today. I'll message Monty back later."

"I know you. Your brain is now on this and there won't be any way to get it off of Monty. Go ahead, message him back. Sky wanted to paint our nails today and Max and Arleigh reluctantly agreed, as long as it's a dark color. I'll let Sky front to do that while you make googly eyes towards Monty. I'm still shocked he wrote you back. Girl, you got GAME." Jessie heads off to her bedroom, but I hardly notice because I am already trying to figure out my next message.

@Katrina_Crochet: Morally gray—I'll have to hear more about that. I think I can understand. Personally, I'm such a rule follower, but when rules don't make any sense, I suppose there have been times when I've gone around them. I wouldn't say I'm a deep thinker, really. I just don't like small talk. I like to dive into important topics. Maybe that does make me a deep thinker. I'm a librarian by day—I love learning. So, vampire, what do you do besides VidVibes?

I'm not even going to overthink it anymore. I'm just letting my spontaneous ADHD side take over and hit send. I stare at my phone, willing the little dots to appear that he's reading it and typing back. Surely he's doing something way more important though. I should go see what color Sky picked out to paint her nails. Maybe she'll paint mine too, although I'll just pick off the paint. I love the idea of nail polish but I can't ever keep it on my fingernails for more than an hour or two.

Montgomery

I apply the finishing touches of my eyeliner in preparation to film a video when I decide to check SnapFoto one more time. Not that I've been checking it every five minutes since sending my message. I feel like a seventeen-year-old again, not a 333-year-old. These are the moments, honestly. What's the point of living this long if you can't get excited about a girl sending you a message? Sure enough, there's a new one from Katrina_Crochet. I open the message and see that she's a librarian. Instantly, hot librarian thoughts download into my brain, and I shake them away. I still don't know if she's the redhead or the one with short hair. Heck, she might not be either of the people in that photo, since there was no caption. I wonder if there's a way to ask without being too obvious. Suddenly tonight is looking way more interesting. That is, if she writes right back.

@Montgomery1690: Librarian, I like it. Do you have glasses or is that just a myth—that all librarians have glasses? I've had many jobs over the years. One of my more interesting jobs was doing construction on the White House. But I've been everything from a cobbler, to a doorman at a fancy hotel, IT guy, and more. These days I mostly focus on making VidVibes, and I've started to write a memoir about my life. I know it's too early to trust you, but I've just got a feeling you're trustworthy. Don't mention my book on social media, as I haven't told anyone about it. Actually, if we keep talking, I hope anything I say privately stays in confidence.

@Katrina_Crochet: I wear glasses sometimes, contacts other times. Construction on the White House? That's an oddly specific job—I'd love to hear more about it. Thank you for sharing about writing a book. How's it going for you? I promise I'll keep your secret. I'm glad you make VidVibes. You are my favorite creator. *Smile* I like making VidVibes too, but my account is quite small compared to yours. Still, I just crochet for fun. I end up giving away almost all of my projects when I'm done with them.

@Montgomery1690: Hmm, so I can have the librarian fantasy where you pull down your hair and take off your glasses for me? The book is going well. I just work on it here and there when I'm inspired. I don't even know for sure if I'll try to get it published or not. We'll see. I'm sure your VidVibes are great—I'll go watch a few later. I've never tried crochet but I actually did join a "Men Who Knit" group a few years ago!

@Katrina_Crochet: You know how to knit?! That is so awesome! Surprisingly, I just am not good at knitting. I noticed you seem to have an American accent but you said you were born in England. Have you lived in America for a long time?

@Montgomery1690: You could say that. I moved to America toward the end of the 1700s. I've lived all over America. As a matter of fact, I recently moved to the Portland, Oregon area and I've got to say it suits me. The weather, the people. I've lived in a lot of great cities, but this is probably in the top three. Where do you live? If you don't mind me asking. I understand if you're not comfortable sharing that with me.

@Katrina_Crochet: ARE YOU KIDDING ME? I live in Vancouver, WA. We are practically neighbors?! How is that even possible? I had no idea where you lived. I don't think you've referenced it in any of the videos I've watched of yours. I haven't seen all of your content, but um, well, I have watched quite a few videos. What an incredibly small world it is! Also, 1700s, huh? You sure are dedicated to the character! I love that though.

@Montgomery1690: Uh, we are actual neighbors! As in, same city. By Portland, OR area, I'm actually IN Vancouver. Most people just haven't ever heard of Vancouver. Originally I was going to move to Portland, but a really nice house came for sale in Vancouver and my realtor convinced me to try The Couve even though Portland is trendier. I cannot get over that we live in the same city. That is wild. Absolutely wild. What are the chances? Also, yep, late 1700s. I am a vampire, like I said. *smile* I hate to cut this short, but I need to get some

VidVibes filmed. I hope to see you in my comment section! Hopefully we can chat again soon??

I close out SnapFoto and mount my phone on my tripod. It's time to put Katrina out of my mind, at least for a little while. I understand why she thinks I'm just playing a character. Part of me really wants her to believe that I'm a vampire, but for now I think it's okay she doesn't actually believe me. But I do need to film a few VidVibes. I need to get them done before Nikolai arrives. I really want to keep that conversation going. I can't believe she lives so close to me. I need time to process that information.

After getting back into my vampire clothes, I get comfortable in my leather chair and look at the camera. I hit record and film a short VidVibe:

"Recently someone asked me what else I do besides make these VidVibes for you, and I thought that was an interesting question. During my lifetime, I've had many jobs, but one I hadn't thought about in a long while was when I was on the construction crew for the White House. The year was 1792, when construction finally began after years of debate between the North and the South about where it should be located. It was able to be built after Congress passed the Residence Act in 1790. For me, it was about being at the right place at the right time. I had moved to America in 1785, shortly after the Revolutionary War ended. I had been living in Philadelphia but made my way down towards the Potomac River where I heard they were looking for crews to build a huge mansion for the president. I was available and willing to learn, so they handed me a hammer and I got to work.

I met a lot of interesting people during that time. Much of the White House was built with slave labor, which likely won't surprise anyone. Many of the enslaved workers were owned by George Washington and Thomas Jefferson. Alongside them were Irish immigrants, eager to do whatever it took to earn a living. Interestingly, the head architect of the project, a man named James Hoban, was also Irish. He hired many skilled artisans to craft the beautiful details that make the White House so striking, from the intricate stonework to the fine wood carvings. I was hired as a blacksmith, working around the forge at night. We hand made the nails, hinges, and other metal fittings that were used by the day crew."

I stop recording and save the video to my drafts. Sometimes it takes me a couple of tries, but often I can make a video in one go. I decide to film one more video of my time in Washington D.C. and then I'll go change into my regular clothes. As I'm pulling my hair back into a low ponytail, the front door creaks open.

"Nik, how was your night?" I greet him as he enters.

"Fairly tame Friday night," he replies, following me towards the game room.

"Hmm, meet anyone interesting?" I prod him.

"No, it was a fairly tame Friday night. A few regulars came by, but nothing exciting. I did sit in a booth with a tourist for a while and showed him how a vampire has a good time, if you know what I mean!" he says as he flops down on the couch in his favorite spot. "I also had the opportunity to save a damsel in distress. There was this slick guy hitting on her at the next booth over. I was keeping an eye on the situation when I heard her practically screaming in her mind, 'How can I safely get away from this creep!' Telepathy can come in handy. I finished up with my new friend, and stood

62

up to tower over Mr. Slick. I turned to the girl and said, 'Hey sis, I didn't expect to run into you tonight. Who's your friend, hopefully someone your big brother is going to like.' Mr. Slick turned tail and practically ran out of the bar. The girl was really thankful. It was fun being a hero."

"And here I was drinking cow blood, but that's okay. I'm glad you were able to scare off that creep. You won't believe it, but I met someone interesting tonight and I haven't even left the house!"

"How, exactly, did you manage that?" Clearly intrigued, he leans forward eager to hear more since it's been some time since I brought up anyone new.

I sit down and turn on the TV and Nintendo. Nikolai has brought his gaming laptop, so we may log on and play *Warcraft* together later. "You know how I did that Live event on VidVibe last night?"

"Yeah, how did it go?"

"It was great. Right at the beginning, I received a really interesting question. Something about the perception of reality. I don't know, I made up some fancy-sounding answer. But the question just stuck with me. I wanted to know more about who asked it, but I couldn't remember their username, so I was trying to put it out of my head, but then she sent me a DM on SnapFoto."

"Really? You don't have your DMs turned off?"

"That's your takeaway? No, I don't have them turned off. I actually get a lot less than you'd think I would. Most are spam and easy enough to delete and sometimes people do want to contact me for legitimate collabs."

"Huh, well you know more than I do. I'm not that social media savvy. So what did her DM say?"

I proceed to get Nik all caught up on our exchange, while trying to tamper some of my excitement. I mean, a few DMs with someone shouldn't get me this excited to begin with, and I feel like I'm setting myself up for disappointment. However, the fact she's local to me makes me feel as if eventually we could potentially even meet each other.

Chapter 8
Boy Next Door

Katrina

"Jessie! He's been writing back. He lives in Vancouver! Not Canada, but somewhere here in this city. Our city! Can you believe it? I can't. I absolutely cannot believe that. What are the odds?" This has me a little worried because Autistic people sometimes form friendships or attachments pretty quickly. We struggle to read social cues, such as how another person might feel about us, and we can mentally jump from seeing someone as a stranger, to "this person is a close friend" too quickly. It has happened to me over and over. I don't do well with acquaintance-level relationships. In my mind, people are either strangers or close friends, and I have to remind myself that isn't always how other people think. Especially neurotypicals. Knowing Monty literally lives within driving distance of me, my mind immediately is jumping to us becoming long lost friends. I need to put on the mental breaks!

I look up and Sky is painting her nails at the coffee table. "Have you been here all along?"

"Um hum, Jessie realized you weren't going to be focused enough to watch *Doctor Who*, so I took the opportunity to . . . " she trails off as she holds up her hand and wiggles her now purple finger tips at me. "I've been enjoying watching you try to figure out what to say back to your vampire. It seems like you two were going back and forth quite a bit there."

"He's still sticking to the vampire bit, but I'll play along for a while. If he keeps it up, it'll get old. I mean, assuming he's not another DID System with a vampire alter, because there's only so many coincidences I can take in one day. You know I love Arleigh and her beautiful elf self."

"Yeah, we know. Don't get all in knots about it."

"Okay, sometimes I just like to check in with you."

"I know, and that's why we all love you so dearly, Katrina. You are the kindest, most open, most understanding person we've ever met. And even though we love you so very dearly, we're kicking you out because it's getting late and I want to get ready for bed." Sky screws the lid closed on her nail polish.

"Thanks for letting me hang out here for a while, even if we didn't really end up doing much." I feel grateful to have a friend that I feel comfortable enough to be around without always having a reason. "Before I go, earlier I gave Jessie a Junimo that I crocheted for you! I think she put it on a shelf in your room. I'm going to Michaels tomorrow to pick out some yarn for my next crochet project. I think I'm going to make a Yoshi. Goodnight! Talk to you tomorrow, I'm sure."

"Don't stay up too late chatting with Monty!"

"Only if he answers back again!" I say with a giggle before pulling the front door closed behind me and practically skipping to my car—a sapphire blue Kia that I named Charlie Zoom Zoom. Yes, I named my car, didn't everyone?

I step through the door of my townhome, shake off my raincoat, hang it up, and then look for Data, who is sound asleep on his cat tree. Eagerly, I rush to my bedroom to change into my pajamas. I know it's late but I want to send

Monty another message before going to bed. I pull out pajamas with cute little panda bears all over them, brush my teeth, and wash my face. Some nights it is extremely difficult to get myself to do these basic self-care tasks because the sensory experience of water on my face and the feeling of toothpaste is just enough for my brain to tell me not to do it. Tonight though, I'm more focused on getting into bed so I can pull out my phone and message Monty, and I'm not as focused on the icky feeling of water being splashed on my face.

@Katrina_Crochet: I'm very excited to see your next VidVibe. I'll make a point to leave a comment. I'll admit, I've probably watched most of the videos you've posted since I found you on the app a couple months ago, but I don't always comment. My favorite ones are the historical videos. I still can't get over the fact we live in the same city. What are some of your favorite things to do here? Do you go into Portland often?

@Montgomery1690: I'll admit, I often get so many comments I don't see them all—I might have read yours before. Vancouver is a bit of a sleepy town, but I do like living here. I go into Portland fairly often because the nightlife is more active across the bridge. What kinds of things do you like to do?

@Katrina_Crochet: Well, I do like to hike, but only when the weather is absolutely perfect. I hate being too cold or wet. But honestly, I'm not a nightlife kind of girl. I lead a pretty quiet lifestyle. My big plan for tomorrow is going to the craft store. You probably think I'm so boring!

@Montgomery1690: Life is lived in the mundane. If everything was always exciting, then that would become the norm and people would start reaching for even more thrill. There's nothing wrong with a quiet, content life.

@Katrina_Crochet: That's very beautifully said and I really appreciate it. Another get-to-know you question: if you could have dinner with any historical figure, dead or alive, who would it be and why?

I have no idea what I'm doing. I didn't think this through. I just wanted to see if I could catch the attention of a super cute creator on VidVibe. I never expected him to actually answer, and there's no way I actually expected him to continue a conversation with me. Yet, I'm sitting here with bated breath, wondering if he'll keep chatting with me. I really should get to bed, but I'm having too much fun.

@Montgomery1690: I actually got to meet Sir Isaac Newton back around 1720. He was pretty old, but it was exciting nevertheless. I ran into him at a pub, where he liked to go on occasion. By the end of his life, though, he was quite a paranoid old man, and our conversation wasn't that amazing. Still, I hold it in quite high esteem that I got to meet one of the great minds of our civilization. But the guy I'd really love the chance to meet is Allan Alcorn.

@Katrina_Crochet: I have so many thoughts about this answer. For one, I hope one day you'll drop the vampire act with me. I get it, I'm a fan, but also, I'd like to be a friend if you'd let me. Two, who's Alcorn?

Oh my goodness, I'm dying. I can't believe I told Monty I'd like to be his friend and would he please drop the vampire act. How did I get that brave? But again, it's just all a bit too confusing for me. I need things to be communicated to me straight. I'm not quite ready to tell him I'm Autistic. Like I said before, there is still a lot of stigma around Autism and ADHD and while I'm not ashamed of who I am, I just don't feel like disclosing it yet.

@Montgomery1690: Katrina, I'm not doing a bit. I *am* a vampire. I'll have to tell you more about it one day. I really would like to be your friend. I don't usually say that to someone I only just met, but I'm compelled to know you better. I am deeply enjoying our conversation. As for Alcorn . . . well he's the inventor of *Pong* and I have reasons for wanting to meet him!

@Katrina_Crochet: Well, I'll admit the vampire thing has me confused but I'll go along with it for now. I'm a pretty understanding girl. And somehow I absolutely love that you want to meet the inventor of *Pong*. I am thinking of the right *Pong* right? It's like a simple video game from the seventies, right?

@Montgomery1690: Thank you for trying to understand. And yes. Yes, it's THE first video game! Well, technically a game called *Spacewar!* was the first video game in the 1960s by a man named Steve Russell, and he'd be cool to meet too, but *Pong* was the first widely accessible video game. Hey, it's only 9 p.m. Would you want to meet up? It's okay to say no, I just felt like I had to ask. I still can't get over the fact you could actually be my literal neighbor for all I know. Of this entire world, how are we in the same city?

@Katrina_Crochet: I'm already in my pajamas! Do you even know what I look like? I don't think there's any photos of me on SnapFoto. I'm impressed you asked to meet me without knowing what I look like. That's a green flag, sir.

I try to stall because now I'm REALLY freaking out. I really, really like to stick to my routine and go to bed at a fairly regular time. But I haven't had something this exciting happen in a long time. I rarely get invited out. I should consider that even though he's a big content creator on VidVibe, shouldn't I be careful about meeting strange "vampires" off the internet? I can't even decide what to do. I am frustrated he hasn't dropped the vampire act. What if he doesn't drop it in person? That would be so weird. I think I need to talk to him about it again. My brain is malfunctioning. I switch quickly over to my ChatBox app and pull up the general chat window I use when I don't know who is fronting.

Me: Rainbow, 911. Are you asleep right now? Okay, maybe not 911 but we don't have a dating emergency code!

Max responds on his ChatBox chat channel with the following:

Max: Katrina, what's going on? Are you okay? I'm not asleep yet.

Me: Oh hi, Max, I figured maybe Sky would still be around.

Max: Well when I saw Dating Emergency, I pulled to the front. You know me, I go into protector mode with my friends. Are you safe?

Me: Yes, I'm sorry, I didn't mean to scare you.

Just as I hit send back to Max, I get a notification from SnapPhoto popping up from Monty again. My ADHD makes it really easy for me to switch back and forth between multiple conversations like a pro.

@Montgomery1690: Katrina? It's okay to say no. I'm sorry, I was probably too fast. Never mind, let's pretend I didn't ask.

@Katrina_Crochet: Uh, no, I was just surprised. Give me a quick second, okay? I'll BRB.

Me: I'm fine. Did Sky or Jessie tell you about the guy on VidVibe I've been messaging all day? Well, he wants to meet up RIGHT NOW! Now. I'm trying to decide if I should. I mean, I'm already in my pj's!

Max: No, no, no, you should NOT meet a man off VidVibe for the first time at 9 p.m. at night. This is something you should NOT do, Katrina.

Me: Would Sky or Jessie say the same thing? Arleigh probably is on your side . . .

Max: To be fair, Sky probably would be rushing over to do your makeup really quick, but no, Katrina. If he's interested, he'll plan a real date with you, not a quick meetup. Please listen to me.

Me: You're probably right. Thank you, Max. I can always count on you to help me make a decision.

@Katrina_Crochet: Monty? Sorry, I was texting a friend. He advised me that it would not be a smart idea to meet someone off VidVibe for the first time spur-of-the-moment. I really want to, but honestly, I'd probably just get a bit overwhelmed. I'm more of a planner type person. Is that okay?

@Montgomery1690: Yes, yes. I'm sorry again. I really shouldn't have thrown that at you. I would like to meet you, but it can wait. Take your time. Can you chat for a few more minutes? What kind of pj's are you wearing? *wink*

@Katrina_Crochet: Yes, a few more minutes and then I better head off to bed. I'm guessing you're a night "vampire." I'm more of a morning person. Haha. My pajamas are more of the comfortable variety, not the sexy variety! I'm wearing a soft black T-shirt and cotton pants with little pandas on them.

I have no idea if Monty is flirting with me or just being nice—Autistic people aren't exactly known for picking up on this stuff. But since he's been chatting with me and even suggested meeting, I'm leaning toward probably flirting. Maybe. And if he is, after him asking about my pajamas, I was probably supposed to say something like: *Ohhh this little thing? Just a silk and lace tank top with silky boy shorts. *kissey face**. Or something. But one, how can anyone

ACTUALLY sleep in that? I shudder at the thought. And two, I'm NOT wearing a sexy outfit, and saying so would feel disingenuous. I simply can't tell lies that way, even in the name of flirting. Which I have zero practice at.

We end up chatting back and forth for the next half hour before I tell him I need to go to bed. I have a feeling it's going to be hard to fall asleep tonight, as my brain will be busy replaying our conversation.

Chapter 9
Unexpected Turn

Montgomery

I look up from my phone in a bit of a daze. Nikolai is on my couch playing the new Zelda game tonight. He notices me sitting up and says, "Hey, welcome back from the land of DMs, bro. I guess we aren't playing *World of Warcraft* tonight?"

Trying not to look sheepish but not really succeeding I say, "What can I say, this girl has me captivated. I can't explain it. She sounds incredibly sweet. I'm so used to girls throwing themselves at me, and while she's a fan, she actually seems more interested in what I have to say than what I look like, or my persona."

"You said she's local, right? Are you going to hook up with her?"

"I don't think Katrina is a 'hook up' kind of girl. If we meet, it'll be a much more old-fashioned sort of meeting, I suspect. So yeah, let's boot up *World of Warcraft*."

Over the next week, Katrina and I send a couple DMs a day, getting to know each other a little more. I spend my days mostly asleep but send her a message when I wake up, as she's getting ready for bed. We chat for a few minutes and then repeat the next day. I learn to look forward to her questions—she is always asking me seemingly random but thought-provoking things.

Once she asked me, if I could travel anywhere in the world right at that moment, where would I go and why? I almost told her I could teleport anywhere I wanted, but I found myself sort of backing off mentioning things that highlighted the fact I'm a vampire. I think it just felt good to pretend to be a normal human infatuated with a beautiful girl. She did send me a photo (she *was* the redhead!) and I've watched a few of her VidVibes. She has a way of describing and talking about crochet that is captivating, but to be fair, she could be talking about paint drying and I'd find her fascinating. Other than a short foray into trying to learn to knit during a fit of ennui several years ago, I haven't been into fiber arts. But I could listen to her talk about hook sizes, treble, and bobble stitches for hours. There is no denying I am "hooked" on Katrina, and I really wanted to work up the courage to ask her out again. You'd think that a 333-year-old vampire wouldn't have confidence issues, but it's been multiple decades since I had this much interest in a girl—and that is scary!

A little over a week after my last Live and the first time I DM'd Katrina I'm trying to find a way to ask her if she'd like to meet up in person. It is a fairly warm spring evening and I am sitting on my porch staring at the flames dancing in the propane firepit in front of me. I am rotating my phone around in my hands, absentmindedly trying to think of a way to bring up the subject without sounding too eager or pushy, when I hear the ping of my notification bell.

@Katrina_Crochet: You know, we should exchange phone numbers instead of just using SnapFoto DMs. Somehow that feels next-level, doesn't it? We could even, I don't know, call each other?

Of course I'll give her my phone number! I am about to type it back to her when another message comes in.

@Katrina_Crochet: Or, well, if you still want to, maybe you could give me your phone number in person?

What? She asked me out! I immediately start typing, totally forgetting to play it cool at all . . .

@Montgomery1690: Yes, yes, I'd love to meet up with you! When and where, and I'm there!

@Katrina_Crochet: How about lunch on Thursday? I'd feel better if our first meetup was casual and had a time limit, because I'll have to get back to work.

@Montgomery 1690: Well, technically, I can go out in the afternoon, especially if it's a cloudy day, but it is difficult for me and we'd have to pick a restaurant where we can sit away from the windows. And, well, I don't eat. But I don't mind visiting with you while you eat at all! What library do you work at? Maybe we can find a place nearby?

@Katrina_Crochet: Really? You're keeping up the vampire bit, still? Monty, I've tried to be so patient. I get that it's your thing on VidVibe but I'm interested in you for you, not the character you've created! I want to meet you, but I just don't know if I can handle this.

@Montgomery1690: It's complicated. It'd be easier to explain in person. I can make an afternoon meeting work if that's what makes you the most comfortable.

@Katrina_Crochet: Honestly? I just don't know right now. Give me some time to think about this. I'm going to go work on my Yoshi crochet project and film a short video before heading to bed. I'll message you after I've had time to think about this more.

I stare silently down at my phone, unable to believe how quickly that went south. One second we were about to meet, and the next she changed her mind. I get it, she thinks I'm still cosplaying and I can see how someone never dropping their act would be annoying. But damn it, I *am* a vampire. I never wanted to let her believe otherwise. Even though I know over the last week I did sidestep most of the conversations we had where I could have reminded her again. I think, deep down, I knew it was frustrating her and I didn't want this to end prematurely.

I need to focus on something else. I turn off the firepit and head back inside. It's now fully dark out. I'm feeling restless. It's probably time for me to feed again. Days like this, I really do wish I could just eat food. Yes, being almost immortal with powers is nice, but also, it makes dating hard. I'm feeling pretty darn pathetic and pitiful. I need a distraction. I decide to call Nik.

"Hey Nik, what are you doing right now?" I ask him over the phone, although I have a pretty good guess that he's at the bar because loud music is coming through the speaker.

"WHAT? I can't hear you!" Nik screams into my ear. "I'm at the bar!"

"Yeah, I guessed that." I try saying it loudly enough for him to hear me. "I'll join you!" I hang up and then teleport to a spot behind the bar. Teleporting is handy but it does have a limitation. I have to know where I'm teleporting to. In the old days that meant I usually couldn't teleport to a place that I'd never been. That could end up with me in a lake, a wall, or some other not ideal place, like the time I ended up in a woman's locker room in the 1980's and almost got arrested. But with modern technology, I can pull up street view on maps and see photos of places, and then I just have to think purposefully about teleporting there. It's just another reason why I really know I am meant for this era.

I pull my hoodie more tightly around my shoulders. I really didn't dress for going to a bar tonight. I normally don't glamor other than to hide my teeth when I'm hunting a meal. Yes, I know that sounds just so . . . predatory? I guess because it is—there's really no way to sugarcoat it. For vampires, feeding and sex can all go very much hand in hand. But it can also just be a meal. I don't want cold bovine blood tonight. I'm upset I may have ruined things with Katrina and I want warm hot blood to fire me up. I'm feeling the undead that I actually am, and for just a few minutes, I want warmth instead. I pull my hair out of its tie and shake it loose. Then I put on a light glamor to make it look as if I'm at least wearing club clothes. My jeans now appear black instead of their faded denim color and my nerdy "What doesn't kill you gives you XP" gamer shirt appears as just a plain black T-shirt. My hoodie transforms into a leather jacket. Holding a glamor is second nature to vampires. It's not something we really even have to give much thought to, like breathing for humans. Humans can control their breath intentionally or just forget about it and the body takes over, a glamor is similar. We manipulate our physical space with barely a thought.
78

Sometimes more intentional, sometimes fairly subconsciously.

I make my way into the entrance. Since I'm a regular here, the bouncer just gives me a nod and I sit at the bar to scan the room for a few minutes. It doesn't take long. The glamor works and a tall woman with lots of curves approaches me. I like a girl with confidence. I'll spare you the details, but we end up going to a booth in the back corner. After a few minutes of small talk, I drop the glamor hiding my fangs and ask her if she'd like to be bitten by a vampire. By this point most girls say yes willingly. If they don't, I just start the process over. I drink from her neck, and all she feels is pleasure. A few minutes after I say goodbye, she won't even remember me. I didn't even get her name. Instead of making me feel warm inside, feeding on a lovely lady had the opposite effect. Now I just feel even more empty and alone. This is why I usually just stick to blood bags. I don't ever enjoy these nameless encounters.

I wave at Nikolai behind the bar. I had intended to spend some time with him after feeding but I'm just not in the mood for being around people after all. Nik looks up at me across the room, and with just a glance he understands how I'm feeling and gives me a look of sympathy. He can't use telepathy on me, but we've been friends for long enough to read each other anyway. I go back home full, but not satisfied. I shouldn't be this sad over a girl I haven't even met, but I'm sad at what could have been. The potential for more.

I have several hours left to fill until dawn. I don't think I'll be able to focus on working on my memoir, like I want to do. Maybe I'll just make some VidVibes focusing on morose topics to match my mood. I don't have the energy to change into my usual outfit, so I just glamor my way into my vampire costume. Usually, I prefer to actually get dressed because it's part of my whole thing, but tonight, I just don't have what it takes to make the effort.

Settling into my set, I put my camera on the tripod and look deeply into the lens. *"Hey VidVibe, Monty here. I guess even vampires can have bad days. Let me tell you a story about one of my worst times. It was a scorching hot summer in 1864 outside Atlanta, Georgia, right after what was known as The Battle of Atlanta. General William T. Sherman and his Union army had defeated Confederate General John Bell Hood's army. I had been lying low in an abandoned farmhouse. The smell of gunpowder lingered in the air, which was still thick with smoke. I was doing my best to stay out of the way of humans, and spent my days buried under a haystack in an old rickety barn, hoping not to be found. Pieces of the barn had been broken off for the army to make campfires, and sunlight streamed through the broken slats. The younger a vampire is, the more dangerous the sun is. Back then, I could tolerate some sun, but not direct rays. I spent my nights feeding off rats and chickens. At the time, I wasn't getting any news. I had no idea what was going on in the outside world. I was just trying to stay alive. If I came across a Confederate soldier, I'd do my part to win the war and use him as a meal, except instead of stopping once I was satiated, I'd drain him. During the nights, I'd try to work myself back up towards the North. I'm glad I eventually made my way back to Pennsylvania for a time."*

After filming, I did feel a lot better, and made my way into the game room to my desk in the corner. It's just a small little computer desk, as most of my room is focused on my gaming consoles, but it's where I keep my laptop. I take it out, boot it up, and start typing away some more at my memoir.

Talking about my time in the Civil War inspired me to write the next section of my story, and for a few precious minutes, Katrina isn't on my mind.

Chapter 10
The Olive Branch

Katrina

I stare down at my phone and just let the big fat tears that are starting to form roll down my cheeks. A few at first, and then more and more until I can't control them. Monty doesn't deserve these tears—I barely know him! I cry instead for all the years, all the struggles trying and failing to make friends as an Autistic individual. It's a constant, never-ending struggle. It's like this almost every single time. I find someone who seems nice and as if they might be a friend, but most of the time, something goes wrong. I don't think it was me this time. Why wouldn't he drop the vampire act? Maybe he's neurodivergent too. Maybe it helps him be social, but it's too much for me. My brain has to understand the "why" behind something. I just need some time. Maybe it's not completely over, but unless he can open up with me a little more, I can't figure out how to talk to him.

It's so different with Rainbow. I understand DID. Their brain basically fractured when they were very young to protect them from things no kid should ever have to experience. Their brain categorized and created amnesia barriers so that part of it could function in daily life, protected from their harsh reality. So if part of them is an elf, it makes sense in a neuroscience way. I'm sure Monty has some explanation like that and maybe he just isn't ready to talk about it. Rainbow doesn't often disclose their diagnosis because of stigmas. Speaking of Rainbow, I think I'm going to go over to their house. I just need to be with a friend tonight.

"Rainbow! I'm letting myself in!" I call once I arrive. I'd never do this with anyone else but Rainbow and I often will stop by without warning. With anyone else, it'd probably just shut me down. I practically need advanced notice in writing five days in advance. I almost trip over yet another Amazon package. I wonder who ordered something this time.

"Come in the kitchen," I hear Max's voice call out. It'll never cease to amaze me that each alter has a different voice. "I'm making a late dinner tonight—we had an emergency surgery on a German shepherd. There were some growths on his throat causing him to have trouble breathing, and they had to be removed right away. Doc let me assist! It was so cool. I mostly got to watch and hand him tools, but still, it was great being in the operating room. Oh, the dog is going to be fine. His name is Geronimo." Max added the last part because he knows that I love animals and I'm always curious what people name their pets.

"Geronimo is a great name for a German shepherd! I wonder if they call him Gerry." For someone who hated nicknames when I was little, now I love them so much. What can I say? Once I understood the why, they were awesome.

"What's up? You look like you've been crying. Want some spaghetti while we talk? It's almost done. Pixie is ready for her dinner too." Rainbow's cat, Pixie, wove her way around his legs as he tried to finish cooking. Pixie can tell when different alters are fronting. She loves Arleigh and Max the best I think. She's a bit standoffish towards Sky and she comes around for Jessie but isn't overly cuddly with her.

I walk over to the cabinet with the bowls and say, "Yeah, I'll have a small bowl. I'm not going to turn down your spaghetti. You are the best cook ever. And yes, I was crying. I got my hopes up about Monty and well, now I don't think it's going anywhere. It's fine. I'll be fine. Especially since you're feeding me."

"What happened? You two have been messaging each other all week, right?"

"Yeah, I even asked him to lunch, but that's when everything went wrong."

"You did pick a public place, right?" Max, ever the protector. He often fronts whenever there's something potentially confrontational that needs to be handled. His alter was formed to protect the Rainbow System, and as the System's best friend, he's very protective of me too. Kind of like the big brother I never had.

"Yes, Max, I picked a public place, but it doesn't matter because we aren't going to meet."

"What went wrong?"

I tell Max about our conversation and how Monty won't drop the vampire bit, saying he couldn't meet me for lunch at noon because of the sunlight.

"Katrina, you are the kindest, most non-judgmental and understanding person I've ever met. I also will support you over Monty one hundred percent. But . . .well, how much of this is him not dropping a bit and you being a little worried it won't work out so you're ending it before it has a chance to start? You haven't dated in a long time and it can be scary. Not that we're one to talk, but this isn't about us," he said, using the collective pronoun for a System.

As you can imagine, dating as a System comes with its own set of complications. He did sort of have a point—one that I wasn't willing to concede just yet.

84

"But don't you think it's weird that he's keeping up the cosplay outside of VidVibe? He even said he wouldn't eat lunch but that he'd keep me company while I ate!"

"Maybe he has extreme food allergies? Sometimes people don't like to get into details about their medical stuff when they are trying to get to know someone. Have you told him you're Autistic?"

"No, it hasn't come up. I'm not hiding it though, you know I'm open about being Autistic."

"In all that chatting, you didn't work it into a conversation? That seems unlike you. Maybe . . ." Max said slyly, "even though I know you aren't ashamed to be Autistic, you are a weee little bit afraid that'd he'll have preconceived notions about your Autism before meeting you in person so you decided to just not work it in subconsciously on purpose? Just maybe?" Having a friend who also faces daily discrimination due to their disability is so helpful because they aren't afraid to call you out on similar insecurities.

"Hurumph! Why do you have to be wise *and* right? Honestly when I saw you were fronting tonight, I figured you'd tell me it was for the best and to ignore the loser," I pouted.

"No, because that isn't in your best interest. You deserve the best. I don't know if that's Monty or not. But he didn't just ghost you when you needed time to think and he stuck around to get to know you with all the messaging. He did say he *would* meet you for lunch in a public place, even though it wasn't his ideal situation. I think he might be worth giving a try, at least to meet once. But also, I haven't been the one staying up late chatting with him. You've got to go with what your gut says."

"Max, but that's what's so hard. I trust so easily and I always look for the good in people and I have a hard time trusting my gut. Guts aren't logical. Guts really have nothing to do with any of this."

"You know what I mean, Kat."

"I do. You're such a good friend. Let me help you clean up. I better get back home. Tomorrow is my shift in the children's section and I need good sleep to have the energy to match theirs."

The next couple of days I just try to focus on work and my crochet. Of course Data is there to give me lots of attention and cheer me up a little. My Yoshi project is coming along and it will only be a few more days before I sew all the pieces together to complete the little dinosaur. He's one of my favorite Mario characters and I always choose him whenever I play *Mario Kart*. Which has been a while, now that I think about it. I should ask Sky if she wants to play with me soon—she has a Nintendo at her house. Other than posting a couple of VidVibes on the progress of my project, I try to stay off the app. I need a break from Monty and the algorithm doesn't know I don't want to come across his content. I also spend time thinking hard about what Max said. If Max thinks it's okay to give Monty a chance, it is something for me to really ponder. Because Max is always the overprotective kind of person, his opinion weighs very heavily in my decisions.

I'd even had a chance to talk to Arleigh about it the other day. Arleigh always has a wise perspective to bring to the table. I was a little nervous to talk to her because she is an elf and since I'm struggling with Monty calling himself a vampire, I didn't want her to think I didn't believe her. But per usual, I didn't have to worry. Arleigh knew it wasn't the same thing. She told me she understood that I respected her as an elf in a DID System and that we both knew the body wasn't an elf, but in her headspace she embodies everything that an elf is. It was only when she fronted in the body that the limitations of actually being human applied to her. And that the entire thing was a phenomenon of the brain, not an actual mythical creature. I love being able to have talks like that with Arleigh. She knows that my Autistic brain needs for things to make sense in a logical way. Often I need repeated reassurances. We've had variations of this conversation a few times during our friendship.

Which makes me think again to what Max said about me not sharing the fact I'm Autistic with Monty. He's so right—that isn't my normal way of doing things. Often I lead with the fact I'm Autistic. So there must be something to him saying that perhaps, just once, I wanted to meet someone and have them accept me how I am without revealing my Autism to explain away my weird quirks and social awkwardness.

As I put away my yarn, with the "help" of Data of course, I decide that tomorrow I'll watch some more of Monty's videos and at the very least leave him a comment. I'm not sure about sending him a message again yet. But the fact that he has given me the space I asked for means a lot. Unless of course it just means he wasn't that interested. I'm sure he's got hundreds of girls throwing themselves at him. He probably forgot about me five minutes after I told him I couldn't handle his vampire act. I need to put him out of my head again before I psych myself out and decide not to leave him a comment after all. Instead, I go to my closet and pull out my yoga mat. A thirty-minute yoga session before bed should clear my head, and tomorrow is a new day.

After work on Friday, I let myself into my house and shed my work clothes piece by piece. I kick my shoes off at the door and hang my purse up on the hook nearby. I give Data a good scratch under his chin as I pull my curls up into a messy bun on top of my head and roll my neck a few times. In the bedroom, I take off my clothes and throw them into the hamper and immediately put on my pajamas, not caring it is only 6 p.m. I then debate whether to wash the makeup off my face or start cooking dinner, but my stomach's growl answers that dilemma. I really want pizza but that'd take at least half an hour to get here and I am not that patient, so I pull out some bread to make myself a sandwich. Putting it in my panini press makes it feel fancier than it really is. But honestly, I am exhausted after working all day. Even though my job is neurodivergent affirming, it still takes a lot of mental energy for me to get through a workday. Eating dinner, such that it is, gives me a bit of a boost, and I head with determination to my comfy red chair.

I am going to watch some Monty videos and re-evaluate this whole situation. I almost did it at lunch today, but I didn't want to spend the afternoon distracted. After pulling out my tablet, I see he's posted several videos in the past few days since our last message.

Per usual, he stayed in character. The guy is consistent, I'll give him that. And so captivating. I can almost smell the smoky air as he describes what it was like to be in the Civil War. Then he has a video on his trek up North, talking about how he stowed away on a steamboat traveling up the Chattahoochee River. He describes how he would hide among cargo containing supplies for Union troops, occasionally donning a uniform at night and pretending to be part of the night crew. Everything he said conveys so much detail—he obviously is a great researcher. It is a really creative approach to· teaching history. No wonder, he has such a large following.

I watch two more videos. The last one is him reaching Pennsylvania and trying to find a nighttime job as a textile factory worker. He talks about how he was tired of hiding and wanted to re-establish himself as part of society. It meant establishing a residence and procuring work without any references. He ended up getting a job as a maintenance man at the textile factory (so he said) working on the machines in the night so that during the day the women could come in and work the looms to produce fabric. He even found some photos of restored machines and added them to his videos during editing. I decide to leave a comment on this video.

@Katrina_Crochet - Such an interesting video, Montgomery. I'm guessing those machines broke often with all the moving pieces. What was the fabric used for? Do you still have any of it?

There. That was my olive branch. I wasn't quite brave enough to send him another message in case he had moved on. There was also a good chance he wouldn't even see my comment since he gets so many. But that was all I could do for now. I give Data a good scratch under his chin, the softness of his silky gray fur soothing my fingers. He looks at me through squinty eyes and purrs loudly in satisfaction. I give him a quick kiss on his head, tuck my tablet away and reach for my yarn bag. It was Yoshi time!

Chapter 11

Making Plans

Montgomery

I stretch slowly as I wake from the sleep of the dead. No pun intended. My bedroom is obviously very dark to keep the daylight out. I have top-notch blackout curtains and a four-poster bed with what some would consider a very old-fashioned curtain around it. The look isn't very modern, but it helps. Like I've said before, I can deal with a bit of sunlight, but if I don't have to, then I prefer not to. I reach over to grab my phone as I do when I wake up every evening. Some days, I still marvel over smartphones. I know there are a lot of vampires who complain about the new technology and long for the simpler days, but I love it. Yes, modern technology makes it harder to disappear when it's time for us to move on to a new life, but I wouldn't trade it.

Since my last message with Katrina, I've developed a new habit of checking my SnapFoto DMs first thing. To think, until recently I was only opening SnapFoto every couple of weeks and now it's the first app I open each day. Still no message from her, but a few from various brands. For some reason, Nike wants to work with me, but I am not an athlete. I shake my head. I don't see their vision in that one. There's a DM from Rolex, which, if that's legit, would be a cool brand to work with. I save that one to look into more later.

I open VidVibe and scan through my comments slowly, trying not to get my hopes up. Suddenly, I jerk up in bed. Sure enough, Katrina_Crochet has left a new comment. I read it and then reread it, trying to decipher if there's any hidden message in her very ordinary comment. I look over at the clock. It's only 6:45—if I leave a response, she might still answer me back tonight. But I feel that there's only one chance at this and I'm perplexed at how to respond. I actually do have a handkerchief that was made in one of the factories I worked in back then. Over the years, I've occasionally kept trinkets or bits of my life. The handkerchief was practical and I used it for many years until it became more sentimental than useful, and I just never threw it out. It's in a trunk at the end of my bed filled with the rest of the knickknacks and odds and ends of my travels.

I respond to Katrina's comment in the VidVibe app:

@MontyTheVampire - I do have a small piece of fabric from my factory days that I've kept, a handkerchief. But we used to make clothes and blankets too. Would you like to see it?

There. Other people will think I'm referring to making a video about it, but maybe she'll get my message asking if she'd like to meet up in person. I really hope she writes back. I check to make sure the sound is turned on my phone in case she DMs me. Notifications are still turned off on my VidVibes or my phone would ping every few minutes which would drive me mad. Then I get dressed and head down my long private driveway and out to the neighborhood street to burn off some of the excessive energy I've got. It's dusk—still a normal time for people to be walking around a neighborhood street. Going for a walk at 2 a.m., I learned, is a good way to have the police called on you. Just as I get back home, I hear the sweet ding of my SnapFoto messenger.

@Katrina_Crochet: I saw you replied to my comment on your video. I wasn't sure if you'd see it. I also wasn't sure if you had moved on, but you've been on my mind all week.

@Montgomery1690: You've been on my mind all week too, but I didn't want to push you or make you more uncomfortable than you seemed to be. I will admit to watching more crochet videos in the past week than ever in my entire life. Haha.

@Katrina_Crochet: I think I owe you an apology. I would like to give you a chance to explain the whole vampire thing in person. Also, I actually really would love to see that handkerchief, if it's that old. I love history and old things!

@Montgomery1690: Dare I ask, when and where you'd be comfortable meeting?

@Katrina_Crochet: There's a little bakery that stays open late near the library. Would you be interested in meeting tonight? I mean of course only if you don't have plans. I don't want to presume you're just sitting home on a Friday night! Would 8 p.m. work? I could only stay out for an hour. I try to stick to my routine as much as possible and I tend to go to bed fairly early.

@Montgomery1690: Eight works for me. I look forward to meeting you, Katrina.

I am in slight disbelief that not only did she agree to meet with me, she is willing to meet tonight. I'm usually a very patient man, something that develops naturally after living for centuries. I haven't felt this alive for as long as I can remember. Even though I'm not human anymore, I was born human and we aren't meant to be such a solitary species. Vampires are more solitary by necessity. We typically spread out because large groups of us cause unwanted attention. We usually travel alone or with one or two of our vampire brethren. Nikolai and I have spent most of our lives together, only occasionally going different ways for a few years here or there for various reasons. During the Civil War we got separated for a few years when we were trying to run away and hide and that was devastating because it's not as if we could just look each other up on FriendLink and check-in "marked safe from the Battle of Atlanta." We finally reconnected, via an underground network of vampires, but it took some time. We are usually loners, but it's easy for us to recognize our own kind. I finally ran into another vampire in South Carolina who had heard a rumor of someone who possibly was Nik a few towns over. It was a dead end, but eventually I did come across someone who had seen Nikolai recently in Virginia . The problem was, he was also looking for me, so when I got there, he'd already left. We finally met up in northern Virginia, both of us realizing that we were both heading North.

I hadn't had a close human companion in many years, and it gets so lonely. Talking with fans in the comment section of my videos is one thing, but connecting one-on-one rarely happens, especially as my account grows bigger. I really don't want to mess this up tonight. Katrina is already extremely wary of me being a vampire. I've got to decide whether to dress how she's used to seeing me on VidVibe or how I normally dress off camera. There's so much riding on this. I consider calling Nik but he won't get it. He's been in the hook-up headspace lately. He meets women or men looking for a fun time, not a relationship. I've never been that way—I'm demisexual—a word I learned in these very modern times. I need a genuine connection before I want to be intimate with someone.

I don't have too much time to figure this out, so I go into my closet and hope inspiration strikes.

Chapter 12
A Pointed Discussion

Katrina

I put the phone down and then just zone out for a minute, feeling very overwhelmed with emotion. I haven't gone on a date in several years and feel very rusty. I know the first thing I should do is send Rainbow a ChatBox message so they know I'm meeting Monty. I feel confident that I'm not going to get kidnapped meeting someone with such a large following, but still, safety comes first. I quickly shoot off a message and then evaluate my clothing options. I want to be comfortable because tugging at your collar or panty line is not usually considered attractive. Also, when clothing is bugging me sensory-wise it just adds to my overwhelm in general. Going into this meeting, I really want to control as much sensory experience as I can, because the social part will be hard enough to navigate.

I go to my closet and pull out a soft and comfortable lightweight, boatneck long-sleeve dark teal T-shirt and pair it with a soft flowy rusty orange overall. I love the contrast of the teal and rusty orange. It is cute, stylish, and most importantly, comfortable! Also, I think it sets off my hair nicely. I didn't take my makeup off after work, so all I need to do is re-powder my nose and add a bit more pink lipstick and I'm set. I have ten minutes to kill and now a ton of excessive emotional energy to burn off. At the risk of messing up my hair, I go over to the small trampoline in the corner of my living room and jump for a few minutes to help settle my nerves. I check that my purse has my noise-dampening earplugs, although this bakery should be quiet enough I won't need them, and then head out the door, calling out to Data, "I won't be long—keep the place safe!"

I arrive a couple minutes early so I can order a peppermint tea and find a seat before Monty arrives. That's one thing I've never quite figured out the social rules for. When you are meeting someone for tea or coffee, are you supposed to wait and order together? I never know. So, I just like to get there early and wait. It's less nerve-wracking to me. That way I can say, "Hey I got us a table," and then have a chance to check the person out from a distance while they wait in line. Although, somehow, I suspect Monty won't order anything in order to keep up the "I don't eat or drink anything except wine," bit he seems overly attached to.

Sure enough, I barely sit down with my mug of tea when the door opens and Monty walks in. I try to stifle a frown because Monty is not dressed how I'm used to seeing him on camera. He's wearing casual street clothes rather than the black pants, silk shirts, and leather jacket he wears on VidVibe or in his SnapFoto pictures. He has on extremely nicely fitted dark-wash jeans, a dark gray T-shirt, and dark brown sneakers. Even though I'm surprised by what he's wearing, it just fits him so well, and he looks both comfortable and stylish, my favorite combo. It makes sense—I'm sure he doesn't want to dress inconspicuously in his day-to-day life, but this is the first time he's broken character, which is promising. His jet black hair falls just past his shoulders and has been brushed away from his face. He's got a five o'clock shadow and I might just swoon like a southern belle if I keep staring at him. I lift my hand in a wave as he looks across the small bakery towards me.

"Hi," I say suddenly, incredibly super shy. Why did I agree to do this? It must be his intriguing charm and obvious intelligence that compelled me to meet with him. I know I'm smart—I'm not trying to put myself down—but next to him, I feel as if I'll get my words all mixed up. I need to find a way to calm down. I slip my hand into my purse and pull out one of my fidget toys. It's a silicone stretchy ball that is both smooth and squishy at the same time. I roll it between my hands, now under the table, and focus my nervous energy into the soothing back and forth motion of the fidget toy.

"Katrina. Katrina. I don't want to blink and have you disappear like a mirage. You are absolutely stunning. I wasn't prepared for your beauty."

"Uh, thanks, I guess?" I never know how to take a compliment. Ever. People are always complimenting my hair, and I get it, it's my favorite feature. I love my red curls. But I was simply born with them, so I guess I got lucky? That's why I never know how to respond.

"You took me by surprise, that's all. I have watched your VidVibes, but the video is mostly focused on your hands and yarn—you aren't always fully in the shot. I knew you were pretty, but I was drawn by our conversations. I hadn't really spent that much time thinking about your looks. Is that bad? I probably shouldn't say that, right?" He pulls out the chair across from me and causally settles into it with an amazing amount of grace.

"It's the perfect thing to say. I much prefer to talk about interesting histories and philosophical questions than what someone looks like. Don't you?" I ask, still nervous but determined to just be myself.

"Exactly. Have you finished the Yoshi? I really can't wait to see him. I love Mario and all the Mario characters.

Goomba is my favorite. Such a grumpy little mushroom, and he has fangs." Monty grins.

"Speaking of fangs, should we dive into the elephant, or should I say, vampire, in the room?" I kind of wanted to ignore it and have fun talking but if I don't work up the nerve to ask him to clarify the vampire thing, I'll regret it. "Why do you never drop character?"

"Getting right into it. I guess it's for the best. I don't drop the character because it's not a character. I actually, really, absolutely am a vampire. The biggest secret I have is that I'm not an 'edgy' vampire. I'm actually a really big nerd. Ever since the early 1990s, I've been obsessed with Nintendo. Before that, as I mentioned to you, I was into *Atari* and *Pong*. I followed the development of PC vs. Mac computers and I love D&D. Back when I was a farm kid in 1700s England, I used to sneak into the church to gawk at the vicar's Bible and his prized Latin books he had hidden in a cabinet. That was nerd behavior—before we even had a word for it. So . . . now you know all my secrets. I won't hide anything from you, or lie to you," he says with the utmost sincerity in his voice.

I lean back in my chair away from the table and just stare at him silently for a few very long seconds. My brain frantically tries to process all of this information without overloading. Sitting in front of me, is an extremely handsome, well-spoken man who appears to be close in age to me and also fully believes he's a vampire. What does one even SAY to that? I thought back to when I first met Rainbow System. Truth be told, when I first met Rainbow, I was hesitant around them and not quite trusting either. I met them when Data was a kitten and had to go to the vet a few times in a row in a short period of time for various vaccinations. Every time I went in, the vet tech, Sarah, seemed a little different. I couldn't quite put my finger on it, but my Autistic spidey-sense picked up on it, if you will. As an Autistic, I'm always watching people, trying to understand how to navigate social situations and often masking my Autism to get through interactions with the least amount of stress. But each day Sarah seemed oddly "different." Most people don't pick up on it because each of the alters are really good at masking to be the body known as "Sarah."

One day, I got stuck in an exam room waiting for the vet to come in and Sarah was waiting with me and we got to talking. When I'm nervous, I often ramble on and say things I'll probably regret later. But this time it worked out for the best. "Do you mind if I ask a personal question?" I asked her. Asking someone if you can ask them a question has always been annoying, but I was trying to follow standard social patterns and that is a common way people start a new subject. When she said "sure," I continued on, "I hope you don't take this the wrong way, but every time I've come in with Data, you seem like you're in a very different mood. Once I thought you were probably an intern because you seemed so young even though you appeared to be very capable. Another time I thought you were older than you looked, but very different from the first time. I'm Autistic"—yep, just threw that right out there because of my nerves—"and well, I just can't figure you out and my brain wants to understand!"

Rainbow looked at me with total surprise and said, "Wow, you really are perceptive. I don't share this with many people but I actually have a disorder called DID. Have you heard of it?" I had heard of it in passing, but didn't know much about it. We ended up going out to dinner that night, and the rest is best friend history. But even then, when I learned one of the alters was an elf, it did take some time to get used to. Eventually it all became logical in my brain and I was able to accept all of Rainbow. Which brings me right back to this bakery with a man who thinks he is—or actually is?— a vampire.

I lean forward, staring him in the eye, which isn't usual for me. I rarely look people in the eye, as it's extremely uncomfortable for me. This time, though, I can't look away. Slowly, I lean back again. I'm pretty sure my mouth opens and closes a few times, trying to get some words out, but nothing emerges. Leaning forward again, I say, "I think I'm going to need some more information."

"Fair enough," Monty says. "I'm an open book. What do you want to know?"

"I don't do well with open-ended questions. But let me try to narrow some things down. Do you have a mental disorder? I say that with the utmost kindness. My best friend does and I have a neurodevelopmental disorder, which I can get into later. But do you perhaps fit into some category like that?"

"No, nothing like that," Monty says with a smile. "And no offense was taken."

"So are you just really into role-play as a lifestyle?" I continue.

"No, I am a real vampire—no role-playing. I did hear about the cosplay niche on VidVibe a couple of years ago and I figured it'd be fun to jump on to VidVibe to talk about my life as a vampire and that people would naturally assume it was cosplay. I never corrected that assumption, until tonight with you, and yes, I did play into it a bit with the stereotypical vampire set and what I call my costume. Because I'm really just a down-to-earth guy who happens to be a vampire. I was actually nervous meeting you. See, I wasn't sure how much of

100

my vampire persona you liked and if you would like the real me. The one who loves Yoshi and video games."

I take a slow sip of my tea, trying to buy some time so I can process his words. I'm glad I ordered peppermint, the scent calms me and I take a moment to breathe it in. I really, really wish Max was here with me. I can be so gullible. I want to believe him—he seems so sincere. But vampires aren't real. One thing that is very important in the disability community is to just believe someone when they tell you they are disabled. Unless you are a business, government, or doctor that needs actual proof to provide adequate accommodations, just believe people. More disabled people get harmed from people not believing their disability than there are people out there who might be faking a disability for attention. People who are faking for attention often suffer from a mental illness anyway. There are actual disabled people who won't use accessible parking spots because non-disabled people will spit on them or yell at them because they don't see their disability. Allies to the disability community just need to believe us. So I really don't want to ask him for proof. Disabled people should never have to prove their disability and many disabilities are dynamic or invisible. But he's not saying he's disabled. He's saying he's a vampire. It's not the same thing, I tell myself. One thing my Autistic mind does is desperately take in data and try to make it all make sense. And the data currently being input into my brain is not making any sort of sense with what I know of the world.

Feeling as if this may be a circumstance where it is okay to commit a social faux pas, I tentatively ask, "Can you tell me more about being a vampire? What does that mean, exactly? Like, are we talking Anne Rice? Bram Stoker? Do vampires not have fangs? You said you could meet me at lunch—it just wasn't easy for you. You can be on camera? Okay, I'll stop talking now."

"Rice and Stoker probably knew a little of vampire culture. They got some things right and some things wrong. I can be seen in mirrors and cameras. Young vampires are more sensitive to sunlight and can perish if exposed. The older a vampire gets, the more we can tolerate the sun, but still not all day long. Vampires do have powers and heightened senses. I cannot turn into a bat. I do have fangs, but can hide them behind a glamor. I do live off blood, but it doesn't have to be human." Monty says this all in a very calm, steady voice.

I sense he's trying not to scare me. I glance around the bakery to see if anyone else might be eavesdropping. It's pretty empty—the teenager behind the cash register is playing on their phone and the only other couple sits a few booths away, deep in their own conversation. "I'm not sure I should ask, but can you show me your fangs?" I do ask in a very tentative voice. A very large part of me really wants this to be a prank. I hate pranks with every fiber of my being, but just this one time, can it just pretty please be a prank?

I keep my eyes on Monty and he gives me a smile and, sure enough, right where his canine teeth were perfectly normal and human a few seconds ago, two very long, very white pointy fangs appear in their place. I blink, and blink again. Then in a flash, they disappear again.

What I know of the world may now include vampires.

Chapter 13
Origins

Montgomery

I put my glamor back in place quickly. Feeding can be . . . well, kind of a lot sometimes. A little intense. Maybe even weirdly sexual, which I definitely wasn't thinking about until just now. I should've had some blood from cold storage before meeting Katrina. My last feed was a week ago at the bar, and just having my fangs out kicked up this whole fluttery, electric thing I wasn't ready for. And of course, she's sitting right across from me, being gorgeous and skeptical and very, very real. Chatting with her these past weeks has already established the beginnings of an emotional connection. And my vampire instincts are apparently showing up uninvited. While I nervously wait for her reaction, a couple a few tables away gets up and says goodbye loudly, like we're not in the middle of a possibly life-altering moment over here.

The teen at the counter looks up from their phone at us and sighs. We are their last customers and I can tell they wanted to start their cleaning routine so they can go home. I'm mad at myself. I should have postponed our first meeting for when we didn't have to feel rushed. But there is half an hour before the shop closes, so we're not going anywhere just yet.

"Wow," Katrina says, leaning away from me in her chair. Then what felt like an eternity later, but was really only a few seconds, she leans back toward me and continues on, "I'm not sure what else to say. My mind is sort of reeling right now. What other powers do you have?"

"Mostly teleportation and telekinesis. I also have heightened senses, but I can control how sensitive I need them to be. And things like super strength and speed."

"Telekinesis? Is that moving stuff with your mind?"

I put up a glamor around our table so if the teen looks up again we'll appear to just be a normal couple still talking, and then I make Katrina's tea mug slide across the table. I admit, at this point it feels as if I am showing off a little bit, but she seems to take it all in pretty well. I haven't disclosed in a very real way that I am a vampire to anyone who has actually mattered to me in several decades.

Katrina whips her head towards the cashier as the teacup stops moving.

"Don't worry. All they see is two people sitting at the table. I can extend my glamor to my environment," I reassure her.

"Wow. Okay, I'm sounding like a broken record at this point. I'm starting to believe you are either an actual vampire or a really good up-close magician. I'm sorry I'm still doubting you, but things just have to be logical to my brain and I've never heard of vampires outside of mythological stories!" She starts to sound a little bit more upset. I need to reel this back in quickly before she goes into actual freak-out mode. Remembering she loves history, I figure I'll ground her with some facts.

"Vampires have been around almost as long as humans. From what the Elder Vampires say, there were some very early humans which probably carried a unique gene. In a serendipitous turn of events, if a certain human carrying a certain gene was in the throes of death and fed off raw blood—we are unclear if this was human or animal—they would turn. They became an undead, a vampire. Their dormant vampire gene was activated. At some point, a few of the Original Vampires had been formed this way. Vampires can turn other vampires and that is how our species perpetuates today, distinct from humans, but also intrinsically linked to humans. We are almost immortal, but not actually. There are ways for us to be destroyed." Maybe if I get her talking about herself for a minute that'll help. "You mentioned you had a neurodevelopmental disorder that we might circle back to later. Do you want to talk about it?"

"Oh!" she says with surprise, possibly at the subject change. "Yes, of course. I'm Autistic and have ADHD. I was late-diagnosed a few years ago. It's unfortunately too common for girls to get missed for diagnosis because our traits quite often present differently than in boys." This all rolls off her tongue as if it's something she's used to explaining over and over to people.

I relax into my seat a bit more, now that the conversation is off of me for a minute. "That's why you've referenced wanting to stick to your routine a couple of times when we've chatted, right?"

She looks up at me quickly. "Yes, actually. Routines are very important to me. My Autistic side thrives on routine, but sometimes my ADHD side wins out, like meeting you tonight was a bit spontaneous. It can be such a duality in my head."

"You never did answer my question about the Yoshi," I remind her, the grin back in my voice. "Have you finished it yet? I don't think I caught a finished video, but maybe you just haven't posted it." The bakery is going to close soon and

I'd like to end the conversation on a lighter topic if we can. I think tonight went really well. I hope Katrina thinks so too.

She is now done with her tea and moving a small ball between her hands. It had been under the table but now she is just absentmindedly rolling it back and forth and also occasionally giving it a squeeze, seemingly without noticing. "Almost. That was my plan for tomorrow morning: to finish sewing his arms on and posting the video. Then I work a couple of hours in the afternoon at the library. I guess after we leave here, my day will be ending but yours will be beginning?"

Back to vampire stuff. But that's okay. I want her to feel comfortable asking me anything. "Yes, after we say goodbye tonight, I'll head home and make a VidVibe. You've just now inspired me. I think I'll do a video on my turning. It isn't something I usually talk about much."

"When were you born, then? Was it actually in 1690? Is that what your SnapFoto handle hints at? Did you bring that handkerchief?"

"Yes, I was born in 1690," I say as I pull the handkerchief out of a plastic bag that was in my back pocket. "Here it is. It's fairly delicate, from around 1865. I really should have it in glass, but it was just a simple little hanky to me for so long. It never seemed special."

"Wow, this is actually really amazing. It obviously doesn't prove you've had it since 1865, but it's still really cool you own it. Although, I am starting to believe your story. I don't know how and I don't know why. Max, one of my friends, said I should trust my gut. I guess that's what I'm doing. Trusting my gut, as apparently people do."

"Trust isn't easy for you?" I ask, watching her carefully.

"Actually, the opposite," she says, and there's a flicker of something vulnerable behind her words. "Trust is too easy for me. I've had to learn to stop giving it away so freely, because . . . it usually backfires."

"I get that," I say quietly. "And I won't ask for your trust all at once. But I'd be honored if I could earn it . . . a little at a time."

She doesn't respond right away, but her expression softens.

Then I hold the handkerchief out again. "Would you like to keep it?"

Her eyes widen. "Seriously? You'd give this to me?"

"I'll miss it," I say with a small, nervous smile. "But giving it to you feels right. Even if we never see each other again—which, to be clear, I really hope we do—I like the idea of you having something of mine."

She actually blushes. Blushes. I might be 333 years old and technically undead, but that does something to me.

"Thank you," she says, gently taking the bag. "I'll take good care of it. This . . . this is really special."

She holds it to her chest for a moment like she's trying to decide what it means, then tucks away her fidget ball and picks up her purse from the back of the chair.

"I've got to get home. Like I said, I don't really like to be out too late. You've given me a lot to think about." She starts to stand up and take her cup to the cleaning station. "I'm not very good at goodbyes—they always seem awkward to me. Did you drive or um, teleport?" She whispers the last part.

With a low chuckle I say, "I drove. Let me walk you to your car." And with hope filling my voice, I ask, "I hope this won't be our only meeting?"

"I don't think so," she says, making her way toward the door. "I quite enjoyed this evening. I'm pretty sure I'd want to get together again."

"But you don't know?" I open the door for her. It is a cool late spring evening. Still cool enough for the cardigan she paired with her adorable overalls. I never thought of overalls as stylish, but they absolutely go with her personality. She stops in front of a blue Kia. "Is this yours?"

She nods. "Like I said, you gave me a lot to think about. I am pretty sure I believe you, but if you look up gullibility in the dictionary, you'll see my photo. Just because I am aware of how gullible I am, it doesn't stop it from being true. I want to run this all by my friend and process this evening."

"I have never met someone who was so upfront. Usually people just are coy or placating and then ghost you."

"Autistic bluntness is another character trait I have, right up there next to being gullible!" She laughs.

"Goodnight, Katrina. It was an absolute pleasure to spend tonight with you. I hope you sleep well and I'll also hope that I'll hear from you soon."

On the drive home, I think about our conversation and about the VidVibe I am now inspired to film. I assume our talk went well. I sense that I just need to be as transparent as I can with Katrina, and when she told me she was Autistic, I was glad I went with that instinct. I'll need to do some reading up on Autism, but from what I know, Autistic people tend to like things explained clearly and directly. I tried to convey that I was willing to answer anything she wanted to ask me. As for the VidVibe, talking about early vampires made me nostalgic to tell my own beginning story.

Now back home, and have taken the time to drink a bit of porcine blood, I settle into my chair, full vampire costume on, no glamor hiding my teeth. I never hide my teeth on VidVibe, and it amuses me that everyone thinks my teeth are just costume accessories. I have had some people ask if I had permanent cosmetic dental work done on them. Apparently that is a thing some humans do. Yeah, I don't get it either. I grab my phone, setup the camera, and hit record.

"Tonight I spent time with the most amazing human ever. We were talking a bit about vampire origins and it got me thinking about my own story. I haven't really talked about it here on my page in a long while. So tonight I'll share the story again. I was born in a rural area outside Berkhamsted, England, about thirty miles from London. One day, most of the town gathered at the Taylor farm to rebuild a barn that had burned down the previous winter. The men were just finishing building for the day, as it was getting to dusk, and the women gathered around a large fire, cooking a stew and catching up on the latest village news. The children were running through the gardens, eating their fill of apples from the orchard. Suddenly, four ominous people appeared out of what seemed to be thin air. They possessed unnatural speed and indescribable powers. It all happened so fast. People were screaming as they died— these strangers started ruthlessly killing without mercy. There were three men and what appeared to be a fairly young lady. But she was just as vicious as the others. I remember my friend, Nikolai (back then was known as Nicholas), my neighbor Henry, and I were trying to run towards the women to save them—not that we stood a chance. But then everything went black and we woke up in Berkhamsted Castle, which was a few miles from the farm. The strangers were nowhere to be seen and the three of us felt sicker than we'd ever felt in our lives. We spent days in

misery, in and out of consciousness. Not sure what had happened to us. Eventually we would learn we had become vampires. Uncovering what that truly meant, is a story I'll save for another day."

I've learned to sometimes break stories up into two parts because people's attention spans are short, and it also keeps some of them coming back for part two. I debate with myself whether I should keep filming or call it a night. I didn't realize how tired I was. Between finally meeting Katrina, worrying if I made a good impression, and reliving the single most terrifying day of my life, even if it was centuries ago, I feel exhausted. I press on because I don't think I want to come back to this topic tomorrow. I put the first video in the drafts folder to publish later. I keep the same costume on since it's all part of the same story, and then I settle back into my chair and continue.

"Yesterday I started telling you how I became a vampire. If you haven't seen that video, you may want to watch it before this one. I left off with a friend, a neighbor, and I huddled together in an abandoned castle a few miles from the farm we had been at earlier that day. We were cold and felt as if we possessed the worst fever we'd ever had in our lives. Our skin prickled with an icy burn, while at the same time a sheen of sweat clung to us making us feel clammy. Every shiver rattled our bones, leaving us with a dull ache that seemed to seep deeper with each moment. We were too weak to move and so we just stayed huddled together in a cold stone corner for what felt like days. At one point, I realized none of us had eaten or drunk anything in what was probably too long, and when a rat ran by, I grabbed it on instinct. Again, pure instinct led me to feed on this rat, which saved my undead life, if you will. Nikolai ended up doing the same, but Henry refused. He somehow
110

gathered his strength enough to go outside. He wanted to look for water. None of us knew what we had become at this point. We didn't know that sun was a sudden death to our infant vampire status. We didn't know we'd never eat human food again. That we'd only need blood to survive. Unfortunately it was in the early afternoon and as soon as Henry went outside, he started burning until there was nothing but ash. Nikolai and I were sitting in the shadow and saw it from a window. Young vampires cannot be in the sun, but of course we didn't know that. Nikolai and I were terrified. We lived in that castle off of rats for a couple of weeks, trying to figure out what had happened. Not daring to go outside in case we'd burn like Henry did. One evening, another vampire found us. Apparently word had gotten around about the rogue vampires who had illegally turned us and massacred our village, and an Elder had come to assess the damage. He found us, and became our teacher and taught us everything we needed to know about surviving as an undead."

I hit stop, saved the video to my drafts, and went to change out of my vampire outfit into my jeans. It was time to lose myself in a video game for the rest of the night.

Chapter 14
Lucky Strike

Katrina

The morning after meeting Monty, I slowly stretch myself awake and reach over to where Data sleeps next to me. He purrs gently in my hands for a few minutes before turning it into some love bites. I know I have only seconds before the love bites turn into "FEED ME HUMAN" bites, so I get out of bed and add some kibble to his bowl. "I know you only love me for food, Data, but I'll pretend it's because you actually love me. I can stay delusional." He rubs up against my legs in what I could only assume was agreement. Agreeing to which part? I let the answer hang in the air.

Ideally, I would stay in bed and dwell on my meeting with Monty but I also want to finish up my crochet project before work. The thing about Autism and ADHD is that I want routine (Autism) but when novelty (ADHD) takes over, sometimes plans have to change because my brain will only focus on what it's decided to focus on. After messing up several stitches in a row, I give up. I know Rainbow is off today, so I send them a quick message in ChatBox.

Me: Can I come over?
Rainbow: Sure, I'll start a pot of tea.
Me: Jessie today?
Rainbow: Nope, Arleigh this morning. See you soon.

I arrive shortly after and make myself cozy in Rainbow's beanbag chair while Arleigh hands me a mug of tea and settles on the nearby couch. "Did Max tell you I met up with Monty and he thought it was a good idea?" Sometimes System members will communicate with each other in the innerworld, but other times I need to update each alter with bits and pieces of recent events.

"Max has informed me of recent events, I'll ask questions if something doesn't connect for me. So, how did your enchanting evening go?" Arleigh asks in her musical voice. "You were very mysterious last night when you checked in with us. Illuminate me on the details."

"This might sound crazy, but . . . ," I pause, not believing what I'm about to admit to, " . . . I think he's actually a real vampire." As I say this, I bury my eyes in my hands. I am still having a hard time wrapping my mind around it. "He showed me his fangs and they looked very real. He told me he can use a sort of power to hide them from human view. He also has telekinesis, and he moved my teacup across the table. I assumed maybe he was just an illusionist, but I really don't think so. I think I believe him. You know, I had plans today to finish up my latest project before work, but this is all I can concentrate on right now. I'm so glad you were home."

"Will you be seeing him again?" Arleigh asks, peering at me over the rim of her delicate china tea cup.

"I don't know. I think so. Maybe. Yes. Probably not," I say almost all at once and then have to laugh at how utterly ridiculous that all sounded.

"I think if you had fun and felt safe, that is important. Are there any other concerns you have with seeing Monty again?"

"Well, he doesn't go out much in the daytime. He said he can a little but that he mostly avoids sunlight. He's over three hundred years old, or so he says. See, a part of me just can't believe him. But if he *is* three hundred years old, I'm a baby to him. What would we even have in common?"

"I think you'll find that if it's meant to be, it will find a way to flourish. I'm a timeless elf—you don't seem to struggle with my age or elvish nature," Arleigh reminds me.

"You're right. You are always so wise. I think I will see him again. I'm usually quick to dive into friendships at full force, but it probably wouldn't hurt anything to see him a couple more times without feeling as if I'm committing myself to him forever. My brain clings to the extremes. This is, of course, assuming he wants to see me again, but I'm pretty sure he does. He said he did want to see me again, but you know how people say things they don't mean when they are trying to be nice." I finish my tea and get up to put it in Arleigh's kitchen sink. "Has Max baked anything else recently? I'm sure those cookies from the other day are all gone now."

"Most definitely. Sky brought those delights into the veterinary clinic the other day, and everyone was so enthralled, yet she claimed the laurels for herself, of course! Much to Max's chagrin. Yet, we knowing folk acknowledge his craft. Although, everyone at the clinic thinks our vessel, Sarah, is just the bearer of myriad talents. And yes, I'm pretty sure he crafted some ambrosial fudge—it should be atop the counter."

It's surprising how normal it feels to hear my friend refer to her other alters. It's become our little normal. I'm sure hanging out with a vampire might feel weird at first, too, but it could be normal after a while. I find the fudge, and eat a piece, moaning as it melts in my mouth.

114

"Do you ever get sad that you can't eat chocolate but the other alters can?" I ask Arleigh as I gather up my purse. I'm thrilled we live so close to each other and can pop in for short visits. "I need to head back home and change before my library shift. I really appreciate you talking to me about this." One thing that I often do is the drawn-out goodbye. I'll ask a question as I'm leaving. My head is always doing two things at once.

"Not really. Someone needs to give this vessel vegetables and I don't mind that toil. I prefer my healthy ways when I'm fronting. And you know I always love a tête-à-tête like this. I will talk with you soon!"

That night after my shower, I work up the courage to text Monty using the number he gave me before we parted ways at the coffee shop. "Here's my number if you want an easier way to chat," he had said, handing me a scrap piece of paper he had written his name and number on.

Katrina: Hi, Monty. I get off work around 4 p.m. tomorrow. What time do you usually wake up? Maybe we can chat or meet up again if you like?

Monty: I'd really love that. I'm glad you reached out — I wasn't sure if I'd scared you off with all the . . . vampire talk honesty. LOL. Do you like bowling? I've got a bit of a competitive streak, what about you? Or, if you'd prefer something low-key, we could video chat. I'd be happy just seeing your face again, in any format.

Katrina: Bowling sounds fun! I haven't done that in a long time. Oh yeah, I definitely play to win! Sunday night shouldn't be too crowded. I don't do well with crowds. I have Monday off, so I can stay out a little later.

Monty: Let's meet at six. I've heard that Big Al's has good food and I can get you some dinner while we bowl too.

Katrina: See you then.

I have a second date with Monty. I can't believe it! And bowling should be fun. I'll bring my noise-dampening earplugs. I bet he's got some kind of super precision when it comes to knocking over the pins—I'll have to talk to him about keeping it fair!

The next day goes by at a snail's pace because I am eager to see Monty again. I still have reservations, but as Arleigh said, I should just take it slowly, and as long as I'm safe and having fun, then what is there to worry about? I shelve a few last books in my stack as Mrs. Humphrey walks by, leaning on her cane, and says hi.

"Katrina, my dear, you look like you've got a sparkle in your eye and a pep in your step. Is that Tokky-Tokky app doing good things for you?" Librarians are really up to date on the latest technology—don't let her misuse of VidVibe's name fool you. I think she does it on purpose. It's all part of her charm.

"Actually, Mrs. Humphrey, it really is." I don't need to tell her that it is doing great because I met an amazingly clever and extraordinarily handsome vampire from the app.

"How many followers do you have now?" she inquires. "You are being safe, right? Never tell them where you live or give out personal information."

"No, of course not. I don't do that. I'm getting close to 3,100 followers, and it is very exciting. I also just finished my latest crochet project and need to upload the video showing it off soon."

"Well, dear, it looks like it's about time to close up the library for the day. I'll see you on Tuesday. You have a good day off and stay safe!"

At home, I feed Data, text Rainbow on ChatBox so all the alters know I am going on another date tonight, and then contemplate what to wear. I had worn a knee-length dress with amazing pockets and a print with books all over it to work, but it just doesn't feel like a bowling outfit. I decide instead on a loose linen shirt and a pair of my harem pants. Loose, flowy, comfortable, but still really cute. I braid my hair so it'll be out of my way, touch up my makeup a bit, and then headed to Big Al's.

I get to the parking lot and then have a bout of Autistic anxiety. We didn't say if we'd meet IN the building or OUT of the building. If I go in and he's waiting outside, that's weird, but what if he's already in and I'm standing out and he thinks I'm late? Do neurotypical people just have a system for this that I'm not aware of? I didn't get the memo. The windows are darkly tinted meaning I can't peer inside to see if he's already in the lobby area. I should have had him pick me up, but I don't want him to know where I live quite yet. I decide to do the text thing.

Katrina: Hey Monty, I just got here. Are you already inside?
Monty: I just pulled up too. I'll meet you at the door.

I get out of my car and see him climbing out of a Mercedes-Benz a few rows over. His car is sleek without being flashy. It did seem out of place among all the minivans and Toyotas. We walk towards the door together. He's wearing jeans and a T-shirt that features Yoshi, Mario, Luigi, and a little red Toad. I'm thinking if we go on a few more dates, I might just have to give my Yoshi to him. I'm getting the feeling he'd love it. "Good morning," I say playfully, knowing he only recently woke up. "I want to ask how your day was, but since it's just now starting, that seems wrong."

"Getting to start it with you is the best way for it to begin," he says with a big grin. "Sorry for being so cheesy, but I couldn't resist." He opens the door for me, and we enter and get shoes and lanes. I look at the menu while answering some questions about my job at the library. I fidget and wish for one of my stim toys as he orders a glass of red wine and I get a chicken tender basket. "Now before we begin," I start to ask him, "do you have some sort of super bowling power I need to know about?"

"Well, I do have super strength, but I can reel it in. And I could move the ball with telekinesis, but we're just here to have fun. I promise not to show off."

"Hum . . . we'll see about that. I'm keeping my eye on you," I say playfully. "I can get quite competitive!" I remind him with a challenge in my voice. I find a bubble gum pink ball and tell him there is no way I can lose with such a perfect ball. "Ladies or Fangs first?" I ask him.

"Is that my nickname? Fangs? I don't think anyone has ever been brave enough to call me that before!"

"Well now it sure is! I'm going to go first." I pick up my lucky ball and try to channel Sky's confident saunter over to the lane. I don't quite granny-bowl, but I can't do that run-

and-let-go coordinated bowler's maneuver. I throw my ball down with as much power as I can muster and will it to stay in a straight line. Halfway down the lane, it kind of wiggles to the left but then I notice it straightens back up and knocks down eight of the ten pins. I frown and blink a few times. Did I just see my ball defy physics? Then it dawns on me.

Hands on hips, I stomp back towards him, when I'm close enough to ensure no one else hears, I say, "Monty! You can't cheat to help me either! That's not fair! I want to beat you on my own merit. No telekinesis for my benefit!"

"Katrina, you look absolutely adorable when you are so rightfully angry. I'm sorry. I won't do it again. I just couldn't help myself. I want you to be happy!" He reaches out to shake my hand. "Let's make a deal—I won't use any of my powers and I'll beat you fair and square."

I reach out to grab his hand and it is as if the world starts spinning for a brief second. A zap of energy courses through our fingers. His hand feels cool to the touch and mine feels overheated. I realize this is the first time we've touched. "Did you feel that?" I whisper.

"Yeah, I don't have an explanation." He gently reaches out both hands to me, and I slowly interlock my fingers with his. The bowling alley seemingly disappears. I am locked in a moment with Monty, just him and me holding hands, in our own little bubble. A pulse of exciting energy hums through me again, but it's smoother, less startling but just as thrilling. It makes me want to touch him more and more while simultaneously feeling extremely overwhelming. I want to stay in this moment forever but also, I need to back away before it becomes too much.

Pulling back and trying to lighten the mood I say, "Okay, I'm going to knock down my other two pins. Psychic powers to yourself!"

"Yes, ma'am!"

The next several rounds go well, leaving us almost tied. Monty is up by a few points. We have three frames left and I really want a turkey— three strikes in a row. It's a long shot, but I've already gotten one strike this evening. I usually have beginner's luck when I haven't played in a long time. Unfortunately, my next ball winds up in the gutter, so no turkey for me this round. Monty ends up winning, but only by a few points, and I'm pleased I held my own and had fun with him. Every time we passed each other I noticed we both kept finding excuses to brush each other's arms or hands. When we touched, little tingles shot across my body wherever we made contact. I couldn't get enough of it. I'm not ready to leave after one game and Monty isn't either, so we queue the scoreboard up for another round.

"I'm going to win this time!" I tell him with a laugh.

During our second round, he tells me he's been living in Vancouver for a couple of years and started his VidVibe channel shortly after he arrived. He tells me about his friend Nikolai and how they both love playing video games. He says he adores modern technology and feels as if he's finally in the right century. In exchange, I tell him that I've lived here my whole life and a little about Rainbow. I reveal how hard it was growing up not knowing I was Autistic and ADHD and not getting diagnosed until after I finished college. But once I got diagnosed it helped me understand myself and know what to look for in a job so I could find one that worked with my social challenges, executive functioning difficulties and sensory struggles. I showed him my noise-dampening earplugs I'd put in before we entered the bowling alley. They are very

120

small and hardly noticeable but they reduce ambient noises quite effectively.

As Monty's galaxy green ball narrowly misses the split pins in his final frame, I let out a delighted squeal because his miss means I win by 2 pins. Jumping up and down, I teasingly say, "Boo-ya! Who's the best now! We'll have to come back again to see who's the ultimate bowler." My excitement fades as I notice the heaviness in my bowling arm. "I had so much fun, but I think I only have two games in me—apparently my arm is weaker than I realized."

"The evening is still early. Would you like to go get some ice cream or something else?" he suggests with the sweetest enthusiasm.

"I do love ice cream, but I'd rather do something you can enjoy too. I never really noticed how much of our entertainment options are focused around food!"

"Yes, the times in my life when I've spent time with humans, trying to avoid food and look inconspicuous can be tricky, because you all really use food to celebrate!" he says with a resigned chuckle.

"Bars and dance clubs are too loud and crowded for me. I did okay at the bowling alley, but only for a short time or it's overstimulating too. The art museum is closed. That's not leaving us many options . . . " I trailed off. I didn't want to be a downer but couldn't think of anything we could do together.

"I don't want to be forward, but I only live a few minutes from here. Would you want to come over?" Monty asks tentatively. "I can show you my VidVibe setup and we can play *Mario Kart*. Beating you on Rainbow Road would be very enjoyable to me!"

Chapter 15
That Escalated Quickly

Montgomery

Did I really just invite a girl over to my house to play *Mario Kart*? Over three hundred years old and that's my smooth move? With Katrina it felt right for some reason. Still, I wait with bated breath to hear her answer.

She tilts her head to the side as if considering my request from multiple angles. I've noticed she does this whenever I pose a question to her. She always takes her time before thoughtfully answering. It is one of the things I am rapidly growing to like about her. "Hum. Would I follow you? Or would you bring me back to my car? Do you live in a house or an apartment? How late would you want me to stay? I'll need to text my friend your address. No, I think I'd rather take my car and follow you." She says all of this while looking past me. I read that was fairly common for Autistic people and so don't think much of it.

"I think it's a great idea for you to follow me. That way you can leave whenever you're comfortable and you don't have to rely on me. Although of course, I'd drive you back to your car whenever you wanted. I live in a house." I give her my address, we bus the dirty dishes, put up our bowling balls and shoes, and head out into the night air. It is a beautiful clear spring night and getting slightly warmer each day. "I'll see you at my place!"

Katrina

I pull up to a large mansion at the end of a private drive located on the Columbia River. I'm glad I came in my own car because it gives me time to collect myself. This place is stunning. Even though the city is right there, the trees surrounding his home offer a sense of privacy, making his property feel miles away from everything else. There is a grand entrance with intricate wood doors and black wrought iron handles surrounded by stone. Over to the right is a covered carpark and what looks to be a side entrance. Further away is a very large garage. Monty climbs out of his car and waves me over to the carpark, so I slowly park my car behind his and get out.

"This place looks like a small castle!" I exclaim.

"I have a fondness for older architecture."

"When was this built?"

"It isn't actually historic, but it was made to look old, and it feels like home. I actually grew up in a little rustic cottage, but this feels comfortable to me now. I spend a lot of time at my house, so I wanted it to be cozy."

"Cozy. Huh?" I let my disbelief linger as my brain tries to cram a giant mansion with a view into a cozy category.

"Come see for yourself. I'll give you a tour if you're interested," he says as he invites me in.

Was I ever! I love looking at fancy houses. We enter through the side door into a charming mudroom just off the kitchen, complete with a bench and hooks for jackets and keys. The kitchen itself is gorgeous, with windows that frame a perfect view of the Columbia River. Everything about the space is modern and sleek: the cabinets are an understated matte black, while the backsplash features classic white subway tiles. An enormous marble countertop with deep grey veining ties the black-and-white theme together beautifully. The dark wood floors add warmth to the room. Naturally, it's spotless—unsurprising, considering he never cooks.

He also shows me a living room with deep leather couches in front of the biggest fireplace I've ever seen in a home. The mantle is dark wood on a stone wall that reaches toward the ceiling. On either side of the fireplace, picture windows once again frame the majestic Pacific Northwest's soaring evergreen trees. There are a couple of spare bedrooms. A quick peek in a few of them show they are modestly appointed. Nice quality furniture, but kept to a minimalist, functional space for guests.

"I don't get that many guests, Nik crashes here occasionally, but he doesn't require anything special, except the black out curtains!" Monty shares with me as we pass the guest rooms.

He points to the doors of his master but says he'll show it to me another day. I tease him that it must be messy, but I doubt it because the entire place is immaculate. There's even an indoor pool! The pool room features ferns and other tropical plants all around the water—it feels like a lush oasis. Past the indoor pool, down another grand hallway and through an arched doorway, the next tour stop is the vampire set, as he calls it. Sure enough, I recognize the leather and wood carved chair he does most of his videos from and the large fireplace I've seen in the background of every one of his Lives. In person, the fireplace refuses to go unnoticed and is an attention grabbing focal point. Smaller than the one in the main living room, it's still impressively large. Honestly, it is unreal to see the room where I've spent months watching Monty. I run over to the chair and sit in it. "I cannot believe

I'm sitting in MontyTheVampire's VidVibe set right now. This is unbelievable. Will you take my picture? Not to post, just to show my friend Rainbow. Sorry, I'm reverting back to a fangirl for just a moment!"

"I trust you, and if you want to post them you can, but it'd come with a lot of possibly unwanted attention," he warns as he takes my camera and snaps a few pics of me sitting in his fancy chair.

After I'm done, he takes me down to the basement where his game room is. The entire space appears to have been designed by a different person altogether. Where everything else in the house is rich, luxurious, and features lots of leather and wood, reminiscent of a castle, this space is all modern. Still a lot of leather, but black leather in squared edges instead of the rich warm brown leather curves from the living room. There is a glass coffee table, LED lights placed in various corners giving off a relaxing purple glow, and gaming paraphernalia everywhere. Lego sculptures, posters of Zelda, a fancy glowing computer, a huge TV, several game consoles. It's Geek Paradise.

"This is my favorite room in my entire house," he says. "I told you I'm a big gamer, and I wasn't joking! I was meant to exist in the 21st century!"

"You weren't kidding! I do like some games, but I wouldn't call myself a gamer, although I do like Mario and Zelda and a few others, mostly Nintendo."

We sit down on the sofa together and Monty turns on the TV. I lean over him to grab one of the game controllers from the side table. Immediately, my brain realizes that I practically crawled into his lap, which absolutely wasn't my intention, but now that I'm here, it feels so nice. His body is cool against my flushed one and he settles back further into the couch to give me more room. Instead of sitting back up, I turn so I am lying down across his lap, my head resting on his thigh as I look up at him. Time seems to stand still for a while as we look at each other. The silence stretches on, but it's a comfortable silence. I glance at his icy blue eyes, but rest my gaze on his red lips, thinking about the fangs hidden behind them. At some point, he removed his hair from his ponytail, and now it falls forward, framing his angular face. He possesses a striking beauty, much like carved marble fashioned by ancient artisans. I know it is his vampire powers that make him look like human perfection—his pheromones encourage the person looking at him to see beauty. But I am at the mercy of my biology. I am very much attracted to him. My lips part as I let out a little sigh. He reaches down and lightly tugs on a curl that has worked its way out of my braid, slowly winding it around his finger.

"I was . . .uh . . .reaching for the controller," I whisper, my voice catching—a little breathy, a little wrecked—like I just leaned too close to a flame and realized a little too late that I liked the burn.

"I can see that," he says, still gently tugging on my curl and then tracing the edge of my face as he tucks it behind my ear. He clears his throat as if it is difficult to speak and says, "Would you like me to hand it to you?"

"Um . . .not really. I'm really enjoying this right now." I slowly reach up and mimic his move, tracing his cheek and then tucking some of his long hair behind his ear.

"I am too." His voice is gravelly and constrained.

As my fingers are tantalized by the stubble on his jaw, I suddenly crave more. It's as if his features are an illusion and I need to feel every contour to believe this moment is real. "May I touch more of your face?" At his nod, I sit slightly more up in his lap and cup both sides of his face between my hands. I trace his brow and the length of his nose. His skin is smooth porcelain, except around his jaw, which reveals the short stubble of a new beard. He slowly wraps both of his hands around my wrists, stopping my movements.

"Katrina," his voice measured and controlled, "I really want to kiss you right now."

I look up at him with wide eyes. This is our second date. Normally, I take so long to get around to letting a guy kiss me that they are long gone before we ever make it to this step. But this time—this time, I want to kiss Monty. I want to kiss Monty more than anything in the entire world. Nothing else is important. Without saying a word, I look right at him and nod very slowly and deliberately.

"Say yes, Katrina. I need you to say I can kiss you. This isn't a vampire thing. I could just take your sweet lips, but I want to hear you say you want this. I don't want to go too fast for you. I didn't invite you to my home for this. I really thought we'd just play video games. But I've wanted to kiss you from the moment you walked into the bakery last week. I've hardly thought of anything else."

"Yes, Monty, please kiss me. Um . . .no bites though?" I say, my voice getting slightly higher at the end. Still, I feel so comfortable right now, sharing what I need from him.

"No bites." Then, with a growl: "For now." The addition makes me shiver with anticipation.

He drops my arms and then gently leans down and presses his lips to mine. At first it is just smooth lips touching smooth lips. The sensation touches the part of my brain that analyzes sensory experiences and puts this into an emphatic "yes, this feels amazing—more please" category. It feels so good, that I lose all shyness and just want more. I surprise myself as I move to straddle Monty's lap, but nothing about this feels rushed—just inevitable. I take control and deepen the kiss. My hands wrap behind his head and I angle my mouth to his and slowly put the tip of my tongue between his lips. I hear his groan, which encourages me along. He moves one of his hands up towards my breast and I pull just enough away to give him more verbal encouragement—"Yes, please, absolutely yes"—and then go back to nibbling on his lips and feeling him kiss me back while he gently kneads my breast, rubbing his thumb over my shirt, making my nipple taut and tingling.

He takes one hand and grabs my ass, slightly lifting me up to his mouth a bit more, and it is exhilarating to feel his strength. He returns my kisses with matched passion. I feel his fangs descend but he is very careful not to mark me in any way. A shiver of excitement runs through my body making my nerves tingle in ways I never thought possible while fully dressed. I'd never been so turned on in my life. I feel his bulge between my legs and I am getting light headed from all the sensations coursing through my body. He slowly reaches for the hem of my shirt as if to lift it up, but I am not ready for that. I shake my head while still kissing him, and he stills his hands and follows my lead. One more last kiss, tongues clashing as if in a war, and I tear myself away from him and sit on the other end of the couch, panting slightly. I'm soaked—and a little squirmy from the sensation—but it's not bad. Just...a lot. "I'm sorry, I . . . I . . . I don't know what came over me."

"You do not need to apologize. I'm in awe of you, Katrina. That was absolutely breathtaking. Did you enjoy it— did anything make you uncomfortable?"

I shake my head.

"Then no one needs to apologize. Come over here and just cuddle me if you'd like. We don't have to do anything you don't want to do."

"I'd like that." This time, I sidle right up next to him. I fit in the crook of his arm and he puts his arm around my shoulders. I lay my head on his chest and we just sit like that for a few more moments, regulating our breath together. I idly start tracing my hand up and down his thigh, noticing the rough texture of his jeans. His muscles tense under my fingers as they travel up and down the length of his thigh. I feel so very relaxed, but even then, I'm just always moving, touching, fidgeting. It's subconscious, I'm not aware that what I am doing is slowly torturing Monty. He just feels so good and so strong.

I hear him clear his throat and say again in a gravelly whisper, "Katrina, that feels really good. Do you want to keep touching me?"

Suddenly I become acutely aware of what I am doing and my cheeks grow warm. I don't normally allow myself to be so comfortable with someone that I don't at least partially mask my Autistic traits. "I wasn't thinking about how that might land. I get fidgety when I'm comfy, and...you're very comfy. You felt so good and I was so relaxed, I didn't think how me rubbing your leg would be interpreted." I lean over and hide my face behind my hands.

"KittyKat—can I call you KittyKat?"

I nod.

"I don't mind in the least. I just want to be clear on what you want tonight—and you can change your mind at any point. We can make out, play Mario Kart, talk about the meaning of life, call it an early night. Whatever feels right to you."

I decide to poke the bear. "What about making love? Hmm? Would you do that if I asked?"

His whole body goes still, but his voice stays calm, sure. "I want that with you—more than you probably realize. But I don't think *tonight* is the night for that. Not because I don't want it, but because I care too much about getting this right with you."

Oh.

I don't even know why I asked. If he'd said yes, I probably would've bolted for the door. How does he already know that? Know me? But the moment is heavy now, and I need a little levity to breathe again—so I grab the Nintendo controller and flash him a grin.

"Good! Because I wasn't gonna ask. I'm going to wipe the floor with you in Mario Kart."

We load up the game. I go straight for Yoshi, and Monty lets me have him, choosing Luigi instead. "No! You can't be Luigi because he's also green," I tell him.

"What's that got to do with anything?"

"Because it's absolutely not fair. I'll start watching Luigi on the screen instead of Yoshi because they are the same   color."

"That sounds like a *you* problem," he teases.

"Oh, mister, you are SO GOING DOWN!" And then we are off. Like I said, I'm not a huge gamer, but *Mario Kart* is my jam. I easily snag first place, although it does take extra effort not to let my eyes drift to Luigi's green head while we play. We keep loading up new races, taking turns winning, until we stop really paying attention to who is ahead, laughing every time someone goes off the course due to a thrown banana. Next thing I know, my phone is buzzing.

Max: Katrina, are you still out? I know it's not that late, but it's late for you and I figured you'd text me when you got home.

I look down at my phone and see that it's 10 p.m. "Wow!" I tell Monty. "I had no idea it'd gotten so late. I guess I really should get home. Data probably thinks he's an orphan by now." I then send a quick text back to Max telling him I am okay and will call him soon.

"Let me walk you to your car," Monty says, setting the controllers on the table. He grabs my hand like a sweet teenager and gently tugs me through his house to the side door. "When can I see you again, KittyKat? Tonight was the most fun I've had in centuries."

I swoon a bit when he says my special nickname again. "Centuries? Hum? That seems like a bit of an exaggeration, Fangs," I tease back.

"I *am* centuries old, so you'll just never know," he replies with a wink.

After calling him 'Fangs' again, the name doesn't seem quite right in my mind. It's fun, flirty and a bit dangerous. But this Monty, holding me against him with his low deep voice that vibrates through my core, this Monty feels like something else entirely. "Maybe I need a new nickname for this version of you," I murmur, half to myself. "Something warmer...like Sunshine."

He looks down at me as we stand on the threshold of the backdoor. "Sunshine?" His voice is dripping with wry amusement tinted with confusion. He's trying to see my vision.

I grin up at him. "Yeah. You may be a vampire, but right now, you're my light."

"Mmm...Sunshine it is." His voice drops, rumbling in my chest. "No one's ever dared call me that. I think I want to hear it again."

Satisfied, I tuck a secret smile away. "Well, *Sunshine*, I don't have work tomorrow. I wish we could get together in the afternoon. Is tomorrow too soon? Should I be playing hard-to-get?"

Monty pulls me up to him in a fierce, protective hug at the back door and in the low growly voice I'm beginning to love, says, "Don't ever feel the need to play games with me, KittyKat. One of the things I like about you most is how genuine and frank you are." Then he leans down to kiss me again. It isn't a gentle kiss, but I don't mind. I needed to feel his need for me. It feels as if I am the only woman in the world. It feels as if I am here in this moment, at this time, and everything that has ever been difficult in my life ceases to exist except this kiss and Monty showing me that he wants to spend as much time with me as I do with him.

"Let me drive you home in your car," he says at last. "I can teleport back to my house, but I'd like to know you got home safely. You drive if that makes you more comfortable, but let me come with you?"

"You just don't want to say goodbye yet," I tease.

"Most definitely not! But it is late, so do this for me?"

"Alright, let's go." We settle down in my car. I do end up driving and he holds my right hand in comfortable silence for the short journey to my townhome.

As we pull up into my driveway, he says, "Tonight will be such a long night. I will count the hours until we can be together again. I'll wake early—can you come over again? Four o'clock?"

"Yes," I say, climbing out of the car and closing the door. "Tomorrow." He comes around, walks me to my door, and with one last chaste kiss, literally disappears right in front of my eyes, leaving me blinking and feeling as if the whole thing was a dream. But then my phone buzzes. I look down and see a text from Monty.

Montgomery: Tomorrow will feel as if it's eons away. Goodnight and sleep well, my sweet KittyKat.

Chapter 16
Debriefing with Friends

Montgomery

I transported back home and still feel Katrina's lips lingering on mine. The evening went better than I could have even imagined. Spending time with Katrina is easy. There's no coyness, no mind games. Just enthusiasm, joy, wonder, and thoughtfulness. You can see her brain working when she's presented with new information and she's trying to sort it out and make it make sense. I've thrown a lot of new things at her too. She'll take it in and contemplate—she doesn't just usually react without consideration. There's something heartwarmingly genuine about that. Her naivety is endearing. Despite the challenges she's faced, there's a certain unguardedness in her that I find deeply compelling. I want to wrap her in Bubble Wrap and protect her from the ugliness of the world but I also know she doesn't need that because she's got a backbone of steel and a tenacity that I admire. Her captivating contradictions blend harmoniously, crafting a unique spirit that continually intrigues me—a mystery I'm compelled to unravel.

I barely have time to grab a quick bottle of blood from the fridge and gulp it down cold when Nik suddenly appears right in front of me. "Whoa, geez, dude, what the heck? Where's the notice?" My voice conveys my irritation.

"Sorry, I have tonight off so I thought I'd see what you were up to."

"Your timing is good because Katrina just left, but dude, what if you'd teleported in while she was still around? I'm going to need you to let me know when you want to come by. I'm hoping she'll soon be a regular around here."

"You told her you're a vampire, right? As in a real one, not just a VidVibe vampire? She didn't flip out? When do I get to meet her?" Nikolai rapidly fired several questions at me.

"Yes, I told her. It felt like the longest week in decades when she went silent on me while she was absorbing that info. She asked more questions and for now seems cool with it. But it's still new, so let's give it a bit before I introduce her to my best friend."

"That's great. I can't wait to meet this special girl." We walk towards the game room and Nik continues on, "Hey, have you given any thought to The Reunion this year?"

The Reunion, as Nik and I like to call it, is a mass meeting of every living vampire. Every four years in Civita di Bagnoregio, Italy, it's held the week before Halloween in a tiny remote village on top of a hill. The only way in or out is by a footbridge, small moped vehicles or, of course, teleportation. It's ancient and picturesque. Everyone in the town is a vampire, friend of a vampire, or human servant that goes through a strict vetting process meaning it's the one location on Earth that serves as a vampire haven. If a tourist wanders in, they'll think the town is largely abandoned, since it mostly shuts down during the day. The only ones about are the few non-vampire friends, occasionally a servant, and some really old vampires that can be out in the sun for longer than most. Most tourists will snap a few photos and then leave before dusk since there's no public hotel. And that's probably in their best interest. Because while Nik and I are very modern and do no harm to humans, not all vampires are the same.

Expectation requires attendance at The Reunion. It lasts for a week and it's a way to spread news quickly, keep updated on any important global changes affecting vampires, and learn of any vampires who have perished or other juicy gossip. Halloween, the last night, is an opportunity to bring a candidate if you want to turn a willing human. This is a fairly new practice, only implemented in the last century. We are trying to modernize. There are newer laws surrounding when and how you can turn someone. It helps keep the vampire population under control. Smaller, yearly meetups are optional, but the big one is almost mandatory.

"Yes, I've started to think about it a bit. There's no reason not to go. I'm not really looking forward to it, but I'll go."

"Yeah me too. I'm trying to decide if I want to make it into a bigger European vacation or just go to the mandatory meetings." Nik looks up at the TV where the *Mario Kart* game is still on. I guess I didn't turn it off after Katrina left. "You were playing *Mario Kart* with her?" he asks incredulously. "I thought you said she was hot?"

"What does 'hot' have to do with anything? She's amazing. She's stunning. But she's also so sweet, perceptive, and genuine. She likes to take things slow and that works for me too."

"Is that why I saw you finishing up a glass of blood, when you had fresh on tap available tonight?"

"You can be so crude, man! She's not ready for that."

"Alright, you do you. Let's play *Halo* tonight." He puts away the Nintendo stuff and pulls out the Xbox controllers.

I think, one day, Nikolai will find a meaningful partner, and who knows, maybe more than one, that he'll want to settle down with. He's always felt as if love should be shared in big ways. He sees himself as someone who wants to build a loving network of support full of both men and women. We are alike in many ways, but this has never been one of them. Still, he's more than just a best friend, he's my non-blood brother. We've been through unimaginable times together.

Katrina

I stand on my front porch for another moment or two just holding in the memory of Monty's face. Like him, I'm looking forward to tomorrow. I go inside to call Rainbow. Before I can even dial, Data is weaving himself between my legs demanding attention and to know where I've been.

"Data, tonight was so fun. I'm sorry your dinner is a smidge late. I promise to make it up to you!" I pull out a can of his favorite flavor and scoop it into his little special dish that has a paw print in the middle. Now that he's happy, I focus once again on my phone and dial Rainbow's number.

After I recognize Max's deep "Hi," I launch into telling him about my evening. "Max, oh my god tonight was perfect! Can I talk girl-talk with you or should I wait to download with Sky? I'm home safe and sound by the way."

"Good, you had me worried there for a bit. I'm about to head to bed, but go ahead and give me the scoop. Go easy on the kissy face details. Was there any kissy face tonight? I think of you as a sister, so kissy details will have to wait for Sky. She definitely will want to hear about that."

"There was kissy face, as you're calling it. So much amazing kissy face! First we went bowling and that was a lot of fun! You and I really should go bowling soon. Anyway, we finished bowling and he wanted to take me to ice cream, but I didn't want to get ice cream just so we could have an excuse to keep talking. He suggested we could go back to his house. That's when I texted you his address. I felt okay going. And, oh my god, his house is ah-mazing. It's like a mini castle straight out of a travel magazine. I'm not even kidding. But we went to his game room and we were going to play *Mario Kart*, which we did, but first lots of kissy face."

"He took you to his house to make out with you?"

"No, we actually were going with only gaming planned. He didn't make the first move. I kinda did!" I exclaim, excitement filling my voice. Even though Max can't see me, I bob up and down on my toes.

"How do you 'kind of' make a move, Katrina? Although, it *is* you. I'm sure you were flirting and didn't even know it. Haha."

"Max, does the word 'flirting' imply intent? I wasn't INTENDING to flirt. I mean, okay, maybe I would have tried flirting if I even knew how to."

"That's what I mean. You probably were just being yourself and he thought it was flirting and you had no idea that's how it was coming across."

"You're probably right, because what happened was I reached over his lap to get the Nintendo controller . . ."

"You reached over his lap and you didn't think that would appear as if you were flirting? Oh Kitty, you are so dang innocent. Continue on."

"Well like I said, I was reaching for the controller and well, that somehow led to kissy face, which I was NOT sad about at all. And before you ask, he didn't dive into kissing me. He was really intent on consent—you would have been proud of him. I did not want to do more than that though, so we did end up stopping and I smashed him at *Mario Kart*. We're getting together again tomorrow! I can't wait."

"Well then you better get some sleep," Max says. "Goodnight. I'll tell the others that you had a good time. I know they'll want more details from you because apparently I don't ask the right questions. Haha."

"Goodnight, Max." I hang up my cell and get ready for bed. Data comes over to me, looking up expectantly. "Data, tonight was the best night of my life I think." And I kiss his furry little face.

Chapter 17
Girls' Night In

Katrina

The next couple of weeks rush by in a blur. I go to work, come home, work on a crochet project or video, and then head over to Monty's, or occasionally he comes to my apartment. The first time was pretty funny. We made plans for him to come over one evening after I'd gotten off work. I was in the bathroom when he arrived. I don't know how long he stood on my stoop before I was finally able to open the door. "Monty, why didn't you just come in?" I had asked him.

He told me, "Tradition dictates I have to be formally invited into someone's home the first time. I've never tested whether or not this would harm me, but it isn't something I've cared to learn the hard way. So, will you please invite me in?"

"Montgomery Ravenscroft, I invite you into my home," I said formally. I smile thinking about it. We don't get together every night, but more nights than not over the past three weeks. I finished the Yoshi but am saving it back as a gift for Monty when the time is right. My current project is Bluey. It's a little dog from a kids show. I don't know much about it, but I did a poll asking my VidVibe followers what they wanted me to make next and that was the overwhelming answer. Apparently, Bluey is pretty popular. I should watch it and see what it's about. As if I had time. I am really starting to overdo it. But I can't help myself. Spending time with

Monty makes me incredibly happy. I also have to find time to carve out for Rainbow, but they have been getting more assists in surgeries at work, so that is keeping them busier than usual anyway.

Although, I can't keep up this pace or I'll burn out. An Autistic burnout isn't like a neurotypical burnout. Going to get a massage and a candle-lit bath isn't the fix for Autistic burnout. It's running your nervous system at max for so long that it starts to cause a trauma response in your brain. I don't want to give up my VidVibe special interest, because it's very important for Autistic people to lose themselves in their special interests. It's one of the things that prevents burnout. But I really need more downtime. Spending time with Monty is great. Unfortunately it's new to my routine and I'm just getting tired.

Last night I had gotten off early and we had met up at dusk for a late stroll around Lacamas Lake. The spring nights were warming up, but I still needed a light jacket. The evening hike was so fun—I'd never been to the lake that late. Monty apparently has excellent night vision, and we brought a flashlight too. Shining the light across the lake and watching the water shimmer was a magical experience. The flashes of light appeared to jump across the water and looked like little dancing fairies. There's one spot across the lake from the parking lot where a rickety wooden dock goes about ten feet into the lake. We walked carefully over the half-rotten boards and stood at the end of the dock and kissed under the moon. I teased him that I was glad he wasn't a werewolf. Then I had to pause and ask, "Wait, werewolves aren't real, right?" He had laughed so hard I thought he was going to fall through one of those rotten boards!

He assured me werewolves were just legends. We had stood there under the big beautiful moon, kissing, with a fair amount of groping too. It started to get really late and we still had half the lake to travel around to get back to the parking lot. He had asked me with big solemn eyes if I trusted him. Without even having to think about it I said, "Absolutely." He then asked if I wanted to teleport with him back to the car. Scared but thrilled, I had to ask my usual assortment of questions. How does it feel? Will I be aware of it? Do you lose time or is it instant? Have non-vampires teleported successfully before? Is it scary? He gave me another deep kiss to soothe my worries, and when I opened my eyes, we were next to my car! I didn't even know we had moved. I think teleportation is my new favorite method of travel, hands down. I was glad he just did it without answering all my questions. It's nice to be with someone who just knows when I need all the questions answered or when I just need help with a decision.

Enough reminiscing, I sleepily try to wake up and get ready for work. I'll be working in the children's section, which means it's going to be a long day. After work, I have my weekly therapy session which I skipped last week to hang out with Monty even though I know that's not a healthy habit. My therapist, Elise, has been such an incredible support in my life and I look forward to our session later today. Monty wants me to come over after dinner tonight to watch a movie with him, but as I stretch out on the bed, I know I'll have to tell him no. I need a couple days to reset myself, not to mention checking in with Rainbow. I promised myself that I wouldn't let a boy take over my life.

Katrina: Hey Monty, you probably already went to bed, as it's already light outside, so you'll get this when you wake up. I've got a busy day at work today, I also have a therapy session and I really want to spend some time with Rainbow. I'll miss you, but I need to reschedule tonight's movie night. Kisses.

Yes, we're now signing our texts with "kisses." We haven't discussed what our relationship is yet, but I've sort of started to think of him as my boyfriend, which is thrilling in its own way. But seriously, I better get to work before Mrs. Humphrey starts to worry about me!

At lunch, I text Rainbow at their job to see if they are available for dinner. Opening ChatBox, I message the Rainbow channel, the one I use when I don't know who is fronting:

Katrina: Hey guys, hoping to catch you at lunch. Anyone around? Was hoping you were available for dinner tonight?

Jessie responded on their private channel with me: Jessie: Hi, it's me! I have a long lunch scheduled today due to a therapy appointment, so I can't chat much. But dinner sounds good. Unless anything happens, I should still be around for the rest of the day.

Moving over to Jessie's channel on ChatBox, I continue the conversation:

Katrina: I have therapy today too! After work from 4–5 p.m. Do you want to come over to my apartment when you get off? I've got to do some laundry and figured you could help. Haha. Jessie: Sounds good, see you around 5:30!

I put my phone away, finish lunch and head back to the children's section. Luckily, the kids keep me so busy that the afternoon flies by. We don't have any kids activities planned but this one little girl asks me to find a book about what it is going to be like to be a big sister. I look over and see her grown-up, and sure enough, I spy an adult over in the reading circle looking like she is trying to take a five-minute mental break to find her inner peace slowly rocking back and forth in the librarian's rocking chair with her eyes closed. Her prominent belly confirms what I suspected, a baby is indeed on the way.

I help the little girl over to some children's books written just for this scenario. I don't have any other kids needing my attention so I sit with her and we read one of the books together. Spending time one-on-one with a library kid reminds me of one of the reasons I love my job so much. The mom seems to have dozed off because she wakes up with a start just as we finish up the book. She apologizes, but I wave her off, telling her everything is perfectly fine. Soon, it is time for me to log out, say goodbye to Mrs. Humphrey, drive home, and log into my telehealth therapy appointment.

I started seeing Elise, my therapist, shortly after my Autistic/ADHD diagnosis. She's really been helpful in helping me talk through frustrations, process the grief stemming from a late diagnosis, and helping me solve various social situations as they come up. I see her almost every week. Today I get her caught up on dating Monty, but I'm not ready to tell her about him being a vampire! I know it's important to trust my therapist, but I just can't go there. I feel confident that talking to Rainbow about him being a vampire is enough to keep me grounded. But I do tell Elise how much fun I am having with him and some of the activities we've been doing. She is really excited for me. I talk to her a little about work too and then it's time to log off and get some dinner going before Jessie shows up.

I am finishing up making tacos when Jessie lets herself in. "How was your day?" we ask each other at the same time, and then burst out laughing.

"Mine was good," I say. "I had an adorable little girl at the library who needed help today. Therapy was good. I still haven't told Elise that Monty is a vampire. Should I tell her? I just don't know how she'd take it."

"You'll know when it's right. Therapists are there to help you, but you aren't obligated to tell them everything. That being said, she can't help you work through complicated emotions you might be having if you don't talk to her about it." Jessie pulls out plates and sets my kitchen table as she talks. "My therapy went well today too. The System has been pretty balanced lately. Even with the changes going on at work and the new responsibility of getting to scrub in on more of the surgeries. I did forget to tell you that my brother tried calling the other day. I was fronting and Max pushed to the front instead, since I was in a spin. He shut our brother down so fast and hung up. We blocked his phone, so I don't know how he got my number." Jessie's brother was a big part of why they had developed DID as a kid. No one in the System talks about their trauma much, and that's okay. I know she talks to her therapist about it and is doing so much healing around it.

"I'm sorry. I hope he leaves you alone. Did Max let him say why he was calling?"

"No, he just told him to leave us alone and reminded him of the restraining order." We start loading up our plates with tacos and guacamole and she says, "This looks so good.

Thanks for having me over tonight. I'm surprised you weren't out with Monty again."

I look up at my friend, a guilty feeling churning in my stomach and say, "I know. I'm sorry I've been so MIA lately! That's why I texted Monty this morning to let him know I needed to reschedule. We haven't gotten to see enough of each other lately and so I knew I needed a Rainbow Night! I feel bad that you didn't even tell me about your brother calling you! You know you can text or call me whenever, right?"

"I know. It just was a weird night. I think it was like two nights ago? You know how I sometimes get fuzzy with time. Max pushed forward and I got shoved to the headspace. Then after that I think the body was blendy for a bit. We texted our therapist right away and she talked to us for a few minutes. I think she was talking to Max and Arleigh co-fronting. Again, it was all kinda blurry. He really triggered us. We ended up going to bed early that night, and by the next morning, I had almost forgotten about it, until wanting to tell you tonight."

"I'm glad you told me, but I'm still sorry I wasn't there for you."

"No worries—I really am so happy you've found Monty. You deserve someone to make you happy, and from what I can tell, Monty does make you very happy," Jessie says through a bite of her taco.

"He really does. I always fall for interesting people, don't I? Do you remember that guy I dated who was really into aliens? He was really nice, but when I found out his dream wedding was at the UFO museum in Roswell, I had to find a way to exit the relationship." The memory brought a chuckle to my lips.

"I think that was before we met. I do remember you went on a date with a guy who talked about himself in third person the entire time. What was his name? Something like Harold Von Hofen wasn't it?" Jessie said the name with an uppity voice.

"Oh my goodness, no it was Arnold Von Hofen the Third. He spent all night saying, 'Arnie likes steak, does Katrina?' I actually slipped away before dessert! Thank goodness Monty is not like either of those guys! Although, to be fair, Levi the alien guy was really nice and I hope he found his special someone, anyone but me! Anyway, do you want to film a VidVibe today? We can film one for your page and Data can be your subject. He needs his teeth brushed, you can do a video on that when we are done eating."

"Yeah, that would be a good one and then you won't have to brush his teeth—I see what you're doing," she says with a laugh. "But that doesn't get you out of laundry either. Let's film a short video so I can take care of Data and then I'll help you fold your laundry."

"You figured me out!" I say, joining in her laughter.

Chapter 18
Unforgivable

Montgomery

I saw Katrina's text when I woke up and I was sad, but we had been spending a lot of time together, and I understood she probably needed some time apart. We really were spending most evenings hanging out, then she'd leave and I still had my whole night to do my VidVibes and spend time with Nik. She had to go home to bed and then go to work in the mornings. It's more than understandable that she wants time to herself or with her friend.

Unexpected extra time meant I could do a special VidVibe. I had ordered a new jacket from Etsy to add to my collection—a long black leather coat that goes down to mid-calf. The collar is high with a large lapel covered in ornate burnished gold designs. There are two rows of decorative buttons along with gold piping embellishing the edging of the coat. The sleeves tuck into metal bracers that I bought to go with it. I pair the jacket with black leather pants and black vest over a cream dress shirt. I wrap a dark brown leather belt around my waist to provide some contrast. It has a secondary piece with gold that loops lower over my thigh and has chains hanging off of it. I'm actually geeking out at how well it portrays "vampire." I think I'll actually film the video standing up at the fireplace to show off the jacket to its fullest potential.

Now to think about what to talk about tonight. Sometimes I plan videos ahead, sometimes I'll do a reply video to a comment, and some nights, I just totally wing it. I haven't eaten in a few days and also need to think about food tonight. I don't mind sustaining myself off my refrigerator blood, but I usually supplement with human blood fairly often. Since dating Katrina, I just haven't wanted to drink from a human. That's something we haven't discussed yet— whether or not we're exclusive. I know I've kept things just between us, and Katrina is not the kind of woman to date more than one man at a time. I should probably eat before filming, but now I'm eager to get started. I take a few minutes to set the tripod up to a new angle and then stand in front of the fireplace, one arm propped up on the mantel holding a carved ornamental dagger for effect and hit record:

"In the early 1900s I was still living on the East Coast. I'd managed to move to Boston around this time. The West was still more rural and I've always preferred city life. Humans are my main prey, after all. But in 1904 there was a lot of talk about a huge fair in St. Louis and it sounded like the place to be. The Louisiana Purchase Exposition also known as The St. Louis World's Fair. As I've mentioned before, vampires have the ability to teleport. The thing is, we have to know where we are teleporting to, so usually the first time we go somewhere, we have to get there by conventional means. After that we can teleport there easily. Otherwise we risk teleporting into a wall, a river, etcetera. I don't know how the physics of it works, but I just have to think about where I want to go, and then I can find myself there. At the time, I was working a job as a nightwatchman for yet another factory in Boston. I didn't have time to travel to St. Louis by train, but I wanted to go to this fair. Because

this fair was a big deal, there were photographs of it in all the local newspapers. I convinced my buddy, Nik, to try teleporting with me with only the photos to go by. Something we'd never attempted before. We had a map and photos and so we decided to try. I'm not sure any other vampire had tried anything like this before either. But it worked! Next thing we knew, we'd gone from Boston to St. Louis, just outside a big exhibition hall. It was thrilling. One thing about me, I've always loved innovation and new technology. And in 1904 anything that was new was at this World's Fair. We spent the night checking out as many exhibits as we could before teleporting back before sunrise in Boston. My favorite exhibit was the huge electric Ferris wheel. Electricity was still fairly novel in 1904. It was a very fond memory indeed. Until the moon rises again, my nocturnal friends. Fangs out, see you in the shadows."

Immediately, I edit the video and post it. I'm not up for filming another one but I am having fun in my costume and don't want to take it off yet. I wish Katrina could see it. Now she's feeling more comfortable with the fact I'm a vampire and understands my whole VidVibe vision, she's also having fun seeing me in my gothic glam look. Glancing over at the clock, I see it's almost 9 p.m. Her plan was to spend the whole evening with Rainbow, but I bet they've already gone home. I know I should probably not call her so she has her whole night to herself, but maybe she wouldn't mind a quick goodnight call. I dial her number and she picks up.

"Hey Monty, I'm getting ready for bed. I had such a fun evening with Jessie. I'm glad you didn't mind rescheduling our date."

"No worries. You need time with your friends too. I get to spend a lot of time with Nik. Too much sometimes!" A genuine chuckle slips out before I continue, "I was just calling to wish you a good night."

"What have you been doing this evening?" Katrina asks. She rustles around in the background and I can hear Data meowing at her.

"I got a new jacket that I'd ordered from one of my favorite Etsy sellers that makes high quality costume pieces, and it inspired me to film a VidVibe about the time I went to The World's Fair in St. Louis. I hear Data meowing—I think he must miss me," I tease.

"I can't wait to watch it! I'm pretty sure I miss you more than Data does."

"I could pop over and stay with you as you fall asleep." I hold my breath to see what she says.

"Hum, no, because I think I'd end up staying up way too late talking to you, and I have work in the morning. But . . ."

"Yes?" I interrupt her as she sort of drifts off.

"But . . ." she continues, "I would enjoy spending the night with you soon. I'd just rather plan for it. Does that work?"

"Absolutely!" I say. Then I ask her, "Are you dressed right now? In your bedroom?"

"Yes, why?"

"I can't stop thinking about you. Can I pop in for a quick goodnight kiss? I promise I'll be gone before you even yawn." I whisper into the phone.

"Monty, you're so ridiculous! I'm in my pj's, my hair is a mess and I'm about to fall asleep. You don't want to see me like this."

"I always want to see you. How about this—I teleport in, give you the quickest, most respectful kiss and then vanish. Just a little surprise before you fall asleep?"

"Hmmm, a quick kiss? I think that would be okay. But then I . . . "

Before she can finish her statement, I teleport into her bedroom, and say, "Thank you for this."

"Monty!" she lets out a little shriek, her phone still pressed up to her ear. "You scared me! I was in the middle of a sentence!"

"I'm sorry! I'm sorry, may I still have the kiss?" I clasp my hands together in a mock-plea, eyes wide and hopeful—full-on puppy dog mode. My voice gets soft and coaxing, like I'm trying to sweet-talk my way out of trouble. "Then I promise I'll go home and we can plan for a proper overnight stay together." I flash her a sheepish grin and tug at my collar. "Plus, I really wanted to show you my new jacket."

"Yes, come here. Your jacket is awesome! You got that handmade off of Etsy? It's really intricate. I bet you'll get a lot of comments on it. Make sure to tag that Etsy shop—they'll get so many orders."

I go to her in a flash, no longer thinking of my jacket, and look down into her hazel eyes which are showing flecks of green tonight. Her curls hang wild behind her, not tamed into a bun or braid like they often are. She is wearing the most adorable cotton pj's with sloths on the pants and a shirt with the phrase "I'm not lazy, I'm a sloth" printed on it.

"Adorable," I whisper. "How can you be sexy as hell and also just as adorable?"

Then I lean down to kiss her. Her lips are soft and supple, parting with a quiet sigh that punches right through my self-control. She tastes like a wildfire, and I want to burn. I feel the unwavering trust in the way she quietly gives herself over to me. That trust hits something deep and hidden inside me, something I thought was long gone.

Suddenly, she intensifies the kiss, her mouth slants against mine, her tongue slips between my lips. As her fingers curl into my shirt, my entire body roars to life like it's been waiting for this—for her.

Something stirs within me, primeval and instinctual. The fragile humanity I've begun to feel snaps out of existence as the sound of the blood in her veins sounds like a rushing river to my sensitive ears. A hunger coils low and hot in my gut. Her heartbeat throbs in her neck, a rhythm my body can't ignore. I'm starving. I haven't eaten in days, and the hunger surges up so fast it steals my breath. It doesn't feel like a choice anymore. It's instinct. Pure and feral.

My fangs unsheathe. My tongue trails down her neck. My mouth closes over that sweet, tender, fragile spot where all it would take is the slightest pressure—and I'd be sipping nectar of the gods.

I don't even register what I'm doing. Until I hear her whimper.

No. No. NO.

My eyes snap open. I jerk back like I've been burned. My breath comes ragged. "Oh fuck . . . " The room spins.

"Sorry, I'm sorry. I'm so sorry." My voice cracks. I stumble backward, the feel of her warm body still imprinted on my skin. My instincts claw at me to continue. To feed. My hands shake. I tremble. What the hell is wrong with me?

And before I can see the confusion—or worse, the hurt—on her face, I teleport back home, sick with shame. The cowardly monster I am.

Furious with myself, I storm to the kitchen and rip open a bag of bovine blood. I drink it cold as a punishment for being so careless. The last thing I want to do is scare Katrina. Almost biting her without consent is unforgivable.

For the first time in decades, I am angry that I'm a vampire. That I have to sustain myself on blood while living in the shadows. I want to be with Katrina out in the sunlight, eating brunch with her at a sidewalk café, followed by an afternoon holding her hand while we window shop together. I want to do mundane, everyday things with her—not lose myself and ravish her like some feral beast. I am a monster.

I sit down on the floor with the bag of blood in my hands and hang my head. Huge sobs wrack my body. I haven't cried for the human life I lost in a long, long time.

Katrina

I stand in the middle of my room as waves of shock roll off my body, trying to process what the hell just happened. I was talking on the phone with Monty, then he was inches away kissing me, and then he apologized and left before I had wrapped my head around the fact that he'd come to surprise me with a kiss goodnight. I know he said he'd kiss and then leave quickly, but this felt wrong. He kissed me, backed away saying sorry, and left without even a goodbye. He looked devastated or maybe scared. But that didn't make any sense. Unsettled, I try calling him, but he doesn't pick up. I feel as if I should get in my car to drive to his house and have him explain what just happened. But also, routine and work. I stand there for a few more minutes in what I call buffering mode, trying to figure out what the best move is. There's no way I'm going to get sleep after what just happened, so it's best to confront Monty. If he won't answer his phone, then I'll go to his house, pj's and all.

I pull up to his driveway, slam my car door shut, and let myself in the side door. If he can just appear in my bedroom willy nilly, then I sure as hell don't have to knock either. I storm through the mudroom and head toward the kitchen, ready to yell his name. But then I see him.

He's sitting on the floor, still in his full vampire costume, face buried in his hands, thick black hair falling around them. His shoulders shake with sobs. I freeze. Whatever I was about to say evaporates from my lips. This— this is not what I expected. Then, suddenly, he goes still. Like he's sensed me.

"Monty?" I whisper, stepping carefully toward him.

He's holding a bag of what I'm guessing is blood. We've been dating for weeks and somehow managed to keep dodging the topic of how he eats. This is the first time I've actually seen it. I kneel down in front of him, slowly, and reach out to gently touch his knee.

"What's wrong?" I ask softly. "What happened earlier? How can I help you?"

"Katrina," he breathes my name like a prayer—or maybe a curse. His voice is raw. "Go home. You're too special. Too good. I should never have gotten this close to you."

Chapter 19
We Need to Talk

Katrina

"Monty, you're scaring me. What's wrong? I don't want to go home. I want to help. You sounded so happy earlier tonight. We were laughing together, and you wanted to spend the night with me. You kissed me, I was really enjoying the kiss. Then you were just . . . gone. I don't understand. I need to understand. Please talk to me."

I need to get through to him. The thing that hurts me the most is when I don't understand why someone stops talking to me. It happens to me so often. I'll get close to a new friend, but eventually I'm too much, or too pushy, or too rigid—then they ghost me. I'm left picking up pieces of my broken heart and never understanding what went wrong. I can't bear that happening with Monty. I haven't felt this comfortable around someone since meeting Rainbow. In the short time I've known Monty, he's become more important to me than I had even realized. I'm not ready to lose him without a fight.

Monty finally looks up at me—his fangs still out, blood on them. No glamor this time. I admit, it's a bit scary, but also, the fangs are incredibly hot. The vulnerability in his eyes smooths away any fear. He's not hiding. He's hurting.

"Katrina, I was a heartbeat away from losing control tonight. I am a monster. I almost bit you—without asking. I couldn't live with myself if I hurt you. I got so into filming and wanting to catch you before you fell asleep tonight, I forgot I hadn't fed in a while." He pauses, swallowing hard. "Feeding can often be a very sexual experience for vampires. Not always—sometimes it's just food. But sometimes, it's tied up in intimacy. When I saw you there tonight, you were beautiful, and when I started to kiss you, my fangs came out, and I lost control, I almost bit you. Something came over me." He closed his eyes. "It took everything I had to pull away. And I'm terrified that almost wasn't enough. I had to leave. I had to. I'm so ashamed. I'm not a fledgling—I should have better control than this."

I reached for him, cupping my hand on his scruffy cheek, "Monty, baby, you didn't lose control. You stopped. I didn't even know you were about to bite me. You didn't even ask if I wanted it. You just left."

I took his hand in mine, "We haven't talked about this. It's been looming between us. I think it's about time we talked. Of course I know some from your VidVibes, but that's for all your fans. We need to talk, just the two of us. Do you want my blood? Would that turn me? You said you don't kill humans. Tell me. Let's talk about this, please."

His thumb works small circles on the back of my hand in a soft, tender massage, "It's late, Katrina. Don't you want to go to bed so you aren't too tired for work tomorrow?"

There he is again, always putting me first.

"No Monty, this is more important. If I have to call in sick tomorrow, I will. Mrs. Humphrey won't mind. I rarely call in sick."

He raises my hand to his lips, and kisses it gently. "You are so precious to me, KittyKat. Okay. Hold on, let's at least get comfortable. Bedroom or living room?"

"Bedroom," I say.

He closes his eyes, and next thing I know, we are in his bedroom. I've seen it before but we haven't spent time in here yet. Now we are under the canopy of the huge four-poster bed that I've only seen from the doorway. Little lights hang tucked around the posts, creating a warm, cozy, and very intimate setting. Silk pillows are piled high across the headboard and I lean back into them, getting very comfortable.

Monty lies down next to me, and I sidle in beside him. "I literally dream of how you'd taste, Katrina. I know it sounds strange. But like I said, sometimes feeding and sex can be connected. For the past decade or so, ever since online ordering has become easier, I've mostly subsisted on bovine or porcine blood. I used to go to blood banks on occasion, but I don't do that as much anymore, for ethical reasons. Before meeting you, I'd occasionally meet a woman, or even a man, at a bar and have a meal. That wasn't sexual. It was just feeding. For it to be sexual there has to be an emotional connection too, at least for me. But you'd be surprised at how many people love the idea of getting bitten by a vampire. They enjoy it, and the process actually creates pleasure for the um, well donor, if you will. Then I can erase their memory afterwards, just to keep things easy. Turning a vampire is an entirely different process than feeding."

He pauses at this point and looks at me to see if I have any questions. Monty knows I always have questions.

"We haven't talked about being exclusive. Have you been, um, feeding from other women?" I am scared to ask—I don't really want the answer to be yes. I'm a one man kind of girl and I know he said it wasn't sexual but still, it had to be somewhat intimate.

He turns towards me in the bed and brushes a curl away from my forehead. "No, since right after we met for tea that first time, I've only been eating blood from bags. It's not the best, but it gets the job done."

I wiggle up close to him, my head resting in the crook of his arm, staring up at the canopy in silence for a moment. Just processing everything he said. He's gotten used to me doing this and I really appreciate it. Oftentimes people need me to answer or react to something right away and that's just not how my brain works. The space under the canopied bed is peaceful, intimate really. Once again, being with Monty, it feels as if the entire rest of the world doesn't exist. It is just Monty and me for eternity, both of us lying together in silence except for the quiet air passing through our lungs and the beating of my heart. I hear the blood rushing through my ears in the dead silence between us, and I am sure his vampire senses detect the pulse of blood in my veins. And yet, there he is giving me time to think.

It is at this moment that I fall in love with Monty. Unabashedly, without reservation. I trust him with my life, my heart, and my body. It was crystal clear and incredibly simple, once I saw it. Without any doubt or urge to meticulously plan ahead, I break the silence and say, "Monty, I want you to feed from me. I want you to make love to me tonight."

His entire body stills. Then, moving slowly, as if not to scare me, he props himself up on one arm. His gaze sweeps over me—my red hair spread out across his silky black sheets—before locking onto my eyes. His voice is low and steady when he asks, "Are you sure?"

"I've never been so sure of anything in my whole life."

As soon as the last syllable escapes my lips, he leans down and kisses me—his lips soft and silky. He starts at the corner of my mouth, going slow, as if testing my statement.

To show him I am serious, I reach up, put my hands in his hair, and direct him to a full-on kiss, parting my mouth and pulling his lower lip between mine. I playfully nibble on it and he growls deep in his throat. "I want you Monty. I really want you."

That's all it takes and all of a sudden Monty is no longer hesitant. He starts kissing back with abandon, then he reaches one arm down to the hem of my night shirt and splays his hand across my soft belly. The touch feels amazing—electrifying. I moan into his mouth, whimpering a little too. He strokes my breast and instinctively my back arches up slightly from the bed. He is now half laying on top of me, keeping his weight on the bed. I wrap my hands around his biceps as he trails kisses from my mouth to my ear. His fangs graze my neck. "Monty, what will it feel like?" I whisper, both excited beyond compare and nervous too.

"It'll feel amazing, my KittyKat. And you can stop me at any time." He nestles his mouth at the beating pulse on my throat. I get really still as he licks my neck. His tongue sends a shiver down my entire body. Then, surprisingly without any pain, his teeth puncture into my skin and he begins to suck. Next thing I know, I see flashes of white and it feels as if I'm spinning out of control, but not in a bad way. Overcome with the most intense pleasure I've ever felt in my life, each nerve in my body begs for the sensation to continue. After just a few minutes, although who knows how long it really was, he licks my neck again, sealing the wound, and works his way down to my belly. Monty pulls my shirt off of me, and the sudden rush of cold air stings at first. But then his mouth is on my stomach, and I forget everything else. He laps his tongue around my belly button, sending more and more shivers through me and to my core. Since the moment I cast aside the logical part of my brain and suggested he feed from me, I've moved from one pleasurable sensation to the next and find it hard to focus—let alone gather my wits. Everything feels so incredibly good that I don't know what to do, say, or even think. There are no thoughts, only sensations and pure pleasure.

Montgomery

The thrill of feeding from Katrina is the most intoxicating experience I've ever known. Up until this point, I was merely surviving. Katrina filled me up with life again. As I take from her delicate neck, my cock stiffens almost painfully. I haven't experienced that connection of feeding and sexual desire in a long while. I need more. After a few minutes, I force myself to stop, thanking the gods I'd had some blood earlier in the evening. I don't want to drain her. I'd never live with myself. I need to gather up some control again. A final lap of my tongue seals the punctures on her neck and I methodically work down to her deliciously round belly. The softness there is like coming home. She arches against me, whimpering and moaning, driving me to near madness. I need more, but I also never want this to end. Katrina's shirt off, I pull down her soft pj's pants and cotton panties and just gaze down at her beauty splayed out on my bed. She is mine. I feel it on a primal level. I silently vow to myself that no harm will ever come to her as long as she is in my life. I shed the rest of my clothes, at vampire super speed, and then rejoin her on the bed. "How did that feel?" I ask her, our naked bodies intertwined together as I gently stroke up and down her body as she does the same with me.

"I can't even describe it. There are no words. It was amazing, it was intense, it is something I'll look forward to again." While she talks, she reaches down to grab my swollen cock. It strains in her soft hand and I am starting to have a hard time concentrating on her words.

"Ummm," I barely manage to say and somehow force the rest of my thought out into a mumbled, "That feels phenomenal." I lean down to flick my tongue across her stiff nipple and gently tug at it between my teeth. Her breasts are beautiful—heavy, soft, and smooth. I need more. I reach down between her legs and gently feel between her wet folds into paradise: wet, slippery, and silky. I need my cock to experience this sensation. I am about to turn to position myself between her legs, but before I can, she sits up and straddles me with a laugh. I love how confident she is.

"Um, Monty, hold on," she says, getting suddenly very still. She leans over the edge of the bed and pulls a condom out of her purse. "I just remembered I had this. I sort of went out and bought some last week, just in case."

It's something we should have talked about earlier, but heat has a way of making people reckless. I'm infertile and disease-free—it's part of being a vampire—but blurting all that out now would kill the mood. I want to respect her choices, not make assumptions.

I take the condom from her and roll it on carefully, catching her eye as I do. "Just so you know," I murmur, "this is about respecting you, not about needing it."

She smiles, soft but knowing, and brushes a strand of hair from my face. "I trust you, Monty."

She straddles me again, her slick heat sliding against my cock, and all rational thought slips away. Her hair spills

162

over her shoulders, and when she kisses me, soft and insistent, I know I'd let her ruin me if she wanted to. Her hips begin to move on instinct, a rhythm born not of choreography but of trust, of need. And then, I could feel it hit her—wave after wave, pleasure cresting into something vast and unstoppable.

I feel her body shatter around me pulsing in waves that threaten to undo me completely. She softly cries out, "Monty, I'm . . . I'm coming!"

Her nails dig into my shoulders, and the sharp sting only heightens the pleasure coursing through me. I can't hold back any longer. "KittyKat, I'm with you." I groan, my voice rough and desperate as I thrust deeper, losing myself in the rhythm of her body. Every pulse of her climax pulls me closer to the edge, until I'm spilling into her with a growl that feels torn from the depths of my soul.

As her climax matches mine, I feel her heartbeat like a drum, loud and intoxicating. My fangs ache with the need to taste her but I force myself back. I don't want to risk taking too much. Instead, I focus on the way her body clings to mine. The scent of her arousal is overwhelming, and I bury my face in her neck, breathing in her own unique scent of vanilla and musk. "You're so perfect," I murmur against her skin, my voice thick with longing. "I could lose myself in you forever."

With one last sigh, she collapses on me, her body trembling with small aftershocks of pleasure. I hold her close, my hands stroking her fiery red hair as our breathing slows. Her skin is warm next to my cool body. As she curls into me, her head resting on my chest, I feel a sense of peace I haven't felt in many decades. She presses a kiss to the place my heart should beat. Not out of pity, but love. It signals to me that she's not afraid of what I am—a vampire. She's not afraid of what others think of as cold, macabre. That truth should comfort me.

Instead, it undoes me.

Because her trust is a light I don't know how to stand in yet.

My fingers trace lazy patterns on her skin, and I know without a doubt that I'll never let her go. She's not just my lover—she's my forever. I just hope she feels the same. The thought of her not loving me the way I love her is enough to fracture me. I cannot comprehend facing endless immortality without her by my side. But I will wait. However long it takes, I will wait. She's worth every second of patience, every ounce of restraint. I will never pressure her, never demand more than she's willing to give. Because her heart, freely given, is the only thing I truly need.

Chapter 20

You've Never Eaten Chocolate?

Katrina

Wow. Wow. Wow. I'm not the most experienced. The couple times I had sex were just not that great. Those relationships ended shortly after, as if we just sort of quietly agreed it wasn't something to pursue. I had no idea that making love could be so Earth-shattering. I mean, I've heard people say that, but like a lot of things, I just assumed it was all blown out of proportion or people bragging, talking up the experience. This is what everyone has ever said was amazing about sex, and more. Like way more. I feel like Monty and I are one, like we've merged into this perfect moment. I'm almost afraid to look at him, unsure if he feels the same way. But if I stay really still, maybe this moment can last forever. And then, of course, my mind starts working again. Logic kicks in, ruining the magic.

"Monty? Are you awake?" I look up at him. I had rolled off him and am lying in the crook of his shoulder, my head resting on his bicep.

"Yes." He clears his throat and leans over to press a tender kiss to my forehead. "Katrina, you're a miracle. Stay the night?" His voice drops lower. "It would mean everything, just knowing you're here, asleep in my bed, while I'm working through the night."

"I should probably get home. I can still get a good night's sleep and make it to work tomorrow," I try to convince myself. I am always so responsible. Just for once, I'd like to be irresponsible. However, logic dictates that in the long run, the result of not sticking to my routine is more anxiety. I hope Monty understands. "I really want to stay, I really do. Monty, I have fallen in love with you." I pause for just a breath, needing to say it again, "I. Love. You. How did this happen? You're a vampire. I didn't mean to fall in love with you. I just thought it'd be fun to get to know you. You were so captivating on VidVibe. I can't love a vampire. I haven't even told my therapist about you." I start to spiral. A neurotypical person might stop after confessing their love to allow the other person a chance to respond. Hiding it in the middle of a run-on explanation means that while I desperately want him to notice and say it back, I've given him easy outs by providing plenty of options of other things to respond to first. Everything is happening so fast and I'm quickly going into an Autistic meltdown from being overstimulated and overwhelmed.

"Katrina," Monty sits up next to me and gently holds my hands in his. He pulls me into a tight hug, soothing my soul. "I love you too. I'm not saying it just because you said it. You are my world. I have traveled this Earth for over three hundred years and not found my soulmate, until I met you. You are my soul." He gently cups my face and kisses me with the tenderness of a flower petal dancing across my lips.

I let out a slow sigh. "You're a vampire, I'm a human. You still look twenty-seven. I'm already twenty-nine. I'm just going to get older and older. You won't. It's not fair, Montgomery. It's not fair." Tears start slipping down my cheeks. Love shouldn't hurt this badly. Especially after the magic we just created together. I start putting my pj's on. I really do need to go home and think about all of this.

"KittyKat, we've got time to figure things out. We don't have to decide anything tonight. I don't want to leave you crying, though. I never want to be the cause of your tears. Let's just stay together—we'll figure out things as we go."

"I need you to meet Rainbow and I still haven't met Nik. If we're going to continue to date, we need to get out of our little bubble we've created. Other than our first couple of dates, we've spent every moment at your house or mine. We need to spend time together in real life, not just inside this perfect fantasy."

"I think that's a wonderful idea. Let's go on a double date. Do you think Rainbow would like that? Who do you think would want to go out?"

"I'm guessing Sky, but who knows. Do you think Nik would go out on a double date with Max? He's the System's protector and I'd like you to meet him especially. He's protective of me and if he approves of you, that will say a lot." I told him very seriously.

"Nik is bi so I don't think he'd mind going on a double date with anyone in the System. Nik is really all about just love is love is love," Monty says without missing a beat. "Would Max date a man? Not that this has to be an actual date for them, it could just be our friends meeting."

"Max doesn't date at all, but I bet he'd love to get to know Nik. So you talk to Nik, I'll talk to Rainbow, and let's plan something. As it is now though, it is late and I think I need my routine. I want to stay—making love to you was life-changing. But I think I need to process. I know I love you, but I've got to figure out what that means. Will you drive me home and teleport back?"

"Anything for you."

Over the next couple of days, Monty and I text and call each other a couple of times, but we haven't seen each other since we made love. Now I'm preparing for our big double date. When I invited Rainbow, the chaos that ensued was both endearing and overwhelming. Everyone wanted to go on the date. Well Arleigh said she'd sit it out, unless I really needed her. She was interested in meeting Monty, but not as much interested in the double date aspect. Jessie wanted to meet Nik because I'd shown her a photo of him and he was right up her alley with his preppy nerd style. She was drooling all over him. I was right about Max. He was interested in meeting Nik also. Sky though—really, really, really—wanted to meet a vampire. I kind of was a little worried about her enthusiasm. The conversation proved chaotic. At first Max and Jessie were co-fronting, with Max talking, but Jessie talking to Max in the headspace and making him relay information. But then Sky kept pushing to the front. Let's just say, it was a long conversation that took a lot of patience on my part. In the end, it was decided Sky would front. Max was going to try to co-front, but that isn't always as easy to plan ahead of time. Sky is now over at my house, finishing up getting ready with me, and then Monty and Nik are going to come pick us up.

Monty hired a yacht on the Columbia River for a private dinner cruise. It sounds like a delightful night and I am so excited. A quiet, private date is perfect—Rainbow's like me; we both have a hard time with overstimulating, crowded places. The two of us can eat a nice dinner and the two vampires can just keep us entertained with tantalizing conversation. I am very much looking forward to it. The weather is perfect too. There's a gentle warm breeze carrying the scent of Pacific Northwest pine trees in the air; it feels like an early summer evening. We finish getting ready, and I check myself in the mirror one last time. I am wearing a light blue summer dress with a white cardigan and Sky is wearing an off-the-shoulder short little yellow dress with strappy sandals. She paired it with a sheer floor-length cover-up, although I don't think it'll keep her warm if the breeze turns chilly when the sun goes down. Also, if Max does end up fronting, he'll hate it, which shouldn't be funny, but he is always such a good sport about it that it ends up being funny. Poor guy, sharing a body with so many girls.

A knock on the door sounds, and I pull it open to reveal the vampires have arrived with flowers! A big bouquet of sunflowers for me, and Nik brought tulips for Sky. We put them in water and then leave for the marina.

Less than an hour later, we are out on the river. The captain is at the front of the yacht, we are lounging around the back and there is one chef/waiter who is very discreet and makes himself scarce down below between courses. I think he must have been familiar with Nik and Monty because he doesn't bat an eye when they don't have any food. Speaking of the food, it is divine. Stuffed lobster with a rice pilaf and grilled vegetables, a choice of white wine or sparkling apple juice, and for dessert, chocolate lava cakes.

We are finishing off the lava cakes when I ask Monty, "Don't you miss chocolate? I can't imagine never eating chocolate again."

"Well, you may be surprised, but I've never had it. Between my birth and when I became a vampire in 1717, I never had the chance to eat chocolate. It wasn't very common in England. Wealthy people would have a type of hot chocolate drink on occasion, but it wasn't anything my family ever had."

"You've never had chocolate?! Monty, I'm so, so sad for you. I don't even know what to say to this. You've lived such an amazing life, have done so many incredible things, and I learn that you also have missed out on so much. Have you ever had lobster?"

"I think I know the topic of my next video! No, I haven't had lobster either. Lobster was not a food many people ate in the early 1700s. It was often used in fertilizer or sometimes if you can believe it, prisoner food. It wasn't considered a desirable food until the 19th century, I think." Monty chuckles. "So, basically in my mind, you ate prison food tonight, but it looks like you enjoyed it, so it was a good choice for the menu."

"I had lobster one time before I turned," Nik says. "I was down by the coast to get a delivery for the farm. I don't remember all the details—it wasn't very remarkable. I had stopped at a seedy inn before heading back home and the matron had some sort of lobster stew on the menu. It was eat that or nothing, so I did. I don't remember anything outstanding about it, but seasonings were for rich people, so that's probably why."

"Well, I adore lobster," Sky says. "Thank you both for this tasty meal. I'm stuffed." She lies stretched out on one of the benches, with her feet in Nik's lap. She's gotten comfortable with Nik really fast. Her comfort level in general lets me know both her and Max, who I'm sure is close to the front, both think well of Nik and Monty. That makes me happy. She sighs a deep, content sigh and then asks, "So neither of you two ever got married? That's really hard to believe after three hundred years! And what about kids? Did either of you ever want kids?"

"Sky! That's rude!" I say, mortified she's asking such a personal question. Although, I do perk up to hear the answer. It is a subject that I haven't talked to Monty about. I mean I know he's dated before, but was he ever really serious with anyone? And what about kids? It was a subject on my mind a lot as I was already twenty-nine.

"I never wanted to settle down," Nik says. "The first couple of decades after turning were hard for me, and I mourned the life I could never have as a human. But once I settled into it, I didn't mind. I love change, always have. I've dated a lot, but nothing ever super serious. I also always had to be very circumspect when dating men until more recently. I never wanted kids either. Maybe if I hadn't turned it would have been different, but after I accepted I was a vampire, I just didn't think about kids much anymore."

Sky looks thoughtful. "I used to want kids, but I don't think I do anymore. DID is hard. I know Monty told you a little bit about it. There are a lot of Systems that have kids, and I think that is awesome. But for me, my life is complicated enough. And I'm happy working with animals. In headspace I'm only twenty-two and I feel like I'm not ready to have kids, and I don't think I'll ever want them. Jessie sometimes talks about wanting kids, but I think she agrees with me. Same with Max. Arleigh doesn't want children. She's like me—animals are enough for her. What about you, Monty?" Sky just goes in for those questions. I hold my breath. I need to know his answer. A big boat passes us by on the river and its wake hits ours, tossing us a bit. Sky grabs onto Nik and I fall into Monty's lap, where he wraps his arms around my waist and nuzzles his nose into the hair on the back of my neck.

"It's a moot point. Vampires are infertile," he says very quietly.

I whip my head around to look at him. "What?" Even though the boat is still rocking side to side from the wake, it feels as if my entire world froze. "You can't have kids? Why did I not think to ask you that sooner? Why did you not say anything sooner?"

"It's a subject that isn't easy for me to talk about, though I've briefly mentioned it on VidVibe in the past. Can we discuss it more later? By ourselves?" Monty pleaded.

"I haven't watched all your VidVibes, or, if it was before we were dating, maybe I just didn't pay attention, or thought you were still pretending to be a vampire. I don't know. It's not the same. But yeah, we'll talk later," my voice was cool, but this information has upset me. It is going to be hard to focus on the conversation around me for a while.

Chapter 21
The Friend Analysis

Montgomery

The conversation is awkward for a few minutes after the questions Sky brought up, but honestly, I am grateful. It was a topic I needed to broach with Katrina, but it never felt like the right time. We are getting serious, so we need to start tackling important topics. I am head over heels, punch-me-in-the-gut in love with this extraordinary woman. Every moment with her, I'm drawn into her web of kindness, her joy at the simplest pleasures in life, her exuberant spirit. If we are going to work out long-term, kids and, well, species are two topics we have to discuss. If we decide to stay together, she has the choice to grow old while I stay the same, or turn. Vampire culture limits how many people can be turned. Rogue vampires turned Nik, Henry, and I, which is not the norm. They were punished with execution for what they did when they were caught. By current vampire law, you can turn a human once every three hundred years and not in your first century as a vampire. This is done because sometimes vampires don't end up wanting to spend centuries and centuries together. Some partnerships split off and go separate ways. We are mostly loners, but sometimes live together in small families. A human must be twenty-five to be turned and it can be done only in a special ceremony at The Reunion in Civita di Bagnoregio, Italy. Anything else, unless there are very special circumstances, is against Vampire Law.

Thank goodness for Sky and Nik. They start up a new conversation, more or less saving our evening. I think after a while, Katrina decides to put her concerns aside and just have a good time for the rest of the night. Although, I know, we'll have to have a serious discussion before long.

Too soon, the boat pulls back into the marina and it is time to drive the girls home.

"When did you guys first learn to drive?" Sky asks both Nikolai and I as I drive everyone back to Katrina's house.

"I actually drove an original Model T once," I tell her. "I didn't own it. I owned a small private newspaper printing press around the 1920s in Boston, and my business partner, a human, bought a Model T and he let me drive it. It was so thrilling! I of course was very proficient at driving a horse and buggy, but driving a motor car was absolutely fascinating. I give up a lot being a vampire, but seeing the progression of technology through the years has been something I won't ever tire of. I bought a Model A when it came out in 1927. My printing press took off, and it's when Nik and I started to make a lot of money. Cars were expensive but I just had to have one, so I felt the expense was worth it. We had learned how to invest and we got lucky that the depression didn't hit us hard. I also had foreign investments, which helped us weather the stock market crash followed by the Great Depression."

"Yeah, I'll admit, I was really scared of the first engine cars," Nik adds. "They weren't very stable and I just really loved horses. Monty has always been on the next cutting edge of tech and I usually trail right behind him. I didn't buy a car until many years later—I used Monty's if I needed one." Nik is sitting in the backseat with Sky, the two of them fairly close together. They really seem to have hit it off.

"That is so hard to wrap my head around," Katrina says. "Most of the time, it's easy to forget how much life you've lived before meeting me."

I sense she is starting to withdraw again, and I worry I'll lose her. She isn't completely wrong. I had lived generations of lives prior to her, but for the first time since before turning, I feel alive again. Back in the 1930s I had met a woman who at first I thought was someone I'd want to marry. I was starting to amass a fortune at the time when most people were struggling due to the Great Depression. I was a philanthropist—I set up food banks and did as much as I could to help my neighbors. Shirley, that was her name, acted like she loved me but would complain when I donated money to the poor. Soon I realized she didn't love me—she just wanted my fortune. I was a means to a lifestyle she wanted. My heart was broken. I dated on and off since then, a few times growing fairly close to someone, but nothing like how Katrina caught stole my heart.

As we get closer to her house, I wish I could stay, but I know she'll want to go in with Sky. In front of both Sky and Nik, I say, "Yes, I have lived a lot longer than you have, Katrina, but I didn't know what living actually was until I met you. You've made me come alive again. I love you. You have changed my life for the better in the months we've known each other, and I hope I'll get the chance to continue getting to know you even more." Nik is going to give me hell over that later, but in a good-natured way. He really wants the best for me, as I do for him. But that's how much I don't care. I need Katrina in my life. We pull up to Katrina's house and she starts to get out of the car. I walk her to the door and thankfully Nik and Sky stay back for a minute to give us some privacy.

"I love you too, Monty. I'm also feeling so many things right now."

"Can you call me later after Sky goes home?"

"Yes," she says, pressing her lips to mine, filling me with hope that I am going to cling on to until I hear from her again. It takes everything I have to walk back to the car where Nikolai is waiting for me. Sky gives me a little smile and a thumbs up as we pass. I think I have her vote of approval, which gives me further hope.

Katrina

Sky and I are sitting on the couch for a post-date analysis. Data curls up in my lap as if to say he missed me tonight.

"So, Sky, what did you think of Monty?"

"Katrina, he's perfect for you! I am so happy you met him. I can't believe it all started with a DM to his SnapFoto account. Like, what the hell? That'll be such a cute 'how you met' story to tell people!"

"But that's the thing I'm upset about, Sky! If I stay with him, it won't be a story I tell my children. I'm twenty-nine. I'm not getting any younger. I've never really thought about kids, but I've also always assumed I'd have at least one." Data senses I am getting upset, starting to nudge my chin with the top of his head, and I pet him absentmindedly.

"It's okay not to have kids, and not to even want them, you know. I made peace with that, and our whole System is pretty much on board. I know Jessie sometimes thinks about it, but she's also happy not having kids. Max does not want to be pregnant, and Arleigh is happy being child-free too. And it's not just about being a System. I'm friends online with other Systems who have kids and it works out amazingly for them. It's just not something we're pursuing. But this isn't about me, it's about you."

"Yeah, there's tons of Autistic men and women who have kids. I can imagine it'd be challenging—being pregnant would be a sensory nightmare, and babies are so demanding and loud. But I know I could do it. I guess I just really need to think about it some more. Then there's the whole age thing too. Would I become a vampire? We haven't talked about it much, but I think that's an option. I wouldn't get to eat ever again. But I'd basically be immortal. Wow. Or I could continue to grow old while Monty stays looking twenty-seven forever."

"I mean, Nik was pretty hot and super fun. I'd totally let him bite me and make me a vampire!" Sky jokes. Sometimes the fact that she's barely twenty-two really shows.

"Is Max still near the front? What does he say?" I watch Sky get quiet, as if she's listening to Max inside her head.

"He says he really approves of Monty. He watched Monty very closely all night and was very impressed with how he spoke to you and treated you. You have Max's approval."

"Thanks, Max!" I say to Sky, knowing he is listening. "Can you catch Jessie and Arleigh up on all this later? It's getting late and I need to call Monty. I told him I'd call before I fell asleep."

"You're kicking me out for him?! We've changed our mind. He's no good for you!" Fake indignation drips from her words. Sky knows I don't handle sarcasm well. Before wrapping me in a goodbye hug and leaving me with plenty to process, she gives me a final genuine nod of approval.

After Sky leaves, I reluctantly call Monty and keep the conversation light. The topic of kids or a future together feels much too massive to discuss over the phone. That doesn't mean I actually want to talk about it in person either. I want things to go back to how they were. I want to go back to hanging out in his game room, playing silly video games with him and, yes, even making love to him again.

The next few days, I spend mostly on autopilot. I keep reliving that night over and over in my head. I don't want that to be my only time with him. But I'm not someone who can date for fun. I wouldn't have made love to him if I hadn't already fallen in love with him. Shouldn't that be my answer? Does anything else really matter? Is love enough to carry us through? It feels as if what we have is a tiny rose bud of love— it still needs care so it can bloom fully. Our love is so new and delicate.

"Katrina, I've called your name five times now, girl. Your head's in the clouds today!" Mrs. Humphrey calls out to me. I am supposed to be sorting a new shipment of books we've gotten in. I look down and see my "sort pile" hasn't gotten much smaller.

"I'm sorry, Mrs. Humphrey. I am having a hard time concentrating today. I'll try to focus." That's another consideration too. If I turn into a vampire, I won't be able to keep my job at the library. I do enjoy it here. It's not necessarily my passion, but it's a job that is able to accommodate my Autism and ADHD nicely. Could I live
178

without it? I start putting the new books into piles according to genre and where they are going to go in the library. I'll have to print out barcodes and tape them into the books next.

Using her cane for support, she carefully made her way over to me, "I'm not worried about your work, Katrina." She patted my shoulder like a grandma would do, "You always get things done much more efficiently than anyone else around here, truth be told. We all have off days. I'm just not used to seeing you this way. Is everything okay?" Concern showed in her soft eyes.

"Oh, yes. Actually, things have been marvelous. I've been dating a wonderful man. I guess you caught me daydreaming about him," I confide.

"Well, well, isn't that nice. I always thought you were too special to not have caught a handsome fella by now," her voice beaming with pride. The dichotomy of her being both so progressive and so old-fashioned in one person always amuses me. But that's Mrs. Humphrey for you. She might still use quaint sayings from a different era, but she wouldn't have blinked if I told her I was dating a woman or someone nonbinary. She just wants me to be happy. And honestly, I love her for it.

I think I've kept some distance from Monty because I feel as if I need to sort out for myself if I'd be happy to be child-free for the rest of my life or perhaps eternity? That's a long time, when I hear myself say it. Eternity. Forever. I mull over the impossibility of eons before continuing my thought process. I still have several years before biologically I'd feel pressured to decide if I wanted to have a baby. The decision now feels urgent. I know Monty isn't pressuring me, but there's so many layers to consider. But I needed time to figure this out by myself. Because if Monty's in the room and I'm looking at him looking at me with that deep love in his eyes, there is no way I can think clearly. We've been texting and talking on the phone, but it's been three days since our date. I think tonight I'm ready to go see him again.

Chapter 22
Conversations and Crossroads

Montgomery

Another lap swimming in my pool and I feel like a damn fish—back and forth, back and forth. I'm trying to keep myself busy and my mind off Katrina. Thankfully she's talked to me a few times, but every single time, she's kept the conversation pretty lighthearted and focused on her day or what Rainbow or Mrs. Humphrey have been up to. At one point, she was talking about silly things Data had been doing around her house. And I appreciate it. It's her way of telling me that she cares and she needs time to process without any pressure. I'm determined to give it to her. That's why I'm here in my indoor pool swimming and trying to burn off energy that I really can't burn off. It's also time for me to eat again, but after tasting Katrina, the thought of the bovine blood in my fridge might as well be like, as the humans say, "eating cardboard."

I'm about to get out of the pool when I hear a huge splash at the other end. Immediately I tense up. I must be distracted if someone was able to get into my house without my notice. Then Nik pops his head out of the water.

"Nik, what the hell, dude?! We talked about this. You are not supposed to teleport in my house without notice. What if I'd had Katrina over?"

"Katrina loves me—we hit it off the other night on the boat. She wouldn't mind," Nik says as he floats over towards me. "I hadn't heard from you in a few days and wanted to check in on you."

"How did you know I'd be swimming?" suspicion in my voice.

"Uh, well, I didn't," Nik confessed. "I just wanted to swim. I figured you'd be over at Katrina's house and that's why I hadn't heard from you in a few days."

"You have it all wrong," I say, and splash him in the face. He deserves it. "Katrina hasn't seen me since the yacht. I've talked to her on the phone, but the whole conversation about kids apparently scared her. I'm trying to give her space, but I'm starting to get worried she's going to end it between us."

"Oh dear god, no. It'd be like when you found out Shirley was using you. I don't think I can handle you like that again."

"Wrong. This would be hundreds of times worse than when Shirley and I ended things. I can't imagine not being with Katrina. I just can't, Nik. She's bewitched me." I start to climb out of the pool. I really do need to eat. I almost want to go to the bar with Nik, but I think that would ruin any chance I have with Katrina. Not until I talk to her about things like that more specifically. We haven't talked about if she feels comfortable with me feeding from other people. It isn't a necessity for me, so it's something I'd rather abstain from until I can talk to her about it.

"You always were such a romantic. I admire that about you. I hope you sort things out with Katrina. I wouldn't mind seeing her friend Sky again. Not to mention, I don't want to have you moping around more. Where are you going? Up for some *Mortal Kombat*? We could kill each other on screen. It'd be fun."

"No, I've got to eat and probably film a VidVibe. Rain check?"

"Sure, dude, sure. It'll be fine. You'll talk to Katrina and sort it out. I saw how she looked at you man. That girl was into you. I promise."

"You're a good friend, Nik. I don't say that enough." I towel off and am almost dressed when my phone rings. Katrina's number pops up on the screen, and I scramble to answer it. Nik gets out of the pool behind me and starts to towel himself off. He teleported in his swimsuit, so not sure what he is planning on doing next, but I put him out of my mind and say hello to Katrina.

"Hey," she says to me. "Um, I've been doing a lot of thinking, Monty."

Is she going to break up with me on the phone? I sit down on a lounge chair and hang my head between my knees. I squeeze my eyes shut and wish Nik was not here to see me this way. I stay silent, willing her to continue.

"Can I come over tonight?" she asks me, not giving much away in her voice.

Okay, so she isn't going to break up with me on the phone. Deep breath in. That's a good thing. That's a really good thing.

"You are always welcome here—any time of the day or night. Would you like me to come get you? Car or teleport at your service," I say, trying to keep my voice light.

"I think I'll drive over, if that's okay. I can be there in fifteen minutes?"

"Sure. I'm getting out of the pool, so I'll get dressed and see you soon." I hang up and look over to Nik. "Katrina is coming over—you need to go. We've got important stuff to talk about. Dear god, I hope this goes well. If you see me at the bar later, be warned I won't be in a good mood."

"Good luck, man. You'll be fine. I told you, she loves you." And then he teleports out, wet swimsuit and all.

I rush to my room and throw on some sweatpants and a faded T-shirt. I pull my wet hair back into a low ponytail and then I head to the kitchen. I need to stave off some of my hunger before Katrina arrives. Best-case scenario we work things out and make love and I get to bite her again. No matter what happens, I need to lessen my hunger so I have more control. I'll never hurt her. I'd die first. Knowing I will get to see Katrina soon makes the refrigerator blood slightly more palatable. I really need to visit a blood bank again and get some human blood in stock. A worry for another day.

Knowing she'll be here any minute, I pace up and down the hallway to the front door to the living room, telling myself everything is going to be okay. I hear the side door click open and I go to meet her in the kitchen. Like usual, she is breathtaking and I linger a moment to soak in her vibrance. She's wearing a teal tunic and her tights have little books and cats printed all over them. It's a look Katrina pulls off. Her mass of curls are pulled up on top of her head in what she calls a "messy bun." Which is apt, but it is also adorable, with errant curls sticking out here and there to frame her face. It's not always easy reading her expression because, like she's told me, what she's feeling on the inside doesn't always match her facial expression. It's a common frustration for many Autistic people. "Hey KittyKat, can I give you a hug?" I ask her, craving the feeling of her in my arms. She nods and walks into my embrace.

I stand there holding her tight, leaning down slightly to gently nuzzle my nose in the soft hair near her ear. She
184

wraps her arms around my waist, her cheek on my chest. Neither one of us speaks, and time slows, stretches. I wonder if she feels it too—the way some moments grip you, refusing to let go, anchoring you in place like a checkpoint in an otherwise blurry timeline. Eventually, she breaks the hug by stepping back, but holds out her hand to mine and then leads me to the living room.

"I wish it was cold enough to light a fire in the fireplace tonight, fires always make me happy, but I'm also glad for the warmer weather," she says.

"It is nice tonight. Summer weather will be here any day now," I reply, still following her lead. We both sit on the cool leather couch, and she tucks herself deep into the cushion, cross-legged like usual. I settle near her and wait, but think maybe I need to start the conversation.

"It's so good to see you tonight. You've been on my mind every moment since our double date. Did Sky like Nik? What did Max think of me?" I ask, feeling brave.

A huge grin spreads across her face. "You got Max's stamp of approval, which is one reason why I'm here tonight. Max's opinion means a lot to me. Sky also said you were, and I quote, "dreamy" but she also thought Nikolai was "F-ing Hot." What did Nikolai think about me?" she ended on a timid note.

"He loved you, and said he could see why I won't stop talking about you. Just like Max and the rest of Rainbow, Nik's opinion means a lot to me. I've known him for a mighty long time."

"So. Babies," she says.

"Yeah. Babies," I repeat. The word feels heavier than it should, pressing down on my chest like a weight I can't shift. I've gone over this inevitable conversation so many times in my head these past few days, rehearsing it like a boss fight where I already know the odds are against me. I've lived through wars, plagues, entire societal collapses—but this? This terrifies me. Because this conversation has the potential to break us, and I don't know if I can survive losing her. "I know it's something I probably should have mentioned earlier, but there just never was a good time. I mean, too early would have scared you, leaving you thinking 'why is he talking about kids when we just met!' but waiting too long has you worried 'why did he never bring this up?' You see how hard that is? Do you want kids one day?" I ask, dreading the answer might be yes.

"It's complicated," she says. "I really hadn't thought about it except abstractly. As in, one day I'd fall in love, get married, and have kids. Because that's what people do. So, yeah, I thought I'd probably have a kid, at least in the next couple of years, but I've never been a girl who dreamed of having kids as much as some people I know. It's just not something I thought I'd have to think about right now. I have fallen in love with you. I know we've only been dating for a few months, but I just know deep within, you are my soulmate. It scares me a little though. It's not the life I thought I'd lead." She sits there on my couch, her fidget spinner in her hands, and looks up at me. I know that wasn't easy for her to say, but I'm happy she is opening up. "It's not always easy to trust people or my feelings. I try to, but I've been hurt so many times before. People eventually get tired of my peculiar ways, my endless questions, or my need to have things a certain way. How do I know you won't start to feel that way?"

"There are no guarantees in life, Katrina. I'm not going to lie and say there are. But I will say those things you mentioned are some of the reasons I fell in love with you." As

I say this, my ever wiggly KittyKat leans down to lay her head in my lap so she can look up at me. I take this as a very positive sign indeed. "Your peculiar ways, as you call them, I adore. I love how you do things to make your life work the way you need it to. I love how you don't let the way things have always been stop you from questioning if that's the way they should be. I love that you ask so many deep questions. Your first question to me in that live video a couple of months ago caught my attention. That's what stood out, that's what sparked my interest. As for routine, you need it and that's okay—it's never bothered me at all." I stare down into her big green eyes, and rub her arm the way she likes.

"Did you ever want children? I mean...before you turned?"

"Like you, I figured it was inevitable. It wasn't something I thought too much on. I was the youngest of the family, so it wasn't as if there was a lot of pressure on me to produce an heir. And we were rural farmers so that wasn't really as big of an issue as it was for the aristocracy. I was the baby of the family, and no one really paid much attention to whether I was courting."

She lets out a guffaw at that. "Courting, hum? Oh my goodness, Monty, you really are so ancient. Are you courting me? I don't have a chaperone. Oh no," she says, taking on a mock-British accent. "My virtue is at stake, being alone with such a dashing young man."

"Your virtue is most definitely *not* safe with me— especially if you keep looking at me like that. I could quite literally eat you again."

Her eyes darken. No push glamor, no trick—just the raw pull between us. I want to taste her again. I either need to touch her or get up and put space between us. I'm about to lift her away when she sits up and swings a leg over me, straddling my hips. Tilts her head, bares her pale neck. My cock swells hard against my sweatpants, pressing to her through her tights.

"KittyKat, are you teasing me?" My voice hitches, restraint fraying. My fangs descend and my control hangs on by a thread.

"Take me, Monty. I need you as much as you need me."

That's all I need. I sink my teeth into her soft neck, pierce, and drink. Ambrosia—heat and sweetness flooding my mouth. My hand slides under her tunic to cup her breasts, pinching her nipples as I feed. She moans, gripping my thighs with hers, hips grinding slow and insistent over me. Her hands tangle in my damp hair. She wants more.

When I've had my fill, I lick the wound closed, then take her face in my hands and kiss her, careful with my fangs. She bites my lip, tugging it between her teeth. I groan. "Katrina, I want to make love to you right now."

"Yes." She's already pulling her tunic over her head. Sweet, practical cotton bra—pure Katrina: fire and passion threaded through comfort. I unclasp it, kiss her breasts, kneading them in my palms. She reaches for me through my sweatpants. "These are coming off now."

We strip in seconds. I lean back on the couch, expecting her to climb into my lap again—but she drops to her knees instead. Her hands wrap around me—stroking, teasing, squeezing like a toy she can't quite put down. My head tips back, fists clenching beside me, just waiting to see what she will do next. She appears to be having a wonderful time driving me insane.

Then she leans in and presses an open-mouthed kiss to the tip before sliding me into the heat of her mouth. Slick.

Hot. Perfect. She sucks, licks, and keeps a firm hand on my base so I can't take control. When she hums around me, I reach into her curls, pull out the ponytail so her hair falls wild around her face. Red lips, pale shaft, rhythm quickening. I'm close, too close—but she knows it.

She looks up at me with a grin in her eyes and I can see she feels powerful. She knows she is safe and in control. She has me under her spell. She sits back with a very satisfied look on her face but I am not done yet. I stand up, and lead her over to the fur rug in front of the fireplace. I really wish it was cold enough to have a fire, but the rug is soft and, honestly, at this point, I don't think either of us care about our surroundings.

She lies back, and I kneel between her thighs, sliding a finger into her wet heat. She arches. My other hand cups her breast.

"Monty, now!"

Not yet. I trail my wet finger up her stomach, sketching shapes over her skin. Kiss her belly button. Taste her. Move slowly up her body—tongue along her ribs, lips closing around her nipple—until her moans turn into desperate little gasps.

I part her lower lips, slide just the tip into her as I kiss her mouth, tongues tangling. Then I drive in deep, burying myself to the hilt. Her tight heat grips me, and we find that rhythm older than language. She bites at my neck as we break together, heat flooding through us in a wave that leaves nothing untouched.

I stay over her for a breath, then slip out and gather her against my chest. Her head rests over my heart. I will never take this woman for granted.

"I love you," I whisper in her hair.

Chapter 23
Big Life Decisions

Katrina

I know we have to talk more, but I feel so happy and relaxed after making love with Monty again. My stomach starts rumbling and I realize it's been a while since I had dinner. Monty either heard it or felt it, because he asks if I am hungry.

"I'm starving! I think I worked up an appetite there." I am trying to remember if I have a granola bar in my purse. I usually keep some sort of safe food on me at all times. Autism and sensory issues around food can be tricky!

"Would you like a bagel and cream cheese?" Monty asks.

"Uh, yeah. But why do you have bagels and cream cheese?" I know full well he isn't eating them!

"Because I noticed that was one of your favorite go-to snacks when you're hungry and I just wanted to have it on hand for you."

"But I haven't even been here in a few days. When did you get them?" I tried to puzzle out.

"I've been buying a few groceries to have on hand just in case for a couple of weeks. It just happened that we haven't been over here when you're hungry until now. I've been dropping it all off at the food pantry when it hasn't been eaten."

"Monty, you just keep surprising me, and always in a good way." We get redressed and head to the kitchen. Without thinking about it, I open the refrigerator to grab the cream cheese and see several bottles and bags of blood in there. It hits home how he's never fed in front of me, other than the two times he's fed from me. Seeing the blood right there in the fridge makes everything even more real. When he feeds from me, it feels so good, I am not really actively thinking about it somehow. I am just focused on the pleasure. I know unequivocally he's a vampire. Somehow seeing the full bags of blood sitting in organized rows in his refrigerator is an unexpected shock. I grab the cream cheese out of the door and quickly close the fridge shut, the bags out of sight for the moment. Food first, then definitely more talking next. Monty is behind me, toasting a bagel in his oven because he doesn't own a toaster. There is something kind of charming about that. What a crazy mix of emotions I am feeling. Does the man even own a plate? Curious, I start opening up his cabinets. Sure enough, he has a minimal place setting. It looks like it came from one of those box sets that has four bowls, plates, and silverware packaged together that college kids buy to set up their first apartment. "Did you buy these plates for me too?" I ask him.

"KittyKat you know I'm a multi-millionaire right? A few plates isn't a big deal. I just want you to feel at home here."

Once again, I am overloaded with information. I mean, I knew he was rich, that was obvious. Awesome mini-castle that passes all the vibe checks. Date on a yacht, nice clothes, nice cars, and I'm pretty sure I saw a motorcycle in his garage, but I haven't really thought about how much money he actually has.

I pull out a barstool and sit down with my plate. He puts the toasted bagels on the plate and I take one of the brand-new butter knives and smear cream cheese on my bagel. He leans on the counter and I take a couple of bites without talking, just processing stuff in my head. The one thing I love most about Monty is how patient he is. He knows I need processing time and he'll just wait, but not in that way where I feel as if I need to figure stuff out fast before he walks out of the room or gets bored. He just waits in a quiet, unassuming way with no pressure. Honestly I've never had anyone who is like that. Even Rainbow will try to help me process stuff and move me along a bit when I go into deep thought mode.

"I think this is the best bagel I've ever had in my life," I say. "Where did you get it? I think I need to start buying them."

"Well, um, there's a little bakery that makes them fresh in New York. I sort of teleport there and get them every couple of days."

"How does that not surprise me?!" I now cannot live without the best bagel ever and of course it comes from a bakery across the country. Is there anything about this man that isn't perfect? Other than the glaring problem that he's a vampire, which is kind of a biggie. "Now I'm going to have to keep dating you so I have access to these amazing bagels. I see your plan there," I tease.

"Darn, you figured out my plan," he says as he leans over and wipes a bit of cream cheese off the outer corner of my lips.

"Okay." I say with a sigh. I've delayed us talking about this, but it's not doing either of us any good. My uncertainty is keeping a wall between us. We need to keep hashing this out until we come to a decision that we can both live with. In a rush of words say, "Let's say I don't want children. Because I've now spent the last three days, which granted isn't that much time, but I've obsessively thought of almost nothing else for the past three days except thinking about if having kids is important to me. I like kids. I like other people's kids. I love the kids at the library and answering their questions. I also love sending them back to their grown-up when I'm done with them. I do think I could honestly be happy without having kids. I think I could be happy being child-free. The initial thought was startling, but it is something I took for granted that would happen, not a passion or milestone I am actively working towards, if that makes sense."

He nods, listening but not adding anything to what I say, so I keep going. "But what are we talking about here regarding our relationship? Are we talking forever? Am I being presumptuous?" At this, I do stop talking. It's not as if he asked me to marry him. Do vampires get married? Do I want to be a vampire? What does that entail? Should I ask these questions out loud? Instead I take a few more bites of my bagel. I need him to start talking.

"It's a bit of a paradox, isn't it? If I asked you to marry me without this discussion, you wouldn't have all the information to make an informed decision. But if we don't have marriage, or a long-term partnership, on the table, the concerns would be quite different, wouldn't they? If you're done with your bagel, let's go sit out in the garden. It's a beautiful night. I can turn on the firepit for ambiance."

We move to his backyard. The Columbia River rumbles softly in the background. The early June evening is pretty perfect and now just nippy enough to warrant the firepit. He turns on the sleek modern firepit and we cozy up together on a padded bench. He pulls a blanket out from somewhere and wraps it around our shoulders.

"Do you ever get hot or cold?" I ask. I'm always wondering about these little things that I take for granted, and wonder if his experience is the same as mine.

"I can feel temperature differences, but they don't really bother me. I'm sure extreme temperatures might be uncomfortable though."

I snuggle into his side, realizing it is my favorite place to be in the world. "Okay, so our conundrum," I say. "You still didn't answer my question."

He tilts towards me, and in a low, gravelly voice says, "Katrina, you are my soulmate. There's no reason for me to pretend otherwise. I've walked this Earth for over three hundred years now. I won't pretend I haven't had other loves, other lovers. But no one, not one single person, have I felt was the other half of me. I am almost immortal, but I've never been more scared in my life than I am right now, here in this moment. Knowing that my life will forever be changed after tonight."

"Are we really making big life decisions tonight? I feel ill equipped for it. I didn't have it in my planner. Life just usually happens to you when you aren't really looking. But tonight feels heavy, impossibly important. As if I'm actually living right here in this moment. It feels big. Why is BIG such a small word? It feels tremendous. Monumental. Colossal. Pivotal even. I wish I could tell the future." I feel a panic attack coming on. I get up from the bench and take four large steps to the end of the patio and back. I reach up to the patio ceiling and then down to my toes. Then I jump up and down a few times, wishing I had my trampoline. But I feel a little better, so I settle again beside Monty. Then it hits me: Monty never judges me when I need to stim. He never judges me

194

when I ask a billion questions. He accepts me exactly as I am. He never, ever asks me to change. He gives me time to think. He asks me questions when he doesn't understand what I'm doing. He's smart, he's funny, he's kind and generous to others, and he's curious. I love people who don't just go with the flow, who question societal norms. I realize I do want to grow old with him, or stay with him as long as I can. More questions begin to bubble up.

"Posit: We work under the presumption that for the sake of this conversation we plan to get married, or have a long-term partnership in a forever kind of way," I say. "What does that look like for me? Do I grow older and older while you always look twenty-seven? Won't that be horrible for you? I can't imagine being sixty while you look twenty-seven but you're actually whatever age."

"That is one option, yes," he says carefully. "Another is for you to turn." At that he gets deadly still while he watches for my reaction.

I leap up from the bench again. "Turn! You mean, turn into a vampire?" I had thought of the idea of course, but not fully. Not enough to turn it over in my head like I did the child question. Tonight is shaping up to be a very difficult night. I start literally turning in circles. I hold my arms out and spin around a few times, trying to release some of the emotional energy vibrating inside me. I plop back down. "Okay, break it down for me. I'm about to leap to a bunch of conclusions that probably aren't true, so it's best for you to just be frank with me. Because while I've been watching your VidVibes for a long time, and we've talked here and there about you being a vampire and what it means, I've never applied that knowledge to me. Start off with maybe *how* one turns properly. I know your origin story is unique." It's getting late, but I don't care. Some moments in life are more important than routines, work schedules, and the daily grind. I'll figure out tomorrow when it gets here. Tonight feels like the most important night of my life.

He hugs me tight, as if to absorb some of my excess energy. His arms feel so strong and secure around me. My muscles relax a smidge. His body feels like home. "Have you ever been to Italy?" he asks me, seemingly out of nowhere.

"No. I've been up to Canada, but never to Europe."

"Well, once a year in a tiny remote village in Italy, there is a meeting of vampires. It's where we catch up on current happenings and such. Every four years, it's a bigger production. Although there's been talk about moving the big reunion to every ten years, but that's neither here nor there. What I mean to say is, anyone who wants to turn a willing human to a vampire does it at a special ceremony at our yearly gathering."

"So I'd have to go to Italy?" That sounds extremely daunting. Travel isn't easy for me. "When is the meeting? What is the ceremony? My passport is up to date . . . "

"You wouldn't technically need a passport. I'd teleport you in—there's no airport or anything. One of the pros of being a vampire is getting to move through borders without documentation. We do end up needing to create documentation for daily life—my driver's license cannot say I was born in 1690," he says with a small chuckle. "The meeting is during the last week of October. The ceremony takes place on Halloween. You wouldn't have to go all week. I could come back for you and collect you just for the ceremony at the end, if you like. I know you don't love big parties, and most of the meetings won't have much relevance to you yet. There is a class, of sorts, that happens before the ceremony. It's a fairly modern invention from the Vampire

Council. It makes sure that any human is there fully at their own accord, that they understand what they are signing up for, and covers some basics they need to know. Of course the vampire turning them is their full mentor." He stops to check if I am getting all of this.

I feel both antsy and sleepy all at once. "I brought an overnight bag," I say. "Just in case I wanted to stay the night. Data will miss me, but he'll be fine overnight. I left him plenty of food and water. I know you aren't sleepy, but I am. Can we get in your bed and keep talking?"

"Good idea. I'd love that." He gets up to turn off the firepit, and I go out to my car, get my bag, and then make my way to the main bedroom.

A few minutes later, curled up in the luxurious bed next to Monty, I continue the conversation. "So what does the ceremony entail?" I'm really nervous about this part. "I can't imagine never eating food again. I don't really like the idea of eating blood—no offense."

"None taken. Don't worry about that part. I mean, I understand not wanting to give up food. But it really isn't that bad, because after turning you won't want human food again. It won't appeal to you. Except wine. I don't get that. But for some reason, we've found that vampires can drink wine and many like it. I like it on occasion. After you turn, blood will taste good. You'll want it. It's what your vampire body needs. How much do you know? I have talked about it on VidVibe some."

"Well, I've heard you eat cow and pig blood, right? And of course humans. There's a couple stories where you've said you've lived off of smaller animals too on occasion."

"Yep, all true."

He then goes into more detail about the logistics of procuring blood in the modern age, explaining it's really not as difficult as one would think.

"And the ceremony?"

Monty goes on to tell me more about the ceremony and everything it entails. As he talks, I start to drift off in his big, cozy bed. Right before I fall asleep, I hear him say, "I'll let you sleep — I'll be around the house all night. If you wake up later and I'm asleep, don't be scared. I really do sleep like 'the dead.'" I half wonder if he's trying to make a joke, but I'm too sleepy to care.

Chapter 24
How Vampires are Born

Montgomery

Katrina falls asleep so fast it makes me smile. I stay for a few minutes, just lying beside her, soaking it all in. She looks peaceful. Content. Like she actually feels safe with me. I can't help it, I gently pull the blanket higher around her, like it'll somehow keep the happiness from leaking out. Then I slip out of the room, feeling lighter on my feet than I have in . . . maybe decades.

It's just past midnight—practically the start of a brand-new day—and I'm too wired to even think about resting. Instead, I head to the den to film a VidVibe. Talking about the ceremony could be fun. If I really ham it up, make it sound like cosplay, maybe no one will notice how much truth I'm actually slipping in. The Elders don't know I'm on VidVibe—and they definitely wouldn't understand why anyone would pretend to be a vampire online—but if they ever found out, they'd probably have a thing or two to say about it and it wouldn't be good.

Since Katrina's sleeping in my room, I don't bother changing—just throw a glamor over myself and get to work.

I make it look like I am wearing leather pants and a dark purple satin shirt with a hunter green vest topped with a black peacoat. Less of a goth look and more of a posh vampire vibe. I also glamor some smokey makeup around my eyes as the finishing touch. I need a gold goblet to make this particular VidVibe convincing, so I head to the kitchen and grab a wine glass, fill it with wine, and glamor it to look like some old artifact chalice.

I settle into my leather chair in my vampire den and set the camera up to start filming.

"I don't think I've talked about how vampires are born. My turning was done by rogue vampires in a horrid fashion that I barely survived. We have vampire laws and customs to keep our species safe, secret, and our population in check.

A vampire can turn a human once every three hundred years and not until they've been a vampire for a full century. I've never turned a human into a vampire. When you turn a human, you become bonded to them and become their mentor. There are ways to undo the bond, but once a vampire, always a vampire. There are a variety of reasons why a vampire and human would choose to be bonded. It is usually a romantic pairing, but some vampires turn friends they want as a long-term companion.

Like a human wedding ceremony, the Vampire Ceremony can be simple or elaborate. Rather than exchanging rings, the human is given a special dagger. It symbolizes that they have the choice to kill the vampire at that moment. It'd be an unwise choice, because they'd be surrounded by vampires witnessing the ceremony, but you know—symbolism. These days humans are not turned without consent.

Pausing my speech, I let my gaze smolder as I look directly into the camera. My voice drops just slightly as I say, *"Consent is sexy,"* punctuating the words with a slow, deliberate wink. I reach for my glass, taking a measured sip of the deep red wine, tilting my head just enough for the movement of my throat to catch the light. The slow, deep swallow is controlled, deliberate. A single drop of wine escapes, trailing crimson down to the curve of my lip. I hold back, letting the wet drop sit there for just a moment before sweeping my tongue over it, slow and purposefully, flashing just the hint of fang as I savor the taste. Then, as if nothing happened, I continue on.

The human takes the dagger and slices it across the vampire's palm. Their blood will drip in a chalice such as this one." I lift the glamored cup up to the camera and take another drink for effect. *"Next it is time for the human to be cut. There is a choice of dagger or teeth. The vampire either bites the human's wrist or cuts it with the dagger, and their blood will mix with the vampire's in the cup. The vampire then seals the wound. Next, the human drinks from the chalice and falls into a deep sleep and is left to transform into a vampire. When they wake, they will be a fledgling vampire. Until the moon rises again, my nocturnal friends. Fangs out, see you in the shadows"*

I finish up my wine, edit, and upload the video. I stayed true, but still feel confident most people will think I'm storytelling, cosplaying. No one will actually believe me. Then I make my way back to the bedroom. I just want to be near Katrina, so I strip down to my boxers, climb into bed next to her, and pull up a book to read quietly in bed beside her for the next couple of hours. I can't think of any other way I'd want to spend my night. But as daylight starts to brighten on the other side of the curtains, I get sleepy. I send a text for Katrina to find when she wakes up, to make herself at home and stay as long as she wants, and then I drift off into a deep deep slumber.

Katrina

After waking up way past my normal time, I stretch and glance over at Monty. He looks so peaceful and vulnerable lying there. I grab my phone and discover he sent me a sweet text message that says he'll miss me today, which makes me smile. I quickly call Mrs. Humphrey just before my shift is about to start to tell her I can't make it in today. That isn't something I ever do, but I am exhausted both mentally and physically from the previous evening. Luckily she is understanding and doesn't ask any questions. I am going to have to spend more time considering my job if I decide to become a vampire. I won't be able to be a librarian anymore. There are other jobs I could do, like become a researcher. I'm sure that would be something I would enjoy. Putting all of that out of my mind for a moment, I slide quietly out of bed and remove some clothes from the bag I packed. I get dressed and then wander into the ensuite bathroom. I unpack my toothbrush, a comb, and a few other bathroom supplies. I thought it might make Monty happy to wake up to see some of my things in his space.

I make my way to the kitchen and see not only yummy bagels, there's cereal, oatmeal, and some apples. I grab the cereal and pour a bowl, and catch up on some social media while eating. While scrolling, I come across the VidVibe he must have filmed after our conversation last night, and that makes me smile. The comments are ridiculous—no wonder my comment stood out to him. Most of them are women begging him to make them a vampire. Glad I'm not the jealous type. I'm also glad my crochet channel doesn't bring out the groupies or fanatics. I finish up, clean up my mess, and let myself out, locking the door with the key Monty had left on the counter for me. Last night I really wasn't sure where I'd end up today, but I'm feeling cautiously confident in the direction we're headed. I haven't made any final life choices, but I'm trying to think more and more on what it'd be like to give up my humanity and become a vampire. The idea is scary, but I think I would lead a happy life with Monty beside me.

The next couple of days go by quickly. I spend every evening over at Monty's house. I am really feeling bad for Data, so one day I bring it up to Monty. We are actually at my house for once, mostly because I just can't leave Data alone for another evening. I'd just finished eating dinner and Monty appeared behind me, wrapping his arms around my waist as I was loading dirty dishes in the dishwasher.

I laugh, spiral around to face him, "Did you teleport straight into the kitchen? I didn't hear you come through the door."

He smirks, "I couldn't find good parking tonight, so I'm down the street a bit, and yes, I wanted to surprise you so I teleported in."

I roll my eyes, but kiss him anyway. It hasn't gotten old—every time I look at him I'm just immediately attracted to him all over again. Tonight his hair is down and it looks as if he has smudges of eyeliner still on. "Filmed a VidVibe before you came over tonight? Usually you do them after you say goodnight to me."

"Yeah, just a quick one. I announced I was seeing someone special," he says with a gleam in his eyes. He'd kept from mentioning that he was dating anyone because part of his allure is the fact that he is unattainable. It means a lot to me that he decided keeping up that image wasn't as important as including me in all aspects of his life. "Of course I didn't mention your name or tag your account or anything. I wouldn't do that without asking you first, and I didn't think you'd want a bunch of looky-loos following you just because you're mine."

When he said, "You're mine," I think my insides turned to literal mush. Normally when I hear men get possessive of women, it makes me so angry, but when he does it, there is so much respect and admiration behind the words. I *want* to be his. He is mine too. "Hey Monty," I say, leading him to the living room and pulling out my crochet project. I haven't been working through it at my normal rate—it's been taking forever—but I only have a few more rows on this Bluey. "I need to renew my lease in two weeks. I'm on a yearly lease which renews every July." I want to ask if I can move in with him, but that feels presumptuous. Moving in with Monty would come with pros and cons. Con: I'd be a bit further from Rainbow, but not by a lot. Pro: Getting to spend a lot more time with Monty, and even fall asleep in his arms. Data would move with me, so no more back and forth between Monty's house and mine all the time.

I needn't have worried about overstepping though.

"Don't sign it. Move in with me. Please? I know we are on weird sleep schedules, but we can figure it out. I can help you move. And by helping you move, I mean hire packers and movers for you."

"Can Rainbow come over whenever they want? And of course that means Data comes too, right?"

204

"Absolutely. I can even get Rainbow a key. Your friend is my friend. And I love Data as my own cat. He likes me too, I think." To prove his point, Data jumps up in Monty's lap and starts butting his head to Monty's chin. "See? He adores me."

"That settles it. I'll talk to my landlord tomorrow. This is so exciting!"

With a more serious look on his face, he asks, "Have you given more thought to whether you want to turn? I need you in my life however I can get you. Whether that is for the short time you're on this Earth with me as a human or for eternity as a vampire. I cannot imagine living without you, but I also don't want you to feel pressured in any way. We don't have to decide now. The vampire reunion is a few months away, and if you're not ready to decide, then we can wait until next year."

"I've thought about little else, to tell you the truth. I even started looking into night shift or work-from-home-on-your-own-time type of jobs. Right now it feels right to move in with you. Let's take it one step at a time."

We spend the rest of the evening talking. As our conversation flows, I am repeatedly blown away by what a perfect match up of someone who is 333 years old and full of rich firsthand history is to an Autistic person who loves history, research, and learning new things. We are never at a loss of topics. I ask him why he mostly lived in England and America and didn't live in many other places. He tells me that when you've got potentially hundreds, if not thousands, of years ahead of you, there isn't much rush, and he does travel around the globe fairly often for short visits. Moving to another country requires a lot of paperwork. That makes me laugh so hard! The mighty vampire taken down by paperwork. Oh isn't that the truth of it all—got to love modern day bureaucracy.

I reach a few unique steps on the Bluey project as we are talking and I ask him if he'd help me film a VidVibe. I normally use a tripod, but having someone else help is easier. Jessie especially loves helping me film on occasion, but I figure Monty is an expert too.

"I'd be delighted," he says as he takes my phone and opens up to go into filming mode. I tell him how I want the shot to be framed.

I try not to be self-conscious as I work the stitches in front of the camera and talk out loud, explaining what I am doing. A couple of minutes later, I have a short video ready to post. I save it to drafts so I can post it later. One of the things I love most about Monty is how easy he is to be around. We don't need bars, concerts, or fancy dinners. Give me my cat, some quiet conversation, filming VidVibes together—and him. And all the making out. I set my crochet aside and climb onto his lap, straddling his legs so I can see his face.

"Thank you for helping me," I murmur, and lean in to kiss him. He meets me right there, lips warm, hands already sliding to grip my ass, pulling me closer.

I'm in a dress, just thin panties between us, pressed against the track pants he's wearing. I feel him harden beneath me.

"It's almost my bedtime—just some kisses tonight, Sunshine," I whisper.

He groans, but nods.

"You smell so good." His hands roam up, cupping my breasts through the thin fabric, thumbs brushing over my nipples. I moan, nearly giving in right there. Making love with him would be worth another late night—but I'm moving in soon, and I need at least one full night's sleep.

I pull back, smile at him, and losing some resolve, I say, "Go ahead—have a little snack before you go."

The flash in his eyes is feral. The growl he makes curls heat low in my belly. He pushes my hair aside, fangs sliding down, and sinks them into my neck. Pleasure floods me instantly, stealing my breath. I feel like I'm flying and falling at the same time, spinning in weightless bliss. Colors burst behind my closed eyes. When he seals the wound with a slow, wet lick, heat pools between my thighs.

"Monty, I don't think I can sleep if you don't make me come," I whisper, voice wrecked.

"Is that a yes? I can leave now if you want," he teases, but the look in his eyes says he's caught in this too.

"Monty, I need you inside me. Now."

He doesn't waste time. My dress stays on, panties shoved aside with trembling hands. He fumbles his pants down and then he's pushing into me—deep, easy, like we were made for this.

We kiss like we're starving. Tongues tangling, teeth nipping—it's messy and hot and perfect. I ride him hard, rocking in quick, desperate bursts until we're both breaking apart, shuddering, gasping, falling into that dizzy, star-splattered release.

After, I melt against his chest, muscles soft as butter. He carries me to bed, finds my pajamas without asking, because he knows I can't sleep without them. Tucks me in. These little things make my heart feel too big for my chest.

He kisses my forehead before leaving the room, and for the first time in what feels like forever, I fall asleep smiling.

"Can you check if Data has enough water before you go?" I mumble, already halfway to dreaming.

“Your wish is my command, KittyKat.”

Chapter 25
Unexpected Visitor

Montgomery

I have a nice pep in my step back to my car after checking to make sure Data does in fact have fresh water. On the drive home, I call Nik. "Hey man, what have you been up to? I'm heading home. Are you off tonight?"

"Yes and we have a situation." Nik sounds really strange and I immediately tense up as I try to figure out what is going on.

"Where are you? Is everything okay?"

"I'm at your house and I can't talk. Just get here quickly."

"Nik, dude, you're scaring me. What's going on?" I look down at the clock—it's only 9:30. Not that the time would tell me anything. I hear Nik hang up. What the hell could be going on? I was excited to tell Nik the news about Katrina moving in with me, but I guess that is going to have to wait until I figure out what is going on.

A few minutes later, after what felt like forever, I pull up into my driveway. I probably should have pulled to the side of the road and teleported home, but my brain was too scrambled to think straight. It still is. I let myself in quietly, because by this point, I'm worried maybe someone learned Nikolai was a vampire and is threatening to kill him with a stake. A stake through the heart will definitely kill a vampire. I make my way to the living room where I see Nik is in the chair by the fire, stiff and silent. On the couch, a Vampire Sentinel is stationed like a warning shot—uniform crisp, posture stiff, expression unreadable. My stomach sinks. What is he doing here with him?

I walk in and bow my head in forced respect toward the Sentinel. "Greetings, Sentinel, how am I so honored to have you in my home? Are you comfortable? I apologize I wasn't here when you arrived. Did I miss your calling card?" I try to remain respectful even though I am pissed off that he came without notice. I can't imagine this is good news.

He opens a missive and reads from it in a formal tone, "Montgomery Ravenscroft, we have received word through the Brothers and Sisters that you have engaged in transgressions against the Vampire Code of Law. It has been revealed that you pulled apart the sacred veil that shrouds our kind. That you, Montgomery, have been indiscreet and have ventured unto a place known as 'The Internet,' weaving word of our very existence into a permanent tapestry called Videography, casting aside our cloak of discretion. By decree of the Elders, thou art summoned to answer these grave accusations. The Court awaits thy presence, where The Honored among us will bear witness to thy trial. Tread carefully, the weight of centuries hangs heavy upon those who defy the Code." He rolls up the parchment—yes, actual parchment—and tucks it in an inner pocket of his cloak.

I take that all in, channeling how Katrina would respond to this situation. This vampire is deadly serious, and my brain still feels muddled. What I did gather was that I am in big trouble and that the Elders somehow got wind I was making videos. And that they think I'm "casting aside our cloak of discretion" or whatever. Why the Court is talking about the internet like it is a new thing is strange too. I mean, it has been a blip in all of human history, but still, the Court knows what the internet is. They need to get with the times.

"Sentinel, if I may, what I am doing is harmless. No one believes vampires exist. What I'm doing is just for fun. There are no true secrets being revealed." I measured out my words slowly and carefully. Nik stares at me from across the room, eyes big. I can tell he really doesn't want to be pulled into this. I know he's wanting to say, "I told you so!" so badly it's vibrating off his body.

"Montgomery, the accusations have been entered into the scrolls. You have no choice but to stand before the Court to defend yourself. You may bring this witness." The Sentinel points to Nikolai and then continues on. "We leave henceforth!"

And then, before I know what is happening, I find myself in a cold, ancient throne room. The walls are made of stone, with moss growing in the corners and here and there between various stones. There are a few windows, if you could call them that. They are more like slits at the top of walls that I estimate are three-story high. Actual fire sconces have been set along the walls every few feet. The fairly large room is mostly empty except for some chairs. The Sentinel marches Nik and I over to two chairs. Our footsteps are the only sound I hear as they echo, making the room feel even bigger and more ominous.

"Communication devices," he says in a monotone voice that reverberates through the space. We reluctantly hand him our phones and then he forces us to sit facing five other chairs that are on a slightly raised platform. Behind those chairs on another raised platform is a huge podium with three additional chairs behind it. As we sit down, five vampires file in from a side door and settle into the ancient carved wooden chairs. Three Elders sit behind them in even more elaborate carved thrones.

I wish I'd paid more attention to formal vampire laws. I know the gist, but I never got too involved in vampire politics. We have elections, and I've always done my duty to vote—but that's about it. I do recognize Cedric Porter and Veronica Zane, two vampires I voted for in the last election because they were younger, and I felt the Court needed more modern voices. Cedric is around two hundred years old, and I believe Veronica is only 125. You have to be at least a century to run.

There are also two I don't recognize, but I'd wager they're both over eight hundred, judging by their choice of clothing. Most vampires wear modern styles to blend in—or dress however they like and use a glamor to pass. But with no humans around, there's no need to bother.

Cedric wears a crisp white button-down that pops against his sepia-toned skin, paired with a black leather kilt. Veronica, though young by vampire standards, clings to the fashion popular when she turned—somewhere in the 1920s, if I had to guess. Her flapper-style dress shimmers slightly under the lights, and her short sandy hair and candy-apple red lipstick stand out against her pale, almost translucent skin.

The last vampire is harder to place. Her age is anyone's guess. She's dressed in sleek, modern clothes, her obsidian hair cut into a severe French bob. One arm is a sleek, futuristic prosthetic—no attempt made to mimic flesh. It's built purely for function, and somehow that is the aesthetic.

I glance over at Nik and mouth "I'm sorry!" and he glares at me. I'm also extremely worried about Katrina. My last video mentioned I had a girlfriend (using human terms— the vampire term would be "bonded mate") and I don't know if this Court or the Elders know about her yet. It's not illegal to date humans—that's one way we turn more vampires—but it can still be tricky. Telling one human about vampires is different from broadcasting about vampires, because for instance, if Katrina and I broke up before she turned, I'd have to erase her memory of me being a vampire. We can do that on a one-to-one basis, not on a mass quantity.

How am I going to get these people to understand that even though I'm literally telling everyone everything about vampires, no one believes it's real? I don't think they understand modern humanity's fascination with cosplay. I also don't know how long this will take. I don't want Katrina to miss me. And if I'm found guilty . . . I can't even think about that now. It is then that I see another vampire out of the corner of my eye as he enters the room. He'd be the equivalent of a bailiff in a human court. He approaches me and tells me to stand, so I do.

"Montgomery Ravenscroft, you are formally charged with Lifting the Veil of Secrecy of the Vampire Kingdom in a mass Broadcast on the Internet. How do you plead?" This came from Justice Porter.

"Not guilty, Your Excellence," I say for the record. I'm very much trying not to freak out. I think the fact that I'm in what looks like very human clothes will hopefully help me out. Thank goodness I'm not dressed in a vampire-esque costume. Not that that really exists, because vampires can wear whatever they want, but these Elders probably know what humans think a vampire should look like and, well, let's just say if I was in one of my costumes, I might be in a worse-off place.

Over the next several hours I am questioned in excruciating detail over all my activity for the past five years, even before I started VidVibe. They brought up my SnapFoto account too and thank goodness I never got into FriendLink. Every once in a while, they direct a question to Nikolai, and like the true friend he is, he backs me up all the way. Trying to get these vampires to understand the concept of cosplaying is a challenge. The best I can do is relate it to theater. That was starting to get us somewhere close to an understanding. Some of these guys were around in those early Grecian and Roman days when the first plays were put on. Even still, hours trickle by. Somehow they procured a tablet and are literally playing some of my VidVibes where I am quite plainly speaking of being a vampire. I really can see how damning it is. I wish we could interview a human to explain it to them. At least they haven't sentenced me yet. The High Elder stands up and says, "It is upon the hour when we shall retire for the day, as the sun doth commence its ascent in the heavens." Or, translated, it is time for everyone to go to bed, as it is getting light outside. Trying to translate their older version of English is giving me a headache and I am more than ready to get out of here. Too bad that doesn't mean they are letting me go yet. Apparently they still have a lot more questions.

Uniformed guards take our cell phones and then lead Nikolai and I to a desolate room with two single cots in the corners, a utilitarian toilet room, and a single light bulb. The cots each have a wool blanket and what could possibly pass as a pillow if one was pushed to describe it. The walls are once again stone, and there is no window. The door slams shut. We aren't locked in, because we could teleport out. That would be incredibly unwise, as it'd be an automatic death when they recaptured us. It is the first time all day I am alone with Nikolai.

"What happened?" I exclaim, finally alone with Nikolai. "I mention you from time to time in my videos, but nothing super specific. I can't believe I dragged you into this mess."

"I'm not going to lie, this is definitely now how I'd like to spend my time." Nik says, cracking a wry smile. "But bro, we're good. I've got your back no matter what."

"I wish I could call Katrina or get word to her somehow that I'm safe. Well, I hope I'm safe. I'm actually really freaking out. Everything hinges on if I can get these people to understand that humans do not believe in the supernatural anymore in a real sense of the word. I mean, outliers exist and I'm sure there are some humans that do, but not on a large scale. And even they would assume I'm cosplaying." I sit on the cot and pull my hands through my hair. I am tired, and I feel gross. I wish there was a shower in that small little toilet room.

There is a knock on the door, and someone brings in two goblets of blood. She hands them to us and then without a word turns around and leaves. As we drink the blood, Nik says, "I was hanging out in your game room. I know, I'm supposed to call first, but I knew you were at Katrina's house because your car wasn't there. So I was hanging out at your house waiting for you to get back home. When all of a sudden the Sentinel appeared before me and demanded to know where you were. I figured he'd be more comfortable in your living room rather than the game room, so I took him in there. I offered him some of your blood supply, which he turned down. I was about to call you, when you called me. So that's all I know."

"Well I appreciate you having my back. I'm beyond sorry you got into this. I've got to find a way to make it better.

Even if it means giving up my VidVibe account. I hope it won't come to that, but I always knew it might. I'll have to make this up to you somehow when and if I get us out of this."

"We will get you out of this. You've been my best mate for over three hundred years. I can't imagine life without you. We'll figure this out." He sounds as if he is trying to convince himself just as much as me.

We settle into our cots as best we can to get some sleep, not knowing exactly what the next night will bring.

"We haven't exactly had a sleepover in quite a while now have we, Nik?" I ask, trying to bring a bit of humor to a very humorless situation.

"Remember that time we got stuck on a train going across America? When was that?"

"Hum, it was after the Civil War. Remember, we got separated during the war and finally found each other in Pennsylvania. Trains were getting really popular and we decided it'd be fun to travel across the country in passenger cars around, what was it, 1875 or so? But trying to stay out of the daylight while doing that was extremely tricky and dangerous at times. Oh the fun we had though, you know, the times we weren't almost getting burned from the sunlight."

"We've had more adventures together than we'll ever be able to remember. And we're going to have hundreds, if not thousands, more. We'll convince the Court you aren't causing harm. I know it." Nik said, another feeble attempt to encourage me.

Chapter 26
Missing

Katrina

I wake up with a smile on my lips, remembering the night before. I really hadn't meant to make love with Monty, but it was spontaneous and really fun. I think I'll definitely get used to doing it more often. Not having to worry about birth control or disease is a nice benefit for sure. It did occur to me that if I turned into a vampire, he'd no longer be able to feed from me, or at least I don't think so. Maybe biting play is still part of vampire sex. I need some education that I don't think will be available in any of the books in the library. The very thought of it makes me laugh out loud and Data turns to look at me as if I am disrupting his peace.

"Oh Data, you are the best," I say, petting his soft gray fur. "We're going to be moving soon! I'll miss this little townhome—it really has been perfect for me, but Monty's house is even better. You'll love it there, I promise. And there's even more room for you to run around. I'll call the landlord today. I hate making phone calls, but it'll be worth it! Ah, well, we better stop chatting, Mr. Data, I've got to get ready for work! I want to have time to call Rainbow this morning too!"

I am about to pull up my ChatBox server with Rainbow when my phone rings. Rainbow's number pops up on the screen.

"Good morning. I was just about to message y'all!" I say.

"Great minds and all, it's Jessie today," Jessie says. I can usually tell, but it's early in the morning, so it's nice she just said it that way I don't have to guess.

"I'm glad you called because I can talk and get ready easier than typing. What's up?" I put my phone on speaker so I can get dressed while we talk.

"Well . . . apparently Sky made a date with Nik for tonight. The rest of the System didn't find out until this morning." Those amnesia barriers can cause a lot of System distress. They work really hard at System unity and communication, but sometimes an alter will do something because they want to without talking to the rest of the System. Sharing a body is hard.

"How do you feel about it? I know you were innerworld when Sky and Max met Nik. They both liked him though." I was not expecting this at all, but to be honest, my best friend potentially dating my boyfriend's best friend is pretty exciting.

"I don't know honestly. I don't usually front with Sky, but I'll try to maybe stay close to the front a bit more tonight. I wonder how he'd feel if I switched in for part of the date. I mean, give him the DID experience and all. Honestly, dating as a System is so hard. It's why we rarely even try it. Sky is all excited though. They plan to go to a bar. I told her she better not get the body wasted. I *will* take over if she drinks too much! So what's going on with you?"

"Monty asked me to move in with him last night! The timing is perfect because my lease is up in two weeks. I'm going to call my landlord and give my notice on my way to work. It's a big step, but I think it's the right one. I'm sad we won't be just a minute's drive from each other anymore, but we're still not that far away, and Monty said he'd get a key made for you too, because you're always welcome." I finished dressing and am now trying to make a fried egg while talking and it is getting complicated, so I tell Jessie to call me at lunch if she wants to talk about the date more.

Later that evening, back home, I send Monty a text telling him I am going to jump in the shower if he wants to teleport in with me. Then I have to laugh while I try to picture how that would go. Hopefully he'll teleport to the bathroom and get undressed, not teleport in the nude straight to the shower. Although, that would be exciting.

I am getting out of the shower and toweling off, a little disappointed Monty did not join me, but I figure he must not be awake yet, as it is still fairly early in the evening. I go to the kitchen to figure out dinner options and also think about my next crochet project. I am about to film the final video with Bluey and then do a giveaway to my followers for anyone who'd like to win him. I'll probably spend some time online tonight to get inspired. It'd be kind of cute to crochet a little vampire—that idea has some potential. Putting that out of my head while I stare in my refrigerator, I decide to just go with a comfort meal. An egg sandwich is a common go-to for me when nothing sounds good, but I had a fried egg for breakfast. Why does food have to be so complicated? I just need to eat something. I throw a frozen TV dinner in the microwave and call it a night. Maybe a lifetime with blood as my only choice wouldn't be so bad after all.

I forgot to ask what time Sky had her date tonight, but I hope she has fun. It's looking like tonight I'm on my own.

Monty and I talk almost every night but sometimes he'll get into a game with Nik or I'll be out with Rainbow or occasionally one of my other friends. I do have a few other friends, but I don't get together with them very often. Maintaining lots of friends is something that is very difficult for me.

A few hours later, I am watching TV and cuddling with Data when Sky knocks on my door. I hurry to open it, eyebrows raised. "Hey aren't you supposed to be out with Nik by now?"

"He stood Sky up. The idiot!" When I hear Max's voice come out but see the body dressed in Sky's style, it takes me a second to figure out what has happened. Sky dressed up in a very sexy mini skirt and crop top tee, but when she got stood up, she probably went innerworld, and Max, the System's protector, came to the front, finding himself now wearing very feminine clothes.

"Um, I have some sweatpants and a T-shirt. Would you like to change? And then tell me what happened?" I ask Max.

"Yes, thanks. I came straight here after sitting at the bar for an hour. I can't believe he stood her up!" Max marches into my room, and I pull out some sweatpants and a unisex T-shirt from a bottom drawer, so Max can change out of Sky's clothes. He then goes into the bathroom and washes off her makeup too. "That feels better. I don't think Sky will be coming back out tonight."

We head back to the living room so Max can tell me what happened. "Sky got to the bar in downtown Vancouver where we were going to meet Nik. It's a different one than where he works, which makes sense. Well, after half an hour Sky texted. No answer. She ordered a drink and sipped on it. When she finished it and he still hadn't shown, she went

220

innerworld and I pushed my way to the front. I was so angry on her behalf. We came straight here. It wasn't until I was almost here that I wondered if you were by yourself or if Monty might be around. Maybe dating your boyfriend's best friend isn't a good idea if he's a no-show!"

"I haven't heard from Monty tonight either, which while not unheard of, is unusual. I wonder if something happened to both of them?" I say, starting to worry. "Let me try calling him and see if he knows what happened to Nik. Is that okay?" At Max's nod, I dial Monty's number. But a little bit later, I hang up. "It went to voicemail. This is strange. I'd advise you not to get too upset until we hear from them. It sucks to be stood up, but from everything I know about Nik, it's not something he'd normally do."

"Yeah, I guess I should give him the benefit of the doubt," Max agrees. "Want to watch *Doctor Who*? What were you up to tonight?"

"Mostly watching HGTV, but *Doctor Who* sounds good. It'll take my mind off of worrying if anything is wrong with Monty. I've got therapy tomorrow, and I'm going to tell my therapist I'm planning on moving in with Monty. I think she'll be supportive. I haven't told her he's a vampire. I just don't think it's something I'm going to disclose with her. What do you think?"

"It's hard to say. I think that would be a difficult conversation to have. She's there to support you, so if you need support in that area, I think it might be important, but if you're not feeling any distress about him being a vampire, then don't mention it unless you think it's something you need to talk to her about." I nod as Max starts up the TV. What is it about boys and remote controls? They always want to be the one in charge of it. It makes me smile—I'm just so happy to have Max as a friend.

Montgomery

We wake up the next night in our little cell expecting to be escorted back to the courtroom, but the hours and minutes tick away. I wish I could call Katrina. I wonder if she is worried about me. Nik is pacing the room when suddenly he stops and looks at me, brow furrowed.

"I was supposed to go on a date with Sky tonight," he blurts out.

"Katrina's friend Sky?" I ask, confused. I didn't know he'd talked to her after the yacht.

"Yeah, we exchanged numbers and have been texting a bit."

"When were you going to tell me?"

"I'm telling you now." Nik keeps pacing.

"Sit still! You're driving me crazy. Are you chatting with the whole System or just Sky?" Nik settles back down on the cot.

"Mostly just Sky, but a little bit the whole System. The date was with Sky. But now she's going to think I stood her up and that's going to piss Max off. Are you okay with me going on a date with your girlfriend's best friend?" Nik asks me a little too late.

"I don't have a problem with it, per say, but I do have a problem if you hurt anyone in the System, because that will hurt Katrina. This obviously is out of your control. I'm sure once we can explain it, both Sky and Max will be fine. How about Jessie and Arleigh?"

"I've chatted with them a few times, and I like both of them a lot. It's interesting to get to know them all."

"They mean a lot to Katrina. I wish I could get a message to her." I go over to the door and open it, then stick my head out into the hallway, "HELLO! Is anyone out there?!" I call to the empty space. "It's got to be close to midnight by now—why have they kept us here? Answering their million questions was horrible, but sitting around with literally nothing to do is driving me insane."

"Yeah, it'd be nice if they at least came to tell us what is going on. And no offense, but I'm an innocent bystander in all of this."

I am contemplating going to see if I can find someone to get some answers when we hear shuffling feet coming down the long hallway. I open the door wider and look and, sure enough, the girl who brought us our cups of blood last night is walking towards me.

"Mr. Ravenscroft and Mr. Lockwood, the Court will see you now. Follow me," she says in a small voice.

It is then that I smell her blood. She is human. "What's your name?" I ask, as Nik and I follow her down winding hallways toward the grand courtroom. "Why are you here? Are you paid? There aren't many humans in Civita di Bagnoregio. Are the vampires treating you nicely?" I try to get a look at her neck to see if it shows any signs of repeated feedings. As a culture, us vampires have modernized a lot, but I wouldn't put it past some of the ancient vampires to keep a human slave and for others to look the other way. Her eyes widen at my questions but then she answers them.

"My name is Celeste. I work here, and I do get paid. I know you all are vampires. I have a very specific contract to not talk about what my work entails when I go home. I work here in the city for three months at a time, and then I go home for two months at a time. I enjoy what I do and I'm both paid and treated well."

"Interesting. Well I'm glad you are treated well. How did you ever get this job?" I say, keeping the conversation going. Nikolai listens with full attention too. We've heard of humans in the Vampire City but honestly haven't come across many in our few short stays here in the past.

"The interview process was fairly long. I've heard it isn't unlike getting a job with a spy agency. I didn't learn about vampires until I was well vetted. But the Elders like to keep some humans around to make sure the city contains some normalcy if tourists ever pop in. I'm working a night shift tonight, but I do things during the day too, it just depends."

Suddenly, a thought pops into my head. "How familiar are you with VidVibe?" I ask her quickly as we approach the courtroom.

"I have an account. I don't post, but I like watching videos. Why?"

Nik sees where I am going with this question and he says, "Have you seen cosplayers on the app? People pretending to be robots, mermaids, or even perhaps vampires?" She nods yes so he keeps going. "If you didn't know vampires existed and you came across a cosplayer vampire, would you assume it wasn't real?"

She pauses in the hallway and turns toward us for a moment to consider. "Yes. When I've seen accounts like that I know they are just playing or acting. It's just for fun."

"Do you think you'd mind telling the Elders that for me?" I ask. "It seems I've gotten myself into a lot of trouble. See, I went onto VidVibe to pretend to be a vampire. I actually am a vampire, but the whole point was to have fun. I knew no one would believe me. But the Elders think I'm 'breaking the veil of silence' or something." I said all of this as quickly as possible because Celeste started walking again.

One hand on the door, she turns again. "I'll think about it." She opens the door and the bailiff takes over and ushers us to our seats again. Another round of questioning is about to begin.

Chapter 27
A Last Ditch Defense

Katrina

Two more nights have gone by and I still haven't heard from Monty. No text messages or missed calls. How could he ask me to move in with him and then just completely disappear? I don't have to be at work until 9:30 this morning, so I debate with myself if I should drive over to Monty's house to see if he is okay. I am really trying not to panic. If it hadn't been for the fact I didn't sign my lease, I wouldn't really be that worried, but in less than two weeks I'll be homeless if for some reason Monty does decide to ghost me. The logical part of my brain knows this is highly unlikely and the two days that I haven't heard from him are likely not that big of a deal. Monty would know I'd be worried, though, and so he wouldn't do this if nothing was wrong. That settles it. I am going to his house. I have a key, so it's not as if I'll be invading his privacy.

I quickly pull on a soft cotton dress, some bike shorts, and a pair of comfortable flats. Not wanting to spend time on my hair, I throw it up in one of my famous messy buns, and apply minimal amounts of makeup. I grab a bagel and cream cheese on the way out the door and blow Data some kisses. "We'll get this figured out, Data!"

A few minutes later, I pull up to Monty's house. His car is in the driveway and I open the side garage door to find his motorcycle parked there. Nik's car is also in the driveway,

226

making me even more suspicious something is wrong. They both should be here. The sun is already up, so presumably Monty will be in bed. Did Nik decide to sleep over in a spare bedroom? Why wouldn't he go home? The fact we haven't heard from either of them has me even more concerned. Something isn't adding up. I let myself in very quietly and make my way through his kitchen, down the hall to the wing of bedrooms. So far, nothing really looks out of the ordinary. His bedroom is on the left and so I tiptoe into the room. He'd told me once he slept "like the dead." I wasn't sure if that was literal or if he just slept soundly. Maybe it was some vampire thing and he went into suspended animation or something each day. I still have a lot to learn. It is eerily quiet in the room. I walk over to the end of the huge four-poster bed and gently pull back the drape. No Monty in the bed. The bed is completely made up. This is strange. I wonder if he is maybe spending the day over at Nikolai's house, having teleported there instead of using his car, but that doesn't really make much sense either. Thinking perhaps he fell asleep in the game room, I leave the bedroom and walk to the other side of the house to check. But still no Monty or Nik anywhere.

Triple-checking every room, I retrace my steps through the eerily quiet home back towards the kitchen. Monty said he was going every few days to get bagels from New York for me, even though I still can't get over that he'd do that. I check the pantry, and sure enough, there is a bag of four bagels, but they are hard as rock, not fresh at all. He said he took them to the food pantry before he let them go bad if I hadn't eaten them, so that just adds to the mystery. Without much else I can do, I leave the house and lock up behind me. It is going to be a long day at work and I know I'm going to ruminate on this situation. I don't feel like he'd want me to file a missing person's report, though. I wish I knew what to do!

Montgomery

Waking up on our fourth night in Civita di Bagnoregio, I am restless, beyond angry, and getting sick with worry about Katrina. By now she's probably talked to her landlord and is terrified I've abandoned her right after asking her to move in with me. But things in the courtroom are going well. I'm hoping beyond hope that they'll come to the conclusion that I've caused no harm. The previous evening, I had asked the Court if Celeste—someone they knew and trusted—could answer a few questions about the nature of VidVibe and how humans experience the app. I think her testimony went a long way and I'll be forever grateful to her. She did not have to agree to testify on my, a stranger's, behalf.

Nik and I are waiting for Celeste to come get us again. We haven't been fed since the first night here, and with all the stress, I am feeling as if I need to feed again. I hope she'll bring more blood before court starts back up.

"Nik, I was thinking. When we get in the courtroom, if I ask the council to allow you to teleport home to get Katrina, would you do it, if they let you?"

"What are you talking about? Why would you want to bring Katrina here!?" Nik's eyes widen.

"I think the Court listened to Celeste. If you go to Katrina and explain everything that's happened, maybe she could testify on my behalf too. When we first met, she was so mad at me that I wouldn't 'drop the act,' as she put it. She thought I was cosplaying the entire time we were DMing each other. It wasn't until I finally got her to meet me in person that she believed me, and even then she thought I was using sleight of hand. I think maybe she could convince the Court of my innocence." I pleaded with him.

"You could be right, actually." Nik paused to consider possible ramifications. "Do you think they'd let me go? I'd be willing to teleport to Katrina and bring her back, if she's willing."

"I'm pretty sure she'd do this for me. Either way, I'm getting to the point where I just want the Court to make a decision one way or another. We've been in these same clothes, with nothing but a sink to wash with. I'm starving and exhausted. I hope one day, we can look back at this ordeal and laugh, but for now, it's a horrible experience." With that, Celeste opens the door and thank goodness she has two goblets in her hand. I quickly grab one and hand it to Nik, then take the other and drink it down as fast as I can. I want to get to court quickly so I can ask the Elders if Nikolai can go get Katrina.

Moments later, we are all in our same positions. Half of me wonders if this whole procedure took so long because the court was bored. When you live for thousands of years, time moves at a different pace. Four nights to some of these guys is a blink of an eye. To me, missing my soulmate and worried about her with my entire being, every moment is torture.

"The Court is now in order," Saraphina announces, banging the gavel on the table with her prosthetic arm.

Standing up because I want to say my piece before they launch into another round of questions, I clear my throat and address everyone. "If it pleases the Elders and the High Court, may I please make a request?"

"You may speak," Saraphina says.

"Your, honors, I wanted to ask if my dear friend, Nikolai, could teleport back to my hometown and bring back Katrina Prescott, the human woman I am dating. I believe she can convince the Court that humans do not believe vampires are real on a large scale, even ones who follow my account."

"We will confer," Saraphina announces. I sit back down and the five court vampires turn towards the three Elders and whisper back and forth. One of them must have been using a silence glamor, because I have incredibly good hearing and I can't hear a word they are saying to each other.

"Nikolai Lockwood," Cedric says at last, "you hereby have permission to retrieve one Katrina Prescott and bring her henceforth to the Court. You have one hour. Court is adjourned and will resume in one hour, with or without Ms. Prescott."

I turn to Nik. "Unfortunately with the time difference it's going to be morning in Vancouver. Most likely Katrina will be at work. The library on 136th Avenue, you know the one? Next to the community center. The library has a lot of windows, but she usually works in one of the back rooms. Unless we're unlucky and she's on the children's desk. Let's hope that's not the case. Have you ever been to that library?"

"No, I don't think I've ever been inside that library," Nik says, then adds with a sheepish shrug, "Not really my scene, you know?"

"What about the community center next door?" Fun fact, since a lot of places are closed when we need to frequent them, we sometimes will teleport into facilities and use books at a library for instance, or gym equipment, when places are closed. Nik wasn't exactly a bookworm, he left that to me, but nobody could out-rep him in the gym.

"Yes, I know where you're talking about. Do the buildings connect? Will I have to go out in the sun?"

"I think the buildings do connect. You'll have to do your best. I'll owe you for an eternity. Please go, and be safe!"

Chapter 28
The Verdict

Katrina

I leave Monty's house and head to the library. I almost called in sick, but I don't want to make a habit of it, and there isn't anything I can do at home, except worry even more. Thankfully I have a stack of books that need repairing and I wasn't assigned the children's desk today. As much as I love the kids, I'm going to have a hard enough time focusing today. I have some tea that I made in the break room in a spill-proof mug next to me and I reach for the first book to examine why it is in the repair pile. It looks like the cover is starting to detach, which will be a fairly simple fix. I get out the supplies I need and I am in my own little quiet world when suddenly from the corner of the room I hear a whisper: "Katrina!" I look around, trying to figure out who called my name.

"Katrina!" I hear again. I place the book I was about to start working on back in the repair pile, and walk toward the sound to find Nikolai around the corner in the employee only area.

"What are you doing here?" my befuddled brain doesn't even know where to start.

"We don't have much time—Monty is in trouble."

"What! What happened? I've been trying to reach him, and I wondered where he had gone. I was trying to decide if I should call the police! I've been so worried!" I barely remember to keep my voice down and suddenly wish I had a fidget toy on hand.

"Okay, here's the short version. The vampire Council came and issued Monty a warrant of sorts. But unlike human court, he was teleported immediately to Italy to stand trial. They demanded I come too, as a witness, so we've both been basically prisoners, trying to defend his innocence for the past several days. We think if you testify for him, that will persuade them." Nik is talking very fast, and I still have so many questions.

"What is he being tried for?" I ask.

"For giving out vampire secrets on VidVibe. We need you to tell the Court humans don't believe him, that they think he's cosplaying a vampire. We need you to tell them how long it took you to believe he was real."

"Yes, yes of course—anything for Monty. But I have to go to Italy? I don't know where my passport is. Should I pack? What should I do?" I'm trying not to have a panic attack, but I'm also so relieved that, while in trouble, Monty is okay or at the very least, not missing.

"We don't have time for you to pack—we need to get back as soon as possible. They gave me an hour to collect you and I've already spent half an hour trying to navigate to your office without getting burned by the sun or being seen by your boss. No need for a passport. I'll be teleporting you straight into the courtroom."

"Well, I have to tell Rainbow where I'm going so she can check on Data. That's non-negotiable. Also Sky was really upset you stood her up, but I'm guessing that was all a part of this? You'll also need to apologize to Max, and I don't envy you that job! Then I'll have to tell Mrs. Humphrey I had an emergency and I won't know how long I'll be gone. Give me a few minutes."

I pull out my phone and send a message to Rainbow System on the general chat on ChatBox:

Katrina: Rainbow, emergency, no time to explain. I talked to Nik. He and Monty have basically been prisoners in vampire court. *shocked emoji* Nik didn't stand Sky up on purpose! He's been kidnapped. It's complicated. I'm going with Nik to Italy! He's going to teleport me there. They think I can testify and save Monty. Take care of Data for me, and I'll be back as soon as I can.

Ugh, I wish I had more time to explain. I hope they understand my message. Next I order Nik to wait where he is while I tell Mrs. Humphrey that I needed to go home unexpectedly.

Mrs. Humphrey, the kind, kind woman, is so understanding. And it does help that I look panicked and flustered, as if I've received a distressing phone call. She tells me to take as much time as I need. I make my way back to Nik and he grabs my hand.

Mere moments later, I am not in Kansas any longer, as they say. Or Vancouver, or even the USA. I am in a very ancient stone castle, something the likes of which I've only seen in movies before. We are in a large hallway and there are two massive wooden doors ahead of us with large black wrought iron handles and hinges. "Is Monty in there?" I ask. Nik nods. I almost run toward the doors, but Nik grabs my shoulder.

"Katrina, wait! You are about to enter the presence of vampires that are over two thousand years old. Do you understand that? To them you are a mere bug. You must treat

234

them with utmost respect. Like the pope, the US president, and the Queen of England all mashed into one important person. If you want them to take you seriously, you need to avoid making them angry. Okay?" Nik whispers this so low I can barely hear him, but I'm guessing he did that because of the council's super hearing. I try not to fidget and nod to let him know I understand. "Okay, we only have five minutes left before my deadline is done, so we better get in there. I bet Monty is worried. Try to follow my lead."

Nik walks towards the huge doors, which seem to open on their own accord. I try not to think too much into it. As soon as the doors open, I see Monty. He is wearing the same outfit he had on when he came to see me several days ago. I want to run to him and give him a big hug, but Nik's words hang in my head, so I keep my decorum and walk reverently towards the middle of the courtroom where he is standing in front of a chair. Nik moves to the chair next to him and I am left standing. I try to give Monty a small smile to let him know that I missed him, I love him, I will do anything to protect him. Can all that be conveyed in one slight smile?

I glance around the room, trying to take it all in while at the same time trying not to look like a fish out of water, which I very much am. I feel as if I was transported back in time, not just around the world, although I do take in details that show I am still in the 21st century. Like one of the female vampires up there that has a very modern prosthetic arm. She is sitting in a row of vampires wearing clothing from various time periods. Beside her is another woman, and then there are two men, with the last vampire giving off nonbinary vibes. Behind them are the three Elders Nik warned me about. These guys, even though they look as if they are between thirty to forty years old, have an air about them that is ancient. They've seen stuff and lived to tell the tale. Monty is still standing, so I inch towards him and try to loop my pinky finger around his and give it a little secret squeeze. A bailiff, or at least that's what I assume from all the keys hanging on his hip, brings up a third chair for me to sit in between Monty and Nik.

"Court is back in session—you may all sit," the vampire who looks to be nonbinary calls out. I know I need to focus, but the thought of a nonbinary vampire is just fascinating to me. This whole experience is so surreal, I am having a hard time wrapping my head around the seriousness of it all.

"Montgomery, you may call your witness and explain to the Court why she is here," the vampire continues.

Monty stands. "Your Honor, Rowan," he says, addressing the nonbinary vampire, "may I introduce you to Katrina. I met this human, Katrina Prescott, through the VidVibe app many months ago. She will be able to explain to the Court how she believed I was pretending to be a vampire. It took weeks before she finally believed me when I told her I was, in fact, a real vampire." This is a risk—we're not supposed to go blabbing to just anyone. Discreet, one-on-one conversations are fine, but the Court wants knowledge of vampires kept between tight-knit connections. I told Katrina up front because I knew she needed the truth if I had any shot at getting close.

"Katrina Prescott, is all of this true?" the vampire with the prosthetic arm and positively stylish short black hair calls out.

"Yes, your honor. If I may?" At her nod, I stand up and nervously pace in front of the chairs. I know I should probably stay still, but I literally can't. Hopefully my Autism won't be on trial here. "Yes, several months ago, I was on the app called VidVibe, since I also make videos on it. People make all kinds of videos. My videos teach people a type of fiber art. Other people post silly videos to entertain, some post historical videos, educational ones, funny stories, all sorts of things. Then there are the cosplayers. They are mostly there to entertain. It's like acting. They'll put on a costume and pretend they are a fairy, super hero, famous movie character, mermaid, and yes, even a vampire. No one thinks it's real, but it's fun to pretend it is real. It's a way to spend time in our imagination. When I first came across Monty's page, I saw he was, what I truly believed, a cosplayer teaching history through the guise of a lived-experience vampire. I thought it was a fascinating way to teach people history, to pretend to have experienced it firsthand.

Many humans who study history talk about certain time periods, so it was believable that his content all came from the last three hundred-ish years. Not for one second did I ever believe he was a real vampire."

I take a breath and look around. I wish I had some water, but I don't see any, so I continue on. "I eventually sent Monty, erm, Montgomery, a private message." I pause to see if I can tell if they understand what a private message is. It looks like they are following along with what I'm saying so I continue on. "I wanted to ask him some more questions. He answered and we started talking. I can show you our messages where I kept telling him to 'drop the act.' That if he wanted to be friends with me, he needed to stop pretending to be a vampire—that it was getting old. I even almost stopped talking to him altogether over this. I one hundred percent did not believe he was really a vampire. But I'm the kind of person who likes to give people the benefit of the doubt. At one point, I actually thought maybe he had a mental illness or disability. I agreed to meet him. That's when he showed me his real fangs and used some powers to show me he wasn't kidding. I still didn't believe him at first. I thought he was a magician using sleight of hand. Eventually I did believe him and over time we've fallen in love." At this I look towards Monty with hope in my eyes. I am not sure what else I can say to convince them, but maybe my testimony helps.

The Elder Vampire in the middle stands up and says, "This court hath borne witness to the testimony of Montgomery Ravenscroft, Nikolai Lockwood, Celeste Dunn, and Katrina Prescott concerning the matter of whether Master Ravenscroft hath, by the ancient laws of the Vampire Codes, lifted the sacred veil of secrecy. Let it be known that the Court shall adjourn and reconvene in one hour's time to pronounce its final judgment upon Master Ravenscroft."

Nik, Monty, and I file out and follow a young woman down a hallway in silence. "Hi, my name is Celeste," the young woman says to me. "I'm human, but I work here in Civita di Bagnoregio. I did my best to explain to the vampires how humans treat VidVibe. I hope I was able to help."

She leads us to a small room with just two cots in it. "Do you need anything? I can bring you some water, bread, and cheese."

"Yes, please, that would be lovely. I appreciate your help."

As soon as she closes the door, I throw myself at Monty, not caring at all that Nik is also in the room with us. "Monty, I was so worried! They didn't let you call anyone? What is going to happen?" Before I let him answer, I reached up and cradle his face and kiss him with a passion born from worry.

"Shh, shh. It'll be okay," he tells me even though he has no way of knowing that is true. It does make me feel better just to be in his arms. I pull away and sit on the cot next to him with Nik across from us on his cot.

"Is this where you have been staying?" I ask both of them.

"Yes," Nik replies. "These rich old vamps and they put us in prison quarters to make us feel inferior to them." He sounds pretty angry.

"Why did they make you come too? Are they accusing you of anything?" I lean forward on the cot, dangling my legs over the edge and swinging them back and forth, trying to keep my mind off how small the room is.

"I got to be this guy's witness. They probably would have let me go, but I wanted to stick around to defend him. I am sorry about Sky though. I wish I could have gotten word to her. I am excited to go on a date with her, and hope she'll let me have a second chance when this is all over," Nik says. My heart swells with happiness hearing Nik talk so fondly of my best friend. Not many people are willing to date a DID System. It's complicated and takes a lot of patience and understanding. But Rainbow is the best friend I could ever imagine and I want the world for them. I don't know if Nik is the best, but I do know that Monty trusts him with his life, so that means a lot to me.

"Really?" Nik asks, "You think I'll be good to date Sky?"

Startled, I turn my head and squint at him. "Uh . . . how . . ."

"Oops, telepathy." Nik says sheepishly. "I'm sorry. I try not to intrude unless I have permission, but sometimes I 'hear' something so loud I can't tune it out. I'm happy you think I may have a chance with Sky."

"I guess I'll have to figure out how to 'think' quieter, I guess." I say with a laugh. "You know, telepathy could really come in handy when dating a System! I never thought about that. You could know who was fronting without asking, with permission, of course."

Nik looks to ponder that for a moment, when the door opens and Celeste brings in a tray with some water and food on it. She sets it on the edge of the cot, apologizing for the sparse accommodations. "We have much nicer spaces, but this is where the Elders wanted you," she says, and then ducks back out. She is a strange mousy woman. She obviously has a lot of grit to be able to work for vampires knowingly, but she seems quite shy too. I feel an immediate kinship towards her—I always liked the outcasts of society.

"What do you think your chances are that they'll say you're innocent?" I ask Monty while tearing off a hunk of bread and biting into it.

"I think your testimony may persuade them, actually, along with Celeste's, since she isn't associated with me. The old guys, they *are* old, but I will say they do try to modernize. It's slow going for them, but over the centuries they've created codes of ethics and they've kept rogue vampires in check. I do think they are trying their best to keep our kind secret while also living among humans. I do see where they are coming from, and if they say I have to shut down my account, I will. I met you from it and, well, that makes it all worth it." He smiles. "But I do hope they let me keep it. It is a fun diversion for me for now, and I really don't think it causes any harm."

"What will they do if they find you guilty?" I ask, almost afraid to find out.

240

"I'm not sure. I don't think they'll put me to death. But they may come up with some pretty harsh consequences. I don't even want to dwell on it."

We sit in that small, dark room for the rest of the hour until Celeste comes to collect us again, and then we quietly follow her back to the courtroom, feeling apprehensive but also very hopeful.

Once everyone is settled and the tension in the room becomes palpable, one of the Elders rises. The room is almost completely silent, but I hear the rustling of clothes, Nik and Monty breathing near me, and wind whistling through the small windows up in the top of the walls.

"After much deliberation, wherein testimonies were carefully weighed, even to the extent of pursuing other VidVibe accounts of similar types of these 'cosplayers' and acknowledging the emergence of this novel form of Human Entertainment, the Court doth hereby declare Master Montgomery Ravenscroft Not Guilty of all Charges."

"Not guilty!" I shout and jump up. Nik quickly takes my hand and settles me down. I remember what he said, and I get quiet really quickly, hoping that my outburst won't put Monty in further danger. I am just so happy! I turn to Monty with big eyes. He smiles a huge grin, letting his fangs extend in his happiness. He never looked more handsome to me than at that moment. Despite the fact his hair really needs a wash and his clothes are beyond ripe.

"Court dismissed!" Saraphina pounds a gavel with her prosthetic arm and we all stand. I wish I could tell Celeste thank you for all she did, but she isn't anywhere to be seen. I am still craning my neck around to look for her when Monty takes my hand. A few moments later, we are in his living room. I blink rapidly at the sudden scenery change and adjust

to my new surroundings a second before Nik appears beside
me.

Chapter 29
Reconnecting

Montgomery

I can't believe that the whole ordeal is over with. I stand gaping for a few minutes, trying to orient myself back to the fact I am free—there is no punishment. I am even allowed to keep my VidVibe account. I've got to wonder if the Elders are just bored and looking for problems. But I'm not going to question it too closely, not when everything worked out in my favor. Next up is trying to figure out what day and time it is. Pulling out the cell phone that was finally returned to me, I see it has a small amount of charge remaining. Checking the date and time, it is Friday, just after 1 p.m. local time. I'm so tired, but first, I really need a shower and so does Nik. "Everyone okay? That was a lot. Nik, do you need to call work? We both need showers. I'm also absolutely exhausted."

Nik calls his boss and says he's gotten so sick he is in the hospital and was unable to contact him to let him know earlier. He hopes his boss won't fire him or try to verify his lie, but he isn't that attached to his job, so it isn't a big deal if he gets fired. He decides to head home to shower and teleports out. I turn to Katrina. "I can never thank you enough for going with Nik to help save me. I know how scary that must have been for you."

"I was just so worried. We said we were going to move in together and then you just disappeared. I came here to look for you, and both your car and Nik's were in the driveway, but you weren't here. I wasn't sure what I was going to do. I thought about calling the police and putting in a missing person's report, but I wasn't sure if that was the right move. I didn't want to get you in more trouble. I was still trying to figure out what to do when Nik showed up. Of course I went with him to help you." Katrina squeezes my hands and looks up at me with such sweet eyes. "I can see how exhausted you are. Why don't you go shower, and then head to bed. I'll find Rainbow and get them up to date on what happened. I didn't have time to call them, so I left a very cryptic message. I'm sure they are just as worried. Then this evening I'll come back over and we can catch up. How does that sound?" I nod and she continues, "I'll need to borrow your car. Mine is at the library where Nik found me. Hopefully Mrs. Humphrey didn't notice it in the parking lot. That might be difficult to explain."

"I don't want to let you out of my sight, but I understand. Go take care of what you need. My keys are hanging in the mudroom. I can't wait to see you this evening." I lean down to give her a quick kiss before heading along the hall towards my bedroom.

Katrina

I grab Mony's keys from the mudroom and then climb into his fancy car. This thing is so sleek and futuristic, I'm surprised it doesn't drive itself. I plug my cell phone in and it automatically connects to the car. Nice! I call Rainbow at work, something I usually only do when they are on lunch break. I get their voicemail and leave a message to call me back as soon as possible.

Then I drive home. I don't want to go back to work today. Plus, Mrs. Humphrey said to take as long as I needed.

A few hours later, I finally hear from Rainbow. I had gotten home and decided to take a soak in my bathtub with lavender essential oil to calm my nerves. Data kept watch on the nearby toilet seat, which is adorable and helps lighten my mood too. But now I am dried off, in comfy lounge wear, and sitting on my couch with a tub of ice cream. It is a tub of ice cream kind of moment. My nervous system is just so out of whack. The thought of telling my therapist that I had been teleported to Italy to save my boyfriend from vampire court, just . . . well, the ice cream made sense. I can only imagine her response, and it makes me laugh out loud in the empty room. When my phone rings and I see Rainbow's number, I quickly answer it.

"Hi!" I say a little too enthusiastically. Maybe the bathtub didn't relax me as much as I had hoped. "Who's front today?" I wish there was a way to know who was calling without me having to ask, but it's better just to ask and not get caught up on it.

"Arleigh speaking," she answers matter-of-factly, then, "I'm so grateful to hear your voice, Katrina! Sky got your message when she was taking her lunch hour and it triggered her back to the headspace. I do not think she felt capable of handling this unusual situation. I decided to take over the body. We were planning on checking on Data after work like your urgent message suggested, but it looks like you are back already?"

"Oh my goodness! I'm sorry to have caused a trigger for Sky. It was a very unusual emergency situation. I wouldn't have done that if I'd had any other choice. Is Sky okay now?"

"Oh no worries my friend, Sky is fine and I am happy to help out." Arleigh reassured me.

"I am back, it ended up being a much shorter trip than I thought it would be. Can you still come over? I have ice cream," I tell her. "I think I have some strawberry sorbet in the freezer you can have," I add, knowing Arleigh prefers sorbet to ice cream.

"Yes, of course. Let me stop along the way and procure some salad for us to dine on."

"Uh uh, no salad for me tonight. I declare a junk food night! You can pick me up a chicken sandwich though." Arleigh, always trying to get everyone to eat healthier. It's good to have her around. But tonight I want comfort food all the way.

Later, as we finish up our impromptu dinner, including more ice cream and sorbet than should have been had in one sitting, I catch Arleigh up on all that has happened since this morning. It feels as if it's been at least a couple of days! I am still wrapping my head around the fact that I was in Italy this morning. Not that I got to see anything except the old castle, but still, I was in another country halfway around the world just a few hours ago. And back. If humans learned that vampires could teleport, they would probably abuse it. No wonder the vampires want to keep their veil of secrecy or whatever. Even though vampires are more powerful than humans, humans outnumber them by a lot.

"At least Sky should be happy to know that Nik didn't stand her up, right?"

Arleigh tilts her head to the side a bit, and her eyes lose focus. I'm guessing someone else is about to front, so I just give them time to get sorted. I put up the dinner dishes and start loading the dishwasher when I hear Arleigh speak again.

"I apologize for that—did you say something? Sky was trying to come to front, but I wasn't done. I have not been able to spend much time with you lately and I have been sorely missing your company."

At Arleigh's words, I feel so guilty for spending so much time with Monty lately. I rush over to squeeze her hands. "I'm so sorry, Arleigh. I really haven't been the best friend lately, have I?" I don't mention Nik again because that was what created the trigger for Sky and I don't want to retrigger the System if Arleigh wants to stay in the front. "Tell me, how's work been going?"

Arleigh fills me in on some of the new surgeries they've been assisting on. She then asks me if I have made any plans for my thirtieth birthday. It's not until August, but it's a big year this go-around, so I've got to have time to decide if I want to celebrate it in any particular way. Birthdays in the past have been a tough time for me—many years spent without friends to celebrate alongside.

"I hadn't thought about it, honestly. Can you believe I'll be thirty? Right now I've got to focus on moving out of the townhome. I'm so thankful Monty is going to hire packers and movers for me. Even though I don't own a lot of stuff, packing is so overwhelming. And then there's the Fourth of July. Not sure if I want to celebrate that this year or not."

"Oh, perhaps Montgomery can secure the services of the yacht again and we can watch the firework display from the Columbia River? For the Fourth. That way, we won't be near crowds, but can still have a delightful evening together in our quaint group?"

"That would be perfect! I'll ask him." We spend the next few minutes reminiscing about past summers when suddenly I notice it is getting close to when I told Monty I'd be back at his house. I don't want to end our chat, but I also have so much to still say to him.

I think Arleigh notices me looking at my watch because she starts to gather up her purse and says, "Well, I shall be heading home to Pixie. She's probably meowing for her dinner by now."

"I don't want to rush you out," I say, still feeling guilty. I want to be in both places at once.

"No, no, not at all, my dear. You and Monty have had quite the adventure the past couple of days and more so for you today. I'm sure you've got a lot to talk to him about. I really should get home. I feel Sky is really wanting to call Nik tonight. I think I'll be heading inward soon! I'm so glad you, Monty, and Nik are all safe. I'll talk with you soon."

I give her a hug goodbye. Then I go to check Data's water and food bowl and pack an overnight bag. Something tells me I won't be coming back home tonight.

I park Monty's car back at his house and let myself in. I am worried about my car at the library and hoping he isn't too tired and can help me go get it. I know it is probably fine, but it'll bother my brain until I get it back.

"Monty!" I call out, hoping he is awake from his nap by now.

"In here!" I hear him call from the direction of the game room. Good—he's awake. I practically skip down the hallway towards him. His eyes light up as soon as he sees me.

248

I am wearing a comfy light teal velour tracksuit and I am feeling cute.

"Hey Monty, can we go get my car? It's going to stress me out being parked at the library." I pull up a map on my phone to show him where I am parked, and in a flash, he teleports us right next to my car. I quickly glance around, but no one is around to notice us. "Do you want to see where I work?" I ask spontaneously. "No one will be in the library and I can show you what I do." I've never been in the library after dark, and it feels daring. In the most nerdy way possible."

"Not how I thought I'd spend my evening, but I'm up for it," he says. I lead him toward the library entrance, and he teleports us inside.

"I could really get used to this whole teleporting thing," I say as we head for the book repair station. My mug of tea is still there from this morning. I eye it, half-tempted to clean it up, but hesitate—too much tampering and Mrs. Humphrey will notice. Instead, I gesture to the workbench.

"This is the book repair area. I fix old or damaged books so they can stay in circulation longer. Some of them are really fragile, but we've got amazing equipment to bring them back to life."

I glance at Monty and a mischievous spark lights in my chest. My hand rises to the bun in my hair. "Hey, Sunshine... when we first started DMing, didn't you mention something about a librarian fantasy?"

I pull out the clip and let my hair tumble down my back. No glasses, no sultry outfit, but something in Monty's expression shifts instantly. His eyes darken, gaze locked on me like I've become the only thing in the room worth noticing.

His desire rolls off him in waves—hot, focused, real. I step closer, voice low. "Got any overdue fines? Need to work something off?" The line sounds ridiculous in my own ears, but Monty eats it up. He closes the space between us in two steps, hands sliding to my hips, and leans in.

"I have *very* old fines," he murmurs, voice like a storm, "and I'm willing to do... whatever it takes."

His mouth finds mine, hungry and unguarded. The kiss sends sparks through my entire body. My back hits the wall and he lifts me effortlessly, arms strong beneath me, lips trailing along my jaw as I cling to him. I wrap my legs around his waist, pressed so close I can feel the heat of him even through our clothes. When I tilt my neck, offering him my throat, he doesn't hesitate.

His fangs pierce gently. The pleasure is immediate, dizzying, a wave of light behind my closed eyes. I gasp against his shoulder, body trembling. It's always like this—like falling and flying at once.

When I blink again, we're in his bedroom. I'm still catching my breath.

"I need you, KittyKat," he says, voice hoarse. "Didn't think you'd actually go for it at work."

"Neither did I." My hands move before my brain catches up. I strip him down, fingers greedy, while he does the same to me. When I'm bare in front of him, he pauses— just for a beat—to look. Really look.

He brushes my hair from my breasts, slow and reverent. His palm cups one, thumb circling the nipple until I shiver. His other hand slides between my thighs, fingers exploring, and my knees start to buckle.

I moan, leaning into him. He catches me as I start to fall and lifts me again. My legs wrap around him just as he slides into me. The stretch, the fullness—it steals my breath.
250

I grip his shoulders, head falling back.

"You can scream, KittyKat," he murmurs. "We're alone."

And I do. I let go, body spiraling, pleasure burning through me like wildfire. I clench around him, and he groans, his own release surging through us both. We sink to the floor in a tangled heap, breathless and undone. I kiss his chest—soft, grateful butterfly kisses—and whisper, "Hey Monty?"

"Yeah baby?"

"We forgot my car." I am feeling so relaxed after that orgasm that the thought of moving is not appealing at all. But Monty stands, scoops me up, and sets me down on his bed.

"Do you want your clothes?"

"I'll just lie here naked for a few more minutes," I say, sort of drifting off to sleep.

He kisses my forehead, "Okay, I'll be right back."

"Hmm, hmm . . ." I say, and then fall asleep.

Chapter 30
Nothing to Fix

Montgomery

I look down at my sweet Katrina for a moment longer, then quickly get dressed and teleport to her car. A little while later, I have it parked back at my house. I walk inside fully expecting Katrina to still be asleep but she is in the game room.

"Sorry I didn't leave a note for you. I figured you'd still be asleep. I was retrieving your car," I tell her as I settle beside her on the couch. She has pulled out her crochet bag and is sitting there with a cute expression on her face as she tries to get a complicated stitch done correctly.

"I figured that's where you went. I only drifted off for a couple of minutes, but I've never been able to sleep in the nude. I like the idea; the execution, not so much," she says, laughter in her voice. "I brought an overnight bag because I'm not ready to leave your side. I told Mrs. Humphrey I had a family emergency so I'll not go to work tomorrow either. I need some down time to recover from all the excitement. Plus, we need to figure out moving logistics. You still want me to move in with you, right?"

The uncertainty in her voice activates a primal response in me. "Katrina Prescott, yes, I want you to move in with me. I want you by my side for eternity. Do you need an official proposal? I'll have to pay a jewelry store to stay open late and we can pick out a ring if you'd like."

"This isn't exactly a romantic proposal," she says, laughing.

"I can give you romance—you know that. But I also know you don't like surprises, so I figure it's best to plan it out with you."

"This is true. I'm not even sure I want a ring. A lot of times, jewelry is just irritating to me. Maybe a simple necklace. I'm not sure. Let me give it some thought. There is one big question we haven't put into words yet, however," she says slowly, and I know whatever is coming is hard for her to talk about. I nod encouragingly. "Human marriage or eternal life together?" The words come as a rush out of her mouth.

"That's something you'll have to decide. I will take whatever I can have. I will watch you grow old and mourn your death when you pass or I'll embrace an eternity with you. It's something you get to choose. I never got that choice and I'd never take it away from someone else."

"I turn thirty in a couple of weeks. I'm not getting younger. I've been thinking about it since before you got kidnapped to vampire court. It's been on my mind almost exclusively. I know I don't have to make a decision now. You turned at twenty-seven and so I'm almost three years older than that, but even if I waited a year or two to decide, it wouldn't be that big of a deal. And yet. I feel as if it's putting off the inevitable. I know without a doubt I want to be with you. I do have a few more questions."

"I wouldn't suspect otherwise. You know I'll answer all your questions as best as I can."

"I saw that one vampire at the Court—I think her name was Saraphina? She had a prosthetic arm. Does that mean that turning doesn't take away disabilities? I love my Autistic and ADHD brain. It is who I am. If I wasn't Autistic,

I wouldn't be me. There's nothing to fix. So I'm guessing I'll be an Autistic vampire, right? If not, that would be a deal-breaker for me. It's not always easy being Autistic, but I wouldn't have it any other way."

"Absolutely. Turning doesn't change who you are as a person. You get powers, and you'll appear more aesthetically pleasing to whoever is looking at you; that's basically so our species can hunt and attract humans. But no, turning wouldn't change your Autism. It would cure chronic illness or pain but not your Autism or ADHD." Katrina's entire body relaxes with this idea—it must have really been eating at her. "What's your next question?"

"Um." She gets shy again.

"It's okay, sweetie, you can talk to me about anything. No judgments here."

"Well. Um. I-actually-really-like-it-when-you-bite-me," she says so fast I almost can't make it out.

I repeat her words back to make sure. "You like it when I bite you? Yes, we deliver pleasure hormones with our bites."

"But if I turn, and I'm a vampire, you can't feed from me anymore, right?" She snuggles into my shoulder. I love cuddling with this sweet woman—both innocent and adventurous all in one.

"Yes and no. I wouldn't feed from you, but we can still have fun bite play after turning. I've never actually done that with another vampire, but I know it's not a problem." My cock starts to get tight as I talk about biting and sex again. I can never get enough of Katrina. We'll need an eternity together.

"Mmm . . . well I'm glad we won't lose that then," she murmurs.

"Does that mean you're thinking of turning?" I ask her tentatively, stroking a hand up and down her arm. I absolutely love feeling her body snuggled up to mine, tucked in like the perfect piece I didn't know was missing from my life.

"I am thinking that I will. I have until October to decide, right? That is, if I want to do it this year? I think moving in with you is the next big step, and I'm excited for that, although we'll have to scramble to find movers who will be available that soon. I'll try to call some places tomorrow."

She turns to look up at me and asks, "So are we engaged? We don't need a ring to be engaged, do we?"

"Katrina, if you say yes, we are engaged. Will you marry me? We can figure the rest out as we go."

"Absolutely, yes, Montgomery. Absolutely." Her smile makes me feel like I won the lottery. I feel like I fumbled this proposal, but I'll make it up to her over and over, I promise myself.

"It's getting late though. How about I head to bed? Will you stay up and make VidVibes? Do you even still feel like you should, or do you want to lie low for a while?" she asks me, trying to stifle a yawn.

"Yes, if you want to turn this year, the end of October is the next ceremony. As for VidVibe, I've thought about it. I was found 'not guilty,' so I don't want to act as if I am guilty now. What story would you like to wake up to? I can upload some while you're sleeping." She pulls away from me and starts to clean up her crochet project that she had abandoned while we were talking.

"Tell a story about what you were like as a new vampire after you had accepted what you'd become. I think that would be interesting." We make our way towards the main bedroom together. She tucks her crochet bag into her duffel and pulls out her pj's. These have cats printed all over the legs, and the top says "I'd spend all nine lives with you." That has to be the most fitting T-shirt ever after the conversation we just had. I don't think she was even aware of that.

I give her a big smile and say, "Look at what shirt you brought over. Is it a secret message?"

She looks down at it as she pulls it over her head, and does "little happy toes," a move she does when she's excited about something. It's like she sort of bounces on her tiptoes a few times. Not a complete jump or a hop, just a burst of energy that leaves her bouncy. It's the most fucking adorable thing I've ever seen and it just fills me with happiness.

While she's brushing her teeth, she asks around the toothbrush, "Do vampires have to brush their fangs? I hate brushing my teeth with a passion. Do vampires go to vampire dentists? How does that work?"

Her questions are never-ending. I wondered if I'd have asked so many if I'd been given the choice of turning. "Well yes and no? We possess natural healing, so we don't get cavities. But I guess a lot of vampires do brush their teeth for fresh breath? I mean, I guess we don't have to. I just started to brush my teeth regularly in the 1940s I think? The modern toothbrush wasn't really around before then . . ."

"What?" she interrupts me. "How did I not know that?" She spits in the sink. "People have been brushing for hundreds of years, surely?"

"Well, people would chew twigs or other fibers to clean their teeth. Some cultures did invent types of paste. But the modern toothbrush as we know it isn't very old, relatively speaking. As for vampire dentists, since we are self-healing, we don't really need to go to the dentist."

256

"Well that's a relief. Seriously, toothpaste is a sensory nightmare. I do it because I have to, but I hate it so much. Sorry if that's gross."

"I understand. It's okay." While she finishes up, I pick out an outfit for the VidVibe. "What do you think about this one?" I ask her, holding up dark blue jeans, a black long-sleeve T-shirt, black leather vest, and my ankh necklace. I also pull out several rings.

"Yeah, that'll work nicely," she says. "You put that on and let me rip it right back off of you."

"Not going to happen! You've got to be beyond exhausted. Go curl up in my—no, OUR, bed—and have sweet dreams. I'm going to put on a bit of eyeliner and go film. Hopefully I'll see you when you wake up. Give me a kiss, but hands off!" I tease.

She climbs in bed and arranges her hair in a halo above her head. She can't stand it on her neck while sleeping, but it makes her look angelic with her hair spread across the pillow like that. It takes everything I have not to climb into bed with her. I lean over, give her a good-night kiss, and then head out of the room.

It is going to be hard to focus knowing Katrina is cozied up in my bed down the hall. Being on different sleep schedules is frustrating, but we're making it work for now. I debate whether or not I want a glass of wine tonight, but I think I'll skip it. I wonder how Nik is doing and consider sending him a text, but after spending the past several days cooped up in a small cell-like room with him, as much as I love him, I figure a nice break is good.

After sinking into my leather chair, I set my phone in my tripod and lean back, steepling my fingers together to think. Katrina wanted a video of my early days. I could tell the story of how I dressed up like a viscount and crashed a debutante ball. It was a masquerade ball and Nik and I had thought it would be hilarious to rub elbows with the nobility. It was a fun night, but since I never learned how to read the code of fans, it made for a confusing experience. Young girls would send signals to suitors by placing their fans in certain positions or flicking them with their wrists a certain way. This practice was known as the code of fans. We made fools of ourselves a couple of different times. The hilarity of it all. And one young maiden wanted me to dance with her, but I hadn't learned how to waltz yet, as it wasn't a needed skill as a farmer.

But I don't know, perhaps telling a story of other young women when your girlfriend asks about your past maybe isn't the best to go to. I close my eyes for a few minutes, allowing myself time to think back to those early days. I'm thankful my memory has stayed pretty fresh, even all these years later. Some details fade here and there, but when I have a quiet moment and relax, I can bring back some really fun times. It's been helping me write my book. Which, now that I think about it, I probably can't publish. The VidVibes are one thing, but a memoir of a vampire may not go over so well with the Court. Even so, it's been a pleasure to write.

Then suddenly it comes to me. The time that Nik and I accidentally stumbled into a gay bar in the early 1700s. That surely will get my fans smiling and make my lovely Katrina giggle. I turn on the camera and settle in.

"In a recent video, I told you I have found my soulmate. At this time, I want to respect her privacy, so I'm

258

not saying her name, but she asked me to film a funny story from my past, so this video is for her. Let me tell you about the time that my friend, Nik, and I accidentally stumbled into a gay bar around the year 1720. Yes, gay bars did exist, but I was a country lad, I hadn't been a vampire for long, and I had never heard of one. We got quite the education that night, and I think it was both life-changing and eye-opening for Nik. These early years, these types of things were well hidden and not talked about openly.

They were called Molly Houses and they were very secret. One night, Nik and I were out walking the streets of London when we saw these two blokes stroll out of a bar together. They looked happy, tipsy, and as if they'd had a good time inside. As they passed us, they said, "You two make quite the couple. Going in? Tell them Danny vouches for you!" Again, we had no idea what he was talking about, but we were looking for fun.

We walked up to the door and a lady—we learned later she was a Madame of the establishment—asked who vouched for us. So we said, "Danny!" in unison. That got us in. We learned very quickly that not all taverns were alike! The room was filled with a rowdy, lively crowd. But when we looked closer, we saw, tucked in the corners of the rooms, men getting very intimate with each other. Everyone assumed Nik and I were together, and we didn't want to let on we weren't a couple. So we danced together and pretended we were a couple for the evening. We got hit on a few times, which Nik found he quite enjoyed. We met some really amazing people that night. They were in a place where they were welcome and accepted and you know, that's all any of us ever want. Until the moon rises again, my nocturnal friends. Fangs out—see you in the shadows"

I turn off the camera, quite happy with the video. I know Katrina will find it hilarious that we got ourselves in that situation. Nik will be amused that I decided to share the story—he's very open about his sexuality these days. I think that night was a significant part of his bisexual awakening. I edit the video and upload it to VidVibe for her to find in the morning. After changing back into some comfortable clothes, I head to the game room and settle at my computer. I want to research some packers and movers and print out a few numbers for Katrina to call when she wakes up.

Chapter 31
Moving Day

Katrina

Tomorrow is my last day in my townhouse. The past week and a half flew by faster than I ever thought possible. When I made it back to work after the vampire trial, I needed a good story to tell Mrs. Humphrey, but lying is not something that comes easily to me; as an Autistic person, I default to the truth. I needed to come up with some realistic reasons why I had to bolt so quickly yesterday. Technically, I could just say it was an emergency and leave it at that, but while Mrs. Humphrey is my boss, I still think of her as a somewhat friend too. I ended up telling her a white lie: I had gotten a call that my townhouse had a possible break-in and I had to deal with the police. She was worried for me, but I told her everything ended up being okay and that I had gotten my locks changed and was actually going to be moving in with my boyfriend soon anyway. That seemed to satisfy her. Still, I hated the white lie.

The packers Monty helped me find came yesterday, and all my belongings are now in boxes stacked in neat little rows for the movers to come get tomorrow. Most of my furniture will be temporarily stored in his garage, even my big red chair. I debated about finding a spot for it in Monty's house, but his furniture is really comfortable, and I don't need it. However, since I don't always handle change gracefully, storing my furniture in his garage means it'll be around—in case I change my mind on anything while I transition to new stuff. My mini trampoline is definitely coming along and will probably go in the game room. I'm so excited! Data is being absolutely hilarious and climbing all over the boxes, playing hide-and-seek and just being a silly kitty. Monty's coming over soon and he's going to take Data back to his house tonight so he'll be out of the way of the movers. I'm spending the night on the floor in a sleeping bag, as my bed was disassembled for transport. Monty thinks it's silly, but I told him I wanted one last night in my townhome.

Living independently all these years really does mean a lot to me. It hasn't always been easy, but this little house was my home and I will miss it. What's coming up is exciting in a different way, but that doesn't mean that I'm not sad to leave. Learning that two opposite things can be true at once was a big lesson for me, and this is a perfect example. I'm both so very sad to move and also ecstatic to start this new chapter of my life.

The door clicks open and both Monty and Rainbow walk in. I invited them over for a final pizza picnic on my living room floor. Obviously, the pizza is for the non-vampires in the room. "Where's Nik?" I ask, since I invited him too.

"He was right behind me. He came in his own car," Monty says.

"Jessie, did Sky ever go on her date with Nik? I mean surely she would have told me? I've been so focused on moving that I haven't really had much time to hang out with any of you!" That's the thing with ADHD—sometimes you experience a lot of out-of-sight-out-of-mind moments, and important things that are happening in your friends' lives will completely slip your brain and you feel terrible. I'm used to it, and so is Rainbow, so it's better to just ask when you finally do remember.

"No. After he got back from Italy helping Monty, he had to suck up to his boss a bit for leaving for so many days without a word. He's been busy and I've been slammed at work. It's that time of year when the lakes turn and get algae, and people let their dogs swim and they get sick. No matter how many signs are up!" Jessie's voice drips with exasperation. "It'll be good to meet Nik tonight. I haven't met him yet, just heard what Sky and Max said about him."

We all make our way into the living room and have to move a few boxes to clear space. Monty stacks four next to each other in the middle of the room for an impromptu table as Nik walks in holding a big pizza box. "I saw the guy on the sidewalk, so I got the pizza from him. You'd think he'd check I was the right person, especially since the order is for Katrina and I just don't think I give off 'Katrina' vibes," he says with a chuckle.

I take the box and open it on our temporary table. The smell of the yeasty dough, the herby oregano, and the savory sausage and pepperoni hit my nose and tell my brain that my stomach it is starving! Did I forget to eat lunch today in all the hullabaloo? I probably did.

"I brought some kombucha Arleigh made last week," Jessie says, pulling two glass bottles filled with the fermented tea out of her bag. I'm obsessed with the fizzy sweetness of Arleigh's healthy concoctions.

"Oh! What flavor. . .do you know?" Arleigh likes to experiment with lots of different flavors but isn't always the best at labeling.

As Jessie hands me a bottle, she says, "I think it's peach? But it might be raspberry ginger? Let's taste it and see if we can figure it out."

I take a sip, feeling the bubbles tickle down my throat. "Oh definitely ginger something! That burns, in a good way!" I laugh. The kombucha will pair nicely with the rich cheesy pizza.

"I wish I could taste it," Nik says as he settles on the floor leaning casually against a stack of boxes. "I honestly don't miss human foods or drinks often, but I do get curious."

"What happens if you do eat something other than blood or wine?" Jessie asks.

"Well, we get really sick. Depending on what it is and how much, determines how sick. I won't go into details while you are eating!"

"Oh, Monty," I say as I suddenly remember to ask, "were you able to get the yacht again for our Fourth of July celebration?" I am excited to see fireworks this way. In general, fireworks can be overstimulating for me. I love watching them, but the constant barrage of noise leaves me feeling drained by the end of the night. But being able to watch them without crowds would be ideal.

"Yes, it's all booked. I'm looking forward to it," he says.

I take a bite of pizza as he wanders around the small townhome peeking his head in the bedroom and bathroom, "So it looks like you're all packed up here. Ready for tomorrow? The movers come first thing in the morning. I wish I could be here to help you direct them!" Now apparently satisfied I didn't miss anything, he lowers himself behind me on the floor and gives me a gentle back rub. Pizza, back rub, and my closest friends? I'm having a terrific night.

Instead of being sad I'm moving, I've got a warm glow of satisfaction filling me up.

"I know, and it's okay. I've got it all handled. It was so much help having packers. I don't think I could have done it without their help!"

The rest of the evening goes by in a flash, our comfortable little group sitting on the floor talking non-stop with a lot of laughter, the pizza long devoured, Data darting around and climbing over everything as if it is the best playground ever. I look around at my small group and just feel an immense swelling in my heart. I'm so incredibly lucky to have these amazing people in my life.

It isn't too long before Jessie has to go home and then Nik takes that as a sign to leave too, leaving me alone with Monty. "My last night living single," I say.

"You haven't been 'single' for many months," he says with a possessive growl to his voice that sends trembles of desire through me. I want no man to possess me, unless I choose to be possessed by him. And I do. I really do with this one.

"You know what I meant, Sunshine. It's my last night living by myself." I look around my townhome, which doesn't really feel like my home anymore. Spending time among the boxes helped with this big transition. To be in the space and have it not feel like mine any longer. It'll be easier in the morning if I'm already here when the movers arrive. I stand up to start gathering up Data's things: his litterbox, food and water, and a couple toys. Then I scoop him up and put him in his carrying backpack. "Put Data in the main bedroom with you. You can put his litter box in the bathroom for now. Then keep the door closed. That way he can get used to the new house slowly and he'll be in there while the movers are there.

I'll have them put all my clothes boxes outside the bedroom door and tell them they can't open it because of the cat."

"Now you go have a good evening and I'll be there with you tomorrow night when you wake up." I stand on my tiptoes and kiss him gently, our soft lips pressing together in a way that will never get old and always feels like home.

The move is both exhausting and exhilarating. I can't believe Monty's house is now my house too. I spend the morning directing the movers where to put boxes. I don't own that much stuff, so they are done by lunchtime. I have a quick bite to eat and then book it to the library and tell Mrs. Humphrey I can do a half day today.

With moving in with Monty on my mind, I start to think seriously about the next step. My mind keeps playing different scenarios over and over. I feel like I am in some sci-fi show where I can look at a pivotal moment and see two ways my life could go. Become a vampire, stay forever thirty, never eat food again, and have very limited sunlight, or grow old like normal and watch my love not age along with me. The choice is gnawing on me. I know I don't have to make an immediate choice, but not making a decision is, in the end, a decision.

In preparation, I am trying to figure out what I'd want to do as a career if I become a vampire. I know I wouldn't have to work. Monty has enough money and he's got investments on top of investments. I'd still like to do some sort of work. I think I could spend some time this afternoon doing some research on night jobs I'd be suitable for. Perhaps even talk to Mrs. Humphrey. Not that I'd mention it'd be a night job, but I am thinking about work-from-home jobs that maybe don't require particular set hours.

It is a quiet Monday afternoon at the library and I am working the children's desk. It is the hour of most kids' naptime, so there are just a few elementary-age kids, probably homeschoolers, browsing the stacks in the children's area. I use the time to look up jobs on the internet. I have a couple websites pulled up and I am reading about a few different careers when Mrs. Humphrey walks by. "Hello dear," she says.

"Hello Mrs. Humphrey. How was your weekend?" Neurotypical people love that question with a passion I'll never understand.

Sure enough, her eyes light up. "Oh, it was so delightful! My daughter brought the grandchildren by and we all got to go to the Portland Zoo together! It was such a good time seeing their excitement over the animals." She takes a seat in the chair next to my desk, usually used by library patrons when I'm helping them do a computer search and leans her cane against her knee

"Which was their favorite?" I am nailing the small talk today, but trying to figure out how to steer the conversation to what I want to talk to Mrs. Humphrey about without causing her alarm is going to take deftness, and I'm not sure I can pull it off.

"Definitely the elephants. One of the mother elephants was giving her calf a dust bath. It was the sweetest thing." Mrs. Humphrey smiles.

I decide an abrupt change of subject is the best way to go. "I'm engaged! I moved in with my boyfriend this morning! We've been dating for quite some time now and my lease was up and the timing was just perfect," I blurt out.

Where am I going with this? Mrs. Humphrey looks at me and is trying to figure out how to respond, but I just press forward. "The move has me thinking of my future, of course. I don't plan on making any changes currently—I do love my job here," I emphasize. "But I was starting to think about the future. I don't know if I want to be a librarian forever. Um, not that there's anything wrong with that of course." Why did I decide to bring this up? My brain is screaming "abort, abort!" But it is now too late.

"Oh, oh . . . Congratulations, my dear! I'm glad you are so happy. What kind of career change were you thinking about?" Mrs. Humphrey asks.

"I'm not quite sure. I'm thinking about traveling more. I'd like a job with a lot of flexibility in the hours, maybe something I'd be able to do from various locations. My boyfriend travels a lot and so it might be nice to be able to go with him. This is all just me looking ahead, you know?"

"I see. Well, I'll be sad if and when you decide to leave us here. But I understand. Young folks these days—they don't stay in one career like my generation did. And having the opportunity to travel sounds wonderful while you're young enough to enjoy it. I'll give it some thought. But it looks like you've got a patron needing your attention, so let's continue this later." Mrs. Humphrey uses her cane to help her stand, then pats me on the back before she returns to the front desk.

A little boy with blonde spiky hair, a scrape on his nose, and a big grin missing several teeth approaches my desk. "Ms. Librarian Ma'am," he says in his most sincere, polite voice, "I need help finding a book on spiders so I can scare my little brother. Can you help me?"

"I think I can," I say, standing up and directing him towards the books on arachnids.

Chapter 32

New Alter

Katrina

On the Fourth of July, I leave a peacefully sleeping Monty and head over to Rainbow's house for the afternoon. I let myself in, and a very upset Pixie comes running towards me, meowing in alarm. She jumps up into my arms and I know something is very wrong. "Rainbow!" I call out and walk through the apartment. I finally find them huddled in a corner of their bedroom, looking very small and afraid.

"Hey, it's me," I say quietly. I glance around the apartment and nothing looks out of place or gives any indication as to what could be wrong. I slowly approach Rainbow and sit down next to them without touching them. "Are you hurt?" I am not sure who is fronting.

"I'm scared," a small voice says. It isn't a voice I recognize. I'm beginning to understand what might be happening, and I know the next few minutes are going to be crucial to navigate with care.

"You're safe now. I'm your friend, Katrina. Do you remember me?" I ask the huddled body on the floor. I want to wrap my arms around them, but I know that could be very upsetting, so I stay back.

"I don't know you," they say. Yep, I'm pretty sure I know what happened. A new alter formed. It happens with Dissociative Identity Disorder. Usually after a traumatic event. I didn't talk to Rainbow yesterday, but something must have happened. Sometimes alters are formed wholly with certain memories from the System and sometimes they form almost like a blank slate with just the memories the body needs to function. First and foremost, DID is a protective and survival mechanism. I've never been around for a new alter to form in the Rainbow System, but Arleigh has told me about it and potentially what to expect. It's important I stay calm even though internally I'm freaking out. I don't want to make things worse.

"It's very nice to meet you. I am your friend, but you just forgot, and that's okay. Do you know your name?" I say this in a very calm voice, and they slowly turn a bit more towards me, pulling their knees up to their chest and hugging them but peering over the top. They shake their head no to my question, so I continue on. "Do you know what happened before you were in this spot on the floor?"

"No, but I think I've been here for a while," they tell me.

"Okay, first things first. Let's take care of your body. I'm going to show you the bathroom. I bet you need to go to the restroom." At that, they nod their head yes. I walk towards the bathroom and then give them some privacy and head to the kitchen to get a glass of water and a small snack. I find some fruit, cheese, and a couple of crackers in Rainbow's fridge and pantry. Then I call Monty and leave a message on his phone because I know he'll still be asleep, but it looks as if we are going to have to cancel Fourth of July. I briefly tell him what is happening and then ask him to call me when he wakes up, but if I don't answer, I'll call him back when I can. Pixie follows me everywhere—I think she's still upset about her owner acting strange. I check, and her food and water dish are both full so that's good at least.

I head back to the bedroom, my intuition is that staying in one room will feel the safest for them right now. Rainbow is still in the bathroom, so I leave a message with their therapist too. They've given me their therapist's number in case something like this ever happens. But for now, I'm just going to have to do the best I can. I knock on the bathroom door and ask them to come back out when they are done.

Rainbow joins me on the bed this time. They sit near the headboard and I sit facing them at the end of the bed. I hand them some water and tell them to drink. Then I pass them a plate of food.

"This apple is really good. I think I was really hungry."

Looks like they know the names of foods—this is good. What a new alter will know or not can be really tricky to navigate. "Do you trust me?" I ask. I really need to establish some trust to get this going. They tentatively nod. "Okay, I'm going to ask you some questions to see what it is you do and don't remember. It seems as if maybe you have forgotten some things, right? Like who I am."

"You seem very familiar and I feel as if you're safe, but I don't remember you," they say, taking another slow bite of the fruit.

"That's okay. We'll figure this out. Do you remember your job?" This will matter. If Rainbow remembers how to work, how to move through the world, we're not in crisis territory.

They get still for a moment, tilt their head a bit, and slowly say, "Yes! I do know that. I'm a vet tech. Wow, I know a LOT about animals. How do I not know my name, but I know my job? I'm scared." Her apple set aside now, her fingers twist into the blanket telegraphing her fear.

"I know. I probably would be really scared too. But look, we're figuring it out. I know you're off work today for the 4th, and we'll probably call you in sick tomorrow. Do you remember if you work this weekend?"

"I don't think so, no." She pauses to reflect more closely, then says, "I actually remember I don't work tomorrow either. I have four days off," they say confidently.

"That's good. It'll give you some time to adjust. Do you remember your cat, Pixie?" They nod. Okay time for me to dive into some more difficult questions. "Take a moment before you answer the next question. It may seem strange at first, but that's okay. Just take your time. If I get really quiet, can you hear other people talking to you in your head? I'm going to be quiet, so just listen for a minute."

We sit together in silence for a few moments. Rainbow stops eating and slowly closes her eyes. Then their eyes pop wide open. "Uh, yes. Actually? "Um...there's someone in my head. They say their name is Max—and that I should trust you."

I take a deep breath of relief. Knowing Max is close to the front is really, really good news. That will make this all much easier and I feel as if he's an invisible safety net. He may not be able to front, but knowing he's listening is reassuring to me. "That's really good actually! Is he saying anything else?"

"He wants me to relax for a second—I don't know. It feels all fuzzy. I don't like this." They grab their head and squeeze their eyes shut. The plate of food drops onto the covers. I am not quite sure what to do, so I just sit there for a moment to see what will happen next. I am not sure if Max is trying to front or if something else is happening.

Then, sure enough, I hear Max's voice. "Katrina, thank god you're here. Yesterday, the body's brother showed up at the house demanding to see us. He was drunk and he smelled horrible and was slurring all his words. He kept screaming vile things at Sky and demanding money. I don't know how he got our address. Sky was fronting and she got frightened. I tried to front, but then I guess the brain decided to create a new alter. They shoved the brother out the door, locked it, and then ran to the bedroom where they have been all night. I was able to be sort of co-conscious for time, but I didn't have control of the body. I don't think I'm going to be able to stay in front. I feel the new alter being pushed towards me now."

And just like that, Rainbow blinks again a few times and the new alter is back. "What just happened? I could hear someone else using my mouth? What is going on?!"

They are starting to get a bit panicky, breathing in and out very quickly, which is understandable. "That was Max. It's okay. Let me explain. Remember, I'm your friend, right?" I hold their hand, steady and calm. They say yes, so I continue on. "You have a disability called Dissociative Identity Disorder. It means that your one body shares a couple of different identities, or alters. It's very unique. Your brain created you into existence last night when something bad happened." I specifically don't want to bring up their brother right now and risk a retrigger.

"I sort of remember yelling at someone."

"Yes, you got yourself safe. That is the important thing. So next, we have to learn more about who you are. Do you know if you are a woman or a man?"

"I don't think I'm either. I don't feel like I'm a man or woman." They stretch their arms out in front of themselves and look at their hands, flipping them back and forth.

"Don't worry if you don't match what your body looks like. One of the special things about DID is that who you are doesn't always match your body's appearance."

"That's interesting because, yeah, I don't feel as if I'm a girl or a boy. I'm a neither."

"That's often called 'nonbinary'. Does that sound right to you?" They nod again. "Some alters aren't even human, so when you think about what you look like, do you look human in your head?" I ask, hoping I am using all the right words.

"Yes, I'm human. I definitely am human. I have short wavy silver hair. I think my septum is pierced." Once again, they reach up to their nose, and notice it isn't pierced. "Maybe not?"

"Remember, what you look like and what your body looks like is probably going to be very different. That's okay. Keep going if you'd like."

"I think that's why I don't feel like a girl or boy. I think I have a very androgynous face. But it's more than that. I think I just want the freedom to express myself however I feel. That seems very important, for some reason. This body's face seems round, but I think my face is longer?"

I nod in encouragement. "You're doing great. Do you think you have a name you'd like to be called?" I ask.

"Does Quinn sound nice? I think my name is Quinn," they say. They pick up the plate from the bed and scoop up the dropped crackers and cheese. The cheese has cat fur on it and is discarded, but they brush off the crackers and absentmindedly start munching on it.

"Quinn it is! You don't have to stick with that. See how it feels and let me know if you think it's different later. So what other things do you think you can remember? You like apples, you said. Do you remember other foods you might like?" Sometimes newly formed alters remember foods, but not always. Sometimes they know they'll like something but not remember what it tastes like.

"I don't think I'm picky. I think I like most food. I think I also like music a lot. Mostly pop music. Ed Sheeran, Taylor Swift. Popular stuff."

"Would you like to turn some on? Would it help, you think?" Quinn says yes, so I take their phone and open Spotify. I find an Ed Sheeran channel and it starts playing softly out of the Ultimate Ears Bluetooth speaker on the bedside table. I normally do not like background music when I'm talking to someone since it's too distracting for me, but this isn't about me. Today is all about getting Quinn and the Rainbow System in a balanced emotional place. "Are you still hungry?" It is getting close to dinner time—a little early, but I could eat. "We can order something, but do you know if you remember how to cook?"

Once again, Quinn takes a minute to think and says, "Yes, I think I'm a fairly skilled cook. I mean, at least for basic things. I think if I went into the kitchen I'd know how to cook. That doesn't seem foreign to me. But at the same time, everything is foreign. Like I've never cooked before, but somehow I know how? This is so confusing."

"It can be, but you're doing a great job. Would you like to know more about your headmates? I can tell you more about them after we order in some food. What kind of food sounds good to you? Chinese, Mexican, hamburgers?" I rarely use DoorDash, but tonight seems like a night for it, although with it being the 4th of July, places might be busy. "Do you remember how to DoorDash?"

"I do! I'll place an order. Hamburgers sound good? I think I like hamburgers."

Quinn pulls out their phone and starts placing the order for us. I check my phone and see I missed a call, I say, "I'm going to call Monty, my boyfriend, really quickly. After we eat, we may need to talk about going somewhere quiet. Do you remember past 4th of July celebrations?"

While typing in the app, they look up at me and say, "Um, no? I know there are fireworks on the 4th, but I don't remember what that is like."

"It gets very, very loud. We had originally planned to go watch the fireworks with my boyfriend and his friend, but now I think we'll need alternate plans. Is it okay if I ask Monty to come over?"

"Um, sure. I think so. Should I get him a burger?"

Oh dear. Quinn doesn't remember Monty's a vampire. One problem at a time. "No, that's okay. He'll be fine—I'll explain later."

I walk into the kitchen for a bit of privacy and call Monty back. I tell him a little more of what is going on, explain that Quinn's memory is very patchy and that they don't remember he's a vampire, but that I'm going to try to explain it to them in a few minutes. I tell Monty that because of how dysregulated Quinn is, I think it would be best if we teleported somewhere quiet during the fireworks. I tell him to give us another hour to eat and talk before he comes over. Then I head back to the bedroom.

Quinn is lying back on the bed with their eyes closed, but I am not sure if they've fallen asleep. I approach quietly and see on their phone that the order has been put through. I hear Quinn snoring softly, so I tiptoe back out of the room to give them a few minutes while I wait on the food. Pixie follows me and I pick her up and sit on the couch. "Oh Pixie, I'm feeling a lot of very big feelings tonight. I hope Rainbow will be okay, and I wonder if this new alter will be around for a long time. This is hard, but we can do this, right, Pixie? Rainbow needs us right now." Then I take those same minutes to close my eyes and mindlessly pet Pixie in my lap.

Chapter 33

Fourth of July

Katrina

It isn't that much longer before there is a knock on the door and the delivery is left on the doorstep. I bring the food into the house, immediately feeling hungry as the salty grease smell hits the air. I figure eating at Quinn's little two-seater table will be easier than in their bed with the messy burgers and fries. I get out some plates and pull out our meals. Then I go to check on Quinn. I guess the knock or the smell of food woke them up because they are sitting up in bed, rubbing their eyes.

"I guess I fell asleep. I'm sorry," they say.

"No worries at all. I think you needed it. The food is here. Let's eat, and I'll tell you more about your headmates."

We go into the kitchen and sit down at the table, and not a moment too soon, because Pixie is getting mighty curious about the smells too. "Pixie, your food is over there," I say to her, laughing.

We take a big bite of our hamburgers at the same time and both say, "This is soooo good." Then we share a tired laugh.

"I'm not an expert, but I've been your friend for a while, so I have some understanding. Your brain has something called Dissociative Identity Disorder, DID for short. When you were a child, your brain split into several people," I specifically leave out the word "trauma" because I do not want to trigger any bad memories at this point. I'll leave that to their therapist. "You, Jessie, Max, Sky, and Arleigh all share a body. You take turns getting to be 'in the front.'" I use air quotes around "in the front," to explain being in control of the body. "Sometimes people with DID will form a new alter—that's what happened last night—and sometimes alters will merge. That hasn't happened since I've known you all. You all refer to yourself as a System. And as a System you are called The Rainbow System. You all came up with the name because it reminded you of happy times, bright cheery colors, and how many colors come together to make one beautiful phenomenon."

While I am talking, Quinn is listening intently and eating. "So, when I heard Max earlier, that was one of my headmates?"

"Yes, there are many amnesia barriers between the alters, and some alters only hold on to specific memories. This is the way your brain formed." Again, I don't want to go into how it is a survival method because a child can't handle the amount of trauma and so splits to compartmentalize what is happening to them. "Sometimes you can talk to each other in the innerworld, or headspace. Sometimes two alters can be co-conscious, also known as co-con. Usually only one alter controls the body at once, as far as I know. At some point you may gain access to the innerworld and be able to meet the rest of the alters. You all often write lots of notes to each other to find another way to communicate. It seems like right now, for some reason, your brain is wanting you to be fairly separate from the others.

"Usually you all take turns being in the front. When your System is fairly regulated, you all have a bit more control over who might want to be in front at any given time. But something happened last night that dysregulated your System, and right now your brain needs you to be in the front. So we'll figure it all out together. I texted your therapist and she just texted back while you were asleep to say you can have an appointment with her tomorrow. She'll be able to guide you a bit better than I can on some of this." I keep eating my burger. I want to talk a bit about Monty and the fireworks too. It is getting late and we've already heard a few random fireworks that someone set off early and which made us both jump.

"I think I'm following . . . It's a lot to take in." Quinn looked down, pushing french fries around their plate. "I feel a lot better now that I ate something. And a little more . . . confident, too." They glanced up briefly before looking away again. "You're really helping me. I'm so glad you came over. I just . . . I'm sorry I don't remember you—you seem like such a good friend."

It's really, really hard to be looking at your very best friend in the whole world and realize they don't remember you. But that is part of DID, and it's okay. I know Quinn and I will be good friends soon too, I just know it. "You hear the fireworks? Well it's about to get a whole lot louder. People here in Vancouver set them off nonstop until about 2 a.m. I think it's about time I tell you a bit more about Monty." Quinn has had so much thrown at them tonight, what's learning about vampires going to do? I'm worried, but I think it's best for me to tell them. It could be possible they won't think anything weird about it at all.

"What do you know about vampires?" I ask, trying to figure out how to start the conversation.

"Not much? I thought you were going to tell me about Monty. Is he really into vampire lore or something?"

"Well, no. Monty is a vampire." I kind of wish I had a camera to capture Quinn's face. I'm telling them all this stuff about DID and they can sense it's true, because it makes sense and because they can hear Max, it feels true. But vampires? They can't tell if I'm now gone mad or trying to joke with them.

"I know it's a lot to take in, but he can help us get away from the loud fireworks easily so we can get you more settled. You'll like him. He's generous, kind, incredibly smart, and quite good-looking too," I add with a giggle. "He should be here soon. But that is why he doesn't eat hamburgers."

"Wow. Well, that was unexpected." Quinn starts cleaning up the trash and putting the plates in the sink. We head into the living room just as another round of fireworks goes off, making us both jump. "It's not even all the way dark yet!"

"I know and it's just going to get worse. The fireworks are quite nice when you're in the right frame of mind, but tonight isn't the best time for them." I hear a knock on the door. "I bet that's Monty. Let me go get him. Since it's not fully dark out, he can't be outside for too long, you know, because of the whole he's a vampire thing."

I get up to go open the door and when I see Monty, I just launch myself at him in the biggest, tightest, most needed hug ever. Holding on to him allows a moment of peace to pass through my body and also makes me aware of how anxious I had become this afternoon, and what an afternoon it's been. "I'm so glad you're here," I whisper up to him. He leans down to give me a kiss.

"Of course. I wish I could have come sooner."

"No, it's okay. I had to go over a lot of new stuff with Quinn. They are doing pretty awesome, all things considered, but there's been a lot of new information. I did get to talk to Max briefly. He was able to front for just a few minutes, but it seems as if the brain wants Quinn in front for now."

Over my shoulder, I call out to Quinn, "Can you invite him in? He can't come in unless you invite him inside since it's your apartment."

"Uh, sure, please come in, Monty," Quinn calls from the kitchen.

I lead Monty to the kitchen so I can introduce my best friend to my boyfriend all over again.

A few minutes later, after the introductions are done, the fireworks pick up in intensity. "We can stay in, maybe play some games or something, or Monty can take us somewhere where there are no fireworks. Perhaps Vancouver, BC. I've always wanted to go there. It'll be nice and quiet. What do you think, Quinn?"

"Hold on, I think Max is trying to tell me something again." Quinn gets really still and then nods. "Max says go. Should we pack a bag?"

"No, let's find a hotel. We can check in, watch a movie or two, and then we'll come back home after most of the fireworks are done. What do you think, Monty?" Monty rubs my back gently, and I am grateful knowing I can count on him to help me when my friend needs assistance. I am sad we won't be able to do that yacht date though. "Was Nik okay with the abrupt change of plans?" I ask Monty.

"Yeah. He was bummed for like half a second but then decided to go party in downtown Portland. He'll be fine. He was disappointed that every time he tries to plan something with Rainbow, it gets delayed, but he knows that it couldn't be helped."

"Who is Nik? Are we dating? Is that a weird question?" Quinn asks.

"Nik is my best friend. He's a vampire too. He and Sky hit it off. Max and him are friends too. Eventually he'd like to get to know the whole System," Monty tells Quinn. "But he's fine—don't worry about him. Tonight the three of us will have our own fun, non-traditional celebration."

We spend a few minutes searching for a hotel, then looking at online maps and photos so Monty can teleport us there. As soon as he gets a handle on where he should land us, he holds our hands, and in moments, we are in Canada.

It is crazy to know we are in another country without paperwork. It's technically illegal, which kind of drives my Autistic side crazy, but I know I am going to have to get used to this aspect of vampire culture. If I become a vampire, I'll have to think about it as if I am adopting a new set of laws.

We end up finding a five-star hotel, Monty checks us in, and we head upstairs and look up comedies to watch, because after this day, comedy is very much needed. I am feeling so tired and my routine is out of whack, but I remind myself I was planning on staying up late tonight anyway. The room Monty rented is a suite, which is so over-the-top for the few hours we are planning on using it. Quinn and I order room service desserts and we all sit on the couch and laugh the night away while watching comedies from the 1990s and early 2000s.

A couple movies later, it is getting close to 2 a.m. I don't think Quinn slept much the night before and my eyelids droop as I yawn. Monty is able to do some sort of virtual checkout and we teleport straight from the room back to Quinn's apartment. I take a few minutes getting them settled in for the night, telling them to call me at all if anything happens. They say they are fine and thank us both for everything. It ends up being a really fun evening.

I look up at Monty and say, "Take me home. I'll figure out how to get my car another day and I'm sure there are drunk drivers out there."

Moments later, we are back in our bedroom. "I know it's the middle of the day for you, but will you stay in here with me for a bit as I fall asleep?" I ask him, and he replies with the "of course" that I knew he would.

After I get in my pajamas, I turn around to see him out of his clothes and in nothing but low-slung cotton pajama pants that show off the kind of muscle definition that really shouldn't be legal in pajama pants. I love how broad his shoulders are, perfect for wrapping me in tight hugs. He has a nicely sculpted chest, toned but not bulky. Enough so that when he moves you can see his muscles ripple under his smooth pale skin. His hair is out of his ponytail and he drags a hand through it so it falls framing his face. He looks sinfully edible and suddenly I am not as sleepy as I had been a few moments ago.

I walk over to him slowly, and he says with feigned curiosity, "I thought you were going to get in bed."

"As a matter of fact, I don't feel sleepy right at this moment. You look good enough to eat." I pull slightly back from my embrace and lick his nipple until it hardens. Then I do the other one, playfully biting and tugging at it too.

"Oh, really?" Then he continues, "You're going to bite me? I think it's the other way around, my dear." The shirt that I had just put on, he deftly pulls over my head and tosses to the ground. He then pulls down my pants and panties all at once, picks me up, and carries me over to the bed.

I playfully shriek at him, but am loving every moment of it. I lie back onto the pillows, my hair piled high on my head in a bun, fully naked in front of his hungry gaze. I am still sleepy, but consensual sleepy sex can be so delightful. He

284

pulls off his clothes and then crawls almost on top of me, keeping his weight on the mattress. He stops halfway up and suckles on my aching breasts, gently biting without his fangs, his fingers tugging at the other nipple. Then he moves towards my lips. I reach down between us to verify that, yes, indeed, he is just as turned on as I am. His lips meet mine as I stroke his hard cock between us. Our lips clash together until we are both moaning.

I turn my head to the side, exposing my neck. I need that rush that his bite gives me. Nothing else compares to it. He sees my need and moves his mouth over the pulsing vein in my neck, extends his fangs, and slides them in. There is no pain, just that pleasure that I've become addicted to. He feeds from me, and I am in another world. The only thing that exists for me is touch, pleasure, his mouth, his cock. Everything else melts away. He seals the wound when he's had his fill, and reaches a hand down between us and moves his fingers between my wet folds, making sure I am ready for him. Am I ever. When he slides a finger in, I almost don't feel it, but when he uses his thumb to rub my clit, I scream out, "Yes! Monty, now. I want you now!"

With his lips back on mine again, he moves into place and slides into my warmth with ease. He fills me up and I feel whole. We are one. We are meant to be together. He is my other half. Thrusting together, we bring each other to the brink of an orgasm. I nip the base of his neck as we go over the edge together. When we come back into our bodies, we are lightly panting and every muscle feels lax.

"Monty, my love, I think I'm going to sleep forever now," I say to him. He chuckles and gets up to bring my pajamas over to me. I get redressed, give him one more goodnight kiss, turn over, and fall into a deep slumber.

Chapter 34
To Turn or Not?

Montgomery

A couple weeks later, Katrina and I have fallen into a comfortable routine. She's now been living with me for about three weeks. The first week was all about unpacking her belongings and figuring out how to blend her stuff with mine. Then the Fourth of July happened—and while everything turned out okay, the night was full of surprises, especially with Quinn showing up. Katrina said it was the first time she'd seen Rainbow form a new alter. She's been in touch with them a lot since. Their latest therapy session went well, and eventually Max was able to front again, followed by the others. Looks like Quinn is sticking around. That's part of how DID works: when someone new shows up, they start figuring out how to fit into the system. According to Katrina, Quinn seems to be another protector. Max's role is physical—he's pulled forward when the system feels physically threatened. Quinn, though, is an emotional protector. They came forward during the emotional overload Rainbow felt after seeing their brother again. Now, Quinn carries that weight so Sky, Arleigh, and Jessie don't have to. It's how the brain fractures to protect itself.

As for Katrina and I, we are adjusting to living together. We cherish the moments we are awake at the same time. I love getting to know even more about her, and in particular to watch various rituals and routines she creates for herself. The hardest thing is our schedule. I don't get to spend nearly as much time with her as I like with me sleeping days and her sleeping nights, but we make it work. My VidVibe page is doing great, I'm getting close to 1.8 million followers. It still gives me something to do, along with the book I'm writing that I still never know if I'll publish. Thankfully I haven't heard another peep out of the vampire court, so I think that crazy experience is finally over with. Katrina's birthday is a couple weeks away. She's turning thirty, and I think it has her feeling all kinds of emotions. She doesn't want her body to keep growing older than mine. For my part, I know I'll love her no matter what she looks like. Of course, I want her to turn so we can enjoy many more years together, but I'd never pressure this life on anyone. I wasn't given the choice, and that haunts me to this day. I'm not saying I wouldn't choose it, I like being a vampire. But the fact the choice wasn't mine to make is something I'll never get over. These were all the thoughts I woke up with this evening. I lie in bed for a few more moments, listening to the house. I hear Katrina rummaging around in the kitchen, so I get up to join her.

"Hey Monty, did you sleep well?" she asks me as I walk in to see her making dinner. It is weird seeing my kitchen being used for real since she moved in—in a good way of course. I love her humanity, but want her to be a vampire too. Life is always so complicated. I have no idea why I woke up with such heavy thoughts today. I guess her upcoming birthday and its significance is in my head too.

I walk over to where she is stirring something on the stove and wrap my arms around her from the back. Her head fits perfectly under my chin. I give her a good squeeze, then step back. I know she can't get too distracted while cooking, or she'll burn everything. "I slept great, but woke up thinking about your birthday. Have you decided how you want to celebrate?"

She turns towards me, her cute little nose wrinkled up in a pout, and says, "Nope. I don't want to think about it." And then she turns back to her dish.

"What are you making? It smells terrific. I wish I could taste it."

"Chicken tortilla soup. It's my favorite. I'm so glad the vampire garlic thing is a myth. I love garlic. This is almost done. What do you want to do tonight?"

"You really don't want to talk about your birthday?" I ask.

She lets out a deep sigh. "Not really. You, Rainbow, and Nik are my only real friends. I have a couple friends I go to lunch with on occasion, but they aren't really people I want to spend my birthday with. And dear Mrs. Humphrey is sweet as can be, but again, not someone I want to socialize with outside of work. And since you and Nik can't eat, going to a restaurant is kinda lame."

"Did you forget I'm a vampire that can teleport us just about anywhere? You've got the entire world at your disposal, if you like." I walk behind her, wrap her in my arms, and smell her fiery red curls.

"You make it sound like you wouldn't take me to Paris anytime I asked," she teases as she turns around in my embrace to face me.

She has me there. There isn't much I wouldn't do for her. "True, true. But still. We could go to Mexico and you could get some authentic chicken tortilla soup. I'm sure we could find a place open after dark, and I wouldn't mind not eating, especially since I can have you for dessert," I add cheekily.

"While that is tempting, I'm not so sure. Do you speak Spanish?"

"Si, un poco—yes, a little bit. I have lived for 333 years, and I've picked up some of the major languages."

Katrina has scooped out her soup, added a dollop of sour cream, some cheese, and a few tortilla chips, and sits down at the bar. She takes a bite and closes her eyes. "Live for eternity, but never get to eat this again? Why the hard choices?" She sighs.

"Have you given more thought to turning?" I ask her. "The ceremony is only a few months away if you want to decide by this year. But again, I support whatever you want to do."

"I like the idea of freezing time at thirty. I'm Autistic— do you think I could be thirty-one for eternity? I think not. There is nothing good about the number thirty-one. And I know it doesn't matter in the grand scheme of things, but I just can't imagine being frozen at thirty-one."

"Is twenty-seven better? Just curious."

"Well at least two plus seven equals nine, and nine is a square number and square numbers are good," she says with confidence.

"If you say so, Kitty Kat. I'll just have to believe you. So is that it? Are we doing it? Are you going to turn for me in October? Become my bonded mate? I know it sounds archaic— we've modernized a lot, but I actually like it. You'll be mine." She takes her time answering me, finishing her soup, getting every single last bite out of the bowl.

She looks me in the eyes. Again, something she only occasionally does, and says, "Yes, Montgomery, I will turn. I will bond with you for all eternity." Then she sassily gets up from her stool like she didn't just say the sexiest, most amazing thing I've ever heard in my entire life, and takes her bowl to the sink. "But for now, I'll race you to the game room for a *Mario Kart* tournament!" And then she takes off down the hall.

"We've *got* to teach you more games, Kitty Kat." I let her lighten the mood. She probably needs time to process what she's said to me. But I want to scream with joy and celebrate somehow.

We load up the game and I let her have Yoshi without argument and pick Mario so I won't trip her up. She knows what I am doing though. "You can't go easy on me just because I said I'd be your woman for all of time, Monty, that's gross. Treat me equal, or else."

"Okay so you want me to be Luigi?" I ask her.

"Absolutely not! You know the rules. I'm Yoshi and you are not Luigi."

"But that's what I did!" I exclaim.

"Yeah, but only because you're giddy with happiness and love. In *Mario Kart*, we fight to the death!" And while I'm not looking, she starts the race and takes off. Oh my god, I love this woman.

As we finish the race, I ask her how her latest crochet project is going.

"I know you're trying to distract me because you can't win otherwise, but I can multitask," she says as she tosses a red shell at me. "It's almost finished."

"Are you still not going to tell me what it is?" She's been working on it while I've been asleep and told me not to look because it was a surprise. She'd already given me the Yoshi she made as a move-in gift. It is sitting in a prominent place on my bookshelf and it brings a smile to my face every time it catches my eye.

"I'm almost done with it. I'll tell you what it is if you win the next race," she challenges me, voice brimming with laughter. I love that I fill her with that much happiness.

We play another race, and this time I do take Luigi so I'll have a chance. She's not a gamer, but with this game, she is an expert. I beat her by milliseconds. "You made me work for that," I tell her, "but 'fess up! What project are you working on? A Mario to go with the Yoshi?"

"Nope, and you cheated."

"I did not cheat. How do you cheat at *Mario Kart*?"

"You took Luigi."

"That's not cheating."

"Fine. Hurumph. I'm just teasing anyway. Well, sort of—house rules and all." She looks over at me with a smile and sets her controller down. Good, maybe she is done, I'm not sure I have another game in me. "I'm making a crochet little vampire! He's so cute. You're going to love him."

"Does he look like me?" I ask.

"I mean, he's a cartoon, but I gave him your hair color and eye color, of course."

"I can't wait to see him." I lean back on the couch and she leans back into me. Data comes into the room and sees that as a perfect opportunity to join in on the cuddles too. "This reminds me of our first bowling date. Remember? We ended up here on this couch."

"Yep. It was a good night," she says, her voice softer, almost hesitant. Then, like she caught herself showing too much, she brightens. "So! How is your channel going? I've been so busy, I actually haven't watched your last couple of VidVibes."

I raise an eyebrow, catching the pivot, but let it slide. "What? My biggest fan has skipped some of my content? I think my ego has a bruise!"

"Actually, I was wondering if you'd be interested in coming on as my girlfriend. Would you be interested in doing a video with me? Or a Live. I haven't been doing as many of them since we started dating. We could link your account—or not, depending on whether you'd want that."

"Hum," she says as she rubs her hands up and down my arms, always moving, always fidgeting, my girl. "That could be interesting. I'm sure your fans would either love me or hate that you have a girlfriend. I don't think I'd want to mention my name—we can come up with an alias. I don't want people following my account who aren't into crochet and are there just because of you. It's getting late tonight though, and I need to shower and then head to bed. Why don't you do a VidVibe mentioning it is upcoming? We'll talk out a plan. This will be fun!"

We spend a couple more hours together in the game room. Katrina texting with Rainbow and watching VidVibes and I spend some time working on my book. I wrap up a chapter and go sit back on the couch near her. She turns around to face me, nuzzling in like the kitty I often call her. I wrap my arms around her in a big hug and nestle my nose in her hair, inhaling the minty scent of her shampoo. We exchange a long, lingering goodnight kiss and she bounds off down the hall to get ready for bed. I will film a VidVibe video once she's asleep, but I'm feeling lazy tonight and will just glamor instead of actually change. I feel more in character when I actually put on my costumes, but I'm glad I have the option to use my glamor too, because even vampires can feel lazy.

I turn on the fireplace in my vampire den and set my phone up on my tripod. I set my glamor, just by thinking about it. Fangs out, eyeliner on. I do pull my hair down. It's a bit messy today but that just adds to the look, I think. I make my Spiderman shirt appear as a silky black shirt, laughing to myself as I wonder what my fans would think if they could see it. I add a choker to my glamor and keep it simple otherwise. I sit in my chair with my legs spread in that masculine way, lean back, and begin my video.

"Many of you have been asking to meet my soulmate, and so I wanted to share with you that in either an upcoming video or perhaps a Live, she'll be on, so you all have that to look forward to. She's very excited to meet you.

Today, I'm going to bring you to a bit of a more modern time. I had made my way out to Hollywood—it was 1952. I was looking for some excitement. As many of you know, I've always loved the forward progress of technology and in the 1950s, TVs were starting to become more widely available. There wasn't much programming on, but one type of show available was cartoons. I'm not the most amazing artist, but a lot of animation work relies on just copying other people's work using transparent sheets of celluloid and just changing one small aspect of the drawing.

Other jobs included the tedious task of moving an image frame-by-frame and taking photos of it in these big frames that would help line up the artwork. We'd move a drawing by a fraction of an inch and take the photo. We'd take twenty-four individual photos for one second of video. As you can imagine, this took many hours of work, so I was on the night shift, working quietly through the night to help the early animators. The studio I worked for was the Walter Lanz Productions studio and I was involved with the early

Woody Woodpecker animations. Old Woody was one of the first televised cartoons.

None of my coworkers had any idea I was a vampire—we are really good at blending in. The majority of us live in and around humans peacefully, just doing our own thing. So if you ever work a night shift and your coworker never seems to eat around you, maybe they are a vampire! Most likely not. We are pretty rare, but just maybe . . . Until the moon rises again, my nocturnal friends. Fangs out—see you in the shadows."

I hope my history buff fans like that one. Being part of early TV was pretty cool, actually. I turn off the electric fireplace and call Nik to see if he is available to play *World of Warcraft.*

Chapter 35
Shutdown

Katrina

Two nights after I told Monty that I'd do a video with him, I am standing in my closet trying to figure out what to wear. Quinn is looking through my clothes with a bit of a curled nose and they say exactly what I've been thinking, "Katrina, none of this is giving off 'vampire's girlfriend' cosplay."

"I know. I figure Monty's fans will think I'm a sexy vixen or something, and I don't really think of myself that way. I could pull it off with my long curly red hair, with the right makeup though, but what to wear? Monty's just blinded by love. He literally said he didn't care if I showed up wearing a potato sack. And while I appreciate the sentiment, I need more theatrical direction than that. He plays a part—I want to play the part too!"

"What if you wear this black bra, black tank top, and one of Monty's chokers. Hum . . . you don't have black jeans, do you?" I shake my head and they continue, "Wear black leggings. You'll probably just film from the waist up. I'll do your hair in some braids. I brought Sky's makeup. She's got some vibrant red lipstick, and we can do your eyes with green eyeshadow and smokey black eyeliner. I think it'll do." We spend the next few minutes getting me somewhat dressed in the best vampire costume on short notice. His audience knows I'm not a vampire, but still, I think they'll be expecting a certain look. I peer into the mirror and am quite impressed.

"I've got these emerald green earrings too." I show Quinn and get a nod of approval. "I think this look will work! Thank you so much, Quinn! I really appreciate it. Monty should be waking up soon, and then we'll be getting ready to go Live. I'm so nervous! We've got a short session planned, just twenty to thirty minutes, but I think his fans will be happy. They've been wanting to 'meet,'" I said in air quotes, "Monty's girlfriend. I hope they approve! And if they don't, oh well." I give Quinn a hug around the neck and then see them out the front door. I go back into the bedroom just as Monty opens the curtain around the bed. He catches sight of me in my dark sexy makeup and his eyes immediately go feral. I think my man likes a little dress-up!

"You like what you see, Sunshine?"

"I sure do. Come over here—you look good enough to eat and I need a snack." His low, sexy, sleepy voice has me scurrying towards him.

"Don't mess up my makeup—Quinn did it!" I say to him, and stand between his thighs as he sits on the edge of the bed. He pulls me into a hug and then starts kissing my neck and the tops of my breasts that I had pushed up in my bra to a point where they are almost spilling out. His tongue traces circles across my flesh as I lean my head back in pleasure. He takes advantage of that and starts suckling on my neck. I feel his fangs descend and he whispers, "May I have a little snack, Kitty Kat?"

"Mmm, humm. Yessss!" I moan. He sinks his teeth into me and puts his hands on my rear to bring me close to his body. Familiar waves of pleasure wash over my body. Then he licks the wound closed and slowly runs his tongue over his lips. I want to kiss him so badly but I am not going to mess this makeup up until after our Live.

"Well, with that, are you ready to get dressed so we can do our live video?" I ask. "I'm so nervous!"

"I want more. Screw the Live—let's just make love," he says with an adorable pout.

"Uh, no, I psyched myself up for this. We aren't going to leave your fans disappointed. Let's do this, and then we can have our own fun." I take his hand and lead him through the ensuite bathroom, past the vanity and into the walk-in closet. Data must have been sleeping with him, because he peeks out from behind the bed curtain and follows us to see what all the fuss is about. "Oh, maybe Data can make an appearance, but we'll have to give him an alias too. 'Data' doesn't sound very vampire-y. Speaking of which, what should my alias be? Let me think about it while we're getting ready." I pick Data up and sit on a stool in the closet while I watch Monty pick out clothes.

Monty finishes getting dressed and then we head to the vampire den. There's only the one chair, so we discuss what would make for the best camera angles. "How about we get the fur rug from the living room and put it in front of the fireplace and sit on the floor together on the rug?" I suggest. "I think that would be a cool vibe, don't you?"

"It is August. Won't you get too hot?"

"We can sit far enough away, and we're only going for half an hour at most, right? It should be fine." He agrees and grabs the rug as I set the tripod up to frame the best shot. "Okay, names . . . Scarlett? What do you think? Data can be Stormy. Simple and sweet and not geeky."

"Sounds good to me. Although, I think Data took off towards the game room. I doubt he'll join us. But if he does I'll call him Stormy, and I'll introduce you as Scarlett."

"ACCCCKKKKKK!" I let out a nervous squeal.

"You alright? You don't have to do this if you don't want to," he reminds me, his voice steady, supportive and calm.

"No, I do. I'm excited and I'm happy you want to introduce me to your fans. It really means a lot. We can even play up that you're going to turn me, and all that. I don't want to come on all the time, but I think it'd be fun to join you on occasion. Let's see how tonight goes."

We settle on the rug in front of the fire and Monty reaches over to turn on the camera.

Montgomery

"Let's get this Live started! I'm sorry I haven't been doing Lives as much lately, but I think you all will agree I've had a very good reason. So in my last couple of videos I've mentioned that after three hundred plus years, I've found my soulmate. We met just a few months ago. I'm elated that Scarlett has become part of my life, and I think she feels the same."

The comments are already starting to pour in.

@CatDragon839 - Do you drink her blood?
@Starry_Poe - I want to meet you Monty! Are you doing any meet and greets?

@user876284160 - You're such a freak! Get a life!

@user4938751098 - Hey Monty! Scarlett is so pretty! Where did you two meet?

@MinxMinx22 - How old is Scarlett? Is she going to become a vampire? Or is she already a vampire?

@TheGrassIsGreener - I want to be your girlfriend Monty! Can you make me a vampire?

It is a mix of the usual: some nice questions, some fangirls, the angry person who doesn't know how to have fun. They are coming in so fast, it is hard to read them. I glance over at Katrina and she isn't looking too good. "Do you want to tell everyone how we met?" She rocks back and forth ever so slightly, fingers clenched in the fur rug, her breathing extremely shallow. My vampire hearing picks up her pulse beating at a very fast rate, and her pupils are dilated. She stares at the ground as she twirls her rings. Something is not right. I focus back up towards the camera and say, *"Hey everyone, it looks like we need to end this transmission. I don't think Scarlett is feeling well. We'll be back on later if we can and if not, until the next time, good evening."*

I switch off the camera and turn to Katrina, who is rocking even more now the camera is off. Tears begin to roll down her face. "Kitty Kat, what's wrong? Are you okay?" She just hugs her knees to her chest and buries her face into her knees. Her arms are wrapped around her legs and she's made herself as small a ball as she can. She still hasn't said a word. I'm at a loss. I want to help her but I don't know what to do. I tentatively reach out to touch her, but she flinches away. Not knowing what else to do, I get up and bring her a blanket and fetch Data. Data starts to rub against her legs, purring. But Katrina ignores him too.

I step into the living room and dial Rainbow's number—maybe they will be able to help.

"Hello?" they answer. I've never called them before and I don't know if they even have my phone number.

"Hey Rainbow? This is Monty. I need some help."

"This is Max—what is going on? Is Katrina okay? Did you hurt her?"

"No, no, I didn't hurt her! Why would you think that? I think she's okay, but I don't know what happened. We decided to do a VidVibe Live on my account together. She was laughing and having fun getting dressed. Didn't Quinn tell you that part? They were over earlier helping her." I still don't understand DID and when the different alters possess awareness and when they don't.

"No, I was deep innerworld until a few minutes ago. I don't remember earlier this evening. Sorry, I know you wouldn't hurt her. I am just protective of her. It's in my nature. So you were doing a Live? What happened?

"As soon as the camera turned on, I started talking, people started leaving comments, and when I looked down at her, she had gotten very withdrawn. Her pulse was racing and she started rocking. I ended the Live. Now she's in a little ball, still rocking back and forth, and crying. She won't talk to me and she's also ignoring Data."

"She's having an Autistic shutdown. She got overwhelmed and her nervous system took over. Sometimes that affects speech too. It's not that she won't talk to you—it's that she *can't* talk to you right now." Max starts to explain to me.

"Oh, like when my computer starts to process too fast because I've given it too many commands at once? It'll slow way down, until the processors can catch back up." I ask, thinking I get what Max is saying.

"Yes, it's very much like that. Just sit with her, and only touch her if she indicates it's okay. When she seems like she's starting to listen to you, try to get her to do a few deep breaths. The rocking is good—it'll help regulate her too. She'll probably feel really tired afterwards and just need some quiet recovery time once the biggest stress passes. Just sit near her and follow her lead."

"Okay, thanks man. I appreciate it." I tell Max goodbye and hang up the phone before walking back into the den and sitting on the floor a couple feet away from Katrina. I set a tissue box next to her. "Hey baby, I just got off the phone with Max. He told me you were having a shutdown. That's okay. Take your time. I'm here for you." It is heart-wrenching to see her suffering and not be able to hold her. But after a few minutes of quiet, except for her crying, she looks up at me and reaches out a hand. I quickly go over to her, and she curls up in my lap. I hug her tight and rock both of us together. I rub her back firmly and massage her nape. Her entire body lets out a huge shudder of release, and she takes in a gasping breath.

"I'm so, so sorry Monty," she says in a small shaky voice. "I didn't know that would be so hard."

"It's okay, baby. It's okay. I love you. It's not a big deal at all. It was just something to do for fun. If it's not fun, we won't do it." I smooth down her hair as I talk.

"I ruined Quinn's makeup job," she says.

My heart swells to protect her, she looks so lost and I want to smooth all her frets away. "That's nothing to be worried about. Do you want to talk about it?" I ask gently.

"I just got overwhelmed out of nowhere. I was fine, but when I saw the comments scrolling so fast I could hardly read them, my brain just couldn't process everything. We'd only been on for not even two minutes and I couldn't keep up. How do you do that? And then when I wanted to say something, I couldn't get my voice to work, and when I realized so many people were watching me, that made me more flustered , so I tried harder to talk, but that of course made it worse. I'm so embarrassed! Your fans are going to think I'm dumb."

"Who cares what they think? I know how amazing you are. I bet anyone who thinks you're dumb would also struggle doing a VidVibe Live with half the people we had. It can be overwhelming. I miss most of the questions and don't worry about it. When I'm ready to read one, I do, but I probably don't even see the majority of them. People know that their question may not be answered. I bet you thought the same thing when you talked to me the first time, right? Did you expect me to answer it?"

"No, I guess not. It just feels so different when you're on the other side of the camera."

"It really does. Now what do you want to do? We don't have to go back on VidVibe. I can post a Story later and explain however you want. And if I don't say anything at all, it's not anyone's business. Just however you want to handle it."

"I don't hide my Autism, but also sometimes it's just frustrating that I can't do anything without having to explain I act the way I do because I'm Autistic. I don't want to have a neurotypical brain. I love my Autistic brain, even when I struggle like this, but it's exhausting having to explain it to other people all the time."

"Do you want to disclose your Autism? You can just say you got overwhelmed. It's up to you. Or like I said, I can just post a Story and say, 'Apologies the Live got cut short tonight. I'll be back soon with more content' and leave it at that. No one is entitled to your response."

"Let's just film a short video together and post it. Just introduce me as your girlfriend or soulmate, as you love to call it, and be vague. I'll say I work a job with my local city and that I enjoy fiber arts and animals. I think part of my problem was we didn't exactly prepare what kinds of responses I was going to give. I don't know why I thought I could just wing it. I never wing anything! I'll go touch up my makeup and be right back." Then apparently rejuvenated, she takes off, leaving me alone with Data, who is now sitting in my chair licking his tail.

"Thanks for the assistance tonight, Data. I think you helped her feel calm." He looks over at me with what I'm going to pretend is approval and goes back to his licking. A few minutes later, Katrina returns, her makeup flawless, and says she is ready to try again, just not Live this time. We spend a few minutes creating a video together and end up having a good time. I give her a kiss on camera, knowing that will make my viewers jealous—or cheer me on. We end up having a really good time. I save it to the drafts and tell her I'll post it after she goes to bed tonight. She says the shutdown plus filming wore her out and she wants to go to bed early anyway.

Under the canopied bed, with the twinkle lights casting a warm, soft glow, I start editing while she showers and changes into pajamas. When she climbs in beside me, I run my fingers through her hair until she falls asleep. I'm learning more about her every day, and I'm so thankful she feels safe enough to be fully herself with me. I slip out quietly and head to the game room to finish uploading the video.

Chapter 36
Birthday Shopping

Katrina

I haven't had another shutdown or meltdown since a few nights ago when Monty and I tried to go Live on VidVibe. I am still residually embarrassed—even disabled people struggle with internalized ableism on occasion—but the video we uploaded afterwards got amazing views for him and everyone seemed to not be weirded out that I was Autistic, which I did end up saying in the video. It's nice to feel supported. Of course there were the mean trolls too, but unfortunately that's to be expected. Overall, I am feeling good, Monty is happy, and things are back to normal.

My birthday is only a couple of days away and I still haven't figured out what I want to do. Everyone wants to celebrate me, and if it is going to be my last "official" human birthday, I do kind of want to do something to mark its existence. I spend some time thinking about what kinds of activities we could do that would be fun as a group and which wouldn't involve eating. Then I have it! A musical. I could get dressed up, which I do like to do on occasion. At my next break at work, I log on to one of the computers and look up what musicals are going on in Portland. *The Phantom of the Opera* is playing and that gets me excited, as it's one of my all-time favorite musicals. I feel as if this was meant to be. Now hopefully everyone else thinks it's a good idea and we can get seats together!

I send Rainbow a text in ChatBox. This is one of the benefits of being friends with a System—surely someone in the System will like musicals as much as I do. I wonder if Quinn would enjoy going. They are still getting a feel for who they are as a person. It's such an interesting experience to be created as an adult but only partially formed as far as memories and preferences go. They are learning what they like and don't like at a quick rate and seem to be integrating well with the other alters. I also ask Sky if she wants to go shopping with me, because I want to buy a formal outfit for the evening.

I know Monty would totally be on board, but am not as sure about Nik, so I send him a text message too. Now that I have a good plan, I can't wait to get home to talk to Monty. The clock on the wall mocks me when I glance up at it and notice my break is over but I still have a little over two hours left of work. Too antsy to sit behind a desk, I go check if any books are ready to be re-shelved. The minutes tick by until it is finally time to go home.

On the way home, I stop at Sushi Ninja, my favorite sushi restaurant, to get a to-go order. I've started looking forward to turning into a vampire, but the food part is something I'm struggling with. I'll be starting a new and very different life, but every meal feels like my last. Will this be my last time eating sushi? Nothing is ever guaranteed in life, but with October drawing closer and closer, every meal feels special and as if it needs to be burned into my memory. The same with sunshine. At work on nice sunny days, I've been taking most of my breaks in the courtyard so I can spend as much time in the sun as possible.

I practically skip in the door, hoping Monty is awake. The sun is still up, but he's fine as long as he's not standing directly in a window. "Monty, are you up?" I call as I walk in. I hang my purse on the hook by the door and set my sushi on the kitchen counter before practically skipping down the hall towards the game room, knowing that's where he'll be if he is up. Sure enough, there he is, sitting at his computer wearing loose jeans and a maroon shirt with an emoji smile with fangs. Cute. "I like your shirt," I say. He is now facing towards me, and I launch myself into his lap and give him a big kiss. "Sleep well?"

"Yep. Just woke up a few minutes ago and was catching up on social media stuff. You look excited about something."

"Yeah, come sit with me in the kitchen while I eat and I'll tell you my exciting plan." Then I take back off towards the kitchen, knowing he'll follow me.

"Sushi is another food I've never had. I don't think many people were eating raw fish in seventeenth-century England," he says with a smirk. "I can't imagine it tasting good at all."

"It's so good. I'm definitely going to miss it. Actually, maybe I should just stay human forever so I never have to give up sushi," I tease.

His eyes narrow and then his lips turn down in a pout. "You'd pick some stinky raw fish over me? I think I'm offended."

"That's just because you've never had it," I say. "Let me tell you my idea!" But before I give him a chance to reply, I say, "I figured out what I want to do for my thirtieth birthday."

"Oh really? I was beginning to wonder if we were going to celebrate at all. What's your idea? Morocco? Paris? Tokyo for fresh sushi?"

"All very good ideas, but I didn't want to do anything centered around food since you can't eat. It's not fair if everyone can't participate. I want to go to a musical! We can get all dressed up and it'll be fun. *Phantom of the Opera* is playing in Portland. Now the issue is whether or not we can get four seats together."

"No worries on that. I'll make some calls. The theater should still be open, so I'll go do that right now. I think this is an excellent idea!"

He heads to the other room to make the call, just as my phone rings and Rainbow's name fills the screen. I pop my last piece of sushi into my mouth and answer, "Hwwerrwo!"

"Hi? Katrina? Is that you?" It's Sky's voice.

I swallow my bite and say, "Yes, sorry, was just finishing up my dinner. Did you get my message from earlier?"

"Yes, I'm so excited!"

"You want to go to the musical?" My eyes widen. I really figured it'd be Jessie, possibly Arleigh, or maybe Quinn who would wind up coming along.

"Ew, no. I do not like musicals. But I want to take you shopping! Can you go now? The mall is still open. We don't have much time to find the perfect dress, if you are trying to get tickets for this weekend."

I glance down at what I'm wearing. Leggings, a belted tunic, comfy shoes. I could probably go to the mall like this. "Plot twist, huh. You know I hate last-minute plans, but I think you're right. Sigh. Have you eaten? I can pick you up since you're on the way to the mall. Monty's on the phone calling for tickets now. He seems confident we can get some. Hopefully Nik will be able to come too."

"Nik's going?" Sky asks with interest. "Maybe I *will* go to the musical . . ."

"I think one of the other alters would enjoy it more. You should do something else with Nik that you'd actually like. Although, of course I'd love to spend time with you on my birthday, but I also wouldn't want you to be bored." I say as I twist a curl through my fingers, absentmindedly.

"Ug, true story. I would be totes bored. But shopping? Heck yeah! I have already eaten. Come pick me up. I'll wait outside for you so we can leave immediately." Her line clicks to silence before either of us says a formal goodbye.

I clean up my trash and go to tell Monty my new plan. He is hanging up the phone too.

"Four seats, middle, about four rows back. Sound good?" he asks me with a smile that lights up the room.

"How did you do that?"

"Let a man have his secrets, okay?"

"Sure, whatever. I'm just happy you got them. I'm heading out. Sky wants to take me to the mall to pick out an outfit for the evening. Letting her 'dress' me for the evening is kind of my gift to her. It's one of her absolute favorite things to do. I was looking forward to staying in with you tonight. I was hoping we could go swimming. But the musical is a few days away, so shopping it is! Can you try calling Nik to make sure he's on board? I left him a message earlier." I stand on my tiptoes to try to kiss Monty without him having to bend over, but I'm still too short. He laughs, picks me up, and kisses me hard. His fangs start to descend, and I whisper, "Save that for later, Fangs." The returning growl makes me smile, and I jump out of his arms, start toward the door but turn back one last time to blow him a kiss with a wink. He reaches up to pretend to grab my kiss, and then he tucks it into his pocket. *Seriously? He is such a keeper.*

308

Sky and I enter the Vancouver Mall, and I immediately put in my noise-dampening earplugs. I enjoy shopping, but the loud noises, conflicting smells, and bright lights can be a lot for my senses to handle. Ear protection helps, at least a little. Thankfully, this isn't a huge mall, and it's not too crowded tonight. With limited time and limited stores here, I'm hoping we'll get lucky. There is a formal wear store, but I was hoping I'd find something nice to wear at Macy's. Sky knows the mall like the back of her hand and takes me straight to the formal section in Macy's. I definitely think she is having more fun than I am, but that's okay by me. Surprisingly, they actually have several formal dresses and she leads me straight to a ball gown first.

"No, Sky. This is way too fancy. I want to dress up, but a ball gown is not practical for a musical. We need to rein it in a little bit!" But she isn't having any of it, and she pulls an emerald green dress off the rack and holds it up to me.

"Katrina, this goes perfectly with your red hair!" she says.

"Sky, it makes me look like Merida. And while I love Merida, I'm not going to a character ball." It *is* a gorgeous dress. Some sort of silky material, off-the-shoulder, princess waist with a big poofy skirt that would need a petticoat. This dress is for an actual ball, not for sitting in a musical. She puts it back on the rack and we keep looking. Sky is wearing her hair in two tiny buns on the top of her head—her short hair isn't really conducive to full buns like I know she probably wants. She is wearing a faux nose ring, bright blue eyeshadow and little star stickers above her eyebrows. She's paired a black tank top and a shirt that looks as if it's been through a paper shredder with a pleated black skirt that features two silver buckles on the side, and big chunky black boots. She is embracing a very gothic vibe today and the juxtaposition of her gothic outfit and these fancy dresses is pretty funny.

In a whirlwind, she pulls off a slinky sapphire blue evening gown, a classic little black dress, and a nude dress with black lace details off the racks and then directs me towards the changing rooms. I am worried the blue gown is still too fancy, but it is absolutely gorgeous. I put it on first because the color is stunning. When I emerge to model it for Sky, she snaps photos of me to send to Monty.

"Don't do that!" I protest. "We aren't sure which dress I'm going to buy yet! What do you think of this one?" It is very pretty, but I think it's still too fancy. It has one thick strap across my left shoulder, leaving the right shoulder bare. It sheaths down, forming to my body, with a thigh-high split on the left side—elegant and simple.

"It is stunning on you, Katrina. You could wear your hair in a soft braid over your right shoulder. But I agree, maybe too fancy. Perhaps for an opera. Try the black one next!"

I try on the black dress, which is just your basic black safe-bet dress. It isn't anything special but it is a contender if we can't find anything else. It was the type of dress where you let the accessories shine. I like it, but I am eager to try on the nude dress. On the hanger it doesn't look that special, but when I put it on, I know it's the one. It is elegant without looking too out-of-place for a musical. The dress features a deep V neckline and a full A-line skirt that stops just above the ankles. A layer of fine black lace lies over the nude material and makes the dress shimmer in a luxurious way. There is a thick black band at the waist, cinching in the middle, and the top is black floral lace that forms a bodice, with some of the floral pattern flowing down the skirt too. The dress has long sleeves that are made entirely out of the black lace. The garment makes my hair look stunning—I know I'll have to wear it down and flowing, maybe pulling up two side pieces into a twist in the back and perhaps pairing it with nude flat ballet slippers, because I never wear heels, as they are a sensory "no" for me. A black ring and a simple necklace is all the dress needs. I take one last look in the mirror in my small dressing room and then step out to show Sky.

Her jaw drops open and she says, "Well, looks like we found the dress." I perform a little twirl for her and we both grin. For me, it is such a weird feeling to shop without even looking at the price tag, but I know Monty would want me to have this no matter how much it costs.

"Do you know if Jessie or Max plans on coming to the musical? I ask because do y'all have a dress or suit to wear?"

"I think Jessie really wants to go," Sky says. "Maybe I should try on the black dress for her. I think she'd like it."

"Yes, do that and I'll buy it—my treat!" I tell her as I hang the dress back up in the dressing room so that Sky can try it on.

She comes out and does her own twirl. "Well, it's not my style at all—does not show enough boob—but I think Jessie will like it. And if Max does end up going, he's got some nice slacks, a button-down, and a tie he can wear. I'm not sure what Quinn's style is yet, but I'm sure if they end up going, they can figure something out from our closet."

"Okay, change back into your clothes and let's go check out."

We take the two dresses up to the register to pay and then hit the boba tea place on the way out of the mall.

Back in my car I say, "Thanks for shopping with me, Sky. This really meant a lot to me. So, have you and Nik actually gone on a date together yet?"

"No, we've been texting a lot though. But our timing has been off. That's okay—he's been busy and I've been busy. If it works, it'll work out, but if not, that's okay too," she says with a maturity that is good to see. I drop her off at her apartment and then head back home to Monty.

Chapter 37
Turning Thirty

Montgomery

Late Saturday afternoon, I wake up early so we can get ready for the musical. The tickets have been purchased, Nik finally got back to me and said he was interested in going, Rainbow decided that Jessie wanted to go see the musical the most, but Max is going to try to co-front because he also wants to see it, and Katrina is super excited. I know she is off work today and has planned to spend most of her birthday relaxing and working on her latest crochet project. She's finished her vampire, which she did not give to me, much to my chagrin, because he did look like a little cartoon of me and I thought that was pretty fun. She kept it for herself, something she doesn't do very often.

I dress in dark gray slacks, a black button-down dress shirt, a rose gold tie, and a black coat. It is very sleek, if I do say so myself.

I enter the living room just as Nik teleports in. He's wearing a navy suit and a silver bow tie. Nik and I have just settled on the couches and started talking about some new downloadable content for some of our favorite games when Katrina comes into the room looking like an absolute goddess. The nude dress with black lace fits her to perfection. Her curly red hair looks to be styled in a half-up, half-down hairdo that compliments the cut of her dress. As she comes into the room and does a little twirl, the skirt flows around her. She looks elegant and extremely kissable. I stand and pull her into a hug. "You look stunning, Kitty Kat. Happy Birthday!" I ask Nik to take our picture in front of the fireplace, which he does. I'll post some of these to my VidVibe stories later. "Are we ready to go pick up Jessie and then head to the musical?" I ask everyone.

"Yep, Jessie texted me just as I was finishing my hair. She's ready and excited too!" Katrina announces.

Several hours later, we are all back in the car to drive back to Vancouver from the Keller Auditorium in Portland. The energy in the car is full of excitement.

I reach over and squeeze Katrina's hand and say, "That was a performance to remember! That was such a good idea, Kitty Kat. I hope you had a great birthday celebration."

"I can't believe you managed to get us backstage passes to greet the performers in such a short time. That was such an unexpected surprise!" She turns towards the backseat and asks, "What did you think of the show, Jessie?"

"The Phantom was so alluring, and his story was tragic. The actors were incredibly talented. I was a little starstruck to meet Christine. She was an amazing performer." Jessie says. Her head is leaned back on the headrest and her eyes are closed, like she's taking in the performance all over again.

"I think Christine should have gone with the Phantom over Raoul. The dark, mysterious man should have won!" Monty says as he drives.

"Of course you'd say that," Katrina says with a laugh. "Being a mysterious man yourself. No worries, dear, I pick you. You also aren't manipulative like the Phantom. He tries

314

to deceive her, isolate her from her friends, manipulate her emotions, and even endangers innocent people."

From the back seat next to Jessie, Nik says, "Do you see the Phantom more as an anti-hero or a tragic villain?"

"I think he's an anti-hero," Jessie says. "He does evoke a lot of sympathy with his story, and his actions are driven by love and acceptance, even if it was expressed in misguided and dangerous ways."

"I can see that," Nik agrees.

"Thank you so much, Monty. It was an amazing birthday. My last birthday as a human. Isn't that crazy?" Katrina says. She'd told Rainbow a few days ago about her decision, and everyone in the System, including Max, was supportive. I know that means a lot to her. If they hadn't been supportive of her decision to turn into a vampire, I'm not sure she'd have chosen to go through with it.

"It's going to be so weird," Jessie says. "Like, I know you'll still be my friend, but it also seems as if, somehow, you'll be different."

"It'll take some getting used to, that's for sure," Katrina says. "But we'll always be friends. I promise."

"I know that." Jessie reaches up between the seats and squeezes Katrina's hand.

Watching the two friends, a thought forms and I decide I need to find a way for Jessie or someone in Rainbow System to attend the turning. It's not something that is typically done, but it has been done before and so I bet I could get permission. I'll have to see what I can find out. It's mid-August now—only two and a half more months until the ceremony. I think it would mean a lot to Katrina to have her friend there with her.

A few minutes later, we drop Jessie off. Nik walks her to the door and gives her a hug goodnight. I'm really curious to see if that ends up going anywhere. Nik seems to really like all the alters in the System, and I wouldn't mind having Rainbow as a future sister-in-law. I mean, Nik isn't my real brother, but he's my brother in all meaningful ways.

Nik climbs back in the car and we drive off. "That was such a fun evening," he says. "I've now gone on two double dates with the System: Sky and Jessie. The best part is that they are so different and yet, it just makes sense that they also belong together. I'm a lucky dude if I can keep dating them."

"As long as you don't hurt them. You better be honest with all of them, okay? You hurt Rainbow and you'll answer to me!" My sweet little Katrina standing up to a very powerful vampire is a sight to see!

"I wouldn't. I promise!" Nik says. "Yo, well, I think I'm gonna go ahead and teleport home now. I'm going to get out of this monkey suit and head to the bar for a late shift. Thanks for the ticket, Monty. I had a great time tonight. Happy Birthday again, Katrina. I'm glad I got to celebrate with you." And with that, he teleports out of the car and I have Katrina all to myself.

"What did you think of the evening as a whole?" Katrina asks as we approach home.

"I think it was a very fun evening and now that I know you like musicals, I think it's something we'll have to do more often."

"I wouldn't mind that at all!" she says, beaming.

Chapter 38
Hard Goodbyes

<hr>

Katrina

It's now been a little over a month since my birthday and it is drawing towards the end of September. There is just over a month until the ceremony that will turn me from human to vampire permanently. Anytime I think about it too much, I start to have a panic attack, but also, I know it's what I want to do. Things we want to do in life can be just as scary and hard as things we don't want to do. Honestly, if I wasn't scared, there would probably be something wrong with me.

There is so much to do beforehand. I had put in my two weeks' notice at the library. That was a very hard task and it was accomplished with both sad and happy tears. Mrs. Humphrey was happy for me. I told her I was getting married in Italy—otherwise she'd have wanted an invitation to the wedding. Monty and I are going to have a human exchange of marriage vows along with the Vampire Ceremony.

I spent time looking up different jobs and decided I was going to be a freelance researcher. I learned that a lot of authors will hire researchers to help them work on various projects. Historical researchers, fact-checkers, general content, and more. I can work remotely and set my own hours. After I become a vampire and can teleport, I'll also have really great access to a lot of research facilities after hours. I mean, just saying, it's good to use the resources available to us, right? One thing Monty told me is that while vampires live among humans and follow most of their laws, they have their own code of ethics. I'm sure it'll take some time to adjust to thinking differently but once I am turned, I won't be human. I'll need to adapt to my new species ethics and laws.

Today is my last day of work at the library. Monty stayed up late to see me off, knowing it was going to be a hard day. I had put on my favorite library dress, which features books printed all over the fabric. I couldn't eat breakfast this morning, but Monty tucked one of my favorite bagels into my bag in case I got hungry later.

"It's so hard to have two conflicting emotions at once, Monty." I lean into him, not wanting to let go. "I'm very much looking forward to starting a life with you, but I'm also very sad to leave my job at the library, my co-workers, the kids who call me Misses Librarian Ma'am, and of course, Mrs. Humphrey. She's been more than a boss—she's been a mentor to me for so many years."

"I know, baby. I wish I could make this part easier for you. I don't like to see you upset." Monty rubs my back to soothe me.

"Well, I better get going. I don't want to be late for my last day." My thoughts drift to after work plans and I remind Monty, "Rainbow is coming over this evening. Is Nik still coming? I think I want to have plans so when I get home I have something to distract myself for a bit."

"Yep, Nik said he'd pop over when he wakes up."

"Okay, well here goes nothing. Time for me to clear out my desk. The new librarian they replaced me with is really nice. She started yesterday but it was all paperwork and training. Today she's going to shadow me and ask questions. That should be fun, although I'll probably be tired after having to spend the entire day with a new person." I reach up to give him a kiss goodnight and then head out to my car to start my last day at the library.

Saying goodbye to Monty this morning feels like a distant memory. Today has been so busy and long! But I'm glad for it, because it kept me from having time to cry. The new librarian, Maggie, is going to fit in so well. I make sure to tell her that Mrs. Humphrey is a gem and that she likes to act really old-fashioned but that she really knows her stuff. Maggie already knows how to repair books, but I show her where all the supplies are and how I have them organized. She isn't going to be working the children's desk—I found out today that wasn't really part of my job description. Mrs. Humphrey just worked it into my schedule because she knew how much I had wanted to be a children's librarian but that I couldn't do it full-time because the kids overstimulated me too much. That did set off a round of tears. I don't know how I got lucky enough to have a boss that was highly empathic and accommodating to my disability.

I show Maggie around the library and the breakroom and a few things that are different from her previous library. She transferred here from a very small one-room country library and is excited to be in a bigger, more bustling one. I also tell her where the closest and best restaurants are if she wants to go out for lunch breaks. By the end of the day, I think I taught her everything I could. She seems confident and I'm happy to know that my replacement is someone who loves books as much as I do.

But then it is time to pack up my desk and say my goodbyes. Mrs. Humphrey thinks I'll still be stopping in to say hi all the time; and I might be able to some in the dead of winter when the sun goes down before closing, but it won't be often. I know this is probably a real, final goodbye. I pull a box of chocolates from my bag and head to Mrs. Humphrey's office. "Mrs. Humphrey? I'm about ready to go. I need to hand in my badge." I try to say this without crying, but I am a complete failure and tears stream down my face. "Thank you for being the best boss a girl could ever have hoped to have. You've been more than a boss to me—you've been a friend and a mentor. I've loved working with you, and while I'm very happy to embark on a new phase of my life, I'm going to miss you so much. I got you these chocolates." And I sort of thrust the box at her. I'm not very good at gift-giving. A box of chocolates can't convey all the emotions I'm currently feeling.

"Oh dear, you've taught me more than I've ever taught you, you know that?" she says as I shake my head, because I've learned so much from Mrs. Humphrey. "I have no doubts you'll be amazing at your next adventure, job, or whatever you choose to do. Our library was lucky to have you be a part of it. I can deactivate your badge if you'd like to keep it as a memento?"

"Oh!" I said with surprise, "that would be nice. I do have a sentimental side."

"Let's go out into the lobby and get Maggie to take our photo before you go, okay? Can I give you a hug goodbye? You've always been like a daughter to me."

I stand up and give Mrs. Humphrey a friendly and comfortable hug. She is warm chocolate chip cookies, a lavender field, a pile of kittens, and a hot mug of tea all in one. Everyone should be lucky enough to have a Mrs. Humphrey in their life. "One more thing—I don't know your first name? Can I find out that secret before I leave? I won't tell anyone!"

I say teasingly. She always, always goes by Mrs. Humphrey. She doesn't mind that the younger staff use first names, but it's not for her. I'm sure it is on paperwork somewhere, but in all my years, I never saw it written down.

"Well, okay. Gertrude. My name is Gertrude. I never liked it. When I was younger, I had people call me Trudy, but when I got married, I just decided to go by Mrs. Humphrey, which suited me fine. Now you take that secret to your grave!" she says with a smile. If only she knew how long that was going to be, I think with a silent giggle.

We go out into the lobby, and Maggie takes photos of us with both our phones—I shouldn't have been surprised Mrs. Humphrey has a smartphone. She really is a mix of modern and traditional. Then I turn to look at my library one more time, and then run out the door as more tears rush down my face.

I think about stopping on the way home for more takeout, but I am still crying and I don't want to have to explain to anyone giving me food that I'm okay. I just want to go home and be in Monty's arms.

Monty is still asleep when I get home so I change into my swimsuit and swim in the pool by myself for a bit. It feels strange knowing I no longer have a job. At least for a while. I am not going to start my freelancing as a researcher until after my turning ceremony and giving myself time to adjust as a vampire. There is no hurry. After about an hour relaxing in the pool, I feel better. I get dressed in some comfy lounge clothes and hear someone come in through the side door, so I go to see who it is.

"Hey Max," I say as soon as I see him. Max comes in with a big brown paper bag that he is holding carefully by the bottom. "What do you have there?"

"I figured you wouldn't want to cook tonight, so I made lasagna." He sets the bag on the counter and starts pulling out divided plates with lids. "I went ahead and made up some plates instead of bringing the whole thing over."

"This looks amazing!" I say as I open the lid to the plate he slides over to me. A piping hot cheesy meat lasagna in one section, a green salad in another, and a piece of garlic bread in the last. "Let me get some wine out—do you want some?"

"Sure, unless you have a beer?"

"Beer and lasagna?" I ask, curling my nose up at Max.

"Hey, a guy likes what a guy likes!"

"Sorry, no beer. I'll pour you some wine though. Do you care if we just sit at the bar?"

"Too fancy for beer, but not too fancy to sit at the counter. Sure, that's fine. Where's Monty?" Max likes to tease me.

"He should be waking up soon." I set the wine glasses down, get out some silverware and napkins and start to eat. "Oh my goodness, Max, this is divine. Too bad you guys can't be a vet *and* a chef. That'd probably get too complicated!"

"Yeah, it's all good though. I like working with animals. I think I prefer cooking just for myself or my friends anyway. Plus, everyone in the System is trained to be a vet tech. Can you imagine if Sky was fronting and we had to go to work as a chef? That would be disastrous. We'd get fired on the spot." He chuckles at the thought.

Right then Monty walks into the room. "When I smell your cooking, I actually do wish I could eat," he says as a greeting, then turns to me. "How was your day, baby? Are you okay? I wanted to be up when you got home, but I accidentally slept through it." He comes up behind me and wraps his arms around me. I lean back into him and look up at him. He bends down and gives me a sort of upside down kiss on the forehead.

I sit back up and swivel the chair around. "It was hard. I cried a lot. I found out Mrs. Humphrey's first name. But I told her I'd take it to the grave." That last part makes me smile. "My replacement, Maggie, is really nice." Monty walks around to the other side of the counter so he can talk to us and I can finish up eating.

"Nik should be—" Monty starts to say, when Nik just appears in the kitchen. "Well, hey, I was just saying you were going to be here soon!"

"Yo, Max. Hey Katrina. How was today?" he says as he gives Monty a high-five in greeting.

"It was good and sad all at once. But I'm glad you are here. After we finish eating, I think we should either play *Mario Party* or go bowling. What do you say?" I ask the group.

"Bowling!" the three guys say in unison.

It sounds as if the evening is going to be quite fun and just the distraction I need.

Chapter 39
Panic Attack

Montgomery

Life is settling into a good rhythm. The vampire reunion is less than a month away. I've talked to the officiants and found out that it isn't a big deal at all to have Rainbow come. Apparently it is fairly common to have a human witness, as long as it is done on a small scale. You know, the vampire veil of secrecy and all of that. That and the non-disclosure agreement Rainbow would sign. No one wants to go against a vampire NDA. We are combining a vampire turning ceremony with a human marriage ceremony. The vampire turning will make Katrina and I bonded mates, but she always dreamed of a wedding, so that part is really for her, although I suspect she just wants an excuse to wear a fancy wedding gown.

We've decided to do what we were calling a pre-honeymoon. I have to be in Italy on and off for various functions the entire last week of October but Katrina only needs to be there for the last day. She really doesn't want to be around all of the celebrations and vampires before she turns, but me teleporting back and forth with different time zones sounds hectic. So we found a nearby sleepy little town that we are going to stay in. She plans to bring her crochet and work on it when I have to attend various functions. On the last day, I'll teleport back to get Rainbow and take them both into Civita di Bagnoregio for the ceremony. Nik has decided to stay in the city the whole time—he loves all the parties.

But that brings us to today where Katrina is standing in front of me in the bedroom absolutely stressed out. "Are you sure I don't need a passport? I know I teleported to Canada with you on the Fourth of July, but that was just a couple of hours, and we didn't even leave the hotel. This feels wrong!" She sits down on the trunk at the end of my bed and I move to sit next to her. But before I can, she pops back up and starts pacing again. Patiently, I sit down in a chair in the corner, to let her have room to process.

"You won't need a passport. Passports are pieces of paper for border crossings over imaginary lines dictated by humans. We won't be using any human forms of transportation or be anywhere near customs or border patrol officers, I promise. I've traveled all over the world. It's really fine. I only need forged documents for my permanent residency so I can work if I want, buy a house, pay my taxes, etcetera. And we'll get those for you when you need them in a few years once it's obvious you don't match the age on your driver's license anymore. We have top-notch vampire forgers who specialize in this. It's part of our culture—part of our rules. You'll now be a blend of cultures, we live in the human world, but we also have our own laws."

"What about my food?" she asks. "I like Italian food, but I also need safe foods. Does Italy have bagels? I need my bagels."

"It's just a week. You can pack a few bagels, if you'd like. I mean, if you need me to, I can always go get more things for you, but I think you'll be fine. What is all this about?" I've seen her upset before, but not like this. "Do you still want to turn? To marry me? Are you having second thoughts?"

"No! Yes! I mean, no, I'm not having second thoughts, and, yes, I do want to turn and to get married to you. But traveling makes me so anxious. I like my routine. Everything is changing. I want to travel. The idea sounds so awesome and when I see other people post vacation photos, I always get a little jealous, but traveling is so hard for me. Everything is different: my bed, the food, the time zone, the sounds and smells around me. I'm also going to miss Data. I know it's only a week and Rainbow will take care of him while we're gone, but I don't like being away from him for so long. And just by the time I acclimate, the vacation will be over."

This is another reason why we've decided to go early— she had told me that when she travels it sometimes takes a while to get used to the new place, but I had no idea it was this hard. By now, Katrina is pacing back and forth at the end of the bed. She reaches the windows and turns around and walks towards the bedroom door, back and forth, as I watch her from a side chair next to our dresser.

"How about if we write down all of your concerns and see if we can find solutions?" I ask her.

"We can and we can't. We can do some things to accommodate me, but some things are just going to be hard and there's nothing I can do about it. Teleporting actually is a really nice accommodation. You should see me if I have to go through an airport. Airports are sensory nightmares, and so are the planes. How do people sit still for that many hours?" She stops in front of me, her tone accusatory, as if something is wrong with me for being able to sit still while she's my constant bundle of wiggly energy.

"Am I supposed to answer that?" I ask her in a lighthearted tone. I don't want to dismiss her concerns—I know they are very real for her—but these are things I've literally never had to think about. I just go with the flow and figure things out. Not to mention, food preferences aren't really an issue when your entire diet is blood.

And as if she can read my mind, the next thing out of her mouth is, "That will be my last week to ever eat food. What if I don't want Italian food? What if I want Chinese food? Why does it feel as if I'm planning my last meal before my execution? Monty, I'm so overwhelmed."

She stops in front of me and kneels down between my legs and rests her head on my lap. I hug her tight to me. I am at a loss for words, so I sit there silently, smoothing out her hair as she clings to me. "We'll figure it all out, Kitty Kat. I know it's hard to imagine right now, but you won't miss human food. Your body won't need it, so it'd be like you missing the taste of, say, motor oil. Or like how a cow doesn't miss the taste of eating meat because all they need is grass and hay. I also understand your last human meal does feel like a big deal. It *is* a big deal, and I'll teleport anywhere in the world and get you the last meal you want. How does that sound?"

"But how do you choose that?" she asks me. "You didn't have to think about all of this. You assume that giving me a choice to change is better, and it is, but also, you didn't have to think about all of these things."

"Believe me, you wouldn't have missed the meals I was eating back in 1717 on a small farm. I mean, my mom was a good cook, but it's not like I was debating chocolate, sushi, Italian, or any other cuisine. Mom made a mean rabbit barley stew, but let's just say, I wasn't really giving up that much when it came to cuisine." I hope I am lightening the mood a bit. I do take her concerns seriously, but there aren't really any good answers either.

"How's your dress selection coming along?" I ask her, changing the topic. "Have you picked out a wedding dress yet? I imagine Jessie had a good time selecting it with you. I bet Sky wanted to be there too." Katrina gets up and goes to sit on the bed next to a sleeping Data as we continue to talk.

"Oh yeah, they actually got fairly switchy in the bridal shop. I think our shopping attendant was confused because we'd be in the dressing room and Sky and Jessie kept switching, and you know their voices are different, and those walls are very thin. She kept looking around for a third person. It really became funny. But I needed Jessie because Sky would have had me in a dress that is not my style at all! She loves shopping so much, though, and I'm glad she was able to switch in to be a part of it. I can't wait for you to see it!"

"Is there anything I can do right now to help you feel less anxious about the upcoming ceremonies?" I ask her, since talking about the dress seems to ease her mind a little bit at least.

"I don't think so. I wish I could just be cavalier about traveling, but it never fails: I get worked up every time. I love the idea of traveling, but actually doing it always stresses me out. I hope maybe now that airports won't be an issue and food won't be an issue in the future, maybe traveling will get easier for me. I'm sure sometimes we'd even be able to take Data with us, depending on where we were going. I love the idea of traveling the world with you."

"Me too. We're going to have so much fun together," I promise her. "Are you up for a swim? Or maybe an evening stroll? The weather's still pretty nice."

"Yeah, let's go for a dip in the pool—bathing suits optional?" She tosses me a knowing grin.

"I like the way you think!" And like that, she darts off down the hallway to my pool, taking off pieces of her clothes as she goes and tossing them behind her. The next hour is going to be a lot of fun.

Chapter 40
Last Sunsets

Katrina

My suitcase lies open on the bed as I frantically overpack it. I'd double-checked the weather in Italy. The temperatures are going to be fairly mild, in the 55–60 °F range and so I had planned to pack clothes I could layer if it ended up being colder or hotter than I was expecting. I did stuff a few bagels, my favorite brand of tea, some granola bars, and some peanut butter crackers in my suitcase. Monty has been showing me the utmost patience. Even if I don't end up eating any of that, I know I'll feel better having some of my favorite foods available if I need them. We'd found a small villa to rent for the week. It has a cute little porch and sits on top of a hill overlooking a vineyard. The photos showed amazing sunsets, and I can't wait to see them. I just have to actually finish packing and get to the rest of my to-do list, which includes dropping Data off at Rainbow's house.

I actually need to do that next. After leaving my job at the library, I switched over to a night sleeping schedule. So even though I just woke up, Rainbow should be off work and about ready to eat their dinner. I pick up my cell phone to give them a call. "Hey, who's this?" I ask as soon as they answer.

"'Tis Arleigh. How do thee fare? Are you prepared for thy journey to Italy? I'm astounded that it's almost that time. I'm happy for you, but this transformation weighs heavily upon us all." I hear the distress in her voice, even though she really is trying to be upbeat.

"I know. Every few seconds I feel as if I'm going back and forth between whether or not I'm doing the right thing. There aren't that many choices a person has to make in life that aren't irreversible, but this is definitely one of them and it's not like there's much literature on the subject for me to have done research on! I just have to go with my heart and my instinct on this one. I know I'm doing the right thing."

"We extend our support unto you throughout your journey. You leave at first light, correct? We requested to be off work on the thirty-first so that Monty can retrieve us and whisk us away to Italy for your ceremony. The entire System is in chaos over whom shall emerge to the front during the ceremonies. I hope you weren't expecting the presence of just one alter."

"Oh Arleigh, I'll be so happy to have the System there however you guys can. I know you'll probably be blendy, but that's okay. I was calling to ask if it's okay for me to bring Data on by and so I can give you one last hug before I go."

"Yes, yes of course. I am tucked in for the evening, toiling away at our domestic duties. Sky was fronting earlier and I swear she was a whirling dervish leaving chaos in her wake, I found one of her bras slung over a lamp—how does she do it? Also, I found a missive here on the counter that notes Max baked some cookies for you to pack and take along with you."

"Of course he did! He's so sweet. Alright, I'll head over and see you soon."

A few hours later, Monty is back from running his errands, Data has been dropped off, and my suitcase is as packed as it is ever going to be. My gorgeous wedding dress is in a special bag along with my shoes, a tiara, and jewelry. It is weird to think that if I do forget something, Monty can just pop back home and retrieve it, but I don't want to have him go back and forth too much. The villa we will be staying at has remote check-in, no human interaction needed. We have a code to unlock the door, but we aren't supposed to arrive until 4 p.m. local time. Our plan is to teleport here at 7 a.m., which is 4 p.m. in Italy, with our bags, then Monty will come back for the wedding gown because we can't carry it all at once.

"Are you ready to go?" he asks me. I take one last look around the room. Everything is set.

"Yep," I reply. "Let's do this!" He takes my hand and holds onto his bag. I already have my purse around my shoulders and grab my suitcase in my other hand. He gives me a kiss, which is not part of the teleportation process. It's simply something he likes to do when whisking me from one place to the next, a tradition he started that night at Lacamas Lake all those months ago. Next thing I know, we are standing on the porch of a villa in Italy. I can't imagine the amazement of instant transportation will ever get old. "Squeee!" I let out an exclamation of excitement. "We're here! We're actually here." Monty types in the passcode to unlock the door, and I swing it open.

Immediately my nose picks up the scent of lived history. A comforting musty scent of old wood beams, plaster walls, and the stories of generations of people laughing and living in the welcoming space. Walking into this 19th century villa we had found to rent is like taking a step back into time. Sure, I can see it's been updated with electricity, and thank goodness for indoor plumbing, but the history of the house hugs me as I pass through the solid wood antique door. The floor is a red clay tile laid out in a herringbone pattern, and the ceiling is low and wooden, with massive beams running the length of the room. The walls are a warm golden-yellow plaster. Everything feels cozy and inviting. The furniture has a worn, lived in feeling. The villa feels welcoming, like home—not sterile like a fancy hotel with no personality. It is absolutely perfect.

I walk into the kitchen and find a bottle of wine on the counter, alongside a corkscrew and two beautiful tall-stemmed wineglasses. I don't drink often, but somehow, looking out over what seems like miles and miles of rolling vineyards out the big picture window in the living room, it is fitting to sip on and enjoy a glass of wine. Monty doesn't have to report to the Reunion until tomorrow. We've been up all night, but it's only 4 p.m. here and we need to adjust to local time. I hear Monty putting our suitcases in the main bedroom for us to unpack in a little while. "I'm going to open this bottle of red wine, while you pop back for the wedding dress." He doesn't have to go get it today, but it just makes me feel better to have it here in Italy with us. "It'd be nice to drink this on the back patio, but the sun's still too high in the sky for you, so we'll have to go out there later." I open the wine to let it breathe, and pull all the curtains shut for Monty. It is a shame to have to close off the amazing views around us, but I understand it is necessary.

A few days later, I am up early so I can go for a walk in the vineyard. I feel a bit melancholy that I won't be able to go outside in the sun for any length of time for the next several years. It is actually impossible to wrap my head around. Monty is still asleep, but he'll be up around dusk. He and Nik have plans to go to some of the scheduled vampire political meetings. Tomorrow is vampire election day. It is really interesting to hear all about the new culture I am effectively marrying into. They have the High Elder who serves a half-century term. Then there are several different councils that all have elected spots that help advise the High Elder. There is the court system, which I of course already know a little bit about. They also have enforcers and executioners. Monty said a lot of this was more modern, because as the vampire population grew, it was important to keep things in check. It is important that humans don't find out about vampires on a wide scale. I'm glad it's not completely locked down, because if I had to give up my friendship with Rainbow, I'm not sure I could do it. Luckily, that is something I don't have to think about.

These are the thoughts in my mind as I stroll aimlessly through the rows of grapes still growing on the vine. Everything is lush and green, and I can see mountains off in the distance and birds flying up above me. The sky is starting to turn a golden warm yellow with hints of pink at the horizon as the sun sets. It is also getting fairly chilly, so I turn to head back to the villa. The villa is at the top of a slight hill and my timing is perfect, because when I turn around, the sunset is in full effect and I can see the landscape stretching out in front of me lit up with the most amazing sunset I've ever seen. I take out my camera and snap a few photos, knowing that they'll never compare to this actual moment in time. I only wish Monty was standing here with me. As the sun dips below the horizon, I hear the door open behind me and a sleepy Monty joins me on the porch. He wraps his arms around my belly and gently rests his head on top of mine. I love how I fit into his arms this way. I wiggle around until I am facing him, still tight in his embrace. "You missed a fiery, brilliant sunset. I wish you had been able to see it."

"Me too—how long have you been up?" He still sounds sleepy.

"Not too long. I wanted to go for a walk and enjoy one of my last sunsets."

He steps back a bit so he can look into my eyes. "No regrets? You do not have to go through with this. I'd understand," he says, his voice full of love. "I of course want you to be with me, by my side, forever, but I absolutely would never blame you if you decided not to turn for me."

"No regrets," I say with confidence. "But at the same time, I feel as if I'm trying to squeeze in the last of my humanity. I'll probably spend all night eating. I saw you stocked the fridge really well yesterday when I wasn't looking! So you and Nik are going to listen to some of the vampire's running for elected positions tonight? Anything else going on?" We settle on the outdoor couch. Fireflies start to emerge, and their little twinkles are flittering around, keeping my interest as we talk.

"There's a big ball tonight. There will be one tonight and tomorrow. If you want to go to one, you'll have to go to tonight's because tomorrow, after the turning ceremony, you'll basically need to sleep for several hours. That ball isn't for newly-turned vampires, which is why you do have an invitation to the one tonight. I know you said you weren't interested in going, and that's totally fine, but I'm just checking to see if you changed your mind."

"Do you want me to go? Are you going to go stag with Nik?" I ask.

"Oh no. I'm not really interested either, and Nik ran into Celeste from the trial and invited her. This is the one event that is more open. The human allies haven't been allowed at most of the events this week."

"I'm glad he found someone to go with. I wonder if he's interested in Celeste. I was kind of hoping things would work out between him and Rainbow," I ponder out loud.

"There's nothing to say that they won't. I don't think Nik is serious about Celeste—she was just really nice to us during the trial, and he didn't want to go to the ball alone. But I better get ready—the first meeting starts soon." He leans over and kisses me. I dart my tongue out, and sure enough, feel the tip of his very sharp fang. I just barely touch it with the tip of my tongue—not hard enough to pierce it, just to see if they'll extend when he kisses me. It makes me smile into the kiss, because I know that happens when he is turned on. I deepen the kiss, straddling him on the wicker couch. It makes a creaking sound as the fibers adjust to my shifting motion. Monty pulls away just for a moment. "What are you doing? I need to go, but I'd much rather be here doing this with you," he says, adding in his own groan.

"Mmmm, one more thing before you go," I say as I tilt my neck to him and wrap my arms around his neck.

"You're killing me, Kitty Kat," he groans, and then— those beautiful fangs sink into my neck, and the world turns molten. I sincerely hope this feels just as good after turning as it does now. I know scientifically he's injecting some sort of pleasure toxin into me, but I have zero cares about it. It feels like lightning and ice all at once. While he is sucking, he reaches around to my front, putting his hands under my shirt and massages my breasts. His thumbs find my nipples, and he rubs them until they are taut peaks. He licks the wound and goes back to kissing me. Before I know what is

336

happening, he has teleported us to our villa room and he quickly pulls off the pajamas I am still wearing and tugs down his sweatpants. His cock stands up, straight and stiff. I know this is going to happen fast. He gives me a look, asking silently how I want to proceed.

I bend over the edge of the bed. He groans behind me—a raw, hungry sound—as he takes in the sight of me, already slick and aching. He takes a finger and rubs me up and down, testing my readiness. But I am more than ready for him. Standing behind me, with his hands on my rear, he enters me with a slow, easy motion, making sure I can take him from this position. I hug a pillow and start to call out, "More, Monty—God, this is so good—please, now. I need you." He reaches under me and uses his fingers on my most sensitive spots to send electric jolts through my body.

"Kitty Kat, you are so amazing!" Monty calls out as his thrusts pick up in pace as he gets closer and closer to his release. My whole body coils, sensation blurring thought, every nerve alight as pleasure crashes into me. With one last thrust uniting us as one, we go over the edge together, coming hard with panting breaths. As he comes down from his high, he lies across my back and we both take a few seconds to collect ourselves.

"I don't want to go now— I want to spend the next hour cuddling with you," he says.

"Go. Nik's waiting. We have a lifetime to cuddle together. I'll see you later. I've got plenty to keep me busy tonight."

Monty gets dressed, and with one last chaste kiss this time, he poofs out of the room to go find Nik.

Chapter 41
Vampire Class is in Session

Katrina

As I wake up on my last night to ever be human, a flood of emotions fills me. The first is excitement. It is going to be a big night. Yesterday, I had my last meal. I had decided on seafood pasta. Monty had teleported to a restaurant in Sicily to bring me back the most mouthwatering mixed seafood pasta dish I've ever had. It contained lobster, prawns, scallops, and mussels, along with delicious mushrooms in a creamy white sauce. It is a dish I'll remember eating for a long time. I won't eat anything else again, needing an empty stomach for the transformation to go smoother.

I have a class I'm attending in an hour to go over everything Monty's told me, but this reassures the Vampire Council I'm a willing participant in this exchange. After the class, Monty is going to teleport back to Vancouver to get Rainbow, and we'll have a few hours to hang out and prepare before the ceremony, which takes place at 3 a.m. on October thirty-first. I'll be forever thirty years old, and more importantly, I'll be married to Monty. It's amazing to think how much my life has changed this past year. I was just a quiet librarian with a crochet hobby. I'm still that, but more, somehow. I wasn't out looking for a life partner—I was very happy with my life. But Monty fits into all the right places and makes what was a full, satisfying life even more complete. I didn't mean to fall in love with a vampire, but here we are.

And to think of all the women Monty's ever known, he chose me to bond with. That feels amazing.

But for now, I reach over and tap on the sleeping vampire next to me. "Hey Fangs, it's time to wake up. Big day today!" He's been extra tired from all the events he's had to attend. He was really glad he skipped out on the ball last night, but he heard from Nik that it was a fun event.

Monty rolls over towards me and gives me a big grin, extending his fangs down to tease me since I'd called him Fangs.

I laugh and brush my fingers along his jaw, "Sunshine, my love, you are so hot. I wish I had time to make love to you this morning. I'm a nervous wreck about the class I have to go to. I wish you could be there with me. I know they want to know you aren't influencing me, but new environments make me so anxious. I've got my fidgets and my earplugs. I can't have snacks, which really sucks, but do you think gum would be okay? Never mind, I don't have any gum. What should I wear? Will the other humans speak English? How many of us are turning this year?"

"I already asked, knowing you'd have some of these questions. There are ten initiates this year, including you. Six are women, three are men, and one is enby. They all speak English, although one is Deaf and will have an American Sign Language interpreter with them. I heard there was a lot of controversy around that, and that they originally wanted their own human interpreter, but that wasn't going to be allowed. They met a vampire interpreter and hit it off, so things are now okay."

"Will they remain Deaf after turning?" I ask. Monty assured me that I'd remain Autistic ADHD and that was important to me. My neurodivergence hasn't always been easy, but it is an integral part of who I am. If I wasn't AuDHD, I wouldn't be me.

"Yes, they'll remain Deaf. Humans' senses in general become more heightened when they turn, so it's possible if they have any amount of hearing, it could get slightly better. Turning doesn't change things that aren't life-threatening. Our scientists actually have the ability to do so, but we voted many years ago that this wasn't acceptable. There is nothing wrong with being disabled, and it adds to the fabric of who we are as a species, just as it does for humans. If we were all the same, that would not be good."

"Is their vampire partner Deaf?" I ask, getting distracted by the thought of another disabled person in my class.

"Yeah, I don't know him very well personally, but I did see him here and there this week. One of the meetings I had to go to was about how to be a good mentor to my initiate. All of the pairings this year are romantic, which is usually the case. It isn't common for someone to turn for platonic reasons, but it has happened." Monty gets out of bed and pulls me out with him. "As for what to wear, just wear something comfortable for today. The class isn't long—an hour, an hour and half if there's more questions. They aren't there to teach you everything, but to give you a perspective that is outside of the one vampire you met. They want you to know your rights, what to expect at the ceremony, and again to make sure you're here of your own choosing. Since hosting these classes, the number of people who have been turned against their will is almost non-existent and this is a good thing for both humans and vampires." He pulls on some jeans and a plain T-shirt. I notice he didn't pack too many of his funny shirts for this week. I think he is trying to blend in a bit more than he does in the comfort of his own home. Something I understand all too well.

The long mossy green cotton dress feels soft as I pull it from the dresser and over my head, its flowy fabric promising comfort that will ease some of my anxiety. A pair of leggings goes on next and I toss a little sweater next to my bag, just in case the air turns chilly. Standing in front of the mirror, my fingers quickly twist my hair into a bun, securing it out of the way with practiced ease. Minimal makeup goes on next, the barest layer—just a quick powdering of my nose, a couple brushes of mascara, and a pink non-sticky lipstick—since I'll save the bold touches for the ceremony later. As I gather the essentials for the day, a notebook slips into my bag, along with my fidgets. Even though the group will be small, I tuck noise dampening earplugs in, just in case the volume of the space overwhelms me.

"Okay, I'm ready. What are you going to do while I'm in class?" I ask Monty.

"You know, I think I'll film a VidVibe. Tell my viewers that we are getting married later today. Obviously I can't film the real ceremony—there's only so much I can show while still leading people to believe we are just cosplaying. It's going to be a long night for me too. If you're ready, I'll teleport you to the city. Your class is in what is equivalent to our community center. You'll have cell reception. I couldn't call during the trial since the guard took my cell phone. You'll be able to reach me if you need me."

"I'm ready," I say with as much confidence as I can muster. I really hope the teacher is as nice as Monty and Nik. Monty leans over to kiss me, and when he pulls back I am outside a fairly normal-looking building with glass doors.

"Do you want me to walk you to class?" he asks with a grin.

"No, I'll figure it out. Have fun filming. I'll call you when class gets out," I say, and head into the building.

Montgomery

After I drop Katrina off at her class, I return to the villa. I only brought a travel tripod and because it's night the lighting isn't really ideal for a video. But I figured I'd lean into the darkness trope and call it mood lighting. I set the tripod up facing a chair in the corner of the living room. On the wall behind me is a Renaissance-style painting of a vineyard. I turned on the floor lamp near the leather chair and glamored up since I didn't bring any of my costumes.

"Hello, my human friends. As you can see, I'm not filming from my normal location. I'm actually on vacation with my fiancée, and later tonight, we will be getting married. You all know her as Scarlett. I made a video of how a human turns into a vampire, and Scarlett will be participating in that turning ceremony with me tonight as part of our wedding ceremony. Right now she's off doing bride-to-be things, but I'm sure she'll join us in future videos, with her brand-new shiny fangs. I know you all will be excited to have her join in on some of my videos in the future. Most of my content will remain the same, though: me telling stories of what it's been like spending the past three hundred-plus years as a vampire living among humans. Until the moon rises again, my nocturnal friends. Fangs out—see you in the shadows."

342

I decide to keep it short, but I do choose to break character slightly in the description box (just in case the council is still monitoring my activities). I added in the text: No humans were harmed in the marriage between MontyTheVampire and Scarlett. Stay safe, and please, do not try the things I talk about in my videos."

I spend a few minutes editing and uploading the video. Then I text Nik to see what he is up to.

Monty: Hey Nik, what are you doing?
Nik: I'm actually hanging out with Stefano. He's a local vampire and he has an impressive winery. He's showing me his wine cellar. I'm hoping he'll show me more, if you know what I mean. Haha. What's up?
Monty: Katrina should be done with her class soon. Then I've got to pick up Rainbow from back in Vancouver. Katrina and Rainbow plan to spend a couple hours getting ready. Apparently that takes hours. I was wondering if you wanted to play night golf while they are primping. I need something to focus my nerves on. How long will you be with Stefano? He can come too..
Nik: I'll ask him. How about I meet you at the villa in an hour.
Monty: Works for me.

Most vampires have really great night-vision, and there is a course near Civita di Bagnoregio that I want to try out. I wish I had my gaming consoles with me, but other than the Switch, I didn't bring any. Going golfing with Nik, and possibly Stefano, will be fun.

Katrina

"Rainbow!! You're here!" I am so excited. Class ended, Monty came and got me, and then went to pick up Rainbow before heading out to golf with Nik and another vampire. Now the clock is ticking down until wedding-turning time! And just as I suspected, Rainbow seems to be pretty blendy. It's a really hard experience for them to explain, but the brain is trying to switch so much that the alters seem to smash together for a bit, leaving no one distinct experience. It can leave them feeling very dissociative and make it difficult for them to focus or be present. It's not ideal, but it does happen when they are very excited or very stressed about something. "How are you all feeling? Would you like me to stick with 'Rainbow,' or is someone more present?"

"Just give us a moment to settle," they say.

We move to the living room and sit down. Rainbow has a suitcase with them because they are going to stay over after the ceremony, partly to make sure I am okay after the turning. I am expected to be pretty weak for twenty-four to forty-eight hours afterwards. Once I gain strength, we were all going to head back to Vancouver together. Monty and I will have a "proper" honeymoon when I am up to full strength.

"Tell me how your week has gone while we attempt to get grounded," Rainbow instructs me as they sit back and try to focus on being present.

I spend the next couple of minutes catching them up, and I show them the progress on the crochet project I am currently working on. I want something fairly easy this week, so I bought the yarn to make a green 1-Up Mushroom from Mario. I tell them about the amazing food I've eaten all week, along with my last meal. And I get them caught up on the class I had to take earlier this evening. "The Deaf human and I got along really well. I know a little bit of ASL, but not really enough to communicate. Their interpreter was great, and after a few minutes it was easy to talk to them through the interpreter. The class itself wasn't that exciting. Monty pretty much had already told me everything that the class covered, but I do understand why they want us to go to it. There was one girl whose partner I guess did not explain things very well, and she left crying. From what I heard, she had her memory wiped of vampires and got transported back to her life. All she'll remember is breaking up with her fiancé before the ceremony, or so we were told. It was fairly dramatic, but really hit home how important that class is!"

"So now there will be nine of us tonight. It's a mix between a group and individual ceremonies. We'll all be in one big room together, but each have our own little space. How are you feeling now?" I ask, noticing Rainbow seems a little more at ease. I still can't tell if just one alter is fronting though.

"Much better." Rainbow has pulled out a little talisman she keeps in her pocket. They have different ones for different alters. Jessie has a smooth worry stone that she gently massages between her fingers to help ground her to the body. "Okay, feeling much more steady now," Jessie says in her own voice. "Everyone wants to be here, but it's just not possible. Both Sky and Quinn are desperate to do your makeup, and all of us want to be at the ceremony. It's really frustrating, but today is about you and not us."

"That's okay. I'll take you all however you show up today. Let's put your suitcase in your room, and I'll show you around before we start getting ready. I can't decide how I want to wear my hair. Monty asked me if I wanted to hire a professional hairstylist and makeup artist, but I really don't want extra people around. It's funny—if you're rich enough, you can get a hairstylist at one in the morning with no questions asked. Although he said there are vampire stylists too."

I get Jessie set up in her room and give her a tour of the villa. I tell her she'll have to look at the scenery tomorrow in the daylight while I am sleeping. Then we head to my bedroom where all my beauty supplies are. With Monty out golfing with Nik, it means there is no concern of him seeing me before I am ready. Because of the group nature of the ceremony, though, we have decided to do our own private unveiling ceremony here at the villa before heading into the city. Monty has his tux over at Nik's hotel and is going to get ready there before teleporting outside of our villa. I am going to be standing in the living room and he'll come in to get his first look. It will be our private moment, before we teleport to Civita di Bagnoregio together. Nik is going to teleport Jessie, or whoever might be fronting at that point.

I pull out all my beauty things, and Jessie is about to get to work. She flutters her eyes a bit and I know a switch is happening. I have a hunch Sky is not going to sit idly by and let someone else do my hair and makeup. It actually makes me grin. I wait a few moments before, sure enough, Sky says, "I told Jessie I was going to do your styling! I can't believe she tried to take that from me! Ugh!"

"It's fine, Sky, I'd love for you to do it, but keep it elegant, okay?" I ask, only mildly concerned Sky will get a little wild. She has this whole gothic vampire look in her head, but that isn't the look I want to go for. "I just want an elegant smokey eye and red lips with a subtle blush. Simple. No overdoing the eyes."

We decide to pile my hair up on my head in a French twist with tendrils of curls coming down around my neck and at my temples. My tiara will nestle in the curls perfectly.

Once makeup is complete, I pull my wedding dress out of its garment bag and hold it up. I bet Monty was thinking I'd go with a human traditional white gown, but I decided to go all-in. The gown I bought is stunning— a deep red ball gown with a sheer black lace layer on top. It is off-the-shoulders and plunges deep into a sweetheart neckline across my breasts. The waist cinches in to a point, accentuating my curvy hips. It has long sheer black sleeves in a bell shape that flow down as long as the dress, with more black beading spilling down the length of them. There is also black beading across the bodice that shimmers as I move. It is a dramatic, full classic-vampire moment. With my hair up, my neck is highlighted, which I thought was appropriate. I had debated the color, because with my red hair, red clothes were something I normally avoided, but when I saw this dress, it just called to me. I didn't want to wear a necklace—I wanted my pale chest and neck on display. Sky helps me step into the dress and accompanying petticoats. She then takes a bunch of photos with my camera and hers. "Monty should be here soon. I'm going to go to my room to prepare so you two can have some privacy before it's go time!

I stand in the living room, using a long black ribbon as a fidget toy. Thankfully my dress came with pockets, and I can tuck the ribbon away if I need to. But for now, I stand there twisting the long strand in and out of my fingers, keeping myself busy. I know Monty will be arriving any moment. Sure enough, a few seconds later, I hear the front door click open and footsteps crossing the threshold.

Chapter 42
Eternal Choice

Montgomery

I arrive at the villa after showering and changing into my tux over at Nik's. Katrina wanted me to see her in her dress before the ceremony so it would just be the two of us, and I adore the idea. She gave me very specific instructions and I intend to follow them. I know she is already nervous and anxious and I don't want to mess up the procedure she's created for herself in her mind.

I open the door and head down the hallway, calling out, "Kitty Kat, I'm here. Is it okay for me to come in?"

"Yes, I'm in here!" I hear Katrina call to me from the living room.

I walk in, and when I see her, I stop in my tracks. She is always beautiful, every single time I lay eyes on her. Whether she's in pajamas, naked, dressed in her cute librarian outfits, or dressed up for a date, each and every time I see her, she's gorgeous. But nothing prepares me for how stunning she looks in the breathtaking gown she is currently wearing. Her pale skin absolutely glows under the dark red-and-black dress. My desire and devotion for her takes me by surprise. I feel like the luckiest man on the planet. How is it that she agreed to spend all eternity with me? I can't even think of any words to say other than, "I love you. You are so gorgeous. Words can't even begin to describe how I'm feeling right now, my sweet Kitty Kat. How did I ever get so lucky?"

I walk up to her and give her a gentle hug. I am scared to mess up her hair or makeup. I know Katrina isn't fussy about such things, but I don't want Sky to come after me the way I know she would if I displaced even one hair on her head.

"Monty, you look amazing too. I'm the lucky one. I'm so ready to be your bonded mate, your wife, your life partner. Are you ready?"

"I've *been* ready. I fell in love with you the first time I laid eyes on you. I never believed in love at first sight, but it's true. And my love for you has done nothing but grow and grow from that first outing."

Katrina

"Okay you two. We've got to get going." Max steps out of the bedroom.

"Max? You're going to the ceremony?" I ask. He is wearing slacks, a red silk shirt that has undertones of black, depending on how you look at it, and a black coat.

"Yeah, Quinn's co-fronting. We want to make sure everything goes well and that if you change your mind at any point, we're there to protect you," he says with deadly sincerity.

"Oh, Max. I know you've got my back. No need to worry though, I've made my choice and I'm very confident in going through with it," I say as I hold onto Monty's hand.

"Even still. Are we set? You two lovebirds head off. Here's Nik—he's going to teleport me," Max announces as Nik walks into the room.

"Woah! Katrina, you clean up nice!" Nik whistles at me.

"Thanks, Nik. I appreciate it. You try so hard to act like a player and bad boy, but I know you're just a softy," I tease.

"Shhh, don't be giving my secrets away. I'm trying to be cool in front of Max," Nik says with a laugh.

And with that, Monty, not wanting to mess up my lipstick, kisses me on the cheek, and then we are in a huge, grand ballroom, followed a few seconds later by Nik and Max.

The room is stunning. Crystal chandeliers drip from the ceiling, the walls feature rows of arches and paneling for architectural interest, and the floor consists of intricate tile work. Sconces filled with candles have been artfully placed around the room. I bet this venue would cost thousands of dollars to rent out in a normal situation. Which this obviously is not. I now see other people teleporting in. Soon there are nine little groups all around the room. We are all directed to stand around a central podium in a semicircle, each in our little groups, some bigger than others. Around the central podium are nine small tables with black lace tablecloths on them. On each table there is a folded cloth napkin, a candle in a silver pillar, a carved silver dagger, and a matching silver chalice. I notice the dagger in front of me is embedded with emeralds. I can't tell from where I am standing if all of them are the same.

The High Elder Vampire enters the room. Monty says this will probably be one of the only times I'll be this close to him or hear him speak—unless I see a future in vampire politics, which I do not. I'm so curious about him, and knowing I may never get this close again, I take a moment to study him.

I know he's one of the oldest vampires still in existence. Monty said he was turned before birth records existed, so no one knows his exact turning age. At a first glance, he appears to be around thirty, but a closer look reveals the wisdom in his eyes—an almost ageless existence. His gaze pierces my soul, and for a brief moment, I have to glance away. The intensity is unlike anything I've experienced before.

His skin, carrying an almost ethereal glow, is as pale as moonlight. His long, dark hair is immaculately kept, framing a face that is too beautiful. The Elder's movements are measured and deliberate, like a being who has never known haste. Time is meaningless to him, and it shows in the way he moves—graceful yet powerful, effortless yet commanding.

His presence is both soothing—likely his glamour—and unsettling. My still-human brain rebels against the unnatural reality of his immortal existence. I know Monty is 333 years old and that is already hard to comprehend. This vampire is so old it's too much for me to grasp. He wears a high-collared coat adorned with intricate embroidery, designed to impress upon the viewer that he is power. On one of his long slender fingers is a silver ring that glints in the candle light.

When he speaks, his smooth, velvet voice demands authority, sending a shiver down my spine. "Welcome, initiates, to this hallowed meeting. We gather for a rite as ancient as the stars themselves. Among us stand nine souls who will swear to embrace the eternal covenant. Know this, dear mortals, the path you have chosen is irreversible, and an irrevocable pledge to join us in the shadows. Tonight, beneath the cloak of darkness, we will partake in a sacrament of ultimate transformation. Each of you shall be anointed, forever altered to walk among us, bound by the threads of immortality." The High Elder Vampire's voice reverberates throughout the space.

I glance at everyone else. There are now five of us women, three men, and one nonbinary initiate. We are all trying to look confident, even though I'm sure they are as nervous as I am, which is to be expected. Everyone is dressed in stunning formal wear.

The High Elder continues. "Initiates and their companions, draw near to the altar in front of you. Your attendants may stand near you to bear witness." As he says this, everyone shuffles toward the altars. "On this eve, two of our couples also want to exchange human wedding vows, and we will allow abbreviated rites. Katrina Prescott and Montgomery Ravenscroft, along with Amber Jonas and Alexander Blackstone. We will start with Mistress Prescott and Master Ravenscroft and then proceed from there." A very short and precise exchange of vows follows, but I don't really care. It is enough to make me happy. I had decided I didn't want a wedding ring, but Monty surprises me with a simple, elegant diamond necklace. A small round diamond hangs on a thin chain that is whisper-soft. It is simple enough to wear every day if I want to. He fastens it around my neck, and the chain is so thin I barely feel it. I smile up at him, pleased at his surprise. Weeks before he helped me pick out a gold ring for himself, and now I present it to him and help him glide it onto his left ring finger. While nobody decreed it by the power vested in them, with our own vows spoken and trinkets exchanged, we are married! We stand by patiently while Amber and Alexander exchange their vows.

Then I jump a little when the High Elder hits a gong behind his podium that I hadn't noticed was there. Nine vampires in red robes step out through a doorway behind him and file around the inner circle, each coming to a stop on the other side of the small altars—what I had mistakenly thought of as mere tables. I guess "altar" does sound grander. I notice my thoughts are getting away from me, and I try to bring my focus back to Monty and what is going on around me. Standing across from our altar is a very beautiful vampire. She has long straight golden-blonde hair that shimmers in the candlelight. Wordlessly, she picks up the dagger and hands it to me. I take it from her, my hand only trembling slightly. I know I have to cut Monty's palm next, and even though I know he'll heal immediately, I still do not want to do this part.

"Each of you is clutching a sacred dagger chosen by your companion with utmost care. In your grasp, you wield the power to end their existence. A testament to the depth of trust they have bestowed upon you. This trust signifies not only honor and respect, but the profound choice they have made to intertwine destinies with you and forge an unbreakable bond." With that, he pauses and the room grows really quiet. It is then I notice a harpist in the corner has begun to play soft music. The notes fill the room with expectation, the music's pace steadily increasing until my chest feels as if it is going to explode with anticipation. Just as I think I can't take it any longer, the High Elder says, "Take thy dagger and mark your companion!" The music matches the intensity of his words. The nine of us humans take the hands of our mates, and with a confidence driven by nothing other than the music surrounding me, I slash Monty's palm over the chalice. Deep red blood drips slowly into the cup for a few heartbeats of time. Everyone in the room breathes in short, quick, synchronized bursts, matching the frenzied rhythm of the music that reverberates through the space. Then the wound seals itself up before my very eyes as the pacing of the music slows down to match the scene. Max puts his hand on my shoulder to remind me he is there, silently supporting me. He takes it away as the High Elder continues once more.

"Initiates, hold out your wrists. Mates, mark your humans and let them spill their life force into the sacred chalice."

I turn toward Monty, the music still playing in the background. Suddenly I hear a flute joining in with the harpist. Were these vampires teleporting in? They must be. My senses are heady with emotion and I feel a slight dizziness as I take in the sight of Monty, love filling both of our eyes. He reaches out to my hand, and gently, lovingly brings my wrist up to his mouth. I can feel my own pulse beneath his tongue as he gently licks my wrist. He looks at me one last time, as if to silently say, "Speak now or forever hold your peace." I nod to him and mouth, "Please, make me yours," and his fangs sink into my flesh and blood slowly drips down his chin. He holds my wrist over the chalice and we both watch silently as some of my blood mixes in with his. Then, just as carefully, he raises my wrist again to his lips and seals the wound.

The High Elder's voice floods the room. "Behold, as you raise your vessel of eternal life, let it be lifted with reverence. Its contents are a potent elixir of immortality. Bring it to your lips, partake of its mystical essence, and ascend into the realm of the undead, where mortality fades and your eternal life beckons." This guy is really stuck on the immortality side of things. I start to wonder if this is why most people decide to turn. I just want to be with Monty. I don't want to age while he stays young in appearance forever.

354

I don't want there to be a time when he'll live past me. The thought is unbearable. But it isn't immortality specifically that I want—it is simply Monty.

I do as the High Elder says. I can smell the metallic scent of iron in the blood as I lift it to my mouth. In my mind, I jokingly think I should get some Autistic accommodation here. This is a sensory nightmare. But I don't want to push my luck, and it is just a few mouthfuls. Seriously, why couldn't they have come up with a less gross way to do this over the past several decades? One, two, I feel Monty squeeze my right hand as I lift the chalice up with my left. He probably is worried I am hesitating because of second thoughts, when really it is because this blood smells god-awful and if I thought cutting Monty was the hard part, I was severely mistaken because *this* is the hard part. THREE! I mentally exclaim, and squeeze Monty's hand so hard he has to wonder what I am thinking. Then I gulp down the blood. I grab the napkin off the altar and wipe my mouth. I wish I had some water to rinse out my mouth, but before I can ask for some, I slump back into Monty's arms.

Montgomery

The ceremony is over. I teleport Katrina back to the villa and lay her on our bed. Nik brings Max back, who switches to Jessie as soon as she gets here. Katrina is in a deep sleep, not aware of anything going on around her. I direct Jessie to the living room.

"She'll need to sleep for several hours. It could be as few as twelve, but some take closer to forty-eight to make

the conversion. She'll be fine, but we need to just let her be."
She was prepped for what would happen, but I know seeing
it is probably still startling. My already pale Katrina is losing
even more color as the transformation process takes place.
The sun is just starting to peek over the horizon. "There's
still a lot of food in the fridge. I'll be going to sleep too.
Make yourself at home here. Eat, and enjoy the winery.
There's a TV with access to all the channels. You've got the
Wi-Fi password. I'll see you tonight when I wake back up,
okay?" I turn to Nik. "Thank you for being my best man
today. It meant a lot to have you with me. Are you staying
here or going back to your hotel?"

"Of course. One day, I'll find my mate and you'll be
my best man," Nik says. "I'm going to head back to the
hotel. It was really good seeing you, as always, Jessie. I'm
sure we'll see more of each other back in Vancouver." And
then he vanishes. Jessie goes off to change out of the suit
Max had put on and I go to bed. I am a happy vampire,
indeed.

Chapter 43
Unexpected Surprise

Katrina

I start to slowly wake up and become aware of my surroundings. My body feels strange— incredibly powerful and weak all at once. I am also hungry, but it is a hunger I've never experienced before. I lift my hands in front of my face and they look like they always have. Someone swapped my gown for my comfy cotton pajamas. I reach up and touch my face to find it feels the same. But I still feel so different all at once. Then my brand new fangs extend. My fingers find them and touch them. I'd felt Monty's so many times, but to feel fangs in my own mouth is strange. They are wicked sharp too. I accidentally cut my tongue and it stings for a split second before it heals itself. That's handy, but I'll have to remember to be more careful. I have no idea what time it is or really even what day it is. I turn to see if Monty is in bed with me. He is, and I think he feels me shifting around because he opens his eyes and says, "Hello, beautiful. It's about time you joined the land of the living. Or undead, should we say? How do you feel?"

"I'm not quite sure. I feel very powerful but also extremely weak at the same time, which makes no sense. I'm also so hungry, but it feels different than anything I've ever experienced before."

"You're ready for your first real blood meal," he says to me. "How does that sound?"

"Weirdly enough, it does sound good. I know you said it would but it seemed unbelievable."

"Give me a minute and I'll bring you a cup." Monty leaves and comes back a few minutes later with a cup filled with blood. "I warmed it up slightly. It's good to learn to take it cold eventually, but at first warm is probably going to be easier for you."

I take the cup and drink from it. Unlike the blood from the chalice, I am no longer put off by the smell. Now, it smells like sustenance, like something I need to consume. "Was that bovine or porcine?" I ask, figuring I should probably learn the difference.

"Bovine," he replies.

With that taken care of, I swing my legs out of the bed and stand up. I do feel more powerful. He said I wouldn't be able to teleport right away, and it'll take time to learn what other powers I've gained. Telekinesis is likely since that is one of his powers, but it could be a power from anywhere in his vampire genetic line. "Did you see Rainbow? How are they? How long have I been asleep?"

"I think I heard Rainbow up and about when I went to get your blood. You were out for about thirty-six hours. It's 7 p.m. on November 1st."

We walk into the living room and find Quinn sitting on the couch watching HGTV in Italian. "You're awake! How are you?!"

I run towards them to give them a big hug. "Max said you co-fronted—did you see the ceremony? And I'm totally fine." Such an ADHD way of conversation: ask my own question, then take time to answer theirs. "I feel a bit strange, but that's to be expected. Hey, look at my fangs." I concentrate really hard, but nothing happens. I turn to Monty. "How do I make these things work?"

358

"Think about giving Quinn here a little bite."

I do as he says, and sure enough, just thinking about blood has them extending—so cool! I give Quinn a big pointy grin.

"Very nice, now put those away. I do not want to be your lunch. I was able to co-front and to see and hear the entire ceremony."

"Don't worry—I already ate," I tell them. "Are you ready to go back to Vancouver? I miss Data. I know he misses me too, and I bet Pixie misses you. But I do appreciate you staying here and watching over me while I was in my deep slumber. You didn't have to."

"I know, but it made me feel better."

We spend the next hour packing our suitcases. Since I can't teleport yet, Monty makes one trip to take all of our suitcases back to our house in Vancouver, then he returns and we do the auto check-out. I say goodbye to the villa, my last place to be human, and he holds both of our hands until we are back home in our bedroom where he knows it'll be dark. It is eleven in the morning, local time, and I can't be near the sun for several months, at the very least. I need to stay away from windows as much as possible too.

"Okay, now I'll take Quinn and their suitcase back to their home and bring Data back," Monty says. "It may take a few minutes to get him corralled into the carrying case. We'll have to get used to local time again." I give Quinn a big hug and tell them I'll call in a day or two, and then they leave with Monty.

It isn't that much longer before Monty reappears with Data in tow. "Data!" I call out.

"Momma!" he cries.

"Monty! Did you hear that? He called me Momma!" I say in shock.

"No, I just heard him meow," Monty says to me.

"I missed you. Where have you been? Why did you leave me? Pixie was fun to play with but I'm glad I'm back with you, Momma," Data says.

"Monty, I can understand Data!" I say. I turn to Data. "I can understand you. It must be my new powers. I'm back, Data, baby. I'm sorry I had to leave you at Pixie's house, but I'm glad you had fun with her."

"That's incredible! That's a super rare power! I've only heard of a very, very few vampires who can understand animals!" Monty's shock is evident in the huge grin slowly spreading across his face.

"I'm going to check out my house and make sure nothing has changed," Data says, and then he scampers out of the room.

"Wow, that is going to take some getting used to," I say, "but he called me Momma." My eyes start to tear up. I may not ever be a human momma, but I'm a pet momma, and that's good enough.

"While you were going to get Data, I checked your VidVibe. Did you know you hit two million followers?"

"I did? It must have been just in the last day or two. That's amazing. I can't believe that many people like listening to me."

"I'm glad I listened to you and got brave enough to reach out to you," Monty says. He joins me up in the bed and I lay the back of my head across his stomach and gaze up at the twinkle lights in the top of the bed's canopy. Neither of us are very tired. He reaches down, idly playing with my hair the way he loves to do.

"I'm glad I responded too. I'm so happy to be home and to start our life together."

"Me too. We've got so many adventures to plan together. I love you, Montgomery Ravenscroft."

"I love you too, Katrina Ravenscroft." And with that, our eternal love story begins.

The End

About the Author

At the age of forty-two, Amanda Maehill received an Autism and ADHD diagnosis, a profound catalyst that transformed her life into one of advocacy and self-discovery. Her creative work, including this novel and her popular YouTube channel, is dedicated to disability advocacy and exploring the lived experience of neurodivergence.

Over the years, Amanda has immersed herself in various passions, from mastering the art of amigurumi and horseback riding to exploring the culinary world. Writing a novel is just the latest adventure she's embarked on. In the process of unmasking her Autistic traits and discovering the woman behind the mask, she has found a deep sense of belonging within the neurodivergent community and embraces her identity as a bisexual demisexual contributing to the wider queer community.

Social Bites is Amanda's debut novel, written with the hope of sharing her journey and inspiring others to celebrate their true, authentic selves.

People who I want to thank

To Eira and Izzie—Thank you for listening to my story, helping me patch plot holes, and designing my book cover. Eira created the layout. Izzie drew the design. I'm so proud of both of you.

To John—You believed in me even when I forgot how. I never could have done this without your steady support.

To the friend who read my early pages with such enthusiasm it propelled me forward—Thank you. Your encouragement mattered. You may have chosen not to stay, as so often happens to Autistic people who burn bright. But for the time you were here, you were a shining star. You won't be forgotten.

To Nicole—Your thoughtful feedback as a beta reader made this book so much stronger. I'm so grateful.

To my friend with DID—Rainbow System in *Social Bites* isn't based on you, but was inspired by your courage, your insight, and your existence. We need more positive representations of DID in the media, and you helped show me why.

To all my friends who cheered me on, asked for updates, or quietly believed in me—This book made it to press because you held space for me to finish it.

And to **every neurodivergent reader** who's ever been told they're too much—You're not. Your story matters. You're not alone.

Social Bites – Book Club Discussion Questions

Theme 1: Identity, Neurodivergence, and the Self

1. AuDHD and Self-Acceptance

Katrina describes the process of "unmasking" her AuDHD traits. How does her self-acceptance prepare her for accepting the monumental change of becoming a vampire?

2. Dismantling Stereotypes

Social Bites includes characters with Dissociative Identity Disorder (DID) and AuDHD, portrayed with depth and respect. How did the book challenge common media stereotypes about these identities? Were there moments that reshaped or deepened your understanding of disability, plurality, or neurodivergence?

3. Performance and Authenticity

Monty uses his VidVibe platform to perform a vampire identity, and Katrina struggles with masking and the pressure to "perform" wellness. Discuss how this novel explores the balance between authenticity and safety in social settings—both online and in real life.

Theme 2: Consent and Boundaries

4. Layers of Consent

What role does consent play in this story beyond romance or sex? Discuss how the relationship between 333-year-old vampire Monty and human Katrina navigates and reinforces boundaries, both physical and emotional.

> *Places to Look: Focus on the constant, explicit communication, the negotiation of powers, and the way Monty ensures Katrina's bodily autonomy is protected at all times.*

5. The Near-Bite Scene (Ch. 18/19)

When Monty realizes he almost bit Katrina without consent, he teleports away to regain control. Discuss the impact of this moment on their relationship. Why was this act of self-removal more effective than staying and fighting the impulse?

> *Places to Look: Look at the internal conflicts Monty faces in the kitchen scene, and how his immediate reaction prioritizes Katrina's safety over his desire.*

6. The Role of the Vampire Class

The Vampire Council requires Katrina to attend a class as a final layer of consent. What does this bureaucratic step reveal about vampire society's values around human choice and emotional safety?

7. The Unveiling Ceremony and Sensory Input

The turning ceremony includes dramatic rituals and sensory challenges (the smell of blood, the gong, the music). How does Katrina's AuDHD perception of the event heighten the emotional stakes for the reader?

Theme 3: Love, Legacy, and Belonging

8. "Not Immortality, Just Monty"
Katrina realizes she doesn't want immortality—she just doesn't want to live without Monty. How does this reframing of the core vampire trope shift the story from fantasy to a love story?

9. Found Family and Chosen Kinship
Beyond the main couple, how does the book explore the idea of found family—through Katrina and the Rainbow System, and even Monty and Nik?

10. The Unexpected Power
At the end of the story, Katrina gains a rare vampire ability: she can understand animals—including her cat, Data, who calls her "Momma." Why does this gentle, everyday power serve as the perfect, heartwarming conclusion to her transition, rather than a flashier or more dramatic skill?

✦ Bonus Question

Character Growth
Who changed the most in this story, and why? What key lesson do you think each main character—Katrina, Monty, and Rainbow—walked away with?